MODERN HUMANITIES RESEARCH ASSOCIATION
JEWELLED TORTOISE
VOLUME 11

GENERAL EDITORS
STEFANO EVANGELISTA
CATHERINE MAXWELL

MIRDJA

L. ONERVA

MIRDJA
A DECADENT NEW WOMAN

By

L. ONERVA

Translated by

EVA BUCHWALD

Introduction and Notes by

VIOLA PARENTE-ČAPKOVÁ

MODERN HUMANITIES RESEARCH ASSOCIATION
Jewelled Tortoise 11
2025

Published by

The Modern Humanities Research Association

Salisbury House
Station Road
Cambridge CB1 2LA
United Kingdom

First published 2025

ISBN 978-1-83954-126-1 (hardback)
ISBN 978-1-83954-124-7 (paperback)
ISBN 978-1-83954-125-4 (ebook)

Typeset in Minion Pro by Allset Journals & Books, Scarborough, UK

CONTENTS

ACKNOWLEDGEMENTS

Viola Parente-Čapková

I wish to thank a great number of teachers, mentors, colleagues, and friends, who have been accompanying me on my 'Onerva journey', as well as institutions which made the journey possible, from its very beginnings in Prague, London (where I got acquainted with Eva Buchwald's stimulating work on the Finnish and Russian *fin de siècle*), and Helsinki, and continuing in Turku and elsewhere. Their names are listed in the extensive acknowledgements chapter in my book on L. Onerva, *Decadent Women (Un)Bound: Mimetic Strategies in L. Onerva's 'Mirdja'* (2014), which was also my dissertation at the University of Turku. Nevertheless, I would like to thank once more Päivi Lappalainen, Lea Rojola, and Maria-Liisa Nevala whose work on *fin-de-siècle* women writers inspired me so much over the years, and Päivi especially for her interest in this project and for her valuable comments on the introduction and the commentaries. Warm thanks to Pirjo Lyytikäinen for sharing her extensive knowledge of Decadence and Symbolism, and Riikka Rossi for her knowledge of Naturalism: working together, also with Mirjam Hinrikus, on our book on *Nordic Decadence*, was very instructive for this project. I have long thought that *Mirdja* was a work that should be translated into English, and over the last fifteen years, various conferences on Decadence in the Nordic countries and elsewhere in Europe increasingly convinced me it was necessary. More and more international colleagues, whose work has been of great inspiration, showed interest in L. Onerva, for which many thanks: Guri Barstad, Guy Ducrey, Matthew Potolsky, Anne Birgitte Rønning, Juliet Simpson, Katharina Herold, Leire Barrera-Medrano, and many others. I am very grateful to Eva Buchwald for taking up the task of translating L. Onerva's major work. I want to express my sincere and special thanks to Melanie Hawthorn and Stefano Evangelista. Melanie believed in the idea of translating *Mirdja* and did a lot of work to promote it, manifesting sustained interest and concern for finding the right publisher for the novel: finally, it was discovered, with Stefano's help, in MHRA/Jewelled Tortoise — warm thanks to Stefano for that, as well as for the constant encouragement and the enormous help with the whole process.

My work on the edition during 2024 was a part of my work within the Estonian Academy of Sciences project 'Emergence of a Civilised Nation: Decadence and Transitionality in 1905–1940' (PRG1667).

Eva Buchwald

I too would like to thank Pirkko Koski, Pirjo Lyytikäinen, Päivi Lappalainen, and Lea Rojola, not only for their encouragement at various stages of this project, but also for taking the time to write references in support of my translation grant applications. This translation was made possible by a generous grant from the Finnish Cultural Foundation. Translation grants are a rare commodity, and I am very grateful to the Foundation for recognizing the value of this endeavour. I also thank the Finnish Literature Exchange for providing a small sample translation grant in the early stages of this project, which helped to secure our publishing contract. I wish to address a special thanks to Maria-Liisa Nevala for her enlightening answers to my questions concerning some of the novel's trickier turns of phrase, as well as for her long-lasting inspiration and astute insights concerning the work of L. Onerva, and Finnish literature in general. I am very grateful to Viola Parente-Čapková for enlisting me as translator for her vision of a critical edition of L. Onerva's *Mirdja* in English. I am so glad that our mutual fascination for Finnish Decadence has borne fruit with this publication.

*

Together we also thank Stefano Evangelista and Catherine Maxwell for their valuable comments on all the texts submitted. We are thrilled to have our book included in the Jewelled Tortoise series, which seems a perfect home for L. Onerva. We thank Gerard Lowe and Simon Davies for all their work on the production of the book. Many thanks to the Finnish Cultural Foundation, which owns the copyright to Onerva's works, for granting permission to publish *Mirdja* in English. Last but not least, our deepest thanks to our families for their continuous support.

We dedicate this publication to the memory of Michael Branch (1940–2019), who spent over twenty years as Professor of Finnish and Director of the School of Slavonic and East European Studies in London, raising awareness of Finnish language and literature in the English-speaking world. His enthusiasm and commitment to the field were instrumental in our own professional development, and the eventual creation of this book.

INTRODUCTION

L. Onerva's Decadent New Woman Seeker

Viola Parente-Čapková

~

'But because you are complicated, inexplicable, caught up in your own web, contradictory, unnatural, unusual, rare, possibly insane and criminal, you drive people mad with your wonderful dissonance', an admirer says to Mirdja, the protagonist of the eponymous novel by Hilja Onerva Lehtinen (1882–1972), who published her work under the pen name L. Onerva.[1] The musical metaphor of dissonances, cacophonies, and all manner of disharmonies and discords seems to befit Decadent works by women writers of the late nineteenth and early twentieth centuries. Indeed, the title of L. Onerva's debut work, *Sekasointuja* (1904), a collection of poems, can be translated as 'disharmonies', while a reader of Decadent works by women writers publishing in English might recall the cosmopolitan Decadent writer George Egerton's collections of short stories *Discords* from 1894. The protagonist enjoys 'driving others mad', but she also feels tormented by the typically Decadent need for interiority and detached analysis: 'this only served to fuel her eagerness for self-examination [...]. And the more she studied herself, the more complicated the questions before her became' (p. 160).[2]

Although much research has been carried out, in recent decades, on women writers who exploit the Decadent mode,[3] it is still the male canon that

---

[1] All English translations from the novel in the Introduction are from the present edition, translated by Eva Buchwald (here pp. 103-04); subsequent references are given in the text. The original is 'Mutta kun olet monimutkainen, selittämätön, omiin verkkoihisi kietoutunut, ristiriitainen, luonnoton, harvinainen, kenties mielipuoli ja rikollinen, niin saatat ihmiset hulluiksi ihanalla epäsoinnullasi...' (L. Onerva, *Mirdja* (Otava, 1908), p. 99).

[2] 'Mutta sitä kiihkeämmin kääntyi hän senjälkeen taas omaa itseään tarkkaamaan. [...] Ja mitä syvemmälle hän havaintoihinsa painui, sitä monimutkaisempia pulmia löysi hän edestään.' L. Onerva, *Mirdja*, p. 208.

[3] See e.g. the special issue on *Women Writing Decadence* of *Volupté*, 2.1 (2019), ed. by Katharina Herold and Leire Barrera-Medrano. In the Introduction to the volume, Melanie Hawthorne talks about 'an entire "lost generation" of women writers who delved into more or less Decadent matters' (p. 2). Apart from the writers from western parts of Europe, there would be many others, both from northern, eastern and southern parts of the continent (see e.g. Viola Parente-Čapková, 'Decadent Women Telling Nations Differently: The Finnish Writer L. Onerva and Her Motherless Dilettante Upstarts', in *Women Telling Nations*, ed. by. Amelia Sanz, Francesca Scott, and Suzan van Dijk (Rodopi, 2014), pp. 247–70).

dominates scholarly accounts. Moreover, while scholars have addressed
Decadence in the literature of various languages, the discussion tends to
focus mostly on French and English writing. In both these respects Onerva's
Mirdja, written in Finnish by a female author in 1908, stands out. With its
mixture of numerous intertextual references and its evident influence from
French Decadence, *Mirdja* can be firmly placed in the international canon of
Decadent prose works. Thus, this first English translation and critical edition
of the novel aims to contribute to the process of filling in the blank spaces
that still dot our map of European Decadence: it is designed to introduce the
English-speaking public to a Decadent woman writer from north-eastern
Europe and to open a window on Nordic Decadence more broadly.

Mirdja is a typically Decadent work, full of introspection, with the main
character endlessly analysing her elaborate and refined sensations and
emotions. Her extreme subjectivity and egocentricity are immersed in multiple
layers of irony and self-ironizing. Art and dreams have primacy over life and
reality, yet there is also a consciousness of the world as 'an infinitely inter-
pretable image'.[4] All this is set within a dynamic of paradox and ambivalence.
Given the relatively minor importance of plot, as is typical of Decadent works,
the novel is easily accessible on a universal level as an expression of an em-
phatically female consciousness commenting on conventional bourgeois
society as well as on the misogyny often found in Decadent bohemian circles.
However, although the novel can certainly be read on this general plane, the
experience becomes even more rewarding when we situate the text in the
contexts of the author's life and works, Finnish history and culture, and literature written by women around the turn of the twentieth century. In this
introduction, I therefore outline the main features of Onerva's biography,
concentrating on the early period of her writing career, which was marked
by a strong presence of Decadent poetics, and focusing in particular on her
prose work. I then discuss Decadence and *fin-de-siècle* literature in Finland
before zooming in on various aspects of *Mirdja* in order to contextualize the
novel more broadly within European New Woman fiction and Decadent
writing by women.

The Author and her Work

The majority of Onerva's works from the early twentieth century exemplify
the ways in which woman's creativity and authorship were inextricably intertwined with women's subjectivity.[5] Hilja Onerva Lehtinen, whose works

[4] Robert Pynsent, 'Conclusory Essay: Decadence and Innovation', in *Decadence and Innovation: Austro-Hungarian Life and Art at the Turn of the Century*, ed. by Robert Pynsent (Weidenfeld & Nicolson, 1989), pp. 111–248 (p. 142).
[5] See Viola Parente-Čapková, 'Feminisoitu naisestetiikka ja naistekijyys. Naistekijäksi tulemisen mahdollisuudet L. Onervan varhaisteksteissä', in *Tekijyyden tekstit*, ed. by Kaisa Kurikka and Veli-Matti Pynttäri (Suomalaisen Kirjallisuuden Seura, 2006), pp. 194–223;

comprise poetry, prose, drama, essays, art reviews, and translations, was one of the most versatile literary figures of her generation. She was born in the Finnish capital city of Helsinki in 1882, the only child of Johan Lehtinen and his wife Serafina. Johan worked as a clerk and was mainly responsible for Onerva's upbringing, since Serafina was interned in an asylum when Onerva was only seven years old. This was a huge childhood trauma that marked the author's life and work. Serafina was subject to violent fits during which she would physically abuse her daughter.[6] Motherhood, motherlessness, and the search for one's own mother are among the principal themes in *Mirdja*, and they are also present in many of Onerva's other works. In the absence of her mother, Onerva established a close bond with her paternal grandmother and, most of all, with her father, who supported his daughter's studies and encouraged the development of her artistic talent.

However, when Onerva was eleven years old, Johan Lehtinen moved to the town of Kotka on the southern coast of Finland, around 120 km from Helsinki, to become the building manager of a sawmill. Onerva remained alone in the capital and attended the Helsinki Finnish Girls' School (1893–1898), where she excelled in arts and languages, particularly French (she would translate de Musset's poems at the age of fifteen). She continued at the Upper Secondary School (1898–1902), where it was possible to obtain a teacher's degree, as Onerva did. The school did not offer full matriculation, so in 1901 Onerva passed her matriculation exam as a private student in the Helsinki Finnish Co-Educational School, which qualified her for university. The School was founded in 1886 in order to promote girls' and women's education in the Finnish language. Onerva was gifted in painting and music, and at one point also considered an acting career, but in 1902 she enrolled to study at the University in Helsinki (known then as the Imperial Alexander University in Finland). She was one of the first generation of women who, unlike their predecessors, did not need a special permit dispensing 'liberation from the female sex' in order to enrol in the university.[7] She studied aesthetics, art history, Romance philology (French and other Romance languages), and other subjects; one of her teachers and mentors was the renowned aesthetician Yrjö Hirn (1870–1952), later also a diplomat. Hirn's interest in the Catholic

---

and Viola Parente-Čapková, *Decadent New Woman (Un)Bound: Mimetic Strategies in L. Onerva's Mirdja* (University of Turku, 2014).

[6] Onerva's manuscript memoirs, quoted in Anna Kortelainen, *Naisen tie: L. Onervan kapina* (Otava, 2006), p. 469.

[7] Women had to apply for 'liberation from one's sex' ('erivapaus sukupuolesta') if they wanted to sit school-leaving examinations, enrol at the university, or get a job that required a university degree. The need for such a permit in order to enter university was abolished in 1901 but the restrictions on employment were not abolished until 1926. See Arja-Liisa Räisänen, *Onnellisen avioliiton ehdot. Sukupuolijärjestelmän muodostumisprosessi suomalaisissa avioliitto-ja seksuaalivalistusoppaissa 1865–1920* (Suomen Historiallinen Seura, 1995), p. 43.

religion and religion in general, and in theatre, psychology, and sociology, played an important role in Onerva's later development.[8] Hirn also motivated Onerva to take an interest in the work of Germaine de Staël. Onerva planned a scholarly career with a dissertation on the rococo period in art history. However, her time was taken up by writing and other literary activities, so that she never fully pursued scholarly work.

As a Finnish-speaking young woman with cultural interests, Onerva was expected to participate in the 'national cause'. Finnish language culture had only begun to develop in the latter half of the nineteenth century, after acquiring equal status with Swedish in the imperial language edict of 1863. During Onerva's youth Finnish became Finland's second language in the spheres of culture and literature. The 1880s saw the arrival of the first generation of writers who had received their education in the Finnish language. Before this, literature in Finnish had been a very sporadic affair, with most of the books and periodicals published and circulating in Finland written in Swedish. The first critically acclaimed novel in Finnish was not published until 1870.[9] Given this recent history, in the early twentieth century Finnish-speaking writers still felt an urgent need to develop and cultivate Finnish as a literary language. This in turn led to a certain tension between a sense of patriotic duty on one hand and, on the other, a desire to 'open a window onto Europe' (notably Western Europe), as the slogan went.

It is interesting to recall, in this context, the frequently quoted statement by the British writer Virginia Woolf, born in the same year as Onerva and canonized as one of the most significant feminist writers of the twentieth century: 'as a woman I have no country. As a woman I want no country. As a woman, my country is the whole world.'[10] This expression of women's often contradictory relationship to nation and to nationalism is equally pertinent for women writers in countries other than Britain, including the women authors engaging with the Decadent mode, such as Renée Vivien (1877–1909).[11] However, in the case of women writers coming from countries that underwent processes of national revival or 'awakening' the situation is especially complex. Finland did not exist as a separate nation state before 1917, having been first a part of the Swedish realm from *circa* 1150 to 1809, and then existing as a Grand Duchy within the Russian Empire for the following century. At the time of Onerva's life, the country was reaching the culminating phase of its national movement. During the nineteenth century

---

[8] Hirn's *The Origins of Art: A Psychological and Sociological Inquiry* was published in English in 1900; it was also translated into German and Russian.
[9] Aleksis Kivi's *Seitsemän veljestä* ('Seven brothers'). The novel was first published in four volumes as part of the Novellikirjasto series by Suomalaisen Kirjallisuuden Seura, and then reissued as a one-volume novel in 1873.
[10] Virginia Woolf, *Three Guineas* (Hogarth Press, 1938), p. 197.
[11] See Hawthorne, 'Women Writing Decadence', p. 4.

the Finnish language had crystallized as the cornerstone of Finnish identity. It was therefore particularly difficult for Finnish-speaking authors to dismiss the issue of nationalism in their work altogether, as Woolf did, especially if they were at all, even in the smallest way, committed to current affairs.

This was one of the dilemmas Onerva had to face. While she did show an interest in the national cause, she was, at the same time, one of the most cosmopolitan cultural figures of her generation, famous for her interest in French culture and almost bilingual in Finnish and Swedish. She acted as a mediator between France and Finland, translating French literature and embarking on an intense dialogue with French cultural tendencies in her writings. Her French translations include precursors and representatives of the French Romantic and Decadent movements such as Alfred de Musset, Théophile Gautier, Charles Baudelaire, Anatole France, Paul Verlaine, Paul Bourget, Camille Mauclair, Joseph Bédier, and Marcelle Tinayre. In 1912, she published a small selection of her translations of de Musset's, Verlaine's, and Baudelaire's poems under the title *Ranskalaista laulurunoutta* ('French song poetry') and in 1915 she completed one of her major translation works, the Finnish rendering of Hippolyte Taine's *Philosophie de l'Art* (1865–82).[12] In light of such portentous activity, some translation scholars consider Onerva to be perhaps the greatest expert in French literature among Finnish-speaking writers.[13] In *Mirdja* she addresses the work of most of these authors as well as others, including J. W. Goethe and the Swedish author Gustav Fröding.

In this respect, Onerva resembled many European *fin-de-siècle* women writers who acted as cultural mediators in their respective national literary fields.[14] In Britain, for instance, George Egerton introduced the Swedish Decadent Ola Hansson to the English-speaking public.[15] When it came to the literatures of 'small nations' or literatures written in 'minor' languages in particular, these cultural transmitters would typically take on various roles ranging from 'translator [to] reviewer, critic, journalist, literary historian, scholar, teacher, librarian, book seller, collector, literary agent, scout, publisher,

---

[12] Hippolyte Taine, *Taiteen filosofia*, trans. by L. Onerva (Otava, 1915). Apart from French authors, Onerva also translated Swedish, German, and Russian writers; see Ulla-Mari Uusitalo, *L. Onerva — écrivain et traductrice* (MA thesis, University of Turku, 2000).

[13] Janna Kantola and H. K. Riikonen, 'Käännösten merkitys suomalaiselle modernismille', in *Suomennoskirjallisuuden historia*, ed. by H. K. Riikonen and others (Suomalaisen Kirjallisuuden Seura, 2007), pp. 446–60 (p. 448).

[14] See Viola Parente-Čapková and Päivi Lappalainen, 'Transnational Reception: Nordic Women Writers in Fin de Siècle Finland', in *Gender in Literary Exchange*, ed. by Anka Ryall and Anne Birgitte Rønning (Routledge, 2021).

[15] See Stefano Evangelista, 'The Time of Ola Hansson: Translating Scandinavian Decadence in *fin-de-siècle* France and England', in *Nordic Literature of Decadence*, ed. by Pirjo Lyytikäinen and others (Routledge, 2020), pp. 205–22; Stefano Evangelista, 'George Egerton's Scandinavian Breakthrough', in *Literary Cosmopolitanism in the English Fin de Siècle: Citizens of Nowhere* (Oxford University Press, 2021), pp. 117–63.

editor of a journal, writer, travel writer or a counsellor'.[16] These activities, which have since been acknowledged by literary and translation scholars, were also noted by Onerva's contemporaries, but not always appreciated. Some of her contemporaries saw her as too cosmopolitan, criticizing her for not paying sufficient attention to national themes. Finnish critics tended to define such themes very narrowly as directly inspired by Finnish folk poetry,[17] which was considered, in the Herderian spirit, to be the basis of the national culture.

At the beginning of the twentieth century, Onerva lived a hectic life. She studied at the university and participated in student activities. At the very start of her career, she was mentored and helped by the poet J. H. Erkko (1849–1906), who came up with her pen name L. Onerva. The L. is an abbreviation of the author's surname Lehtinen, and does not stand for a first name, as it may appear. In Finnish, it evokes the form 'Lehtisen Onerva', or 'Lehtinen's Onerva', that is, it uses the possesive case of the surname and the first name — here, the middle name — as an informal way to refer to a person.[18] In 1904, Onerva debuted with the aforementioned collection of poems symptomatically titled *Sekasointuja* ('Disharmonies'), marked by the oscillation between ecstatic visions and melancholy tones, typical of the period. The book was for the most part positively received in the contemporary press. During the first decade of the century she also travelled extensively, spending longer periods of time in Berlin, Paris, and Rome. In Finland and abroad, she made the acquaintance of many leading figures on the literary and cultural scene, and found her soul-mates especially in the circles interested in Symbolism, Decadence, and Nietzscheanism.

One such acquaintance was Eino Leino (Armas Einar Leopold Lönnbohm, 1878–1926), a similarly versatile figure, much more acclaimed among both contemporary critics and literary historians than his female counterparts. Leino wrote poetry, prose, and drama mostly in Symbolist and Decadent modes, ranging from light song-like poems to complex, existentially charged

---

[16] Petra Broomans, 'Introduction: Women as Transmitters of Ideas', in *From Darwin to Weil: Women as Transmitters of Ideas*, ed. by Petra Broomans (Barkhuis, 2009), p. 2; Petra Broomans and Marta Ronne, 'Gendering Cultural Transfer and Transmission History', in *Rethinking Cultural Transfer and Transmission: Reflections and New Perspectives*, ed. by Petra Broomans and Sandra van Voorst (Barkhuis, 2012), p. 118. On the broader point about small nations, see *Translating the Literature of Small European Nations*, ed. by Rajendra Chitnis and others (Liverpool University Press, 2019).

[17] Finnish folk poetry and its textualizations, namely the *Kalevala* by Elias Lönnrot (1802–1884), characterized as 'the Finnish national epic', were a major source of inspiration for Finnish national neo-Romanticism (see p. 14).

[18] There is a rather unfortunate history in literary criticism of using first names for women writers and surnames only for male writers, but Onerva's case is different. For the sake of clarity, I refer to the author as 'Onerva', as is customary practice in Finnish scholarly discussions.

works, many of them intended to be read as political allegories. He was also a prolific journalist who commented on cultural and political events, especially during the two 'periods of oppression' (*sortovuodet*), that is, the periods of intensified Russification policies towards Finland around the years 1899 to 1905, and again from 1908 to 1917. Onerva and Leino's close personal relationship lasted until Leino's death in 1926 but they were never married to one another. Both married other partners, Leino three times, Onerva twice. Onerva's first marriage was to Väinö Streng, whom she also met in conjunction with her university studies, at a student society or so-called 'student nation' (*osakunta*), where students gathered according to their region of origin and organized various events, as also described in the novel *Mirdja*. Streng came from a wealthy family: his father was a headmaster of a prestigious secondary school in Helsinki and held important positions in cultural and clerical institutions. The newlywed couple spent their honeymoon in Paris but on their return they moved far from Helsinki, to the small town of Räisälä on the Karelian Isthmus, on the border between Finland and Russia. This is where the Streng family had their estate. During the following years, Onerva continued her studies (writing her thesis on Musset's female characters[19]) and spent her time between Helsinki and Räisälä. Although the couple would later move back to Helsinki, the marriage did not last long: Onerva and Streng separated in 1908 and subsequently divorced. Onerva had begun her relationship with Eino Leino and spent time with him in Rome.

The year 1908 was a prolific one in Onerva's writing career: she published her debut novel, *Mirdja*, and her second collection of poems, entitled simply *Runoja* ('Poems'). Onerva's poems from this period continued to mingle an ecstatic, vital mode with the search for a 'new humanity'. The emphasis is on the transient qualities of life and existence, and the expression is rich in tragic and ironic overtones, Decadent moods, melancholia, and *fin-de-siècle* scepticism. Intertextual allusions range from Greek mythology to 'oriental' subjects. Some of the poems from *Runoja* deal with the same themes or use the same poetic devices as can be found in *Mirdja*: there are musical poems such as 'Resitatiivi' ('Recitative') or 'Barcarola', and there is a poem addressed 'to the stronger one' ('Voimakkaammalleni'), expressing the omnipotent feelings of a femme fatale who, nevertheless, longs to meet someone stronger than herself. There are also poems on strong and 'sinful' female figures from classical mythology and the Bible, including 'Megairan laulu' ('Megaera's song') and the apostrophic poem 'Magdalena'. The same trend continues in her subsequent collection of poems, *Särjetyt jumalat* ('Broken gods') from 1910, where the lyrical subject identifies with such figures, particularly in a long dramatic monologue, 'Geisha'. What is remarkable is that both *Runoja* and *Särjetyt jumalat* include poems about ageing by an author who had not

---

[19] L. Onerva, 'Musset'n naisluonteet' (Laudaturtyö (MA thesis), Helsinki, Archives of the Finnish Literature Society, Literary and Cultural History Collection, 1905).

yet turned thirty. In 'Geisha', the process of ageing acquires a specifically female point of view: 'Don't look at me: I am already old. I am dancing in the glimmer of wine and the silver brooch.'[20] Here Onerva gives a voice of her own to the grotesque figure of an ageing muse, a fading beauty, often described by male Decadent authors with a mixture of fascination and sadistic pleasure as a symbol of over-sophistication and decay.[21] The figure of Mater Dolorosa also appears in *Runoja*, as well as other motifs associated with *Mirdja*, such as 'the dark city in flames'.[22] Though the early collections of poems were dominated by Symbolist and Decadent poetics, what stands out is also Onerva's taste for irony and satire, which was to grow stronger during the following decades.[23]

Between *Runoja*, *Mirdja*, and *Särjetyt jumalat*, Onerva also published her first collection of short stories, entitled *Murtoviivoja* ('Broken lines', 1909), in which she displayed the wide spectrum of her preoccupation with gender. The story 'Kuvittelija' ('Fantasist') depicts a person who identifies absolute beauty with the figure of the androgyne (or 'hermaphrodite', as the contemporary usage would have it). At the same time, the collection includes short stories about the 'fatal' aspects of sexual difference between man and woman. The stories' female subjects oscillate between enjoying the various roles they are styled into and suffering when they feel that these roles prevent them from being fully human. In *Murtoviivoja*, Onerva expands the spectrum of her heroines' social backgrounds: though most of her heroines are middle-class women, (aspiring) artists, or intellectuals, the collection also includes the poor country girl Kati and Russian princess Manja Pavlovna (in the eponymous story). The story that has attracted most attention is 'Itsenäinen nainen' ('An independent woman'), which portrays a woman intellectual who has achieved world fame. While she does not regret her decisions, she cannot help envying her childhood friend who has a child and a traditional family life. An even stronger concern with social issues, particularly upward social mobility, is to be found in Onerva's subsequent collection of short stories, *Nousukkaita* ('Social climbers', 1911), thanks to which the word

---

[20] 'Ällös sa katso mua: | ma vanha jo olen, | ma tanssin vain välkkeessä viinin | ja hopea-solen.' L. Onerva, *Särjetyt jumalat* (Otava, 1910), p. 81. All translations from Onerva's works (other than *Mirdja*) and secondary sources in this Introduction are my own, unless indicated otherwise.

[21] See Viola Parente-Čapková, 'Free Love, Mystical Union, or Prostitution? The Dissonant Love Stories of L. Onerva', in *Changing Scenes: Encounters between European and Finnish Fin de Siècle*, ed. by Pirjo Lyytikäinen (Finnish Literature Society, 2003), pp. 54–84 (p. 58).

[22] 'Kaupunki allani | liekeissä pimeä'. L. Onerva, *Runoja* (Vihtori Kosonen, 1908), p. 126.

[23] See e.g. poems 'Neuvo' ('Advice') or 'Révérence' in *Runoja*, pp. 62 and 66. The number of satiric poems rises in the 1910s and especially in the 1920s. Annikki Yrjänäinen collected Onerva's satires and published them together with the long poem 'Geisha' from *Särjetyt jumalat* into a volume *Puoluepukarit ja Geisha* (Party Bullies and Geisha, TAI-teos 2002).

nousukas became established in the Finnish language.[24] This collection is populated by characters of rural extraction, both male and female, and peasant students familiar from the literatures of other countries.[25] In the tragic short story of the failed peasant student Pentti Korjus, there is evidence of Taine's influence, intertwined with Darwinist ideas, racial theories, and theories of degeneration.[26]

Other upstarts in the same collection could all be characterized as uprooted, transitional, and, as such, destined to suffer: since the development towards the human being of the future cannot be accelerated, no stage can be skipped. In accordance with the nationalist ideology, the future of the country should belong to the Finnish-speaking population, which consisted of country folk and the lower classes, while the Swedish-speaking population was seen as made up mostly of the aristocracy and the upper classes. As a result, within the Finnish national project, the Swedish-speaking classes were often constructed as weak, degenerate, and decaying — in other words, as being caught in a downward transition. This also appears to be Onerva's perception, although she portrays the rising Finnish-speaking folk as not yet ready to assume the status of leaders, either in the cultural or in any other sense of the word. This ambivalence is intensified by her depiction of the gender identities of the characters, which shows the multiple marginalization of women who try to rise socially in order to become students or artists. For instance, the short story 'Raina' describes the tragedy of an aspiring Finnish woman singer in Paris, where she is alienated both from the local, i.e. French, community

---

[24] The term *nousukas* is notoriously difficult to translate: none of the English translations, such as parvenu, arriviste, nouveau riche, upstart, or social climber, seem wholly adequate, given the characters' different ways of 'elevating themselves' socially in various contexts. See Viola Parente-Čapková, 'Gendering Seekers and Upstarts in Early Twentieth-Century Finnish Literature', in *Approaching Religion*, 11.1 (2021), pp. 28–44 (p. 31); and 'La vergogna motivazionale e paralizzante. La figura del parvenu negli scritti di L. Onerva, sullo sfondo storico della Finlandia di inizi Novecento', in *LEA: Lingue e letterature d'Oriente e d'Occidente*, 2 (2013), pp. 423–38.

[25] Within Nordic literature, such characters are especially prominent in the novel *Bondestudentar* ('Peasant students', 1883) by the Norwegian author Arne Garborg (1851–1924). In Finnish Realist, Naturalist, and *fin-de-siècle* literature, this same figure earlier appears as one of the prototypes of patriotic masculinity, and is later demystified and shown as weak and decadent, e.g. in works by Juhani Aho and K. A. Tavastjerna. See Jyrki Nummi, 'Between Time and Eternity: K. A. Tavastjerna's *Barndomsvänner*', in *Changing Scenes*, ed. by Lyytikäinen, pp. 85–120; and Eira Juntti, 'The Student as a Representation of Masculinity in Nineteenth-Century Finnish Literature', *Scandinavian Studies*, 89.3 (2017), pp. 301–25.

[26] Cf. Maria-Liisa Kunnas, 'Ympäristö taiteen ja yksilön muokkaajana. Tainen teoriat L. Onervan tuotannossa', *Kirjallisuudentutkijain vuosikirja*, 33 (1980), pp. 85–97; Päivi Molarius, '"Will the Human Race Degenerate?" The Individual, the Family and the Fearsome Spectre of Degeneracy in Finnish Literature of the Late 19th and Early 20th Century', in *Changing Scenes*, ed. by Lyytikäinen, pp. 121–39.

and from the Nordic artist colony. All in all, therefore, Onerva's *nousukas* appears as 'a deeply ambivalent, mostly melancholic figure, a seeker for the impossible, obsessed with both the search for a — mostly unattainable — ideal and the eternal — mostly abortive — "longing to belong". This last did not necessarily mean longing to belong merely to a higher social rank, but also desire to identify with a particular idea.'[27]

The short stories in *Murtoviivoja* are already an indication of Onerva's inclination towards an extensive use of dialogue or of the juxtaposition of long monologues, in order to show rather than to tell. The same feature is also evident in her other collections of short stories from the early period, as well as in her novels. The 1912 collection entitled *Mies ja nainen* ('Man and woman') contains five short stories as well as two short dramatic pieces referred to as 'stage fantasies' or 'stage images' ('Näyttämö-kuvitelmia'). Following that, her last collection of short stories manifesting strong Decadent features and foregrounding women's difficulties in finding their place in the contemporary world is *Vangittuja sieluja* ('Imprisoned souls') from 1915. The title, which is also the title of one of the stories, suggests that, in Onerva's view, while women in Finland were granted the right to study and to vote (in 1906, the first in Europe), this did not prevent them from experiencing a form of inner imprisonment.

After *Mirdja*, Onerva only published two more novels. *Inari* (1913) is also a fictional work, although it is more directly inspired by the author's life. The novel depicts the protagonist's studies and her plans to write a dissertation, as well as her wavering between two men: Pirkka, who reminds the reader of Eino Leino, and Alvia, who resembles the distinguished Finnish composer Leevi Madetoja (1887–1947), whom Onerva married in 1918 (their marriage lasted till Madetoja's death in 1947). Inari ponders the impossible existence of a female intellectual; she is described as a 'hysteric intellectual' who at the same time suffers from the female 'desire to be a slave'.[28] Inari echoes Nietzsche, Lombroso, and many Decadents when claiming that a woman writer is 'ugly, ridiculous, incorrigibly unaesthetical'.[29] The problem of asynchronous, anachronistic female existence, thematized in the afore-mentioned short story 'Itsenäinen nainen' and resonating with the interme-diate states typical of Decadence, is emphasized again in *Inari*: 'She had the nervous system of the woman of the past, the brains and the will of the woman of the future. She was destined to be unhappy.'[30] Onerva's third and last novel, *Yksinäisiä* ('The lonely ones', 1917), which has been called a *roman*

---

[27] Parente-Čapková, 'Gendering Seekers and Upstarts', p. 32.

[28] 'älyllinen hysteerikko', 'orjuuden kaipaus'. L. Onerva, *Inari* (Kirja, 1913), pp. 10 and 27.

[29] 'hänestä oli kirjallinen nainen ruma, naurettava, auttamattomasti epäesteettinen ilmiö'. L. Onerva, *Inari*, p. 13.

[30] 'Hänellä oli menneisyyden naisen hermosto, tulevaisuuden naisen pää ja tahto. Hän oli luotu onnettomaksi.' L. Onerva, *Inari*, p. 26.

conversant, can also be characterized as a novel of ideas. The author confronts many of the intellectual currents of her day, from nationalism, socialism, and women's emancipation to religion and theosophy. The novel consists mostly of dialogues, inner monologues, memories, diary entries, and polemical exchanges between the characters. The ideas and opinions are so pronouncedly polyphonic that they puzzled and provoked contemporary critics: 'There are many things about which I don't share the opinion that I believe the author holds, if I have read her in the right way.'[31] Particularly remarkable is the author's assessment of the Finns' relationship towards Russia and the Russians, as well as the way she anticipates the horrors of the 1918 Finnish Civil War,[32] foreshadowed by post-1900 events, especially the General Strike of 1905.[33] Although *Yksinäisiä* 'lacks the more pronounced features of Decadent style like the cultivation of the oneiric and the bizarre, it resembles Decadent texts in downplaying the importance of the plot, and in its ecstatic way of expression', typical also of *Mirdja* and *Inari*, 'abundant in intense imagery, exclamations and invocations'.[34]

[31] 'Monessa asiassa olen toista mieltä kuin luulen tekijän olevan, jos olen häntä oikealla tavalla lukenut.' V. A. K. [V. A. Koskenniemi], 'Yksinäisiä', *Uusi Päivä*, 143 (22 December 1917), p. 5. See also Viola Parente-Čapková, 'Effeminate Race? Ideas and Emotions in L. Onerva's Representations of Russianness', *Joutsen/Svanen*, Erikoisjulkaisuja 4 (Suomalaiset ahdistukset), pp. 47–66 (p. 47).

[32] Parente-Čapková, 'Effeminate Race?', p. 62. The Finnish Civil War of 1918 was an armed conflict for the leadership and control of the country. It was the culmination of a complex social situation that developed during the previous decades, when Finland was still a part of the Russian empire, and arose from the political crisis following the First World War. The fighting parties were the so-called White Guards or 'Whites' and the Red Guards or 'Reds', supported by the Russian Bolsheviks. In March 1918, Germany intervened on the side of the Whites, contributing to their victory. The total number of deaths is estimated at around 35,000. The war inflicted a painful wound on Finnish society, which lasted for the following 100 years. In her writings about the national conflict of 1918, Onerva repeatedly emphasized the need for ideals and the danger of a purely materialist world view. Though she considered some social developments during the First World War and the February Revolution in Russia as positive in regard to the possibilities of the liberation of the people and the emancipation of women, she was very critical of later developments in the Soviet Union. See L. Onerva, 'Sota ja naiskysymys', *Sunnuntai*, 8 April 1917; 'Nykyhetken mietteitä', *Sunnuntai*, 16 September 1917; and 'Pois materialismista!', *Sunnuntai*, 19 May 1919. See also Maria-Liisa Kunnas, *Kansalaissodan kirjalliset rintamat eli Kirjallista keskustelua vuonna 1918* (Suomalaisen Kirjallisuuden Seura, 1976).

[33] The 1905 General Strike had some features of a revolutionary movement, and aimed to combat Russian supremacy, but it was also a consequence of Finland's inner political conflicts. The most immediate and far-reaching result of the Strike was the adoption of universal and equal suffrage in 1906, as well as the foundation of the Finnish parliament and the transition towards a more democratic organization of society. However, in the subsequent years, it became clear that the efficiency of the constitutional bodies was low, resulting in the second period of oppression of 1908 to 1917.

[34] Parente-Čapková, 'Effeminate Race?', p. 53.

The 1910s appear to have been the most prolific years of Onerva's life, with publication of various literary works, journalism, and editing activities, as well as translations. From 1918 on, the rest of Onerva's prose production includes other collections of short prose pieces, e.g. *Neitsyt Maarian lahja ynnä muita legendoja* ('The Virgin Mary's gift and other legends', 1918), which is the culmination of her interest in the figure of the Virgin Mary. *Jerusalemin suutari ynnä muita tarukuvia* ('The cobbler of Jerusalem and other mythical tales', 1921) picks up the sometimes-apocryphal use of biblical motifs. The last collections of short stories — *Salainen syy* ('The secret reason', 1923) and *Uponnut maailma ynnä muita satukuvia unen ja toden mailta* ('The sunken world and other fairy-tale pictures from the land of dream and truth', 1925) — continue the inclination towards mysticism and the intensified search for a personal kind of faith. In the 1920s, Onerva also wrote one proper drama, *Syyttäjät* ('Accusers', 1923), in which she continued the strategy she had adopted in *Yksinäisiä* of discussing topical issues, including Finland's relationship with Russia — in those days, already the Soviet Union — and gender equality, as well as pacifism by means of exchanges of opinions between figures representing various approaches to contemporary society. Throughout that decade Onerva drew ever closer to pacifist ideology and in 1926 she unsuccessfully attempted, together with some other cultural personalities, to found a Finnish section of the French Clarté peace movement, inspired by Henri Barbusse, whose novel *Le feu* (1916) she translated into Finnish (*Tuli*, 1922). Poetry was the genre Onerva would continue to write in subsequent decades, right up to her death in 1972. Her last published book, the collection of poems *Iltarusko* ('Afterglow'), came out in 1952. Other unpublished poems, as well as those from her literary bequest, were not published until after 2000.

During the latter half of the 1920s, Onerva worked on an extensive biography of Eino Leino. Published in 1932, the book is still an important source for scholarship on Leino's life and work. It is possible to trace Taine's influence in the biography, which posits the writer as defined by the intellectual and material environment in which he lived.[35] The 1940s were less prolific and, at the same time, a tragic period in the author's life: she and Madetoja suffered from various addictions and underwent treatment, but while Madetoja returned to his normal life, Onerva remained confined to a psychiatric hospital in Nikkilä and was only released after her husband's death in 1947. She survived the period of forced hospitalization thanks to the care staff enabling her to write, draw, and paint.[36] She was thus spared the fate of her

[35] Kunnas, 'Ympäristö taiteen ja yksilön muokkaajana'.
[36] Kortelainen, *Naisen tie*; Hannu Mäkelä and Berndt Arell, *L. Onerva, Valvottu yö. Runoilijan maalauksia pimeydestä valoon* (Minerva Kustannus 2004); Viola Parente-Čapková, '"Oi ystävä, oi kallis sana se!" L. Onervan Nikkilän sairaalan varjossa kirjoittamat ystävyys-invokaatiot', in *Ritvan ystäväkirja*, ed. by Maarit Leskelä-Kärki, Kirsi Tuohela, and Kaisa Vehkalahti (k&h, 2012), pp. 233–46.

mother Serafina, who spent most of her life in psychiatric care, where she also died. Onerva spent her last decades peacefully in her Helsinki apartment, overlooking the sea. She died in 1972, feeling that the surrounding world had forgotten her. However, this was not so. A first biography, by Reetta Nieminen, was published in 1982[37] and she was soon 'rediscovered' during the subsequent decades. The first doctoral dissertation on L. Onerva's *oeuvre* was written in Sweden in 1994.[38] The beginning of the new millennium saw the posthumous publication of two volumes of her poems from the postwar period as well as a second, very extensive biography by the art historian Anna Kortelainen.[39] Although in the popular perception Onerva continues to be overshadowed by the fame of Eino Leino, she was prominently included in the most recent major history of Finnish literature and her works are appreciated and researched by scholars interested in the history of women's writing and the literature of the *fin de siècle*.[40]

Finnish National Neo-Romanticism: Symbolism, Decadence, and Nietzscheanism

In *fin-de-siècle* Finland, literature and the arts were dominated by a melange of artistic currents that used to be referred to as 'national neo-Romanticism', a term originally coined by Eino Leino. On one hand, the allusion to a new version of Romanticism is partly misleading and, in this sense, the term obscures the plurality of the various artistic and philosophical trends that were in play at the time.[41] On the other hand, by highlighting the national, which was rather subdued during the Realism-dominated 1880s, the term brings to the fore an important feature present in many writers' work. As the Finnish literary historian Rafael Koskimies (1898–1977) was the first to show, the aforementioned melange included Naturalism, Symbolism, Decadence, and the Finnish version of Art Nouveau or Jugendstil.[42] Most Finnish writers

---

[37] Reetta Nieminen, *Elämän punainen päivä: L. Onerva 1882–1926* (Suomalaisen Kirjallisuuden Seura, 1982).

[38] Irene Virtala, *Narkissos i inre exil. En studie i begärets paradoxer i L. Onervas 'Mirdja'*, Acta Universitas Stockholmiensis, Studia Fennica Stockholmiensia 4 (Almqvist & Wiksell, 1994).

[39] L. Onerva, *Siivet. Runoja vuosilta 1945–1952*, ed. by Hannu Mäkelä (Otava, 2004); L. Onerva: *Pilvet ja aurinko. Runoja vuosilta 1953–1963*, ed. by Hannu Mäkelä (Otava, 2006); Kortelainen, *Naisen tie*.

[40] Elisabeth Møller Jensen, Margaretha Fahlgren, Beth Juncker, and Anne-Marie Mai (eds), *Nordisk Kvinnolitteraturhistoria 3. Vida Världen* (Bra Böcker AB, 1996); *Suomalaisen kirjallisuuden historia II*, ed. by Lea Rojola (Suomalaisen Kirjallisuuden Seura, 1999).

[41] See Pirjo Lyytikäinen, *Narkissos ja sfinksi. Minä ja toinen vuosisadanvaihteen kirjallisuudessa* (Suomalaisen Kirjallisuuden Seura, 1997), esp. p. 12.

[42] See Rafael Koskimies, 'Dekadenssityyli Suomen kirjallisuudessa', in *Juhlakirja Kauko Kyyrön täyttäessä 60 vuotta* (Tampereen yliopisto, 1967), pp. 1–21; and *Der Nordische Dekadent. Eine Vergleichende Literaturstudie* (Suomalainen tiedeakatemia, B 155, 1968).

would eclectically mix various aesthetic and other trends in their work. Leino's national neo-Romanticism also suggested the importance of inspiration drawn from Finnish-Karelian-Ingrian folk poetry, which he himself cultivated in many of his works. In the words of the British scholar Michael Branch, Leino was able to fuse what Robert Redfield called the 'little tradition' ('folk songs and folk tales, the popular culture of the non-learned and unlettered') and the 'great tradition' ('handed down by education' and 'following closely, even if a short step behind, what was happening elsewhere in Europe') into a kind of personal mythology, which has often been compared to that of W. B. Yeats.[43] With its Nordic variant embodying a kind of 'pantheist mysticism', Symbolism offered Finnish artists and writers 'a form of expression that had a remarkable affinity with the poetry of the little tradition'.[44]

While not all of his contemporaries would employ folk poetry as their intertext, the themes and motifs taken from folk tradition are of huge importance and should not be overlooked. Even the poet Otto Manninen (1872–1950), often regarded as the author of the purest Symbolist writing in the Finnish language, who cultivated Mallarméan poetics and drew inspiration from classical antiquity, would be occasionally inspired by the folk tradition.[45] However, in literary histories of the Nordic countries, the tendency to highlight national characteristics and supposedly unique features (like 'national neo-Romanticism' in Finland or the 'modern breakthrough' in Scandinavia) has at times been accompanied by an over-emphasis on foreign, mostly French models.[46] The key to less one-dimensional interpretations is to try and take into consideration both foreign and local influences and the complex interplay between them. Moreover, the genre that was most commonly identified as the pertinent local tradition was typically epic folk poetry. Thus, the Finnish national epic, the *Kalevala*, collected and compiled by Elias Lönnrot (first version 1835, final version 1849), was exploited for purposes of fostering Finnish national identity, both immediately on publication and over subsequent generations. By contrast, the folk lyric, or lyrical epic, was deemed less

[43] Michael Branch, 'Introduction', in Eino Leino, *Whitsongs*, trans. by Keith Bosley (Menard Press, 1978), pp. 7–8. *Whitsongs* is Leino's major opus of this kind, combining inspiration from folk poetry, European medieval folklore and literature, classical antiquity, legends, and other material.

[44] Branch, 'Introduction', p. 11. Branch notes that Leino was inspired by the Danish poet Johannes Jørgensen (1866–1956), who reflected the ideas of the French Symbolists but developed them 'in the direction of pantheist mysticism, "a secret world in which the artist's or poet's soul is one with the soul of nature"' (p. 11). See also Annamari Sarajas, *Elämän meri* (WSOY, 1961).

[45] See Hanna Karhu, 'De la chanson au poème. Les réécritures de rekilaulu du poète Otto Manninen', *Études finno-ougriennes*, 55 (2023), pp. 211–42.

[46] The concept of the 'modern breakthrough' stems from the Danish critic Georg Brandes (1842–1927) and has been used in Scandinavian literary histories for almost a century and a half. In his writings of the 1880s, Brandes described the Scandinavian writers of the young generation as moralists and idealists, distancing them from Naturalism and Decadence.

suitable for the construction of Finnishness and, as a result, its use in published prose and poetry was less widely celebrated. It followed that texts by women writers drawing on the folk lyric, or Decadent prose works such as Joel Lehtonen's (1881–1934) *Mataleena* (1905), with its allusions to an old Finnish folk ballad modelled on the biblical story of Mary Magdalene, were not deemed as patriotic as Leino's political allegories focusing on heroes recognizable from the folk epic, namely the *Kalevala*.

Both Lehtonen and Leino combined folk poetry material with — at times strongly — Decadent elements. Hence it is not surprising that the figure of Magdalene, who in Lehtonen's prose ballad stands both for the mother of the author's alter ego and for a demonic femme fatale, appears eventually as an old hag, a kind of a repulsive and disgusting *vetula* (old woman), whose process of decay and dying is described in detail.[47] *Mataleena* takes place in the woods, a space that is hardly a typical setting for international Decadent literature but that is in fact significant for Finnish Decadence: for, although Finnish Decadent literature comprises urban landscapes and although, in many cases, writers gesture beyond the physical world, there is a large number of texts containing natural or rural landscapes that can nevertheless be described as Decadent. *Mataleena* is one of the most telling examples of this rural Decadence, as well as of the mode that Pirjo Lyytikäinen has called 'Dionysian decadence', where the action takes place in the wilderness and culminates in a kind of wild and mad bacchanal.[48] Once again, this *fin-de-siècle* genre transposed into Nordic literatures ideas from Continental art and philosophy. Another pole is represented by the early twentieth-century work of Volter Kilpi (1886–1939), 'entirely preoccupied by [an] aesthetic vision of the world', a passive '"beautiful soul" infected by the "poison" of aestheticism'.[49] In Finland's Swedish language circles, aestheticism was promoted by the ultraconservative nobleman Bertel Gripenberg (1878–1947), who, in his early work, produced very subtle symbolist and decadent poetry.

---

[47] Joel Lehtonen, *Mataleena. Laulu synnyinseudulle* (Otava, 1905). See Pirjo Lyytikäinen, 'Passions against the Grain: Decadent Emotions in Finnish Wilderness', in *Nordic Literature of Decadence*, ed. by Lyytikäinen and others, pp. 87–101.

[48] Lyytikäinen, *Narkissos ja sfinksi*, and 'Passions against the Grain', p. 86. For more on 'rural Decadence', see Riikka Rossi, 'The Allure of Disgust: Rural Decadence in Zola's *La Terre*', in *Excavatio*, vol. xxv, ed. by Anna Gural-Migdal (The AIZEN and the University of Alberta, 2015), pp. 1–11; Lyytikäinen and others, 'Decadence in Nordic Literature: An Overview', in *Nordic Literature of Decadence*, ed. by Lyytikäinen and others, pp. 3–37 (pp. 24–27). A different kind of rural Decadence is to be found in Frans Emil Sillanpää's novels of the 1930s; see Riikka Rossi, 'Primitivism and Spiritual Emotions: F. E. Sillanpää's Rural Decadence', in *Nordic Literature of Decadence*, ed. by Lyytikäinen and others, pp. 119–35.

[49] Pirjo Lyytikäinen and others, 'Decadence in Nordic Literature', p. 18. See also Pirjo Lyytikäinen, 'Decadent Tropologies of Sickness', in *Decadence, Degeneration, and the End: Studies in the European Fin de Siècle*, ed. by Marja Härmänmaa and Christopher Nissen (Palgrave Macmillan, 2014), pp. 108–30.

However, some of his poems expressed a decadent racial elitism, and appealed to Finland-Swedes to defend the Swedish-speaking population (representing the 'Germanic race') and save it from Eastern barbarism.[50]

Together with Onerva, Leino, and Aarni Kouta (1884–1924), who was the Finnish translator of Ibsen, Strindberg, and Nietzsche, Lehtonen belongs among the most Nietzschean writers of the generation that entered the Finnish literary scene around 1900. As in other countries, in Finland Nietzsche's philosophy became extremely influential, especially in its emphasis on the individual, in its way of questioning the old ethical values, and in seeking an aesthetic justification for life. Nietzsche inspired philosophical and artistic interventions across Finland's social and political spectrum:[51] academic circles, creators of 'high art', as well as working-class writers and representatives of the women's movement, both Swedish- and Finnish-speaking, all found their own Nietzsches to draw on. The idea of the *Übermensch* was, of course, popular everywhere across the Nordic countries, often crystallizing in the figure of the artist as a creative demon who struggled against authority and the alienation produced by modern society, striving instead for an authentic existence in the Nietzschean sense.[52] Leino's variations on this figure also express existential issues resulting variously from a loss of traditional religious faith, from the weight of knowledge, from the sense of separation from the rest of human existence, and from the burden of responsibility felt by the 'modern bard', that is, by the artist who aspires to educate and guide his own people. The fact that the people did not want to be guided, following their own agenda instead, often resulted in feelings of frustration, disappointment, fatigue, and the Decadent contempt for the masses, as is evident in many of Leino's works.[53] All these feelings overlap and intermingle with the general crisis of the male subject and his sense of self-alienation.

Such feelings and Decadent tendencies were difficult to reconcile with the

[50] See Pirjo Lyytikäinen and others, 'Decadence in Nordic Literature', p. 22. Gripenberg translated Onerva's short stories into Swedish in 1910. In Finland's *fin-de-siècle* Swedish-language prose, the Decadent mode was explored by K. A. Tavastjerna (1860–1898) in his *I förbund med döden* ('In alliance with death', 1893); see George C. Schoolfield, *A Baedeker of Decadence: Charting a Literary Fashion, 1884–1927* (Yale University Press, 2003), pp. 132–46.

[51] Esko Ervasti, *Suomalainen kirjallisuus ja Nietzsche I. 1900-luvun vaihe ja siihen välittömästi liittyvät ilmiöt* (Turun yliopisto, 1960).

[52] See e.g. Antti Ahmala, *Autenttisuus ja itsestä vieraantuminen Joel Lehtosen varhaistuotannossa* (Helsingin yliopisto. Suomen kielen, suomalais-ugrilaisten ja pohjoismaisten kielten ja kirjallisuuksien laitos, Humanistinen tiedekunta, 2016).

[53] A certain approach to the interpretation of Leino's works from the early twentieth century has unequivocally highlighted the motif of disappointment, missing nuances of irony and self-irony. See Jussi Ojajärvi, 'Eräs tulkinta sivistyneistön pettymyksestä', in *Läpikulkuihmisiä. Muotoiluja kansallisuudesta ja sivistyksestä 1900-luvun alun Suomessa*, ed. by Kukku Melkas and others (Suomalaisen Kirjallisuuden Seura, 2009), pp. 197–235; and Parente-Čapková, 'Gendering Seekers and Upstarts'.

national project. Unlike in France and Britain,[54] nationalism in Finland was not associated with bourgeois philistinism and bourgeois gender models — although of course it could be, as we can see in the opening chapter of *Mirdja*. Here, as well as in other works by Onerva and her contemporaries, it is not patriotism or the national ideal per se which is ridiculed, but rather the kind of parochial bourgeois patriotism which has no understanding of art and philosophy. The way in which Decadents in France and Britain would sometimes reject the democratic, 'the secularist, and egalitarian developments of the modern world, preferring instead to seek out the aristocratic and spiritual trappings of an imagined old regime',[55] did have a certain appeal for some Decadent writers in the Nordic countries and Finland; but it was in direct contradiction with the teachings of Johan Vilhelm Snellman (1806–1881), who was later given the attribute of Finland's national philosopher. Snellman embedded the ideas of democracy and equality in the national programme, emphasizing the need to elevate the Finnish-speaking population by means of education and calling for greater unity and cohesion between the Finnish- and Swedish-speaking peoples, between the upper and lower strata of society. In Finland, Snellman acquired the reputation of a literary politician: he created a programme for a national literature, the key to which, he believed, lay in Finnish-language literary productivity. Literature was to have a didactic function and authors were to take on the role of the nation's leaders, a role that Eino Leino, in particular, internalized and struggled with throughout his career. Both Decadence and Naturalism were labelled foreign and un-Finnish, and associated with the 'degenerate' urban centres of Paris in the west and St Petersburg in the east.[56] Such defamation of Naturalism and Decadence, typical of all Nordic literary institutions, was directly connected to the rise of the young, healthy nations on the Nordic margins of Europe. The undesirable phenomena of Decadent and Naturalist art and literature were consequently 'swept under the carpet of the national cause'.[57]

[54] See David Weir, *Decadence and the Making of Modernism* (University of Massachusetts Press, 1995), p. xv.

[55] Liz Constable, Dennis Denisoff, and Matthew Potolsky, 'Introduction', in *Perennial Decay: On the Aesthetics and Politics of Decadence*, ed. by Constable, Denisoff, and Potolsky (University of Pennsylvania Press), pp. 1–32. See also Matthew Potolsky, 'Decadence, Nationalism and the Logic of Canon Formation', *Modern Language Quarterly*, 67.2 (2006), pp. 213–44. For the French Decadent writer Rachilde's stance on nationalism, see Melanie Hawthorne, *Rachilde and French Women's Authorship: From Decadence to Modernism* (University of Nebraska Press, 2001).

[56] See Eva Buchwald, *Ideals of Womanhood in the Literature of Finland and Russia 1894–1914* (PhD thesis, University of London, 1990). At the turn of the twentieth century, St Petersburg was the city with the largest Finnish-speaking population.

[57] Pirjo Lyytikäinen, 'The Allure of Decadence: French Reflections in a Finnish Looking Glass', in *Changing Scenes*, ed. by Lyytikäinen, pp. 12–30; and Lyytikäinen and others, 'Decadence in Nordic Literature'.

Onerva as a Finnish and European
Decadent Woman Writer, and her Mirdja

Among Finnish female as well as male writers, Onerva was, beyond any doubt, the writer who employed the Decadent mode most intensely and innovatively. Indeed, *Mirdja* has been defined as the most Decadent and Nietzschean Finnish novel.[58] In 'The Decay of Lying', Oscar Wilde famously put forward the Decadent paradox that 'life imitates art more than art imitates life'.[59] Onerva read and studied Wilde, claiming that 'Aside from Taine's theory, according to which the environment forms the person and, in that way, also the artist, there exists another theory, contrary to it, supported for example, by Oscar Wilde; one according to which the artist creates his/her environment [...]. According to Wilde's theory, the artist creates the milieu and the culture, not vice versa.'[60] In the concept of *zhiznetvorchestvo* ('life-creation') typical of Russian Silver Age aesthetics art and life were also understood as inseparable. These ideas often originated from the artists themselves but, especially in the case of women writers, they could lead to a restrictive identification of writers with their protagonists. In *Mirdja*'s case, certain elements of the novel do evoke events and people in the author's life: for instance, Mirdja's mentor Rolf Tanne, a Decadent dilettante Pygmalion, points partly to Eino Leino; while Mirdja's husband Runar bears a remote resemblance to Onerva's first husband Väinö Streng. However, the novel is far from being directly autobiographical. This is evident especially in the last part, where Mirdja's degraded marriage is transformed into a mystical marriage of sorts. Here, the old couple sinks into a kind of 'prelinguistic, Edenic space of perfect mutual understanding', giving up linguistic communication, which seemed to be 'the major cause of misunderstanding in their relationship'.[61] This new relationship subverts the idea of radical heterosexuality as well as the plot of romantic love. Earlier in the novel, Mirdja is told by her mentor Rolf that she cannot love woman in man but her fusion with Runar proves Rolf wrong. This new kind of relationship unfortunately happens too late, shortly before Runar's death, and seems to continue after it as well, showing that the ideal love does not belong to this world.

---

[58] Ervasti, *Suomalainen kirjallisuus ja Nietzsche I*.

[59] Oscar Wilde, 'The Decay of Lying', in *The Artist as Critic: Critical Writings of Oscar Wilde*, ed. by Richard Ellmann (W. H. Allen, 1970), pp. 290–319 (p. 307).

[60] 'Paitsi Tainen teoriaa, jonka mukaan ympäristö muodostaa ihmisen ja niin muodoin taiteilijankin, on olemassa toinen aivan päinvastainen, jota esim. Oscar Wilde kannattaa, se niin, että taiteilija luo ympäristönsä. [...] Wilden teorian mukaan luo taiteilija milieun ja kulttuurin eikä päinvastoin.' Quoted in Kortelainen, *Naisen tie*, p. 393, from L. Onerva's manuscripts and notes ('Watteau, Boucher, Fragonard ja ranskalainen taide' and 'Musta muistikirja. Taidehistoria', Tutkimukset ja tutkimusaineistot, Helsinki, Archives of the Finnish Literature Society).

[61] Parente-Čapková, 'Free Love', p. 76.

Although Onerva was not the only Finnish woman writer to engage with Decadent strategies in her work, she was certainly one of a very small number, comprising Selma Anttila (1867–1942) in some of her prose works and Ain'Elisabet Pennanen (1881–1945) in both her published and unpublished texts.[62] Pennanen also engaged with Nietzsche's thought, especially in her novel *Voimaihmisiä* ('People of strength', 1906). Here, a woman writer enters into dialogue with Nietzsche's ideas about the radical, fundamental difference between man and woman and his often contradictory use of the word 'woman' to refer both to mythic figures, metaphors, and actual embodied women. While some women writers rejected Nietzsche as a misogynist due to the expressions of revulsion for the female body to be found in his writings, others found there empowering potential for constructing the figure of a strong woman, capable of love as affirmation and self-assurance — a Dionysian force defying the restrictions of bourgeois society.[63] In this sense, Nietzschean women were supposed to be free and strong in love; however, for some women, as for the German-speaking Latvian writer and cultural mediator Laura Marholm (1854–1928), this still meant that, in love, women should derive their meaning from men. According to Marholm, women were not supposed to fight for equality and give up their 'feminine' nature and instincts; on the contrary, these had to be revalued.[64] The heroine of Pennanen's novel wavers between various models and types of femininity but is eventually unable to join the 'people of strength' of the title, who are portrayed as self-assured egotists and narcissists. She ends up bitterly disappointed, facing a pattern according to which she has, once again, existed only for the sake of man's pleasure. The concept of free love was important for Onerva — indeed the original title of *Mirdja* was *Vapaa rakkaus* ('Free love') — but both Onerva

[62] In terms of style, Pennanen's unpublished novel *Karadja Nikolajevna*, written most probably around the year 1906, manifests many Decadent features. The manuscript abounds in descriptions of interiors and can be easily read as ironizing the idea of home as 'feminine space', since the protagonist feels imprisoned and oppressed. For research on Pennanen, see Ulla-Maija Juutila, 'Voisiko naisenkin tuhkasta nousta feniks-lintu? Naistaiteilija minuutensa rakentajana Ain'Elisabet Pennasen teoksissa *Voimaihmisiä* ja *Kaksi raukkaa*', in *Pakeneva keskipiste. Tutkielmia suomalaisesta taiteilijaromaanista*, ed. by Tarja-Liisa Hypén (Turun yliopisto, Taiteiden tutkimuksen laitos, A 26, 1992), pp. 29–48; Lyytikäinen, *Narkissos ja sfinksi*, pp. 196–201; Suvi Ratinen, 'Huoneen hengettären lumo. Julkaisematon romaanikäsikirjoitus "Karadja Nikolajevna" osana Ain'Elisabet Pennasen tuotantoa', in *Lukemattomat sivut. Kirjallisuuden arkistot käytössä*, ed. by Elsi Hyttinen and Katri Kivilaakso (Suomalaisen Kirjallisuuden Seura, 2010), pp. 181–99.

[63] See Kelly Oliver, *Womanizing Nietzsche: Philosophy's Relation to the Feminine* (Routledge, 1995). Oliver's criticism is a response to Jacques Derrida's *Éperons — les Styles de Nietzsche* (Flammarion, 1978).

[64] This kind of 'female Nietzschean', acting as men's saviours, can be found in various literary works by women, such as *Nietzscheénne* (1907) by the French writer Daniel Lesueur (pseudonym of Alice Jeanne Victoire Loiseau, 1854–1921).

and her heroine refuse to accept the male understanding of free love as 'a pretext for making "free" use' of women's bodies and sexuality, 'without thoroughly questioning the whole system of asymmetry and inequality between the sexes'.[65]

This critique is to be found also elsewhere in Onerva's work, for instance in the short story 'Hävittävää voimaa' ('Destroying power') from the collection *Mies ja nainen* ('Man and woman', 1912). Here, the protagonist Sinikka feels attracted to the 'dark side of her personality', which is associated with eroticism and sexuality. She is fascinated by the 'subterranean, eternal fire, which will one day destroy the world, whose long, inward, secret seething suddenly explodes into lava, into an all-consuming sea of fire'[66] — similar to one of George Egerton's protagonists' celebration of 'the eternal wildness, the untamed primitive savage temperament'.[67] At the same time, Sinikka refuses to identify with only one aspect of herself or accept the idea of free love as woman's sexual availability. She wants to be a complex human being, as men are, 'Apollonian and Dionysian, creative and destructive'.[68]

Nietzsche's ideas on women, femininity, and gender, which are at the same time provocative, infuriating, and stimulating, are of utmost importance in *Mirdja*. Also significant is Nietzsche's complex stance on Decadence.[69] As in the works of many other Decadent women writers inspired by the German philosopher, Nietzschean concepts in Onerva's novel often lead the protagonist to an impasse or, at the very least, their consequences are ambivalent. Mirdja styles herself into the figure of the femme fatale but she suffers from compunction and twinges of conscience. She agrees with her male mentor who blames mothers for raising children according to conservatively oriented, prudish bourgeois values, but she draws little consolation from being motherless herself. Likewise, the fact that her own opinions on women, artistry, genius, love, and society are moulded by Decadent bohemian dilettanti proves to be equally problematic. Woman's attempt to appropriate the figure of the

---

[65] See Parente-Čapková, 'Free Love', pp. 69–70.

[66] 'maan-alainen, ikuinen tuli, joka kerran kaiken hävittää, joka kauan, sisällisesti, salaisesti kumisee, mutta sitten äkkiarvaamatta purkautuu laavaksi ja maailmannieleväksi tulimereksi…'. L. Onerva, *Mies ja nainen*, p. 60. Translation by Eva Buchwald.

[67] George Egerton, 'A Cross Line', in *Keynotes* (Roberts Brothers and Elkin Mathews & John Lane, 1893), pp. 9–44 (p. 30).

[68] L. Onerva, *Mies ja nainen*, p. 60.

[69] See Viola Parente-Čapková, '(Un)Masking Woman: Decadent and Nietzschean Figurations of Woman in the Early Work of L. Onerva', in *The New Woman and the Aesthetic Opening: Gender in Twentieth-Century Texts*, ed. by Ebba Witt-Brattström, Södertörn Academic Studies 20 (Södertörn högskola, 2004), pp. 67–81. For Nietzsche and Decadence in general, see e.g. Charles Bernheimer, 'Nietzsche's Decadence Philosophy', in *Decadent Subjects: The Idea of Decadence in Art, Literature, Philosophy, and Culture of the Fin de Siècle Europe*, ed. by T. Jefferson Kline and Naomi Schor (Johns Hopkins University Press), pp. 7–32.

Übermensch does not lead to success. However, Onerva employs textual strategies that can be called, at least partly, Nietzschean: violating narratological norms, questioning the hierarchy and the very difference between the original and the copy, frequently using irony, parody, and paradox. By employing the strategies of masking and masquerading, by (re)appropriating various figurations of the feminine, embodying them, and exploring them from an explicitly female point of view, Onerva belongs to the wave of early twentieth-century women writers who would open up aesthetic and political pathways that were to be explored by successive generations.[70]

Similarly to Nietzsche, most Decadent writers, both male and female, largely rejected, for various reasons, the idea of women's emancipation. The most notorious is Rachilde's (Marguerite Vallette-Eymery, 1860–1953) way of adopting 'an explicitly anti-feminist public stance'.[71] Rachilde's anti-feminism was caused by, among other things, the typically Decadent sense of seeing oneself as 'an exceptional individual', leading to identification with other Decadents, i.e. men, and not with women.[72] However, many women writers who engaged with Decadence were, at the same time, committed to the cause of women's rights and to the idea of social justice in more general terms, as was Onerva. The 'Woman Question', as the debate addressing woman's position in society was referred to in many parts of Continental and northern Europe, included a broad range of topics and themes: women's suffrage, their right to basic education, their right to study and teach at the university, their free access to work, art, and so on. It included issues related to love both in its 'new' or 'free' and its institutionalized forms, to prostitution, and, of course, to motherhood. The aforementioned Finnish philosopher J. V. Snellman spoke in favour of women's education and even of their literary activities, although his attitude to women writers remained somewhat ambivalent. Snellman's way of supporting the advancement of (patriotic) women had its own strict parameters: for him, it was not a viable option for Finnish women to refrain from the sacred vocation of motherhood, be it biological or 'social'.[73] 'Social motherhood' (*yhteiskunnallinen äitiys*) was women's special task within the Finnish national project. Thus Finnish women were not excluded from the public and political scene, but they were included on

---

[70] Parente-Čapková, '(Un)Masking Woman', p. 76.
[71] Melanie Hawthorne, and Liz Constable, Introduction, in Rachilde, *Monsieur Vénus* (The Modern Language Association of America, 2004), pp. ix–xxxix (p. xvii).
[72] Diane Holmes, *Rachilde: Decadence, Gender and the Woman Writer* (Berg, 2001), p. 76.
[73] See e.g. Päivi Lappalainen, '"Äiti-ilon himo". Naiset ja kansakunnan rakentuminen 1800-luvulla', in *Kaksi tietä nykyisyyteen. Tutkimuksia kirjallisuuden, kansallisuuden ja kansallisten liikkeiden suhteesta Suomessa ja Virossa*, ed. by Tere Koistinen and others (Suomalaisen Kirjallisuuden Seura, 1999), pp. 106–29; Kati Launis, *Kerrotut naiset. Suomen ensimmäiset naisten kirjoittamat romaanit naiseuden määrittelijöinä* (Suomalaisen Kirjallisuuden Seura, 2005), p. 80.

a special basis.[74] If a woman did not have any biological children, she was expected to function in professions which enabled her to carry out her supposedly 'natural' womanly, that is, maternal, inclinations.[75] The notion of 'social motherhood' was also advocated by the mainstream Finnish women's movement.[76]

Mirdja's search for a mother and the secrets of motherhood both literal and mystical (in the form of a female divinity) is one of the central themes in the novel, if not the principal one.[77] A reading that emphasizes a more 'literal' interpretation is most relevant, given the heated contemporary cultural and societal debates about the issue of motherhood. As a motherless, literally or metaphorically orphaned daughter, *Mirdja* enters into a long line of eighteenth-, nineteenth-, and early twentieth-century heroines, including the *fin-de-siècle* ones, e.g. those of Rachilde, Colette's Claudine (1900–1904), and the protagonists of *Una donna* ('A woman', 1906) by the Italian feminist writer Sibilla Aleramo (1876–1960) and *Hellé* (1898) by Marcelle Tinayre. Though returning, over and over again, to the issue of motherhood, Onerva never accepted the ideas of thinkers who were widely read and debated in early twentieth-century Finland, such as the influential Swedish feminist thinker Ellen Key (1849–1926), or the German-speaking novelist and editor Elisabeth Dauthendey (1854–1934), born in St Petersburg and translated into Swedish and Finnish in 1902.[78] Onerva remained sceptical about Dauthendey's and Key's way of associating Eros directly with motherhood, of 'venerating woman's reproductive capacities, while neglecting her intellectual potential' and thus reducing her creative forces.[79]

---

[74] See Räisänen, *Onnellisen avioliiton ehdot*, pp. 116–20; and Lappalainen, 'Äiti-ilon himo'. By means of social motherhood, both mothers and childless women were able to stand for the same ideal and fulfil woman's 'true' vocation. The ideal of social motherhood was connected with that of the brave 'äiti-kansalainen' or mother-citizen; see Irma Sulkunen, 'Naisten järjestäytyminen ja kaksijakoinen kansalaisuus', in *Kansa liikkeessä*, ed. by Risto Alapuro and others, 2nd edn (Kirjayhtymä, 1989), pp. 157–75.

[75] See Sulkunen, 'Naisten järjestäytyminen'.

[76] The Finnish Women's Association (Suomen Naisyhdistys). The ideal of social motherhood was also espoused by Onerva's history teacher and early role model, the writer and feminist Hilda Käkikoski (1864–1912). Käkikoski, who would go on to become an MP, was famous for her Christian (Lutheran) patriotic ethos. This is in the background of Onerva's complex relationship with the women's movement. See below, p. 57, n. 10.

[77] See Lea Rojola, 'Oman sielunsa hullu morsian. Mirdjan matka taiteen maailmassa', *Pakeneva keskipiste. Tutkielmia suomalaisesta taiteilijaromaanista*, ed. by Tarja-Liisa Hypén (Turun yliopisto, Taiteiden tutkimuksen laitos, A 26 1992), pp. 49–73; Viola Parente-Čapková, '"Kuka, kuka sitoi?" Dekadentti äitiys L. Onervan Mirdjassa', trans. by Pirjo Lyytikäinen, in *Dekadenssi vuosisadan vaihteen taiteessa ja kirjallisuudessa*, ed. by Pirjo Lyytikäinen (Suomalaisen Kirjallisuuden Seura, 1998), pp. 95–126.

[78] The work in question is *Vom neuen Weibe und seiner Liebe: Ein Buch für reife Geister* ('Of the New Woman and her love life: A book for mature spirits'), published in 1900.

[79] Parente-Čapková, 'Free Love', p. 77.

The idea of 'social motherhood' remains alien to the main character of *Mirdja*, and the figures which represent it are seen in a rather negative light, be it Elli Kailo in the opening scene, Mirdja's landlady Madam Malenius, or Anna, mother of Mirdja's husband Runar. They impersonate the aforementioned type of narrow-minded patriotism: the incapacity to understand art and culture, the hostility to the intellectual and artistic aspirations of the protagonist — attitudes that stem from the short-sighted nationalist zeal that was typical of provincial bourgeois patriots.[80] Mirdja distances herself from such types, exclaiming: 'We have different souls, different morals!' (p. 66).[81] Yet the 'nation' (*kansa*, meaning also folk, people) is by no means irrelevant to Mirdja's search. Mirdja is a particular kind of *nousukas* or upstart. In spite of her *Übermensch* dreams, she feels the urge to 'merge with the *kansa*' when she chances to visit a folk festival in the third section of the book. The heroine's defiance and her identification with the *Übermensch* figure mix with her longing to belong, to achieve unity with humankind, which was a visionary dream shared by many Decadent authors.[82] The desire to resolve one of the basic conflicts intrinsic to modern humanity, the conflict between individualism and the desire for symbiosis, can be understood to converge with the Decadent tension between the longing for psychological 'wholeness' and a sense of fragmentation and analytical distance from the self.[83] However, Mirdja receives some most unwanted attention while trying to get closer to the people attending the festival: by being called a 'pale and pretty lady of Lumiluoto' and accused of living at the expense of the workers, who claim that it is them to whom '[her] fortune, [her] beauty, [her] delicate figure, [her] fine skin' belong (p. 159),[84] she is delegated to the shameful and strongly gendered position of an outcast, verbally attacked by the crowd. This harsh response of the *kansa* is amplified by what Mirdja experiences almost as a kind of collective rape by the mob, a feeling that 'there was not one spot that they left untouched'.[85] She escapes, overwhelmed by the typically Decadent mixture of contempt and envy directed at the *kansa* as a brutish but healthy force: 'The pale and pretty lady of Lumiluoto was a stranger here, sick and homeless. Where was she born? Where were her roots? Where were her blood relations, her kindred spirits? These people here were neither' (p. 159).[86] The event puts an abrupt end to Mirdja's impossible dream: while she has a

---

[80] Cf. Potolsky 'Decadence, Nationalism and the Logic of Canon Formation', p. 213.

[81] 'meillä on eri sielut ja eri siveys!' L. Onerva, *Mirdja*, p. 28.

[82] Pynsent, *Decadence and Innovation*, p. 110.

[83] Parente-Čapková, *Decadent New Woman (Un)Bound*, p. 59–60.

[84] 'Lumiluodon kalpea ja kaunis neiti [...] [sinun] rahasi, [sinun] kauneutesi, [sinun] sirot muotosi, [sinun] hieno hipiäsi...'. L. Onerva, *Mirdja*, p. 205.

[85] 'ei ainoatakaan kohtaa jättäneet ne koskemattomaksi...'. L. Onerva, *Mirdja*, p. 205.

[86] 'Vieras oli täällä Lumiluodon kalpea ja kaunis neiti, sairas ja koditon. Missä oli hän syntynyt? Missä oli hänen isänmaansa? Missä olivat hänen veri- ja henkiheimonsa? Nämä täällä eivät olleet kumpaistakaan.' L. Onerva, *Mirdja*, p. 207.

'different soul and different morals' compared to bourgeois bores, the *kansa* feels even more alien, so that Mirdja concludes: 'We are each sick in our own way. We cannot help nor understand one another' (p. 159).[87]

The chapter about the folk festival evokes various Decadents' attempts to fuse with an overwhelming force, here, the 'ordinary folk'. Intertextually, it alludes to the short story 'Elämän meri' ('Sea of life', 1901) by the Finnish author Arvid Järnefelt (1861–1932). There, a single water drop finds its fulfilment in union and fusion with the sea, culminating in symbiotic devotion. Intertextual affinities play a key role in *Mirdja*, as in Decadent works in general. Indeed, we can speak of a programmatic intertextuality that takes the form of both indirect allusions and direct quotations from both historical and contemporary writers including Shakespeare, Goethe, Verlaine, Bourget, Leino, and Nietzsche, but also composers and painters. The synaesthetic nature of the novel, characteristic of Symbolist and Decadent writing, is expressed also by means of intertextuality, for example when Mirdja's beloved Selinä quotes a stanza from Verlaine's 'Art poétique' (1874), famous for its synaesthetic images (p. 124). Verlaine's way of placing music above everything resonates strongly throughout *Mirdja*. Indeed, music plays a very important role in the novel on many levels, from references to composers including Leoncavallo, Grieg, and Tschaikovsky, through musical figures like Don Juan, with whom Mirdja tries to identify (in the form of 'one special variation of the type: the female Don Juan', p. 210[88]). Onerva exploits the musical qualities of literary language and uses music as a leitmotif for the whole book. Music thus forms a key structural element of the novel, notably within the section 'Madrigal Tales', where chapters are named after musical terms.[89] Even the folk festival scene has its musical motif, a hymn to which Mirdja reacts strongly. Here and elsewhere, the novel's musical vein is permeated by irony, for instance in the chapters named after the traditional goliard song 'Gaudeamus igitur' ('Let us rejoice'),[90] highlighting the impossible position of a creative woman in the company of (male) Decadent artists, university students, and 'pub philosophers'. One of the most paradoxical moments, expressing, once again, a total gender asymmetry, and destabilizing the Decadent concepts of creative androgyny, is the question allegedly posed by Mirdja, reported by one of the men: 'Must a man really behave like a woman in order to be a

---

[87] 'Me olemme eri lailla sairaita. Me emme voi tosiamme auttaa emmäkä ymmärtää...' L. Onerva, *Mirdja*, p. 206.

[88] 'don Juanista naisen hahmossa'. L. Onerva, *Mirdja*, p. 312.

[89] For a detailed discussion of musical elements and 'musical mimesis' in *Mirdja*, see Parente-Čapková, *Decadent New Woman (Un)Bound*; and Viola Parente-Čapková, 'Musiikillinen mimesis symbolistis-dekadentissa kirjallisuudessa. L. Onervan *Mirdjan* sekasoinnut', in *Kirjallisuuden ja musiikin leikkauspintoja*, ed. by Liisa Steinby, Susanna Välimäki, and Siru Kainulainen (Suomalaisen Kirjallisuuden Seura, 2018), pp. 138–68.

[90] See note 54 to the novel, p. 119. The chapters 'Gaudeamus Igitur' and 'Post Jucundam Juventutem' are found in 'Madrigal Tales', the second part of the novel.

great poet?'; and his own reaction: 'Must a woman really behave like a man in order to be a great woman?' (p. 126)[91]

The synaesthetic features of the novel are compounded with its use of interart aesthetics.[92] Allusions to visual artists (from Leonardo to Rembrandt, Rubens, and Rossetti) culminate with the ekphrastic chapter in which Mirdja visits an art gallery and falls in love with the picture of a female saint, whom she calls Madonna, by the Italian Renaissance painter Carlo Crivelli. Feeling urgent desire for the beautiful woman in the picture, and at the same time narcissistically identifying with her, Onerva's heroine expresses her transgressive affect: 'My God, what a beautiful creature is woman! I almost wish I could be a man for a while, that I might take better pleasure in woman, and for that matter, in myself' (p. 165)[93] The desire to take narcissistic pleasure in enjoying her beauty and sexuality evokes 'A Cross Line' (1893) by George Egerton, 'An Egyptian Cigarette' (1900) by Kate Chopin, as well as works by the Russian-born Lou Andreas Salomé (1861–1937), texts manifesting traits of what Ebba Witt-Brattström has called the 'narcissistic turn' in women's writing.[94] The idea of a female Narcissus, paving 'the way for a new self-conscious female subjectivity'[95] as well as articulating the idea of same-sex love is, in *Mirdja*, subverted by the more Decadent feeling of the essence of the female icons created by men as 'stony', hostile to the aspiring woman artist. Mirdja's sexual and creative transgression, which makes her 'steal' the Crivelli painting by copying it, is punished both by the Madonna-Medusa's petrifying look and by the intervention of a mysterious male figure, who can be read as a fusion of other male characters in the novel. This ghostly presence evokes the figure of the effeminate Decadent artist, the painter Bengt Iro, introduced earlier in the novel, who tries to turn Mirdja back into a model, muse, and object of *his* gaze, *his* creation. Mimicking the divine creation, he claims that God 'was even more decadent than Crivelli' in creating Mirdja

[91] 'Pitääkö miehen välttämättä olla kuin nainen ollakseen suuri runoilija? [...] Pitääkö naisen välttämättä olla kuin mies ollakseen suuri nainen?' L. Onerva, *Mirdja*, p. 137.

[92] See Peter Dayan, *Art as Music, Music as Poetry, Poetry as Art, from Whistler to Stravinsky and Beyond* (Ashgate, 2011).

[93] 'Jumalani, miten nainen sentään voi olla kaunis! Tekisi välistä mieleni olla mies vain sentähden, että voisin enemmän nauttia naisesta, niin, ja miksei silloin myös itsestäni.' L. Onerva, *Mirdja*, p. 221.

[94] See Ebba Witt-Brattström, 'Towards a Feminist Genealogy of Modernism: The Narcissistic Turn in Lou Andreas Salomé and Edith Södergran', in *Gender — Power — Text*, ed. by Helena Forsås-Scott (Norvik Press, 2004), pp. 61–76; Ebba Witt-Brattström, 'Introduction: The New Woman Specter in Modernist Aesthetics', in *The New Woman and the Aesthetic Opening*, ed. by Ebba Witt-Brattström (Södertörns högskola, 2004), pp. 1–14. Witt-Brattström discusses writers such as Lou Andreas Salomé, Laura Marholm, and Ellen Key, as well as the subsequent generation of women writers, including the Finland-Swedish poet Edith Södergran (1892–1923) and the Russian Anna Akhmatova (1889–1966).

[95] Witt-Brattström, 'Introduction: The New Woman Specter', p. 10.

(p. 167).[96] In a Decadent vein, Mirdja sees the event as fatal, confirming her paternal heritage of Decadent dilettantism. At the same time, it is significant that Mirdja feels that she 'managed to capture a little part of her', leaving the meaning of the encounter ambivalent (p. 166).[97]

While Onerva's direct intertextual references in *Mirdja* are mostly drawn from male authors, it is, as already shown, more than relevant to read the novel within the framework of literature written by women. With a few exceptions, it is difficult to establish which women writers Onerva was familiar with; however, there are many shared concerns and many convergences to be found in her work with that of her immediate predecessors and contemporaries, both in the sense of influence and confluence.[98] Onerva's works, especially *Mirdja*, manifest many features typical of New Woman fiction. The term New Woman was first used in conjunction with literature written in English (it was originally coined by the British writer Sarah Grand) but, in recent decades, it has been applied to many other national literatures.[99] The concept of the New Woman is used here to point to the various means by which *fin-de-siècle* thinkers and artists/writers created a progressive idea of female subjectivity that differed from previous conceptions.[100] Such discursive construction was based predominantly on depicting the concerns of middle-class women, which are at the centre of Onerva's attention (if one excepts some lower-class and upper-class women in her short stories). Onerva herself uses the expression 'new woman ' in one of her short prose pieces, called 'Lohduttajat' ('Consolers'), when the protagonists argue whether the 'new woman' can be, at least in some respects, like the 'former one'.[101] Hence

---

[96] 'Jumala on ollut suurempi dekadentti kuin Crivelli luodessaan teidät'. L. Onerva, *Mirdja*, p. 224.

[97] 'Mutta jotakin olen kuitenkin saanut hänestä itselleni…' L. Onerva, *Mirdja*, p. 222.

[98] Kati Launis points to Carol MacKay's efforts to define the proximity of Fredrika Bremer (a Swedish writer born in Finland, 1801–1865) to the novels of her contemporary, Charlotte Brontë (1816–1855). As Launis states, 'what MacKay means by confluence is parallelism: two women writers, writing in different countries in the same period, were interested in the same topics connected with woman's life, such as women's education, and would often use partly similar plot configurations and similar ways of expression.' Launis, *Kerrotut naiset*, p. 62; see also Carol Hanbery MacKay, 'Lines of Confluence in Fredrika Bremer and Charlotta Brontë', *NORA*, 2 (1994), pp. 119–29.

[99] On Onerva as a Decadent New Woman writer, see Parente-Čapková, *Decadent New Woman (Un)Bound*, esp. pp. 15–18.

[100] As Ebba Witt-Brattström has pointed out, much of the New Woman debate could be characterized by means of the Foucauldian term 'reverse discourse', in that it borrows definitions, diagnoses, and categories of femininity from the nineteenth century. The New Woman is thus a figure negotiating the divide between nineteenth-century discourses on sexuality and the contemporary women's movement(s). See Witt-Brattsström, 'Introduction: The New Woman Specter', in *The New Woman and the Aesthetic Opening*, ed. by Witt-Brattström, pp. 1–14.

[101] L. Onerva, 'Lohduttajat', in *Mies ja nainen* (Uusi kirjapaino-osakeyhtiö, 1912), p. 71.

Mirdja's search for new ways of being a woman can be viewed against the backdrop of searches carried out by protagonists in the works of other New Woman writers, Onerva's contemporaries. In Finland, for instance, Maria Jotuni (1880–1943) produced new figurations of female subjectivity in her short stories and theatre plays, manifesting similarities with the laconic expression of the French prose writer and playwright Jeanne Marni (1854–1910). Jotuni employed Decadent imagery mostly in terms of ideas, inclining, in her style, more to Naturalism, and discussing, with a considerable dose of irony, the lives of lower-class women and their life options in urban and rural *milieus*.

The phenomenon of 'rural Decadence', important for Nordic and Finnish *fin-de-siècle* literature, is not relevant in Onerva's *Mirdja*, which takes place mostly in the city. Though the name of the city is never mentioned, it is obvious that Onerva means Helsinki, characterized by the heroine as 'that familiar small town, which is the biggest city of her native country' (p. 176).[102] Mirdja's wandering in the big foreign cities makes her a Decadent *picara*, striving to appropriate the role of *flâneur* but being degraded into a street-walker by the homosocial group of male Decadents in the chapter called 'Nocturno'. While the city is described as 'deceptive' and 'lying under its black shroud' (p. 111),[103] it is still the most natural habitat for the main character, whose union with the marshland at the end of the novel does not stand for the possibility of return to an idyllic, redeeming nature. The way the winter frost on the bog creeps over Mirdja and 'covers her with its white shroud' (p. 286)[104] evokes the concept of 'dual negation' typical of Decadence: this meant 'condemnation not only of a tawdry urban culture but also of the nostalgic yearning for an idyll of unmediated nature',[105] a kind of idyll often cultivated in Finnish literature as the solution to the lifelong quests of many literary protagonists.

Mirdja's quest is manifold, and includes a painful search for spirituality. Hence the character of Mirdja can also be seen as embodying the figure of the seeker, evoked in the novel in various contexts, also with Decadent overtones, as a 'self-seeker', or a 'seeker who has nothing left to seek'. The word seeker (*etsijä*) refers also to the concept of looking for alternatives to traditional forms of religion, widespread in *fin-de-siècle* literature and art.[106] Onerva

[102] 'Taas on Mirdja tuossa tutussa pikkukaupungissa, joka on hänen kotimaansa suurin.' L. Onerva, *Mirdja*, p. 243.
[103] 'petollinen […]. Tuo suuri kaupunki mustien käärinliinojensa alla…'. L. Onerva, *Mirdja*, p. 113.
[104] 'Hallat hiipivät hänen ylitseen ja peittävät hänet valkeaan käärinliinaan…' L. Onerva, *Mirdja*, p. 471.
[105] Rita Felski, *Gender of Modernity* (Harvard University Press, 1995), p. 107. Felski points to A. E. Carter's study of French Decadence, *The Idea of Decadence in French Literature 1830–1900* (University of Toronto Press, 1958).
[106] The concepts of the seeker and 'seekership' (*etsijyys*), adopted from the sociology of

was very critical of the Lutheran Church and any other institutionalized religions as such; although she was interested in Catholicism, which fascinated many Decadent authors, she never converted to it. A very personal, though contested and questioning version of Christianity remained a source of inspiration for her throughout her life; this is something that already the novel *Mirdja*, especially its latter half, strongly suggests. At the same time, Onerva explored the issue of spirituality in a most versatile way, looking for ideas and stimuli in various religions and spiritual currents, including mystic and esoteric trends such as theosophy, as evident especially from her work after *Mirdja*.[107] In *Mirdja*, the Protestant (Lutheran) Church is rejected and the institution of matrimony criticized and ridiculed. Criticism of the Church and concomitant Nietzschean defiance are most evident when Mirdja's mentor Rolf Tanne advises her to despise 'that false idol, that great double dunce, the state and the church' (p. 246).[108] However, Mirdja never gives up her spiritual search, which continues during her travels abroad. She is fascinated by the cult of the Virgin Mary and Catholicism, refusing, however, to separate it from the more literal search for a mother and motherhood: 'Mother of God, have you ever come across my mother among the servants who kneel before you...?' (p. 171).[109] The aesthetic aspect of the Catholic Marian cult is also behind her falling in love with the fatal picture of the Madonna-Medusa. Eventually, the Catholic worship loses hold and Mirdja ends up worshipping the ideal of suffering motherhood, turning, once again, to a flesh and blood figure of an elderly woman.[110] Thus the fusing of Eros and the spiritual, art and worship, hysteria and ecstasy in *Mirdja* does not acquire the mystical overtones that characterize, for instance, the works of the Russian Silver Age writer Zinaida Gippius (1869–1945), whose 'erotic utopia' converts sexual energy into a transfiguration of life in order to transcend gender and attain a new utopian religion.[111]

The wavering between the aesthetic, oneiric, and the real is one of the key elements of *Mirdja*. It is also conveyed by Onerva's style, by means of shifts

religion, were introduced into the *fin-de-siècle* Finnish context by the art historian Nina Kokkinen in her study of occulture in the visual arts. See Nina Kokkinen, *Totuuden etsijät. Vuosisadanvaihteen okkultuuri ja moderni henkisyys Akseli Gallen-Kallelan, Pekka Halosen ja Hugo Simbergin taiteessa* (University of Turku, 2019), esp. p. 52.

[107] Onerva shared this interest with Eino Leino. Their concern with these issues culminated in the 1910s, when together they edited the journal *Sunnuntai* (1915–1918), dedicating major attention to theosophy and other forms of spirituality.

[108] 'tuolle epäjumalaiselle suurkaksois-idiootille, valtiolle ja kirkolle'. L. Onerva, *Mirdja*, p. 389.

[109] 'Jumalan äiti, oletko koskaan nähnyt minun äitiäni polvistuviesi joukossa?' L. Onerva, *Mirdja*, p. 230.

[110] Parente-Čapková, "'Kuka, kuka sitoi?'".

[111] See Olga Matich, *Erotic Utopia: The Decadent Imagination in Russia's Fin de Siècle* (The University of Wisconsin Press, 2005).

in the text from past tense to present tense, blurring the boundaries between dreams, visions, and reality, between past, present, and future. Remarkable also are the constant narratorial shifts: the novel is narrated in the third person with the exception of the section 'Soliloquies Abroad' (pp. 162–75),[112] but all its narration is pronouncedly polyphonic. Various voices compete, as if (often ironically) commenting on the protagonist's thoughts as well as on each other's utterances; this polyphony makes the irony multi-layered.[113] The quarrelling, competing voices seem to illustrate Mirdja's fragmented self. At times, the inner voices rebuke and offend the protagonist, mocking and deriding her: 'What an altruist you are, evil, selfish Mirdja! How stupid you are, unable to find a better answer, wise, self-sufficient Mirdja! How weak you are, slain by a fly, strong, commanding Mirdja!' (p. 232).[114] Natural phenomena such as the waves and inanimate sources of sounds like bells have voices too, in tune with the Nordic 'neo-Romantic' mode.[115] The Decadent cult of ambivalence is present on many levels, both in form and content. The way the style evolves in the course of the novel is also symptomatic: it moves from a relatively realistic narrative in the first chapter to a feverish, decomposing form of expression in the last sections.[116] The fragmentary nature of the narrative is highlighted by the frequent use of ellipses and dashes, in accordance with the Decadent mode.

Read as a kind of a meta-comment on literary mimesis, *Mirdja* enters into a broader dialogue with other novels dealing explicitly with art, the figure of the artist, and female creativity, mainly in the sphere of reproductive arts such as acting and singing. *Mirdja* can be characterized as a female Decadent *Künstlerroman* as well as an ironic mutation of the *Bildungsroman* form. It is also a Decadent dilettante novel with a female protagonist. The theme of dilettantism is prevalent in Decadent works by male authors such as Paul Bourget and J.-K. Huysmans, but in the case of literature written by women and featuring female protagonists, ideas about lack of originality, anxiety of influence, and dilettantism acquire different meanings, as does also the typically Decadent trope of 'copying a copy'.[117] The words of the dilettante Rolf Tanne, 'You see how worn out I am, I can't think of anything new to say.

---

[112] 'Yksinpuheluja maailmalla'. L. Onerva, *Mirdja*, pp. 215–39.
[113] Viola Parente-Čapková, 'Decadent New Woman's Ironic Subversions: L. Onerva's Multi-layered Irony', *Volupté*, 2.1 (2019), pp. 82–99 (p. 86).
[114] 'Mikä altruisti sinä olet, sinä paha, itsekäs Mirdja! — Miten tyhmä sinä olet, kun et löydä parempaa ratkaisua, sinä viisas, itsekylläinen Mirdja! — Miten heikko sinä olet, kun sinut kärpänen kaataa, sinä voimakas, ihmisiä hallitseva Mirdja!' L. Onerva, *Mirdja*, p. 363.
[115] Parente-Čapková, 'Decadent New Woman's Ironic Subversions', p. 87.
[116] See Eva Buchwald's Note on the Text and Translation in this volume.
[117] See e.g. Potolsky, 'Decadence, Nationalism and the Logic of Canon Formation', p. 229.

Always quoting and plagiarizing', are echoed by Mirdja with bitter irony: 'And I plagiarize you. A double honour!' (p. 116).[118]

It is this spectre of double sterility, channelled into the figure of a barren streetwalker, with whom the protagonist obsessively identifies towards the end of the novel. This spectre leads Mirdja on a search, after all her revolt against the expectations of society, for a child she never had. This plot twist gives, once again, a gendered meaning to the 'semi-ironic dilettantism' mentioned in Bourget's *Cosmopolis* (1893) apropos the character of Dorsenne, which, according to Richard Hibbitt, may 'imply that dilettantism *per se* is both ironic and serious'.[119] In *Mirdja*, the bitter gendered irony of the old, sterile, childless dilettante in the figure of the 'aging New Woman'[120] also gives a tragic meaning to the role of *musa inspiratrix*, with which Mirdja struggles as a young woman, a role to which women were so often relegated in the sphere of art.[121] For Onerva, there was also a personal dimension to the fictional role of the muse, given her companionship with a famous poet (Leino) and a no-less-famous composer (Madetoja).

Though cast in Decadent mode, the issue of female creativity connects *Mirdja* to a long tradition of works with similar concerns written by women: from *Corinne, ou l'Italie* (1807) by Germaine de Staël, about whom Onerva wrote a short book in 1920,[122] to *Consuelo* (1842–43) by George Sand, whom Onerva mentions frequently in her 1905 thesis on Musset's female characters. De Staël and Sand can be viewed as conscious role models and sources of inspiration with regard to *Mirdja* (in the case of Sand, her *Lélia* from 1833 also seems to have inspired Onerva considerably). Another possible source of direct influence is the aforementioned novel *Hellé* by Marcelle Tinayre, which Onerva translated from French into Finnish.[123] *Hellé* is not a story of a woman artist but it features an exceptionally erudite female protagonist, raised by her uncle, talented in music and highly intelligent, who, however,

---

[118] 'Siitä nyt näet, miten kulunut minä olen, en keksi enää mitään uutta. Aina minä vain siteeraan ja kopioin. — Ja minä kopioin sinua. Kaksinkertainen kunnia!' L. Onerva, *Mirdja*, p. 123.

[119] Richard Hibbitt, *Dilettantism and its Values: From Weimar Classicism to the fin de siècle* (Legenda, 2006); Paul Bourget, *Cosmopolis*, in *Œuvres completes: Romans*, 7 vols (Plon-Nourrit, 1900–1911), IV, *La Terre promise / Cosmopolis* (1902), pp. 302–03.

[120] The protagonists of the New Woman fiction, especially those best known, tend to be young, and as a novel that follows the heroine from her teens to old age, *Mirdja* might seem an exception. However, a closer look at the production of *fin-de-siècle* women writers shows that this might not have been so exceptional (see e.g. Carol Diethe, *Nietzsche's Women: Beyond the Whip* (Walter de Gruyter, 1996)).

[121] See Buchwald, *Ideals of Womanhood*, and 'Taiteilija ja hänen muusansa. Luova uudelleensyntyminen Aleksandr Blokin ja Eino Leinon tuontannossa', in *Katsomuksen ihanuus. Kirjoituksia vuosisadanvaihteen taiteesta*, ed. by Pirjo Lyytikäinen, Jyrki Kalliokoski, and Mervi Kantokorpi (Suomalaisen Kirjallisuuden Seura, 1996), pp. 91–107.

[122] L. Onerva, *Madame de Staël* (Werner Söderström, 1920).

[123] Marcelle Tinayre, *Hellé*, trans. by L. Onerva (WSOY, 1922).

eventually finds her mission in 'universal love', dedicating herself to social work.

In the Finnish context, *Mirdja* is one of the first *Künstlerromane* or artist's novels to be written by a woman. The earliest examples of this genre date back to the late nineteenth century, beginning with *Framåt* ('Forward', 1894) by the Swedish-speaking Helena Westermarck (1857–1938).[124] Throughout Europe and beyond, women writers in this period shared a preoccupation with the theme of woman's search for an individual identity through art, philosophy, love, or spirituality, but only some of them employed a Decadent style when dealing with it. In Norway, for instance, Dagny Juel Przybyszewska (1868–1901), the 'Bohemian Queen and Cultural Mediator of the Avant-garde',[125] wrote aesthetically refined Decadent prose poems on the subject of female artistry, love, and death. In the English-language context, George Egerton's short stories, strongly inspired by Nietzschean thought, dealt with the theme of female creativity in a variety of ways, while C. P. Gilman's celebrated story 'The Yellow Wallpaper' (1892) presents an allegory of the restrictions imposed on women's talent.

In Italy, interesting points of comparison include the Decadent Regina di Luanto, especially her diary novel *Un martirio* ('A martyrdom', 1894), which depicts the heroine's growing madness within an oppressive marriage caused partly by her thwarted attempts to identify with male fantasies.[126] The 'hysterical', nervous, hypersensitive heroines of all these works partly resemble each other. However, while for some of them the only options are madness and death, the Decadent cult of artifice would lead some of the others to acknowledge their sexual desire but, at the same time, to learn how to control 'coldly and calculatingly, the game between the sexes'. That is the case of the protagonist of the Decadent novel *Berta Funcke* (1884) by the Swedish writer Stella Kleve.[127] Decadent women writers' take on marriage is multi-layered and complex, as shown also by Rachilde's writings;[128] L. Onerva's portrayal of Mirdja and Runar's union only confirms this.

[124] For an overview of Finnish artists' novels written by women, see Jasmine Westerlund, *Murtumia lasikellossa. Naisten kirjoittamat taiteilijaromaanit Suomessa 1900-luvun alkupuolella* (University of Turku, 2013).

[125] Anne-Birgitte Rønning, 'Decadence and Female Subjectivity in Dagny Juel's Prose Poems', in *Nordic Literature of Decadence*, ed. by Lyytikäinen and others, pp. 155–172 (p. 156).

[126] See e.g. Ulla Åkerström, 'Intimacy and Spatiality in Three Novels by Regina di Luanto', in *Women Writing Intimate Spaces: The Long Nineteenth Century at the Fringes of Europe*, ed. by Birgitta Lindh Estelle, Carmen Beatrice Duțu and Viola Parente-Čapková (Brill, 2023), pp. 129–144. Åkestrom compares *Un martirio* to 'The Yellow Wallpaper' on p. 137.

[127] See Birgitta Ney, 'On the Verge of the Forbidden', in *The History of the Nordic Women's Literature*, chief editor Anne-Marie Mai, 2011 <https://nordicwomensliterature.net/2011/07/15/on-the-verge-of-the-forbidden> [accessed 30 September 2024]. Stella Kleve was the pen name of Mathilda Kruse, later known as Mathilda Malling (1864–1942).

[128] See Hawthorne, *Rachilde and French Women's Authorship*, pp. 114–37.

It is reasonable to place Onerva among those authors who operated within the category of 'woman writer' at the turn of the century, and to analyse her strategies for examining how creative genius reflects female beauty and essentialized femininity. However, it is no less important to look at the ways in which she constructed and discussed various forms of gender fluidity, which often appear in dreams and fantasies and are set in stark contrast with the strict binarism of the sexes promoted by bourgeois morality and nationalist figurations of masculinity and femininity. Such dreams and visions celebrate androgyny as an aesthetic ideal, connecting with notions cultivated within esoteric circles and with various *fin-de-siècle* theories of a 'third sex'. As indicated earlier, Onerva also explores woman's potential to love other women,[129] be they flesh and blood or works of art, such as the picture of the Madonna-Medusa in *Mirdja*. As the protagonist's double,[130] this portrait evokes Oscar Wilde's *Picture of Dorian Gray*, but it invites the reader to ask questions about the dynamics of desire and identification.[131] Crivelli's female saint therefore assumes a different role to Dorian's portrait: apart from its mirroring function, it is one of the fatal texts that punctuate the novel, together with Mirdja's father's letter, her husband's 'Diary of a Sick Man', and the play 'Odalisque'. All of those — visual or written — texts shape Mirdja's understanding of herself in a fatal way, for instance by making her believe that her destiny is that of hereditary dilettantism and foregrounding the Decadent tenet that art shapes life.[132] Moreover, 'The Diary of a Sick Man' is at the root of Mirdja's obsession and identification with a woman of ill-repute.

---

[129] This is expressed much more daringly in the manuscripts of the novel held in the Literature and Cultural History Collection, Archives of the Finnish Literature Society. See Parente-Čapková, *Decadent New Woman (Un)Bound*, pp. 87–88, and Viola Parente-Čapková, 'Spaces of Decadence: A Decadent New Woman's Journey from the City to the Bog', in *Nordic Literature of Decadence*, ed. by Lyytikäinen and others, pp. 138–54 (esp. pp. 142–44).

[130] The motif of the double, or various figurations of the doppelgänger, is an important one in *Mirdja* as in many other Decadent works. In Finland, the first explicit mention of Freud and his work appeared in the 1910s, although his theories were only analysed systematically in the 1920s; see e.g. Maria-Liisa Kunnas, *Mielikuvien taistelu. Psykologinen aatetausta Eino Leinon tuotannossa* (Suomalaisen Kirjallisuuden Seura, 1972), esp. pp. 52–60. What we may regard today as Freudian ideas were in the time of L. Onerva's early work often connected with the literary analyses of the divided self, of the 'light' and 'dark' sides of the human psyche.

[131] Cf. Diana Fuss, *Identification Papers* (Routledge, 1995), p. 66; Parente-Čapková, *Decadent New Woman (Un)Bound*, p. 180.

[132] The notion of 'fatal text' is derived from the work of Linda Dowling and Robert Pynsent; the 'cult of the book' points e.g. to the importance of a 'sacred book' for Decadent characters (e.g. Huysmans's *À rebours* for Wilde's Dorian Gray). See Linda Dowling, *Language and Decadence in the Victorian Fin de Siècle* (Princeton University Press, 1986), p. 164; Pynsent, 'Decadence and Innovation', pp. 212–13. See also Parente-Čapková, *Decadent New Woman (Un)Bound*, p. 46.

The cult of ambivalence and in-betweenness also marks the concluding chapter of *Mirdja*. The equivocal image of the marsh, the 'enchanted wilderness', is often used as a symbol of the subconscious in Nordic Decadent writing (p. 286).[133] Often associated with the dark, dangerous side of the human psyche, with the uncanny, and with nocturnal forces and 'subterranean powers',[134] the marsh in *Mirdja*, filled with synaesthetic elements, is symptomatic of the protagonist's last refuge. Its use looks back to Finnish folk poetry, evoking the ancient practice of banishing strange and different individuals by sending them onto the marshes. At the same time, it is important to emphasize that Onerva was one of the women writers opening up the possibility of deconstructing the heavily gendered, patriotic imagery of the Finnish national landscape, engaging with the textual politics of representing and (re)creating place in Decadent writing.[135] In the final scene in *Mirdja*, the mention of pungent marsh herbs creates an association with morbidly veined plants, recalling Baudelaire's flowers of evil and Swedish Decadent Ola Hansson's *Sensitiva amorosa* (1887), 'a strange and singular plant' growing 'in the over-cultivated soil of modern society'.[136] The sinking aspect of the mossy bog adds an ironic twist to the fate of the Decadent type of *nousukas*: 'Given that a bog is an intermediate location (neither land nor water) with ambiguous connotations, it can be seen as both a symbolist soulscape, and as a decadent version of Mother Earth, the Great Mother.'[137] The climax of the novel demonstrates Onerva's ability to combine aesthetics with politics in the broad sense of the word: the finale, which stages woman's search ending in madness, reflects on the opportunities that were available to a woman seeker like Mirdja at the beginning of the twentieth century.

It is a sad truth that literary works written in a 'minor' language only very rarely enter the canon of world literature. In the case of Onerva's *Mirdja*, the marginalization has been manifold: written not only in the Finnish language, but also by a woman writer, and moreover in a Decadent mode generally adopted by men and resented by the proponents of cultural nationalism, the novel had several obstacles stacked against its chances of becoming famous,

---

[133] 'lumottu erämaa.' L. Onerva, *Mirdja*, p. 471. On the symbolism of the marsh, see Koskimies, 'Dekadenssityyli', p. 89.

[134] Cf. the earlier quotation from L. Onerva, *Mies ja nainen*, p. 60.

[135] Cf. Alex Murray, *Landscapes of Decadence: Literature and Place at the Fin de Siècle* (Cambridge University Press, 2016); Parente-Čapková, 'Spaces of Decadence', p. 148; Lea Rojola, 'From High Hills Down to the Marshes: Nature, Nation and Gender in Finnish Literature', in *The Angel of History: Literature, History and Culture. Anthology Based on the Papers Given at the NorLit Conference in Helsinki, August 2007*, ed. by Vesa Haapala and others (Department of Finnish Language and Literature, University of Helsinki, 2009), pp. 102–17.

[136] Ola Hansson, *Sensitiva amorosa*, trans. by Paul Norlén (Department of Scandinavian Studies, University of Wisconsin-Madison, 2002), p. 4.

[137] Parente-Čapková, *Decadent New Woman (Un)Bound*, p. 216.

even in the author's own country. As indicated earlier, Onerva was repeatedly admonished for her lack of originality and her dependence on the models provided by male authors, particularly Eino Leino. In the review included in this critical edition (written for the conservative cultural journal *Aika*), the influential Finnish literary critic V. A. Koskenniemi (1885–1962) observes that 'although it is quite wrong to suppose that only a woman can properly understand and depict her sex, nevertheless it cannot be denied that one would also like to read a woman's description of woman sometimes. In *this* sense,' Koskenniemi continues, 'I think that even "Mirdja" can prove interesting.' However, Koskenniemi is clear about the lack of artistic qualities from which *Mirdja* suffers since, according to him, 'the dimensions of real life are confused, the essential is overshadowed by the inessential, and many trivialities are blown out of all proportion'. For all these reasons he labels the book a 'hopelessly long, embarrassing, and tedious monologue'.[138] The most negative reactions to *Mirdja*, however, came from conservatively oriented women who were outraged by the alleged immorality of the 26-year-old writer: they publicly opposed her receiving the state prize of 1000 marks which the novel had been awarded. Nonetheless, the reception of the novel was not completely dismissive. It received favourable reviews from critics in Onerva's cultural circle, as shown by Aarni Kouta's article, also included in this volume. Kouta appreciated the style of the novel, emphasizing that the author 'does not err into vacant sentimentality, although the danger and opportunity for it are ever present; she has created a poetry in which the crucial developments are new, creating a unique atmosphere and mood'.[139]

In her review of the second edition of *Mirdja* in 1926, Finnish writer and translator Fanny Davidson seemed to fully recognize the merit in Onerva's depiction of the complex spiritual life of an aspiring female artist and of a woman who is developing her personality 'independently and totally volitionally'.[140] However, it would take several more decades before the reception of the novel grew generally more favourable. In 1956 the aforementioned Rafael Koskimies, who had an interest in Decadent writing, edited Onerva's *Valitut teokset* ('Selected works'), comprising *Mirdja* and a selection of short stories.[141] This shifted the attention from Onerva's poetry (which had been, till then, the focus of discussions of her work) to her prose. The next favourable overview of Onerva's *oeuvre* was written in the 1970s, by the Karelian, then Soviet scholar Eino Karhu (1923–2008). In his literary history, published first in Russian and then translated into Finnish, Karhu dedicated considerable

---

[138] See p. 288 of this volume. V. A. Koskenniemi, 'L. Onerva: Mirdja. Romaani. — Otava, Helsinki 1908', *Aika*, 23 (1908), p. 878. Translation by Eva Buchwald.

[139] See p. 291 of this volume. Aarni Kouta, 'L. Onerva: *Mirdja*. Romaani.', *Helsingin Sanomat*, 138 (1908), p. 6. Translation by Eva Buchwald.

[140] 'itsenäisesti ja täysin tietoisesti.' Fanny Davidsson, 'L. Onerva: Mirdja. Romaani. Toinen painos', *Tampereen Sanomat* (26 February 1928), p. 7.

[141] Koskimies, 'L. Onerva', in L. Onerva, *Valitut teokset*, pp. 5–14.

space to Onerva's works, including *Mirdja*.[142] His judgements show some of the ideological burden of official Soviet Marxism, yet he analysed the novel thoroughly and perceptively from several points of view, including its Nietzscheanism. *Mirdja* was then reissued by Onerva's major publisher Otava in 1982, for the centenary of the author's birth, and again in 2002, in the 'classic series' of the Finnish Literature Society, the major publisher of scholarly and critical editions of Finnish literature.[143]

As indicated earlier, a major shift in Onerva's Finnish reception took place thanks to the feminist literary criticism of the 1980s and the 1990s,[144] and the emergence of a new wave of interest in the literature of the turn of the twentieth century.[145] From the vantage point of the new millennium, we can say that *Mirdja* has, at least partly, entered the Finnish literary canon. Looking beyond Finland, there were no translations to other languages before the 1990s, when the novel appeared in Swedish. In 2022, it was translated into Italian.[146] French and Estonian translations are currently under way and, with this volume, *Mirdja* is also finally available to English-language readers.[147] The editor and translator hope that this English edition will broaden the scope of Decadent studies in many ways, proving the fruitfulness of 'widening the lens' in comprehending Decadence as an 'extensive international movement',[148] giving an extra dimension to the '"translational" understanding of decadence',[149] and confirming that many elements of what is customarily called modernist poetics first emerged in Decadent literature.[150] Taking a

[142] Eino Karhu, 'L. Onervan tuotanto', in *Suomen 1900-luvun alun kirjallisuus* (Kansankulttuuri Oy, 1973), pp. 319–59.
[143] L. Onerva, *Mirdja* (Otava, 1982); L. Onerva, *Mirdja* (Suomalaisen Kirjallisuuden Seura, 2002). Some of the editions of the novel would be reprinted during the subsequent years; the most recent dates from 2012.
[144] It was Maria-Liisa Nevala, Päivi Lappalainen, and Lea Rojola who called attention to L. Onerva's seminal role in the history of Finnish literature written by women.
[145] Pirjo Lyytikäinen has been highlighting L. Onerva's place in Finnish and Nordic Decadent writing in her numerous studies of Finnish Decadence, including 'Nordic Cultures: From Wilderness to Metropolitan Decadence', in *The Oxford Handbook of Decadence*, ed. by Jane Desmarais and David Weir (Oxford University Press, 2022), pp. 209–26.
[146] L. Onerva, *Mirdja*, trans. by Sixten Johansson and Irene Virtala (Östlings bokförlag Symposion, 1995); L. Onerva, *Mirdja*, trans. by Marcello Ganassini (Vocifuoriscena, 2022).
[147] So far, only a short extract from *Mirdja* has been available, to the readers of the journal *Books from Finland*, translated by Mary Lomas and introduced by Maria-Liisa Nevala; see L. Onerva: *Mirdja / An extract from the novel 'Mirdja'*, trans. by Mary Lomas, *Books from Finland* 1/1984 <https://www.booksfromfinland.fi/1984/03/mirdja>; Maria-Liisa Nevala, 'A Life of One's Own', *Books from Finland* 1/1984 <https://www.booksfromfinland.fi/1984/03/a-life-of-ones-own>.
[148] Hawthorne, 'Women Writing Decadence', pp. 1–2.
[149] Matthew Creasy and Stefano Evangelista, 'The View from Strasbourg: Translational Readings of Decadence by the Guest Editors', *Volupté*, 3.2 (2020), pp. ii–x (p. vi).
[150] Pirjo Lyytikäinen, Riikka Rossi, Viola Parente-Čapková, and Mirjam Hinrikus,

stance on issues of gender and sexuality, class and age, nationalism, religion, and society, *Mirdja* joins other Decadent works written by women in revealing to us the transnational and politically complex nature of Decadence. *Mirdja* and her author will finally be included in the international and transnational 'Decadent republic of letters',[151] with all the dissonances of longing for a community and celebrating loneliness, wavering between endless nuances and demanding absoluteness, as expressed throughout L. Onerva's work:

> I sense my calling's crescent:
> The smoulder of each solitary while,
> Forged fast into the firmament.[152]

'Afterword: The Spectres of Decadence in Later Nordic Literature', in *Nordic Literature of Decadence*, pp. 257–72.
[151] Matthew Potolsky, *The Decadent Republic of Letters* (University of Pennsylvania Press, 2012).
[152] 'Tunnen elontyöni vanteen: | yksinäisten hetkein hehku | taottava taivaan kanteen.' L. Onerva: *Runoja*, p. 32. Translation by Eva Buchwald.

AN ONERVA BIBLIOGRAPHY

~

Works by L. Onerva

POEMS

Sekasointuja: Runoja (Lilius & Hertzberg, 1904)
Runoja (Vihtori Kosonen, 1908)
Särjetyt jumalat: Runoja (Otava, 1910)
Iltakellot: Runoja (Kirja, 1912)
Kaukainen kevät: Runoja (Otava, 1914)
Liesilauluja: Runoja (Otava, 1916)
Murattiköynnös: Runoja (Ahjo, 1918)
Lyhtylasien laulu ynnä muita runoja (Ahjo, 1919)
Elämän muukalainen: Sikermä unikuvia (Kirja, 1921)
Helkkyvät hetket: Runoja (Otava, 1922)
Sielujen sota: Lyyrillinen sarja (Otava, 1923)
Maan tomu-uurna: Runoja (Otava, 1925)
Liekki: Runoja (Otava, 1927)
Yö ja päivä: Runoja (Otava, 1933)
Rajalla: Runoja (Otava, 1938)
Pursi: Kohtalovirsiä (Otava, 1945)
Kuilu ja tähdet: Runoja (Otava, 1949)
Iltarusko: Runoja (Otava, 1952)
Siivet. Runoja vuosilta 1945–1952, ed. by Hannu Mäkelä (Otava, 2004)
Pilvet ja aurinko. Runoja vuosilta 1953–1963, ed. by Hannu Mäkelä (Otava, 2006)

COLLECTIONS OF SHORT STORIES

Murtoviivoja: Novelleja (Otava, 1909)
Nousukkaita: Luonnekuvia (Yrjö Weilin & Kumpp., 1911)
Mies ja nainen: Novelleja (Kirja, 1912; includes two short dramatic pieces, referred
    to as 'stage fantasies' or 'stage images' (*Näyttämö-kuvitelmia*))
Vangittuja sieluja: Novelleja (Kirja, 1915)
Neitsyt Maarian lahja ynnä muita legendoja (Ahjo, 1918)
Jerusalemin suutari ynnä muita tarukuvia (Otava, 1921)
Salainen syy: Novelleja (Otava, 1923); includes three short dramatic pieces
Uponnut maailma ynnä muita satukuvia unen ja toden mailta (Otava, 1925)
Häistä hautajaisiin: Novelleja (Otava, 1934)

NOVELS

Mirdja: Romaani (Otava, 1908)
Inari: Romaani (Kirja, 1913)
Yksinäisiä: Romaani nykyajalta (Kirja, 1917)

Later editions of *Mirdja*

Mirdja (Otava, 1927)
Mirdja, in *Valitut teokset*, ed. by Rafael Koskimies (Otava, 1956)
Mirdja (Otava, 1982)
Mirdja, Suomalaisen kirjallisuuden klassikoita [Classics of Finnish Literature] (Suomalaisen Kirjallisuuden Seura, 2002)
The original text of the novel is available via Project Gutenberg: <https://www.gutenberg.org/cache/epub/54306/pg54306.html>

DRAMAS

Syyttäjät: 4-näytöksinen draama (Otava, 1923)

LITERARY BIOGRAPHIES

Madame de Staël (WSOY, 1920)
Eino Leino: Runoilija ja ihminen 1–2 (Otava, 1932)

SELECTIONS

Valittuja runoja (Otava, 1919)
Valittuja runoja 1–2 (Otava, 1927)
Valitut teokset, ed. by Rafael Koskimies (Otava, 1956)
L. Onervan kauneimmat runot: Valikoima (Otava, 1956)
Etsin suurta tulta: Valitut runot 1904–1952, ed. by Helena Anhava (Otava, 1984)
Toisillemme: L. Onerva – Eino Leino. Valikoima runoja, ed. by Reetta Nieminen and Jorma Rakkolainen (Otava, 1986)
Puoluepukarit ja Geisha, ed. by Annikki Yrjänäinen (TAI-teos, 2002)
Liekkisydän: Valitut runot 1904–1964, ed. by Hannu Mäkelä (Tammi, 2010)

Works on L. Onerva

BIOGRAPHIES

Nieminen, Reetta, *Elämän punainen päivä: L. Onerva 1882–1926* (Suomalaisen Kirjallisuuden Seura, 1982)
Kortelainen, Anna, *Naisen tie: L. Onervan kapina* (Otava, 2006)

ONERVA AS A CENTRAL FIGURE OF EARLY TWENTIETH-CENTURY CITY LIFE

Kortelainen, Anna, *Eri kivaa! Onerva – kaupungin naiset 1910* (Tammi, 2010)

ONERVA'S PAINTINGS AND DRAWINGS ACCOMPANIED BY CRITICAL ESSAYS

Mäkelä, Hannu, and Berndt Arell, *L. Onerva: valvottu yö. Runoilijan maalauksia pimeydestä valoon* (Minerva kustannus, 2004)

BIOGRAPHICAL, SEMI-BIOGRAPHICAL, AND FICTIONAL TEXTS
INSPIRED BY ONERVA'S LIFE

Mäkelä, Hannu, *Nalle ja Moppe — Eino Leinon ja L. Onervan elämä* (Otava, 2003)
—— *Uponnut pursi: kuvitelma.* Sepitteellinen Onerva-monologi (Otava, 2004)
—— *Onnen maa: L. Onervan elämä ja runot* (Minerva, 2007)

ONERVA'S PUBLISHED LETTERS

Onerva's and Madetoja's correspondence: Makkonen, Anna, and Marja-Leena Tuurna (eds), *Yölauluja: L. Onervan ja Leevi Madetojan kirjeitä 1910–1946* (Suomalaisen Kirjallisuuden Seura, 2006)
Onerva's letters to Eino Leino have not been found; Leino's letters to Onerva were published in 1960: Leino, Eino, *Kirjeet Onervalle*, ed. by Aarre M. Peltonen (Otava, 1960)

Select Bibliography of Critical Works

Jalkanen, Huugo, 'L. Onervan runous', in *Esseitä ja arvosteluja* (Arvi A. Karisto, 1919), pp. 132–44
Karhu, Eino, 'Begstvo iz odinochestva. O tvorchestve finskoi poetessy L. Onerva' ('Бегство из одиночества. О творчестве финской поэтессы Л. Онерва'), Petrozavodsk: *Sever*, 14 (1972), pp. 113–21
—— 'L. Onervan tuotanto', in *Suomen 1900-luvun alun kirjallisuus*, 2nd revised edn (Kansankulttuuri, 1972/1973), pp. 319–59
Karttunen, Päivi, 'Eräs aivan tuntematon laji', in *'Sain roolin johon en mahdu'. Suomalaisen naiskirjallisuuden linjoja*, ed. by Marja-Liisa Nevala (Otava, 1989), pp. 294–302
Koskimies, Rafael, 'L. Onerva', in *L. Onerva: Valitut teokset*, ed. by Rafael Koskimies (Otava, 1956), pp. 5–14
Krohn, Eino, 'L. Onerva — ensimmäinen huomattava naislyyrikkomme', in *Käännekohtia. Esseitä ja tutkielmia* (WSOY, 1967), pp. 90–105
Kunnas, Maria-Liisa, 'L. Onerva 28.4.1882–1.3.1972', in *Työtä ja tuloksia. Suomalaisia vaikuttajanaisia*, ed. by Suoma Pohjanpalo, Tuulikki Jääsalo, Maija Lehtonen, and Irma Rantavaara (WSOY, 1980), pp. 161–72
Lappalainen, Päivi, 'Jotakin vanhaa, jotakin uutta. Naisen subjektiviteetin rakentuminen L. Onervan *Mirdjassa* ja Aino Kallaksen *Sudenmorsiamessa*', in *Vampyyrinainen ja Kenkkuinniemen sauna. Suomalainen kaksikymmenluku ja modernin mahdollisuus*, ed. by Tapio Onnela (Suomalaisen Kirjallisuuden Seura, 1992), pp. 151–68
Laurila, Antti, 'L. Onervan 'Nousukkaita', *Kirjallisuudentutkijain Seuran Vuosikirja*, 18 (Suomalaisen Kirjallisuuden Seura, 1960), pp. 183–90
Lyytikäinen, Pirjo, 'Mirdja — dekadentti nainen', in *Suomen kirjallisuudenhistoria 2. Järkiuskosta vaistojen kapinaan*, ed. by Lea Rojola (Suomalaisen Kirjallisuuden Seura, 1999), pp. 147–48
—— 'Naisen elkeet miesten maailmassa', in L. Onerva, *Mirdja* (Suomalaisen Kirjallisuuden Seura, 2002), pp. vii–xvii
—— 'Naisen peilit', in *Narkissos ja sfinksi: Minä ja Toinen vuosisadanvaihteen kirjallisuudessa* (Suomalaisen Kirjallisuuden Seura, 1997), pp. 153–75

—— 'Nordic Cultures: From Wilderness to Metropolitan Decadence', in *The Oxford Handbook of Decadence*, ed. by Jane Desmarais and David Weir (Oxford University Press, 2022), pp. 209–26

Nevala, Maria-Liisa, 'Naiset arvojen ja asenteiden muuttajina. Minna Canthin, L. Onervan ja Hagar Olssonin tuotannon reaktioita naisen asemaan', *Kirjallisuudentutkijain Seuran Vuosikirja*, 34 (Suomalaisen Kirjallisuuden Seura, 1982), pp. 33–47

—— 'Särjetyt jumalat — L. Onerva', in *'Sain roolin johon en mahdu'. Suomalaisen naiskirjallisuuden linjoja*, ed. by Maria-Liisa Nevala (Otava, 1989), pp. 287–94

—— 'Ympäristö taiteen ja yksilön muokkaajana. Tainen teoriat L. Onervan tuotannossa', *Kirjallisuudentutkijain Seuran vuosikirja*, 33, ed. by Auli Viikari (Suomalaisen Kirjallisuuden Seura, 1980), pp. 85–97

Nieminen, Reetta, 'Naisen tie L. Onervan novelleissa', *Sananjalka — Suomen Kielen Seuran vuosikirja*, 41 (Suomen Kielen Seura, 1999), pp. 221–38

Parente-Čapková, Viola, 'Decadent New Woman?', *NORA - Nordic Journal of Women's Studies*, 6.1 (1998), pp. 6–20

—— 'Decadent New Woman's Ironic Subversions: L. Onerva's Multi-Layered Irony', *Volupté*, 2.1 (2019), pp. 82–99

—— *Decadent New Woman (Un)Bound: Mimetic Strategies in L. Onerva's 'Mirdja'* (Turun yliopisto, 2014)

—— 'Decadent Women Telling Nations Differently: The Finnish Writer L. Onerva and Her Motherless Dilettante Upstarts', in *Women Telling Nations*, ed. by Amelia Sanz, Francesca Scott, and Suzan Van Dijk (Rodopi, 2014), pp. 247–70

—— 'Dekadente Dissonanzen. L. Onerva und die Situation von Frauen im literarische Leben Finnlands um die Jahrhundertwende', in *Jahrbuch für finnisch-deutsche Literaturbeziehungen*, ed. by Hans Fromm, Maria-Liisa Nevala, and Ingrid Schellbach-Kopra (Deutsche Bibliotek Helsinki, 2000), pp. 180–88

—— 'The Effeminate Race? Ideas and Emotions in L. Onerva's Representations of Russianness', in *Joutsen/Svanen*, Erikoisjulkaisuja 4: *Suomalaiset ahdistukset* (2020), pp. 47–66

—— 'Free Love, Mystical Union or Prostitution? The Dissonant Love Stories of L. Onerva', in *Changing Scenes: Encounters between European and Finnish Fin de Siècle*, ed. by Pirjo Lyytikäinen, Studia Fennica Litteraria, 1 (Finnish Literature Society, 2003), pp. 54–84

—— 'Gendering Seekers and Upstarts in Early Twentieth-Century Finnish Literature', *Approaching Religion*, 11.1 (2021), pp. 28–44

—— 'Kuvittelija/tar. Androgyyniset mielikuvat L. Onervan varhaisproosassa', trans. by Päivi Lappalainen, in *Lähikuvassa nainen. Näköaloja 1800-luvun kirjalliseen kulttuuriin*, ed. by Päivi Lappalainen, Heidi Grönstrand, and Kati Launis (Suomalaisen Kirjallisuuden Seura, 2001), pp. 216–37

—— 'Narcissuses, Medusas, Ophelias: Water Imagery and Femininity in the Texts by Two Decadent Women Writers', *Water and Women in Past, Present and Future*, ed. by Zdenka Kalnická (SUNY Cortland, 2007), pp. 196–219

—— 'The Old Woman, Decadent and Folkloristic', in *States of Decadence: On the Aesthetic of Beauty, Decline and Transgression across Time and Space*, 2 vols, ed. by Guri Barstad and Karen P. Knutsen (Cambridge Scholars Publishing, 2016), I, pp. 61–79

—— 'Spaces of Decadence: A Decadent New Woman's Journey from the City to the Bog', in *Nordic Literature of Decadence*, ed. by Pirjo Lyytikäinen, Riikka Rossi, Viola Parente-Čapková, and Mirjam Hinnrikus (Routledge, 2020), pp. 138–54

—— '(Un)Masking Woman: Decadent and Nietzschean Figurations of Woman in the Early Work of L. Onerva', in *The New Woman and the Aesthetic Opening: Unlocking Gender in Twentieth-Century Texts*, ed. by Ebba Witt-Brattström, Södertörn Academic Studies, 20 (Södertörn högskola, 2004), pp. 67–81

—— 'La vergogna motivazionale e paralizzante. La figura del parvenu negli scritti di L. Onerva, sullo sfondo storico della Finlandia di inizi Novecento', *LEA. Lingue e letterature d'Oriente e d'Occidente*, 2, ed. by Beatrice Töttössy (Florence University Press, 2013), pp. 423–38

Rojola, Lea, 'Oman sielunsa hullu morsian. Mirdjan matka taiteen maailmassa', in *Pakeneva keskipiste. Tutkielmia suomalaisesta taiteilijaromaanista*, ed. by Tarja-Liisa Hypén (Turun yliopisto, Taiteiden tutkimuksen laitos, A 26, 1992), pp. 49–73

Schoolfield, George C., *A Baedeker of Decadence: Charting a Literary Fashion, 1884–1927* (Yale University Press, 2003)

Uusitalo, Ulla-Mari, 'L. Onerva: écrivain et traductrice' (unpublished master's thesis, University of Turku, 2000)

CHRONOLOGY OF ONERVA'S LIFE AND WORKS

This timeline lists significant events in Onerva's life in relation to Finnish cultural and political history as well as international Decadent literature, with particular attention to works written by women.

1882   Hilja Onerva Lehtinen is born into the family of Johan and Serafina Lehtinen in Helsinki, their only child. At the time, Helsinki is the capital of Finland existing as the Grand Duchy of the Russian Empire. During Onerva's childhood, the family lived also in the Kymi area east of Helsinki.

          Virginia Woolf is born in the same year.

1884   The French Decadent writer Rachilde publishes *Monsieur Vénus*; Joris-Karl Huysmans publishes *À rebours*.

1885   The Swedish writer Mathilda Malling (b. Kruse, known best by her early pen name Stella Kleve) publishes *Berta Funcke*, a Decadent novel with a female protagonist.

1889   Onerva's mother Serafina is interned in a psychiatric hospital, where she would remain, in different locations, till the end of her life. Onerva is brought up by her father and his mother.

1893–1898   Onerva attends the Finnish Girl's School in Helsinki, studies French and other languages, excels at school.

1893, 1894   George Egerton publishes her collections of short stories *Keynotes* and *Discords*.

1895   The Baltic-German writer with a Danish background Laura Marholm publishes *Das Buch der Frauen: Zeitpsychologische Porträts*.

1896   First production of Oscar Wilde's *Salome* in Paris.

          The Russian author and 'Decadent Madonna' Zinaida Gippius publishes a collection of short stories, *Novyje ljudi*.

1898   The Russian-German psychoanalyst and writer Lou Andreas Salomé publishes her tales *Fenitschka* and *Eine Ausschweifung*.

1898–1902   Onerva attends Upper Secondary school, acquires a teacher's degree.

1899, 1900	The American writer Kate Chopin publishes *Awakening*, a *Künstlerroman* with a female protagonist. The following year, 1900, she publishes her famous short story 'An Egyptian Cigarette'.
1900	The Norwegian Decadent poet, 'bohemian queen', and 'cultural mediator of the avant-garde' Dagny Juel Przybyszewska publishes her Decadent prose poems.
	Friedrich Nietzsche dies.
	Rachilde publishes *La jongleuse*.
1899–1905	First 'period of oppression' (*sortovuodet*), i.e. Russification in Finland. After decades of relative freedom, when Finland, as the Grand Duchy, enjoyed special liberties within the Russian Empire, Russia begins to curtail those liberties, consistent with Russia's policies towards various non-Russian minorities within the Empire. The Russification policies are partially reversed after Russia's defeat in the Russo-Japanese war and episodes of civil unrest within the Empire.
1900–1903	Volter Kilpi, a Finnish writer whose early work was influenced by symbolism and Decadence, publishes his major Decadent works: *Batsheba* (1900), *Parsifal* (1902), and *Antinous* (1903).
1901	Onerva passes her matriculation exam at Helsinki's Finnish Co-Educational School. She manifests a versatile talent, is gifted in literature, music (both as a composer and singer), art, and acting; she is also interested in medicine and mathematics.
1902	Onerva begins to study aesthetics, art history, Romance philology (French and other Romance languages), art history, contemporary European literature (mainly French and German), and other subjects (Italian language and literature, Latin, theology, geography, and mathematics) at the University of Helsinki (Imperial Alexander University in Finland). She is one of the first generation of women who, unlike their predecessors, did not need a special permit dispensing 'liberation from the female sex' in order to enrol at the university.
	At the university, Onerva meets Professor Yrjö Hirn (1870–1952), aesthetician and later also a diplomat. Hirn's interest in the Catholic religion and religion in general, theatre, psychology, and sociology is extremely important for Onerva's later development. Hirn would also motivate Onerva to take an interest in Germaine de Staël. Another important acquaintance is Werner Söderhjelm, professor of German and Romance philology, later also a politician and diplomat.

Onerva begins to publish in newspapers and journals, translates from French and other languages.

1903   Eino Leino publishes his major work, *Helkavirsiä* ('Whitsongs'), combining inspirations from folk poetry, European medieval folklore and literature, classical antiquity, legends, and other material.

1904   Onerva's first journey abroad to Dresden, Berlin, and Paris. She attends lectures on art history and literature at the Collège de France and the Sorbonne.

Onerva's first work, a collection of poems entitled *Sekasointuja* ('Disharmonies') is published under the pen name L. Onerva, suggested by the poet J. H. Erkko.

Joel Lehtonen publishes his Decadent novel *Paholaisen viulu* ('The Devil's violin').

1905   Premiere in Dresden of Richard Strauss's opera *Salome*, based on Oscar Wilde's play.

Premiere of Wilde's *Salomé* in the Finnish National Theatre; the title role was performed by Elli Tompuri, actress, dancer, director, and writer.

General Strike in Finland, a result of events in Russia as well as political conflicts within Finland; the old Diet of Finland is abolished and the modern Parliament of Finland is founded.

Onerva writes her thesis on Alfred de Musset's female characters ('Musset'n naisluonteet').

Onerva marries her first husband, Väinö Streng; for their honeymoon, they travel to Copenhagen and Paris via Hamburg and Cologne.

Publication of three major works of Finnish Decadence: Joel Lehtonen's *Mataleena* ('Magdalene') and *Villi* ('Wild'), Johannes Linnankoski's *Laulu tulipunaisesta kukasta* (*Song of the Blood-Red Flower*, English translation in 1921 by W. J. Alexander Worster).

Aarni Kouta publishes his strongly Nietzschean collection of poetry *Tulijoutsen* ('Fire swan').

1906   Finnish women are granted the right to vote. They are second in the world and the first in Europe to gain this right.

Onerva plans a dissertation on rococo art.

Publication of the first Finnish translation of Oscar Wilde's *Picture of Dorian Gray* by Helmi Setälä.

One of the few other Finnish Decadent women writers, Ain'Elisabet Pennanen, publishes her novel *Voimaihmisiä* ('Powerful people', or 'Strong people').

1907   First free parliamentary election in Finland with universal suffrage; it is the first parliamentary election in the world in which women could be elected.

Aarni Kouta publishes his Finnish translation of Nietzsche's dithyrambs.

Onerva meets Eino Leino, poet, journalist, and versatile cultural figure with whom she maintains a close relationship during the rest of his life, though they never marry.

1908   Onerva separates from Väinö Streng.

She travels via Copenhagen, Germany, and Austria to Rome, where she joins Eino Leino and returns to Finland in the early spring of 1909.

Collection of poems *Runoja* ('Poems').

Onerva's debut novel, *Mirdja*.

Mirdja is awarded a literary prize of 1000 Finnish marks, which provokes criticism and protest from the mainstream Finnish women's movement; the reception of the novel is both negative (mostly in conservative circles) and positive (in the artistic circles close to Onerva).

1908–1917   Second 'period of oppression', i.e. Russification, when the powers of the newly established Finnish Parliament were severely reduced by the Russian czar. The situation changes completely after the February Revolution in Russia in 1917, the October revolution of the same year, and the subsequent Russian Civil War.

1909   Onerva's first collection of short stories, *Murtoviivoja* ('Broken lines').

Onerva begins to work as critic and editor in various news-papers, beginning with the left-wing liberal weekly *Päivä*, publishing reviews of literary works and exhibitions, along with essays on aesthetics; as a divorced woman, she has to make her living by publishing and translating. She also has to help her father financially.

1910   Collection of poems *Särjetyt jumalat* ('Broken Gods').

Onerva meets the composer Leevi Madetoja, her future second husband.

Death of Onerva's father Johan Lehtinen, with whom she was very close.

1911   Collection of short stories *Nousukkaita* ('Social climbers').

Onerva's second thesis on 'Watteau, Boucher, Fragonard, and French art' for Yrjö Hirn.

She publishes translations of Anatole France's *Thaïs* and Camille Mauclair's *L'amour tragique*.

1912   Collection of short stories *Mies ja nainen* ('Man and woman').

Collection of poems *Iltakellot* ('Evening bells').

Selection of French poetry, edited and translated into Finnish by Onerva under the title *Ranskalaista laululyriikka* ('French song poetry'), with poems by Alfred de Musset, Paul Verlaine, and Charles Baudelaire.

1913   Onerva and Leevi Madetoja begin to live together.

Onerva publishes her second novel, *Inari*.

1914   Collection of poems *Kaukainen kevät* ('Distant spring').

1914–1918   First World War (Finland as part of Russia does not participate).

1915   Collection of short stories *Vangittuja sieluja* ('Imprisoned souls').

Publishes a translation of Hippolyte Taine's *Philosophie de l'art* on which she had worked for more than five years.

1915–1918   Onerva works for the newspaper *Sunnuntai* (devoting particular attention to theosophy and other forms of spirituality), which she co-edits with Eino Leino; in *Sunnuntai* she also publishes her articles and translations.

1916   Onerva travels to Moscow.

Collection of poems *Liesilauluja* ('Songs by the hearth').

Edith Södergran, the most well-known Finland-Swedish poet and a major figure in Scandinavian modernism, publishes her first collection of poems *Dikter* ('Poems').

1917   Finland becomes an independent republic in December, after having existed for six and a half centuries as a part of Sweden, and for a century as a part of the Russian Empire.

Onerva publishes the novel *Yksinäisiä* ('The lonely ones').

1918   Finnish Civil War, an armed conflict for the leadership and control over the country and the new republic; it is the culmination of a complex social situation that developed during the previous decades, arising from the political crisis following the First World War. The fighting parties are the so-called White Guards or 'Whites', and the Red Guards or 'Reds', supported by the Russian Bolsheviks. In March 1918, Germany intervenes on the side of the Whites, contributing to their victory.

Onerva and Madetoja are married.

Collection of short prose pieces *Neitsyt Maarian lahja ynnä muita legendoja* ('The Virgin Mary and other legends').

Collection of poems *Murattiköynnös* ('Ivy vine').

1914–*c.* 1928 Onerva publishes other translations from French literature, including Voltaire's *Candide* (1914), Anatole France's 'La chemise' (1915) and 'Les sept femmes de la Barbe-Bleue' (1920), Joseph Bédier's *Tristan et Isolde* (1917), Honoré de Balzac's *Mémoires de deux jeunes mariées* (1917), and Paul Bourget's *Un Divorce* (1925).

1919 Collection of poems *Lyhtylasien laulu* ('Song of the lantern glass').

1920 Short literary biography of Germaine de Staël (*Madame de Staël*).

Collection of poems *Elämän muukalainen* ('Life's stranger').

Onerva and Madetoja travel to London and Paris.

1921 Collection of short prose pieces *Jerusalemin suutari ynnä muita tarukuvia* ('The cobbler of Jerusalem and other mythical tales').

Onerva is awarded the State Prize for literature (and again in 1923 and 1927).

1922 Collection of poems *Helkkyvät hetket* ('Tinkling moments').

Onerva publishes her translations of Henri Barbusse's *Le Feu* and Marcelle Tinayre's *Hellé*.

1923 Collection of short prose pieces *Salainen syy* ('The secret reason').

Collection of poems *Sielujen sota* ('War of souls').

Onerva publishes her only drama, *Syyttäjät* ('Accusers').

1925 Collection of short prose pieces *Uponnut maailma ynnä muita satukuvia unen ja toden mailta* ('The sunken world and other fairy-tale pictures from the land of dream and truth').

Collection of poems *Maan tomu-uurna* ('The dust casket of the earth').

Onerva and Madetoja travel to Paris.

1926 Death of Eino Leino.

Inspired by Barbusse, Onerva attempts, with other writers, to found a Finnish branch of the peace movement *Clarté*.

Onerva and Madetoja buy a villa in the suburbs of Helsinki.

1927   Collection of poems *Liekki* ('Flame').

1928   Virginia Woolf publishes *Orlando*.

              Finnish writer Aino Kallas publishes her novella *Sudenmorsian* ('The wolf's bride'), set partly in the marshes, where the protagonist, a young woman called Aalo, transforms herself into a wolf.

1932   Onerva publishes a biography of Leino, the massive two-volume *Eino Leino, runoilija ja ihminen I.–II.* ('Eino Leino, poet and human being').

1930s   Onerva and Madetoja live permanently in their villa; they experience growing alcohol and drug problems.

1933   Collection of poems *Yö ja päivä* ('Night and day').

1934   Collection of short stories *Häistä hautajaisiin* ('From wedding to funeral').

1936   Onerva and Madetoja move back to Helsinki.

              Onerva's mother, Serafina Lehtinen, dies after spending many years in a psychiatric hospital.

1938   Collection of poems *Rajalla* ('At the border').

1939   Second World War begins. For Finland, it consists of two conflicts with the Soviet Union (Winter War, November 1939–March 1940; Continuation War, on Germany's side, June 1941–September 1944) and one with Germany (Lapland War, September 1944–April 1945). After the armistice with the Soviet Union, Finland has to expel or disarm any German soldiers remaining in its territory.

1942   Onerva and Madetoja are treated for their addiction problems. Onerva is eventually moved to the Nikkilä psychiatric hospital.

1945   Second World War (for Finland, Lapland War) ends.

              Collection of poems *Pursi* ('Barque').

1947   Onerva is released from the Nikkilä hospital after Madetoja's death.

1949   Collection of poems *Kuilu ja tähdet* ('Abyss and stars').

1952   Collection of poems *Iltarusko* ('Evening glow').

1972   Onerva dies and is buried at the Hietaniemi cemetery in Helsinki, next to her second husband Leevi Madetoja.

NOTE ON THE TEXT AND TRANSLATION

Eva Buchwald

⁓

For this translation I have used the original 1908 edition of the novel, published by Otava, on which all subsequent editions are also based (although more recent publications have modernised some of the spelling).

L. Onerva's *Mirdja* is a bold work for its era, unashamed in its psychological and sensual portrayal of the development of a young woman from adolescence to adulthood, and caustic in its criticism of the societal constraints imposed on grown women. The novel's protagonist, Mirdja, is unequivocal in her view of marriage as living death, for both partners, but more so for women because of the notion of marriage as the pinnacle of fulfilment for woman, a career in itself, with no possibility of escape. Times have changed since the novel was written, and women have acquired rights and opportunities that were not available to L. Onerva or to Mirdja. Yet the novel remains very modern in its portrait of a woman learning to navigate the world and confronting its expectations of her. The tendency to proscribe the nature and scope of women's freedom is tenacious even today, and the practice of defining the boundaries of women's morality according to their sex is all too current the world over.

I have tried to keep the feel of the period in certain choices of words and poetic forms, in the text's descriptive ornateness and the structural complexity of Onerva's sentences, as well as in her abundant and purposeful use of dashes and ellipses, but I have also tried to convey the extent to which Onerva's prose remains fresh and accessible to the modern reader. There is an urgency to the heroine's introspection, a comic undertone to much of the dialogue, an engaging rhythm of thought in general. Moreover, many of the issues and concepts that Onerva's heroine contends with are still topical, and the vocabulary for them very contemporary. Onerva makes the connection between woman's self-image and the external gaze that is so central to the modern-day discourse on both political identity and artistic representation. Mirdja struggles to become the subject of her own story, always aware of the male gaze and conscious of the fact that her own self-image is moulded by it. Her bid for independence, as both artist and individual, is thwarted as much by society's conformist values as by her own inability to see herself as anything but mediocre at best, a dilettante. Likewise, Mirdja's search for love is repeatedly undermined by the eternal paradox of her intrinsic desire for autonomy in confrontation with her socially conditioned desire for submission.

All this makes for multiple contradictions, inner tensions, dualities, and divisions in the narrative. Railing against the established church, Mirdja nevertheless knows her Bible well. I have used the King James version for the translation, which seems the best parallel to the author's original usage in terms of vocabulary, style, and tone. If the author uses direct quotations, I have included the equivalent in the text and, if paraphrases, I have provided the relevant biblical quotation in a footnote. Written at the turn of the century, the work contains a wealth of contemporary themes and observations, and Onerva's approach ranges from psychological reflection, moral deliberation, and artistic introspection, to social criticism and political polemic. This is a broad tapestry, rich in linguistic motif and literary allusion. All literary references, if they occur in the source text in Finnish, are translated into English with the original in a footnote. If such references occur in another language (namely French, German, Italian, Swedish, and Latin) I have maintained them as such, and provided an English translation in a footnote, either my own or from other sources as credited.

Onerva's language, often heavily decorative and even pointedly repetitious, can sometimes be challenging for a translator, but it is also rewarding for its inventive turns of phrase, its poetic reverie, and its deeply, sensuously Decadent imagery. The author has a remarkable capacity for mingling intensity of emotion with subtlety of humour. Onerva's style is often lyrical, yet it is also scientific, including for example detailed biological observations from the natural world to conjure exotic imagery or erotic nuance.

For a translator, one of the most fascinating aspects of the novel is the stylistic progression of the text. Written in the third person, the narrative shifts effortlessly between the narrator's objective viewpoint and the protagonist's subjective experience, allowing the author to play with both irony and self-irony in her viewpoint. The narrator's impartiality can give way to sympathy on one hand or to cynicism and ridicule on the other. As the story unfolds and the protagonist ages, the narrator's own form of expression undergoes a parallel transformation. The tale begins with simple confidence and much good-natured humour reflecting the arrogance and dismissiveness of youth. As Mirdja moves into adulthood and faces the increasing contradictions of her self-image, the narrative style acquires poetic complexity and ornamentation. The tone transitions back and forth between social criticism and self-irony. As the bitterness of disappointment engulfs the protagonist, the narrator's irony becomes more trenchant, but there is also a growing note of despair. And as Mirdja struggles with her phantoms in old age, the narrative itself loses cohesion, disintegrating into a lyrically feverish and fragmentary reflection.

An outsider all her life, Mirdja is a surprisingly existentialist character in a surprisingly anarchic work. Just as her protagonist rebels against the constraints of bourgeois norms, so L. Onerva in her day challenged the conventions of prose to create an experimental, vividly individualistic form of expression.

L. Onerva

MIRDJA

Translated by Eva Buchwald

Notes by Viola Parente-Čapková

This translation has been made possible by a generous grant from the Finnish Cultural Foundation and an initial sample grant from the Finnish Literature Exchange.

I

~

Professor Kailo's spacious drawing room was brimming over.[1] The sharpest minds in the Party had come together to discuss the programme for the approaching cultural soirée.[2] At the helm, as always, was professor Kailo's industrious wife who, in all good conscience, could easily have founded her very own Office for the Campaign of Noble Causes. But she chose not to. She was a modest woman who never blew her own trumpet. There were plenty of others to do this for her, and it was generally accepted that she should take the lead whenever the success of some new enterprise was at stake. And so here she was once again, chairing the meeting.[3]

The hum of conversation, which had risen to the level of a din during the coffee break, instantly subsided as Elli Kailo moved to take up her familiar position at the head of the table.

'A good deal of the programme is already confirmed, as we know,' she began. 'Master Pientare will make the opening speech, followed by Doctor Rautanen's presentation, and our good ladies Mrs Pilvenpää and Mrs Aarniheimo will perform an Indian dance. It all sounds splendid. And my attention is

[1] In this context, 'professor' (*lehtori*) means a secondary school teacher (as noted e.g. by Miroslav Hroch in his *Social Preconditions of National Revival in Europe: A Comparative Analysis of the Social Composition of Patriotic Groups among the Smaller European Nations*, trans. by Ben Fowkes (Cambridge University Press, 1985), p. 45, 'described in many continental countries as "professors in gymnasia"'. Secondary school teachers were an important force in the national movements in small European countries, including the Finnish national movement, which was reaching its peak at the time *Mirdja* was written.

[2] Though the name of the party is not mentioned, it is quite obvious that Onerva means the Finnish Party (*Suomalainen Puolue*), a political party that developed from the nineteenth-century Fennoman movement. Based on the doctrine of monolingual nationalism (i.e. the idea that Finnish language should be the basis of Finnish identity) as promoted by the philosopher and politician J. V. Snellman, Fennomania was the most important political movement in the Grand Duchy of Finland, then part of the Russian Empire. In the late nineteenth century, the Fennomans split into two political parties: the Finnish Party (originally the Old Finnish Party) being more conservative than the Young Finnish Party. In the first universal parliamentary election in the Grand Duchy of Finland in 1907, the Finnish Party was the biggest non-socialist party. It lost seats in every subsequent election and was dissolved in 1918, after Finland achieved its independence in December 1917.

[3] Women from Finnish patriotic circles, mostly *fin-de-siècle* Finnish patriots' wives, would frequently organize patriotic social events with cultural programmes, while their husbands were engaged in 'real' politics and art.

particularly drawn to the small but important fact that all the aforementioned have Finnish surnames.[4] I wonder if we might manage, for once, to print a programme in which all the surnames are of Finnish origin.'

'A truly excellent idea,' rallied the ladies.

'Till our own soil,' added one gentleman.

'What is still missing from the programme?' someone asked.

'We will have the student choir of course, and hopefully a short play, but what about a solo performance? A singer would be a delightful addition, but do we have such a talent in our midst?' said Mrs Kailo.

'What about among the student body, is there no young artist of promise we could turn to?'[5] added the elderly but ever flirtatious Mrs Pilvenpää as she turned towards the gentlemen.

Eino Kailo was sitting on the other side of the room surrounded by a whole group of young men. They burst into a flurry of discussion. Finally one of them said:

'There's only one member of our circle whose singing we can recommend.'

'The member's name is another matter,' someone laughed.

'Who is it?' people asked eagerly.

'Mirdja Ast.'[6]

'???'

'She graduated from school six months ago, very young, outstanding talent, wonderful potential…'

'For good as well as bad?' quipped Mrs Pilvenpää.

'Do you know her?' Mrs Kailo inquired with curiosity.

'Not as well as every young man in the city.[7] And it is precisely these young men who have put her name forward,' she added pointedly.

'Her name is indeed quite unfamiliar, from which it follows that her person may equally be a stranger to our common purpose. And it would be preferable

[4] Linguistic nationalism was manifested by the Fennomans' and Finnish Party members' habit of finnicizing their names (i.e. changing Swedish-language names into Finnish-language ones), which remained a widespread trend among late nineteenth- and early twentieth-century patriots. Having a Finnish language surname acquired a symbolic meaning.

[5] Students were also a significant force in the Finnish national movement, as they were elsewhere. At the turn of the twentieth century, most students in Finland were, of course, men. Until 1901, women could study at the university only after being granted a 'special permit', literally a 'liberation' or 'freedom from their sex' (*erivapaus sukupuolesta*). Onerva herself belonged to the first generation of Finnish women who were able to study without this special permit.

[6] L. Onerva never commented on the choice of 'Ast' (a surname of ancient Germanic origin), but in one of her late interviews, she claimed that she invented the name 'Mirdja' on purpose, in order to be able to endow her heroine with an unusual name not to be found anywhere else.

[7] Though Finland's capital Helsinki is not mentioned explicitly in the novel, it is strongly suggested that the novel takes place there.

if all our performers were pledged to the same cause,' said Mrs Kailo, who had sensed a certain reservation behind the remarks of her friend, the pharmacist's wife.[8]

'Surely a singer's purpose is to sing, and to sing well at that?' Eino Kailo remarked.

'But on such an occasion as this, don't you see, the performers must also be chosen internally, so to speak.'

'Yet you seem to be making your choices according to external factors, such as a name. Goodness me, what's a name got to do with a performer's performance!'

Mrs Kailo gave her son a long, disapproving look.

'It really is quite vexing, how you always remain so aloof when it comes to matters of principle. So you too propose that we should choose this Miss.... what was her name again?'

'Quite the contrary. You cannot possibly choose her because she wouldn't agree to come. Mirdja Ast is definitely not your soil to till.'

The voices of both mother and son betrayed a trace of irritation which presaged an argument. But at that moment they were distracted by the general discussion, which had suddenly become very vociferous.

'I think I've heard that name before, Mirdja Ast,' said someone. 'It's an unusual name, it sticks in the mind.'

'There's something very strange about her family circumstances too. Her parents are both long dead and her uncle is her guardian.'

'What does he do?' that typical, gauche society question rang out.

'I think he's a landowner of some sort. He's rich at any rate.'

'He owned some factories.'

'No, he has a university background.'

'But by no means is he a man of good sense. That's his most distinctive characteristic.'

'He's an original...'

During the general hubbub, the pharmacist's wife had drawn the professor's wife into the adjoining room.

'Do you mean to say you really haven't heard of Mirdja Ast, even though your own son is... a university student?' she added nervously.

'Eino hasn't mentioned a word about her before this evening.'

'But the whole town is talking about her. Frankly, she's a very dangerous young woman. I'm only saying this as your friend. As a mother you should know what everyone else knows, namely that your son is head over heels in love with this girl.'

'What are you saying!' Mrs Kallio cried out, jumping up from her chair. 'And this girl is not of good character?'

---

[8] Together with teachers, students, doctors, and other professionals, pharmacists were also among the groups active in the national movement.

'Oh my dear, she is the very epitome of bad character. And it's not just that she herself is totally immoral, she also has a great deal of influence on others.'

'Yes of course, like all bad people. And what's more she's a student, you say?'

'That's what's so wretched about all this! It makes me perfectly miserable to think that now we must beware our female students who, until now, have acted as the best safeguard for our young men. Oh well, this only goes to show that bookish intelligence is of little use where a good upbringing is wanting, not to mention Mirdja Ast, whose behaviour hasn't even had the benefit of a basic school education.'

'And you think that Eino... But Alma dear, you are making my head spin. I still can't comprehend it. Tell me everything you know.'

'Quite by chance, I happen to have heard a thing or two about Mirdja Ast, none of which commends itself. For a start, she is of bad blood. Her father was a strange man, an adventurer who never settled into a respectable profession. In the end he disappeared abroad never to be seen again, leaving his wife and debts behind him. His dissolute life probably killed him. In any event, his brother is still living somewhere in the country, a former university graduate, but now evidently with all his screws loose. He somehow managed to discover his niece, Mirdja, born in some remote who-knows-where corner of the world, no doubt beyond the boundaries of law and decency. And so this uncle apparently brought her up, that is to say, allowed her to grow up a wild thing. She only attended school for one year, can you imagine, one year, and not even that. She was just a young girl at the time and resided with my cousin, Mrs Malenius. She was the one who told me all this and more. While living in her charge, the girl behaved so outrageously that it does not bear repeating, and then one fine day, just like her father, she ran away! And that was that. The old man presumably became her schoolmaster. Apparently, they would go travelling abroad. And now suddenly, if you please, this selfsame runaway, Mirdja, turns up here, does brilliantly in her matriculation exams, and seduces everyone with her giftedness and her diabolical charm, and when I say everyone, I mean all the men. The male students are all mad about her. They have eyes for no one else, they talk of no one else. If intelligence is called for, Mirdja's the one, if beauty is called for, Mirdja's the one, no matter what talent or tendency under the sun is required, Mirdja's the one, always, always, Mirdja's always the only one. All the nicest and most pleasant young girls in society are neglected because of that terrible woman. She has destroyed our boys.'

'But can she be so very immoral?'

'How can you even ask! She doesn't know the first thing about manners and neither does she care. She really is like a common hussy. And she only mixes with men. Did you not hear how they sang her praises just now, your son loudest of all? That is no testimonial for a young woman. And furthermore, I know one or two things about her, as I mentioned, that others don't...'

The pharmacist's wife lowered her voice.

'What would you say about a fellow who keeps company with Rolf Tanne?[9] You would say he's a degenerate, an absolute degenerate. Well, what would you say about a girl who gads about with Mr Tanne? Can there be any further doubt as to her character! And Tanne is Mirdja Ast's most constant companion. Apart from the bars they frequent together, Mirdja Ast has been seen coming out of Tanne's lodgings, in the early hours.'

'Good God, how is this possible! All this going on in our so-called civilized society! But perhaps the poor girl is just being childish! Perhaps she should be warned, reprimanded...?'

'By whom, pray? None of the men would do it, and she doesn't deign to mix with women. And childish, her! She's everything but. She is wicked and poisonous and insults anyone who tries to reason with her. Even my daughter has had a taste of her impudence. Once, my daughter felt duty bound to point out to Mirdja that her lifestyle was totally unsuitable and you know the answer she received? Mirdja just laughed in her face and said: "that only goes to show that I don't suit your company, and you don't suit mine." She is beyond all sense of morality. All I can say is life without discipline leads to death without honour.'

'But can Eino really be besotted with her?' Mrs Kailo's voice trembled.

'So they say.'

'Surely God cannot have hurled such misfortune upon us. Eino is just a child. His eyes must be opened. I cannot believe it of him. But I am glad to have learned everything. I'm very grateful to you. Goodness, life can be hard sometimes.'

Both women returned to the drawing room. Mrs Kailo was clearly put out. Her inner commotion brought a tremor to her lips and an anguished, searching look to her eyes as she surveyed the group of young students. It was a great responsibility to be a mother in these trying times![10]

The conversation had taken a sensible turn. It focused on the programme, on ideals and idealism, but Mrs Kailo was strangely distracted. She felt as if

[9] 'Rolf Tanne' is a pronouncedly un-Finnish name.

[10] Here, Onerva is ironically alluding to women's traditional role, later described as 'social motherhood' (*yhteiskunnallinen äitiys*), which defined women's special task within the Finnish national project. If a woman did not have any biological children, she was supposed to function in professions which enabled her to carry out her 'natural', i.e. womanly, maternal inclinations. In this way, both mothers and childless women could stand for the same ideal and fulfil woman's 'true' vocation.Motherly qualities in women were promoted e.g. by Onerva's early mentor, the teacher, feminist, and later MP Hilda Käkikoski (1864–1912), whose Christian nationalist-feminist ethos had a considerable impact on the young writer. In her letters to Käkikoski (e.g. 1898), the young Onerva showed vivid interest in these ideas, but they soon proved incompatible with her involvement in Decadent literature and art, as well as with her interest in woman's sexuality. See also Introduction, pp. 21–23.

all those people and their ambitions were suddenly distant and irrelevant to her inner being. Her soul was consumed by one idea, one single ambition: to keep hold of her son, whom the big bad world wanted to steal from her, perhaps had already stolen. She was certain that for some time now, something had come between them, something terrible, hostile, and unaccountable. Was it the world, was it a woman…? What secret enemy's soul had Eino brought into their home?

Mrs Kailo sat and stared at Eino. If he made the slightest sudden movement, she jumped, as if she feared he might go astray at any minute, and drift further and further away from her.

Eino seemed to find her gaze unsettling. He stood up and left the room.

'Eino, Eino where are you going?' she called after him in distress, and followed him into the hallway.

'What's the matter with you, mother?' he asked, wide-eyed.

'Where are you going?'

'I have things to attend to, a friend I need to see,' Eino said evasively.

'What can be so important, in the middle of our meeting?'

'It is important… and the meeting is far from amusing.'

'Amusing, amusing… always putting amusement first. I would be very happy to hear what or who does amuse you. Who are you going to visit?'

'Surely, mother, you don't need to follow every step I take! Anyway, you don't even know my friends.'

'But I have a right to know them. I want to know with whom my son keeps company, who are these people stealing you away from me.'

Growing impatient, Eino tapped his cane irritably on the floor, as if to say: will there be much more of this nonsense?

But at that moment Mrs Kailo pulled her son into a side room and shouted unexpectedly:

'Listen to me Eino, you really mustn't see so much of Miss Ast. It is quite unacceptable. Mixing with common street wenches!'

Eino was struck dumb for an instant. Then uncontrollable anger towards his mother surged within him.

'Miss Ast is my friend, and I will not allow you to…'

'One must be able to tell the difference between good and bad friends.'

'You old fogies, you have no understanding of young people today. We have different notions of acceptability.'

'But I've heard very damning reports of Miss Ast.'

'Miss Ast is someone a man can be proud to call his friend.'

'Perhaps every one of them as proud as Mr Tanne, who has enjoyed the privilege of letting her slip out of his rooms in the early hours of the morning. You are right, I don't understand this modern notion of friendship. A young woman who, under the guise of friendship, does as she pleases! I'm sorry but we old fogies reserve the right to call such a girl a bad sort, and we don't want our boys mixing with her kind.'

Mrs Kailo was extremely agitated. Her son slammed the door in her face and took off.

She sighed:

'What are we to do with them, we poor mothers!'

II

~

Mirdja was sitting on a park bench waiting for Eino Kailo.

She was in a bad mood. Eino was taking an age! Mirdja was beginning to feel vexed, thoroughly vexed with the boy. It was a feeling that had been mounting of late, as she became increasingly aware that Eino made a perfectly childish and foolish impression. Or to be precise, this was not Mirdja's own observation. She had once accidentally overheard someone saying that Eino was hardly the type to be found where gunpowder was invented, and at that point she immediately stopped in her tracks, took a step back and placed on her nose the magnifying spectacles of a cold-hearted biologist. And from then on, she saw everything in a new light. Firstly, she couldn't help realizing that Eino really was stupid, but she also realized that all people in love are stupid, and she had been stupidest of all for thinking that she was in love with him. It was love she was in love with and had been for years, and for as many years, her imagination had painted a picture in her mind's eye of her romantic troubadour.[11] And then she had met Eino, and his eyes looked into hers like burning coals and she sensed the soft, dusky caress of the spring night… And Mirdja had felt a strange tremor in her chest and a dizziness in her head, and a sweet suspicion began to formulate in her mind: could this be love? Mirdja had been walking in silence, but Eino had kept talking. First, he told a fairy tale about himself, a very beautiful tale. Then he told a fairy tale about Mirdja, an even more beautiful tale. A tale about a princess with limitless power and a kingdom, about a sceptre borne by a white hand and captives ensnared by jet-black eyes. It had been music to Mirdja's soul. She had shut her eyes and her heart beat like a drum: just so must he sing, the troubadour of my love! — Just then Eino kissed her, the only time. And it made her head spin even more and ever since then, Mirdja had been walking in a dream, bearing in her heart the elation of furtive sinfulness.

But that was some time ago now. The enchantment had long since been broken. But Mirdja had not sent Eino on his way because she had learned to appreciate that a princess must have slaves and that a man was a delightful plaything in a woman's hands.

---

[11] A troubadour was a composer and performer of songs dealing mostly with courtly love and chivalry during the Middle Ages. The phenomenon originated in Occitania but similar movements also existed elsewhere in Europe. The Symbolist artist-aesthetes were sometimes seen as heirs to the medieval troubadours, for whom the worship of their beloved woman was often an excuse for worshiping the abstract idea of love, combining artistry with narcissism.

However, now Mirdja was truly beginning to grow bored with Eino. It was all so old and tired. And furthermore, Eino had begun to entertain all kinds of embarrassing long-term plans for the two of them, some sort of marital prospects... As if such a thing were even possible! Getting married, as one does. What did that entail? First having to petition Eino's parents, whom Mirdja held in prejudicial disdain; and then having to be always and forever together, till the end of time, with Eino, who was so childish and stupid! Never! What did love have to do with any of this? — Yet all good family boys and girls were either stupid or deceitful. — It was a social requirement — and Eino's mother was bound to be nothing but a silly prude.

Mirdja sat, bitter and bad-tempered, tracing figures in the sand with the tip of her umbrella. Then she turned to look up at the clouds through the leaves. They flitted past breezily, hastily. She too would sail through her life as swiftly as they. Her future would rise like a whirl of fire. She herself would soar on wings of flame above the crowds, who would bow to her glory. She was going to be a singer, an actress, she would enchant the world, and she would never have to beg for anything from anyone.

Motivated by these inner fancies, Mirdja had sprung to her feet, but at that moment she remembered Eino and a sudden aversion gripped her soul. She was going to have to break free of this unappealing, insubstantial relationship. Love, love; they never had anything else to talk about but love! Mirdja did not feel it, and undoubtedly neither did Eino. Was there anything to it? It was just the hollow-sounding catchword of two stupid souls. She was going to have to prove it. And so, resolute and acerbic, she sat down again to wait.

She could see Eino approaching. He was walking at a rapid, nervous pace. He was still fuming over the scene at home. The cheap, shameless provocation behind his mother's words! He was smouldering to the very depths of his soul with sheer anger toward the vile and petty morality of good families. But suddenly he felt a cold knife blade cut across his heart: jealousy had reared its ugly, reasoning head. If Mirdja had been visiting Rolf Tanne, how was it she hadn't mentioned a word about it to him? She was hiding something. An absence of love, at the very least. Perhaps Mirdja was in love with Rolf Tanne and was only toying with him, Eino, for whom Mirdja was everything, everything.

'Have you been waiting long?' asked Eino, quite out of breath.

'Indeed I have, and in the meantime wondering why exactly have I been waiting for you, because I have no desire to be with you right now.'

Mirdja's voice was cold and irritable.

She's in love with Tanne, came the whisper of doubt in Eino's heart.

'Who is it you would rather be with then?'

'Not you, isn't that enough information for you!' Mirdja answered indignantly.

'You don't love me, Mirdja. Otherwise you wouldn't be so rude and stubborn.'

Not that old chapter about love again. All right, firstly: love has long tentacles, it is full of suspicion and curiosity, said Mirdja to herself.

'So a lover must reveal all,' she said quietly and cryptically.

'It's only natural. It happens spontaneously. But you haven't done that. Lately you have been almost hiding from me, and rumour has it that you have been spending time with Tanne, in his rooms furthermore, which you haven't mentioned to me at all.'

Secondly: love is coarse and prying, said Mirdja to herself.

'Is that an accusation?'

'Why are you being so cold, so cruel? Confess to me Mirdja, you're in love with Rolf Tanne, not me. You've never been to my place…'

'You've never invited me. You haven't had the nerve. See how well I can see through you. Is that love? Is that chivalry? Needing to keep me hidden? Is love chicken?'

'Mirdja, Mirdja, just say you love me, and I will have the courage to do anything for your sake, I will take on the whole world…'

'Mummy and Daddy too?'

'Don't make fun, nothing is more sacred to me than you. Hang everything, as long as you are here!'

Thirdly: love is a worthless braggart, said Mirdja to herself.

'Why do you make such grand statements that mean nothing!'

'Mean nothing! Mirdja, you must believe me. Look, I could kill myself right here at your feet. Would you believe me then?'

Fourthly: love is childish and insane, said Mirdja to herself.

She laughed.

'Oh Mirdja, why do you torture me so! Don't laugh at my love! I would die for you.'

And Eino threw himself at her feet.

'A pointless exercise.'

'I will lie here till I die. You don't love me, you don't love me. I have nothing left.'

'Get up!'

'Kiss me as a sign of your love for me.'

Two boys were walking by the park. They stopped to stare at the curious scene and laughed. Mirdja felt a dark anger gathering on her brow.

Fifthly: love is ridiculous and cowardly, Mirdja concluded to herself as she stamped her foot with acute impatience. Did Eino really think he could force her to love him like this! To love a madman grovelling on the ground! The stupidity of it!

'Get up, you're mad,' she said, 'quite mad!'

'I will die on the spot if you don't love me.'

'Get up!' said Mirdja dragging him by the arm.

'Kiss me!'

'Never!'

'Then leave me to die.'

Mirdja felt how she despised this man lying before her, who was no man at all.

'Your love is driving me mad, and your madness is making you ridiculous! To love a ridiculous fool! A woman can love an evil man, a deceitful man, why not, but to love a ridiculous man — never! How can you ask of me something that you cannot ask of any woman in the whole world!'

And Mirdja suddenly turned on her heel and walked away without looking back.

III

Mirdja was feeling wretched, very wretched indeed. She sat in her little room looking out at the sea, which was her only friend, indeed more than a friend: her other self, her better, more profound self. At least that is how she often felt. But at present the sea seemed to reflect her poor conscience. It was spilling over, pounding and thrashing, watching her steadily, at times sombre and gentle as sorrow, at others ruthless and fearsome as endless, engulfing loneliness. It drew Mirdja's small, frail soul into its vast, weighty expanse, and magnified her desperate sense of longing.

Then the dusk set in. This intensified her melancholy, focusing its sway into a single emotion, distilling its mists into a single tear.

And so, in the half-light, Mirdja sat and cried —

She felt a compelling need to be good and kind, to take back her recent cruelty. It had all been an empty, arrogant outburst, provoked by a moment's malice. Once again, she felt she was capable of love and she herself craved love and warmth around her, in this terrifying gloom and loneliness.

Dear, dear Eino, how despicable I've been to you! — What if he really has killed himself! Oh if only Rolf were here! But it was precisely Rolf who was the source of Eino's foolish jealousy. 'You're in love with Tanne!' What a ridiculous notion! Such a notion as had never yet entered her head. Rolf meant a lot to her, Mirdja knew that, he was her best, her oldest friend, almost a brother, or an uncle to her... But to be in love with him—? No, Mirdja had never imagined love to be like that. Even if lately, she had been spending more time with Rolf than with Eino, even if she had indeed spent a couple of nights at Rolf's lodgings, it didn't mean anything of the kind. Their relationship had its own mystique, one which should never be defiled by someone's petty jealousy. 'I owe you that much consideration at least, my dear friend!'

And Mirdja fell to thinking about Rolf. It would be easier, far easier, to lose Eino than to lose Rolf. Was love not created precisely in order to be lost, to be renewed each day in the unflagging joy of mutual rediscovery? Was love not a crimson poppy, growing all over the world, losing its leaves every day yet straining forth to be plucked over and again? But friendship? A rare prize, a treasured heartwood exuding a mysterious narcotic, only one per life. Mirdja felt she would never find another Rolf, which is why in her heart she called him her friend. But she could have just as soon called him her guardian, her mentor, her guide to humanity and much more. For it was in the shadow of Rolf's spirit that she had moulded her own self.

Suddenly images of days gone by rose in her mind's eye, from a time when she was still very young and very childish. Images from her brief school career, of which she only held unpleasant memories. She stared and stared into the darkness… Only the phosphorescent glow of her own fantasy world as a child still shone back at her in the dark, and at its centre was the image of Rolf. Mirdja saw herself as she was in her happiest moments, in other words, when she was quite alone in her little schoolgirl's bedchamber. Here, the wild fancy that was in her blood rose to her head. She would adorn herself in white veils and flowers like Ophelia, or dance in the translucent gleam of her bare limbs like Salome.[12] And when she got carried away, she would make up verses whose rhythms and rhymes invented themselves. But Rolf occupied the adjacent room, and he gradually became privy to Mirdja's most intimate, secret impressions. After that, Mirdja was at her happiest when they were together. Back then, Mirdja still called Rolf 'uncle', and when uncle said goodnight, he never forgot to add 'little Mirdja'. Madam Malenius, who ran the boarding house, was a typical, stout busybody of a landlady, and Mirdja couldn't help feeling antipathy toward her, a feeling which inevitably extended to her many tenants. None of them were as good and wise as Rolf. And yet Mirdja often heard them saying that Rolf was a bad, wicked fellow. It so happened that now and then Rolf used to disappear for several days and nights, and when he eventually returned, he looked worn and tired for some time afterwards. It was especially on these occasions that Mirdja would overhear talk of Rolf's dissolute state. Oh, how pained she was by their cruel words. She was sure they were wrong, and she determined to put a stop to their worthless tongues and shield him from their unseeing eyes. From then on, whenever Rolf was out later than usual, Mirdja used to wait up for him. She would wait and wait with her heart in her mouth for fear that someone would notice he was out late and tomorrow there would be malicious gossip again. When Rolf returned, Mirdja would walk ahead of him with soft and silent steps, lighting the way for him and opening doors, and often she would only leave him once she had made sure he was tucked up in bed. In the end, this became a habit. 'Where are you, little Mirdja?' Rolf would ask before she

---

[12] The character of Ophelia from Shakespeare's *Hamlet* (1599–1601), driven to madness by Hamlet's actions and eventually drowning herself, was a very popular figure in *fin-de-siècle* literature and art. The same is true for Salome. A Jewish princess from the first century CE, daughter of Herod II and Herodias, Salome is known from the New Testament for requesting and receiving the head of John the Baptist. Her portrayal in the arts and literature evolved into an image of a treacherous temptress dancing before Herod with the head of the Baptist on a silver platter. Her dance came to be known as the 'dance of the seven veils' after Oscar Wilde's Symbolist play *Salome* (1891) and Richard Strauss's opera *Salome* (1905), which used a German translation of Wilde's play as its libretto. Actresses playing Wilde's Salome in various countries would often be given the label of 'goddess of decadence' and be identified with the role.

even reached the front door. And then he was even gentler and kinder than usual, speaking wisely on many subjects.

'Why do you drink?' Mirdja once asked, following him into his room, 'when it just makes you ill and makes others…'

'You won't understand now, little Mirdja, not yet, only later. But as for those others, they will die before they learn to understand. I know they despise me and call me weak, but I throw all that back in their faces, they haven't the courage to know the human soul, they haven't the courage to experience what millions of people around them experience, they haven't the courage to drink themselves under the table even once, these model citizens who are supposed to be humanity's salvation. They can't help anyone, but you Mirdja, you…'

From then on, Mirdja felt a certain thrill at being able to understand what others couldn't: Rolf was wise and they were stupid, Rolf was brave and they were cowards. And her heart now beat with a secret future ambition: to experience everything in order to understand, and — to heal… And when at the dinner table the discussion revolved around moral rectitude and abstinence and virtuous behaviour, Rolf and Mirdja merely held each other's gaze. Or when the conversation turned to all the depravity and vice in the world, their eyes addressed the others in a different language: you noble humanitarians and keen teetotallers, what do you know about humanity! We have different souls, different morals!

This beautiful, terrible collusion between Rolf and Mirdja lasted quite some time. They formed their own sect. Then disaster struck: the matter came to light! It caused a furore. Mirdja had been in Rolf's room at night! The immorality of it! Madam Malenius almost fainted. But Mirdja remained proud and there was not the slightest flicker of a bad conscience in her soul. What do you know about the human spirit, you morality deaconesses, she felt the words ringing in her ears, we have different souls and different morals!

But that wasn't the end of it. Madam Malenius began to spy on Mirdja. Naturally, a close watch was to be kept on such a wayward child, such bad habits at the age of only fifteen! — And then once, Mirdja was rehearsing the role of Juliet. She imagined herself on the balcony of the Capulet palace, a flimsy mantle draped over her gleaming moonlit shoulders, her arms outstretched… with only the limpid night to dampen those lovesick verses.

Gradually Mirdja forgets herself… Invisible characters answer her, and the drama intensifies. She sees only the shadow images of her dreams, her eyes gleaming, her soulful voice trembling:

— O serpent heart hid with a flowering face!
Did ever dragon keep so fair a cave?
Beautiful tyrant! Fiend angelical!
Dove-feathered raven, wolvish-ravening lamb!
Despisèd substance of divinest show,

Just opposite to what thou justly seem'st,
A damned saint —[13]

'My dear girl, are you quite mad?' A stern voice rings out behind the anguished Juliet. 'Cursing enough to bring the house down! Is that what you call doing your homework?'

'It's Shakespeare,' explains the unmasked actress, with a flash of pride and irritation in her eyes.

'If Shakespeare curses it does not follow that you must,' Madam busybody imparts pedagogically.

At this the young girl laughs scornfully: what do you know about the essence of art, you petty bourgeois souls!

I will never bow to bourgeois mentality, her spirit declares in reckless defiance. Rolf is wise; he despises you. You have no understanding of the human soul.

Soon after this incident, Rolf left town. This was followed by the final calamity: Mirdja ran away to the country, to stay with her uncle. What did she have to do with these stupid people and their rules!

All this Mirdja remembers as if it were yesterday, as she weighs up Rolf's influence on her. Why was it so great? Perhaps because Rolf awakened in her that essential, intrinsic, as yet dormant part of her self... They were made of the same mettle. They understood each other, even better now perhaps than five years ago.

Mirdja suddenly awoke from her old memories. It was almost dark already. She thought of Eino. She had been awful to him. What if Eino was still lying out there? But then he really would be mad...

No, she must visit Rolf and tell him all about it. He would know what to do...

[13] The lines are from William Shakespeare's *Romeo and Juliet*, Act III, Scene 2. Onerva quotes a slightly adapted version of Paavo Cajander's Finnish translation of the play from 1881.

IV

~

Rolf was sitting in the dark, smoking a papirosa when Mirdja walked in breathless, without knocking.[14]

'Ah, it's good you came. I was about to go out. I can't bear to spend these dark autumn nights alone at home, as you know. But what's the matter with you?'

'How fortunate that you are in! I have something very important to tell you. I'm feeling so very wretched, and I have been such a wretch... I have to tell you everything.'

And Mirdja described everything from start to finish: her brief infatuation, her long period of doubt and observation, the unexpected dénouement and her own cruel behaviour.

'Tell me Rolf, what do you think it all means? Is it love? Should I go and find Eino...? But I can't bring myself to apologize, or even regret it and take back my words... He really was a ridiculous idiot... Or you don't think he has killed himself, do you?'

'No,' said Rolf with a brief laugh. 'It was just the giddiness of growing pains.'

'Am I in love with him?'

'Your little act of meanness is not, at any rate, evidence to the contrary...'

'So you do think I am in love...?'

'Why are you asking me for an answer in such a difficult, personal matter? You know I have my own cynical view of the world and it would be rather dangerous for me to fill you with all kinds of preconceptions before you have experienced life for yourself. But if you absolutely insist on hearing my opinion...'

'Do tell Rolf, do!'

'Then I say: no, you are not in love with him. You are simply new to hearing confessions of love, and that is why it makes your head spin at first. You'll get used to it, I can assure you that you'll be hearing such confessions your whole life long. I know this because I know men. Not even the most resilient of men can resist the burning glimmer in your eyes and the delicate, soft, sultry sway in your step. You were born to be a *bayadère*.[15] And yet yours is a

---

[14] *Papirosa* (a Russian loan word) is a type of filterless cigarette. Papirosas were smoked mostly by the lower classes and soldiers, but gradually became popular also among other social strata, particularly bohemian artists.

[15] *Bayadère* means an Indian temple dancer, especially as found in Hindu temples. It is a

masculine spirit, rich and strong-willed and impossible to conquer, unlike those eternal feminine ones.[16] You cannot be taken and left. You will be a hazard to yourself, and to others, a serious hazard. But don't listen to me, listen only to life! It lies before you in all its glory and variety. And you will always dream of finding a prince, but will find only subjects, worms who will crawl at your feet like your recent admirer, and yes, like me too, why not, like all of us…'

Mirdja listened as if listening to her own proud, burning heart. Yes, yes how well you know me: it is a prince I dream of!

'But then is love no more than an arrogant dream, a lie, an evaporating whim?'

'Find out, find out for yourself! So long as you keep walking past it, love is truth looking you in the eye, but as soon as you stop in your tracks, it turns into a lie… But why am I telling you this; I have my own cynical view of life. Don't listen to me, go out and live and find out for yourself!'

'Is there no such thing then, as enduring love?'

'If you were a man, I would answer you in the words of that old French song:

"Plaisir d'amour ne dure qu'un moment
Chagrin d'amour dure toute la vie."[17]

Whomsoever you win, you abandon and forget, whomsoever you fail to win, remains the source of lifelong sorrow.

It's the story of Don Juan,[18] old as life itself and perhaps in the future not

French word of Portuguese origin (*bailar, bailhadera* in Portuguese). *Bayadères* were a favourite subject of rococo paintings of the eighteenth and nineteenth centuries. Onerva studied rococo art and planned a doctoral dissertation on the subject. In Decadent art and writing, *bayadères* belong to the arsenal of exoticized and eroticized 'Oriental' fantasies, as for example in Camille Lemonnier's (1844–1913) *Le Possédé* from 1890.

[16] The eternal feminine (*Ewig-Weibliche* in German) is a concept coined by Johann Wolfgang von Goethe (1749–1832), introduced at the end of *Faust, Part II* (1832). It is an unattainable ideal with metaphysical dimensions, described also as transcendental ideality, detached from the attributes of living women. Goethe was an important figure for Onerva, who reviewed translations of his works (e.g. *Torquato Tasso*, 1790) into Finnish.

[17] Rolf quotes the beginning of the famous song 'Plaisir d'amour' by the French poet and author of novels and fables Jean-Pierre Claris de Florian (1755–1794); the music was composed by Jean-Paul-Égide Martini (1741–1816). The song originates from Claris de Florian's novel *Célestine. Nouvelle espagnole* (1784) and it has survived, in various arrangements, to the present day. 'Love's pleasure lasts but a moment | Love's sorrow lasts a lifetime.'

[18] Don Juan is a legendary Spanish libertine. This figure is known from various works of literature and music, including seventeenth-century plays by Tirso de Molina and Molière, the opera libretto *Don Giovanni* by Lorenzo da Ponte (set to music by W. A. Mozart and premièred in 1787), and an early nineteenth-century satirical epic poem by Lord Byron. For *fin-de-siècle* artists, Don Juan was often a symbol of male narcissism. Decadent figurations of Don Juan include e.g. Charles Baudelaire's poem 'Don Juan aux enfers' (from

unfamiliar to your soul. But remember: Don Juan obtains everything he wants except his dream, he wins his lover, but not love itself.'

'Have you been through all this?'

'At my age one knows a thing or two. When I first met you, I was already well versed in the so-called romantic joys of a young man, those fleeting, far from dreamlike moments, but since then I have regained my dream, my unattainable, enduring dream — thanks to you Mirdja.'

'Thanks to me...?'

'Whomsoever you fail to win, remains the source of lifelong sorrow. You've given me back my beautiful faith, by being unattainable.'

'But what if it isn't true, my being unattainable?

What if you could attain me, to keep for yourself, in the way a man attains a woman... What then, would you abandon and forget me...?'

With an impatient gesture, Rolf answered almost heatedly:

'I'm talking about a dream, don't you understand, only a dream, which can never and must never be anything other than a dream, do you hear me, never! I have had more than my fair share of reality's values in this world, they hold no value for me anymore. But I do need the golden gossamer of dreams, and I am not the kind who desires a magic wand to transform them into ropes of steel — except, possibly, should I need a hanging noose. And just now, I wasn't speaking about us, not about me and you, my friend. If and when you choose a man, you will pick one tall and strong — as for me — I am just an old devil you've had to carry home more than once. Do you think I don't know that, that I haven't always known that, that I haven't enough male pride to refuse a woman I cannot tower above, god-like, because that and that alone is what love between a man and a woman requires.'

This was followed by a long silence. Then Mirdja spoke softly, as if to herself:

'And yet there is more strength in you, more man in you than in Eino. His soul is too weak for me; his love is limp, pathetic, or insane. It dominates him instead of he dominating it, and a man should dominate himself and his woman. Yes, a man should dominate his woman...'

And in her heart, Mirdja repeated over and again her clear, callous thought: now I know I could never love him...

'Are you still feeling wretched?'

'No, you always give me comfort, you know me better than I know myself.'

'But we're sitting here in pitch darkness. Shall we not go somewhere to carry on our conversation? I feel like getting out of myself, in other words, I want to carry on talking nonsense. For which the dark provides an excellent release but — I know an even better one...'

Les fleurs du mal, 1857) and Camille Mauclair's short story 'Don Juan d'automne' (from L'amour tragique, 1908). In her thesis on Musset's female characters ('Musset'n naisluonteet', 1905; see Introduction, p. 7, note 19), Onerva revealed her knowledge of Byron's Don Juan (1819–1824), quoting some verses in the Swedish translation.

They went out and soon they were sitting in a restaurant, amid the bright lights and music.

'Women rarely understand why we men like to sit in bars drinking. They have no idea how fascinating it is to witness souls laid bare,' said Rolf.

'It seems to me there is no better place to be alone together than amid the noise and bustle of a place like this. No walls, no ground rules, just you and me, the two of us, and all around us the immensity of life, so far and yet so very close.'

'Actually, I would like to sleep away the daytime, sleep the daytime and live the nights! It's only then we dreamers feel alive. We dreamers need such strange things to be able to live. We need to fly high on the wings of our imagination, to build castles in the air, to see them sparkle and fade in misty eternities, to imagine worlds more wonderful than what the eye can see — ah, the things we need in order to survive this problem-laden world! The duller and uglier the reality around us, the more keenly we turn our inner gaze towards the beauteous landscapes of our fantasy worlds. They fade away of course, but they are weightless and glittering; we don't kill them by making a living out of them or trying to achieve them. That is for those who have no dreams.'

'But who have the ability to work.'

'The ability of dullards! The insatiable ability to enjoy endless disappointment.'

'But perhaps even dreamers can dream higher than their wings can carry them, and so encounter disappointment.'

'Undoubtedly. It is indeed the dreamer who is doomed to plummet mid-flight. I raise my glass to you!... And with your permission, Mirdja, I will finish my speech. Which is still about those I call dreamers. — They are all as delicate as mimosa blossoms and their inner life is complicated. It conceals a myriad secret nuances, a myriad deliriously weird finesses, of which your average individual knows nothing. They are hot-house saplings, born to flourish in the artificially created humidity, in the intoxicating proximity of exotic flowers, under the shelter of slender palm trees, where no evil wind has ever penetrated. In a cold climate such as ours they need a constant blanket and shelter, which is why they wander through the long winters wearing Mephisto's red fool's cape on their shoulders and the all-deriding, nihilistic mask of the doubter on their face.[19] But when we want to lift the

---

[19] Mephisto or Mephistopheles is a demon figure from German folklore, namely from the Faust legend. The tale has inspired many adaptations over the centuries, one of the earliest being Christopher Marlowe's play *Dr Faustus* (1592). The most famous version of the Faust legend is Goethe's drama *Faust* (1808), where Mephistopheles is a figure acting as the Devil's messenger. His appearance is associated with fire, and in Goethe's version he appears clad in a red and gold cape made of silk. Mephistopheles offers Faust otherwise unachievable powers in exchange for his soul. In *fin-de-siècle* literature a Faustian thirst for knowledge fuses with attributes of the Nietzschean *Übermensch* (see note 72, p. 125).

mask, we say "cheers!" And then we, who are the smallest fry in the land, become as powerful as a bright purifying flame, striking through the blue blood of all those dullards. Because they strike us over and over, and their lies fall upon us as blows from a sabre. But we have all severed society's ugly Medusa-head and we all have our own Pegasus, speeding wildly over Medusa's body.[20] At moments like these it speeds! And what matters eternity in the face of such moments? Do not such moments give us the strength to withstand life's grim greyness, to go hungry, to walk in rags and happily to bear the name of dreg and reject! Surely it is not for the sake of this band of parasites, who in their identical millions crawl into their identical cocoons, that we should give up moments like this!'

'You're not a stupid man, Rolf,' said Mirdja. 'You can shuffle the pack as it suits you, and bedazzle us all with paradoxical word play... and then there is this sincere, endearing pathos about you... which gushes forth like a poem.'

'Like the venom of the vexed...'

'Why don't you proclaim all that to the world? Why haven't you taken up journalism, you could wind the public up like a jack-in-the-box with the tip of your pencil...?'

'And you? Why aren't you the mistress of a prince or diplomat at some suitable point in history, then you could twist this whole little world around your little finger! — But to serve the public and then start twisting it! That's a dangerous game. Society is like a vortex sucking you in, like a vamp, "all this is yours for the asking, if only you fall to your knees and beg me." And anyway, do you think some insignificant journalist has the guts to say "get thee behind me, Satan!"[21] No, he's just one of the mongrel pack, licking the master's fingers, going in for the kill when ordered, and barking till he's hoarse. This country's press is an organized system of curs.'

'I have in mind something else entirely. I have in mind an individual whose unflinching use of scintillating verbal and ideological weaponry would afford an occasion of pleasure. Wounding, provoking, undermining, and quashing

---

[20] In Greek mythology, Medusa (also called Gorgo) was one of the three monster figures known as Gorgons. Medusa was usually depicted as a female creature with snakes instead of hair. She had the power to turn to stone anybody who gazed into her eyes. She was eventually beheaded by Perseus, one of the greatest slayers of monsters in Greek mythology. The Medusa myth has been represented frequently in art and literature, and was used in Freud's psychoanalytical theories. The notion of Medusean beauty as beauty tainted with pain, corruption, destruction, monstrousness, and death, was a popular theme in Romantic and Decadent literature. In Onerva's later work, the more unequivocally negative image of Medusa's head is associated with fate and destiny (e.g. the poem 'Medusan pää', ('Medusa's head'), from the collection *Liesilauluja* ('Songs by the hearth'), 1916). Pegasus was a creature from Greek mythology, represented as a winged horse, usually white. He was born from Medusa's blood mixed with sea foam after Perseus decapitated her. In modern times, Pegasus became an emblem of poetic inspiration.

[21] Matthew 16. 23.

a frenzied adversary with serenity and, above all, disdain, all the while remaining unassailable oneself. That would at least offer the sweet, selfish pleasure of exercising one's own power.'

'That would be ideal. But you have heard of universal law, and universal laws are always mean and brutal. We are not yet civilized enough to uphold such individualistic refinements. But faith in one's own power is not lacking, unfortunately! On the contrary, everyone thinks he's a hero, gadding about like a clown, full of bourgeois eagerness, vulgar stupidity, and vanity. Just think of it! Being a clown and believing yourself a hero! Or perhaps they are all martyrs who began with noble ideals but were overwhelmed by the majority. That's only human! I don't mean to speak ill of them. I take my hat off to all human qualities. Most of us die defeated... when I think of myself...! It is above all falsehood and dissembling that society demands of its public servants, and by devil I could certainly do that! I am telling the truth now and the first truth is that I always lie, and the second is that I am an excellent actor, but if I had to say two words upon a stage it would be a fiasco. There we have it! — But you, "little Mirdja", you're not one to falter through the pantomime. A toast to old memories!'

'Why is it that we all lie and act even when we don't mean to?' said Mirdja, deep in thought.

'You should rather be asking why people are also such fools that they believe in their own lies. And my answer is this. It is because upbringing is in the hands of women. Child-rearing should be taken away from woman who, in her ignorance, can only train the child in the one characteristic she possesses: duplicity, the duplicity of her world-view. She nurses her child living a lie, she prays with her child living a lie, she disciplines and rewards living a lie, she girds and surrounds her child with a lie. Is it a wonder that society is one great lie! Or show me one woman who does not swear by the many blessings of society and all its *comedia*: its high standards of moral propriety, the divine doctrines of the church and all manner of rituals, hierarchies, traditions, prejudices, and any number of practices that have found their way onto the road of progress since the beginning of time. And this will remain so for as long as women hold the sceptre of education. You, Mirdja, are an exception to the rule, you have a mature intellect, and you dare to look truth in the eye. But for that you should thank destiny for preserving you from a woman's influence.'

'If that is worth being thankful for,' said Mirdja sadly. 'I lack something, something essential to being human, I've always felt that. I don't know what it feels like to have a father and a mother... Every creature knows this, but I, I have never even seen them... What is it like, to have a mother...? You are an orphan like me, but you remember your parents, so you've said... Oh Rolf, tell me about you mother!'

Rolf suddenly became very sullen.

'It's a sad story,' he said quietly, 'my mother was very unhappy.'

'Was she kind to you?'

'Yes, very kind…'

'Why was she unhappy?'

'It was fate…'

They both remained quiet.

'I have been meaning to tell you sometime, about what they were like, my mother and father,' Rolf continued, 'I may as well tell you now. They were like me, see… even this is my father's legacy!' — He raised his glass. 'I have mentioned as much before. And I only have one dominant image of my mother, one memory of her, as she was on her deathbed. Even when she was alive, she was the image of death, ashen, long-suffering, and silent, like most unsung, untrained carers, of which there are no small number in this life.'

They fell silent again.

'I wonder what my mother and father were like!' Mirdja said softly. 'Somewhere I feel I've heard a whisper, like the shadow of a voice, saying that my father was not quite in his right mind when he died. If only he were alive, I could share in his madness! Sometimes, when I feel very close to my uncle, I suddenly get this impression: my father was different. Better and wiser he couldn't have been… but he was mad after all…'

They had become very serious.

'What a lot of rubbish I have been spouting to you once again this evening.' Rolf laughed finally, 'I enjoy having someone listen to me.'

'There's a lot of wisdom in your words, and there's often something new for me to think about, but often, very often, you manage to say exactly what I am feeling,' said Mirdja.

'All the wisdom in the world is very old, and yet people get no wiser. Read the lessons and proverbs of Solomon!'[22]

'Luckily people don't live by their wisdoms and that is the greatest wisdom of all.'

They laughed.

'My company is not good for you,' said Rolf, 'I'm just an old scoundrel.'

'Well then I'm just a slightly younger scoundrel, does that help?'

'Maybe.'

They fell quiet again.

They had left the restaurant and were walking along the street in silence. Mirdja tried to imagine what impression she would make in Rolf's mother's eyes… And in her own mother's eyes. And what it must be like for those who have a good, kind mother, but one who does not understand her child's soul.

---

[22] According to the Hebrew Bible and the Old Testament, Solomon was a monarch of Israel, the son and successor of King David. Traditionally, he was considered the author of several biblical books, including Ecclesiastes. Solomon's wisdom was proverbial.

'Did you know that there is a lot of malicious gossip about me?' asked Rolf, once they had reached Mirdja's front gate.

'Yes…'

'Did you know that there is a lot of malicious gossip about you, because of me?'

'Yes.'

'It's women, doing the talking.'

'What difference does it make to me? I don't have a mother who could suffer because of it…'

'You're an astonishing woman…'

They said goodbye and Mirdja walked slowly up the steps to her room.

V

⁓

Mirdja threw herself onto her bed. But she couldn't sleep. All the events and conversations of the evening went round in her mind. She thought of Eino, and Rolf's words: not even the most resilient of men can resist the burning glimmer in your eyes and the sultry sway in your step. You were born to be a *bayadère*! — That was exactly what she thought. After all, there was no denying she had a beautiful body!...

Mirdja undid her clothes and let them drop slowly to the floor. Finally, she lay quite naked on her red coverlet. She allowed her gaze to follow her contours, she placed one leg over the other and enjoyed seeing how the fine, elegant curves of her white calves flowed into the slender grace of her young limbs.

I really am beautiful. What a shame no man can see me, admire me, tell me how beautiful I am... It would alleviate the burden of my self-adulation. — These were the young girl's thoughts.

But soon her thoughts came to a standstill, her tired brain refused to function... Mirdja stared dully at the wall, the plain white wall... Suddenly, she noticed a tiny red dot on its surface. She studied it absent-mindedly. It was a small red spider, twisting and swaying on an invisible silk. It was like a drop of blood. — Could it be that Eino had killed himself after all —?

Now she noticed another dot and soon there were dozens of them. And they all started sliding downwards, slowly and surely they descended their silk strands... They wanted to weave their web over Mirdja's body, to dig their teeth into her beautiful flesh and suck her hot, restless blood dry.

Red dots, dots of blood covered the whole room.

They were upon her now, spreading all over her, binding her, biting her with their blood-sucking fangs which paralysed her — it was like death...

For the first time in her life, Mirdja was in the grip of a nightmare. The red spiders pressed heavily on her chest.[23]

During the night, Mirdja dreamed of an ashen-faced woman... The woman was staring at her, and her lips were moving, but Mirdja couldn't hear what

---

[23] The spider as a symbol has many different, often contradictory — and by no means only negative — connotations. In women's writing, the image of the spider has sometimes functioned as positive, encouraging symbol, pointing to the Arachne myth and the tradition of female creativity and energy. In Decadent literature spiders often symbolized fear of death. Bloodsucking spiders evoke vampires and the *fin-de-siècle* understanding of vampirism as a metaphor for dangerous or corrupted sexuality.

she was saying. She understood that it was Rolf's mother who had come to reprimand her — 'Drunkenness is one of the seven deadly sins and you have not once warned my Rolf. What have you done for him?' — Mirdja's soul filled with panic and pearls of sweat gathered on her brow. 'I have drunk half,' she answered, 'so that Rolf has less.' — At this the woman's face contorted terribly, becoming warped and ugly, and her eyes vanished into a fog of absinthe green[24] and she started to howl like an owl, whoo whoo whoo whoo —

Mirdja awoke with a scream.

---

[24] Absinthe is a highly alcoholic beverage, typically of green colour, made of several plants including green anise. It reached the peak of its popularity at the turn of the twentieth century, when it was associated with bohemian and Decadent culture.

VI

~

The next day was Sunday. Mirdja was tired, it was as if some heavy, pregnant thought were pressing against her forehead, and yet she had never felt as full of vim and vigour for life as she did now. Every cell of her body jolted and stung as if from an electric shock, every nerve of her animate sensory circuit surged with wild exhilaration. Every limb of her body burned with the desire for something new and different, with the yearning for uncharted experience, like a restless thirst for power.

'I'm only an actress,' Mirdja said to herself, 'but I'm a good actress. I have feelings enough for heaven and for hell; I have the means to make you all crawl at my feet!'

Was she being wicked? She didn't know. She had always been this way — never as good as other girls her age. Mirdja took a certain, secret pride in herself. She had always been somewhat shameless and different from the others. — Even as a child she had thought bad thoughts and felt feelings which were not appropriate to a young person's development. She read wicked books and her imagination leapt boldly over even the highest ramparts. — And she remembered that always, when the frenzy in her mind was at its most dangerous, she had taken great pleasure in playing the child: she would look at people with her big, bright eyes, full of innocence and earnestness, and she would attract great cries of admiration from the lips of sympathetic adults. Because Mirdja knew how to act with her eyes: she could have them laughing on the surface like a meadow full of golden daisies, or running deep and still like dark woodland pools, or bursting into sporadic sparkle like fireworks in the night sky. And Mirdja would play with her eyes the way other children would play with the glint in glass globes or shiny toys, but she amused herself with caution and skill, always slipping through the fingers of her observer like a lie, or a shadow. Only once the dusk crept in and solitude settled down for the night with its gentle, understanding hush, only then did Mirdja dare to amuse herself openly, to her heart's content. Only then did she give free rein to her imagination. She would speak her bad thoughts aloud and allow her gestures to express her bad feelings. And she enjoyed it, enjoyed hearing the dulcet tones of her delivery; she took in her own words with obsessive passion. She was both actress and her own audience. She would watch the harmony of her gestures and hues in the mirror, and soon her sensory pleasure and emotional sensitivity blended into a strange kind of intensity of being which could have offered the delirium of happiness, were it not crying out so painfully for recognition, recognition...

All this belonged to the mystery of Mirdja's soul, and it had been so for as long as she could remember. — But now Mirdja was old, much older than many girls of her own age. And this development had not been arrested. Her wicked thoughts had grown even more wicked, her dangerous feelings even more dangerous, and the cry in her breast had become even more painful.

Even now she felt a strange fever in her soul. All her unruly thoughts leapt wild and furious in the confines of her imagination, demanding to be made real. She wanted to do something wild, horrific, reckless… to do a bad deed and enjoy it. She was capable of so much! Deceit, deceiving all those poor fools… She could be their trial, their temptation… She could maintain ten lovers at once and fritter away the nights in scandalous bacchanalia,[25] in the lustful ecstasy of flaming torches and morbid fragrances. And she would kiss them all, and with a smile make them believe her deceit was the truth, supreme, unshakeable, and exclusive. Thus, she would poison them with her embrace and lure them into her web with the arched mesh of her gaze… And then… She would see them out — or no, cast them out of their orgiastic revels into the crisp, clear morning, wan and weary, after which they would wander the streets of the earth as ridiculous fools… But Mirdja would possess their souls… Because she had been given all the power of heaven and earth. She was born to shackle souls. — Even Rolf knew this.

'Oh, why am I not allowed to play dare between death and lust!' Mirdja's entire being begged and screamed for morbid pleasure, for the wild, fervent gratification of the senses, for the light, intoxicating frolic of the spirit; her talent for intrigue craved an outlet!

Mirdja was tortured by the fact that she had no opportunity to commit the level of sin that she would have wished to; but she was even more tortured by the knowledge that even given the opportunity, she would never be capable of committing the magnificent crimes of her imagination. These would require a great deal of ruthlessness, and Mirdja knew that she was fundamentally a good person. Oh, but how pale and insipid was goodness! And Mirdja did so love pleasure and power…

Poor Mirdja!

Anyway, her sins would have required the uncontrollable, erupting passion of primordial times. And Mirdja knew that were she to be summoned, right now, to life's most torrid revels, she would have looked down upon them from a cold, dispassionate height like the Northern Star… Why must one be so reasonable, so circumspect… With such inclinations as hers, to have to be reasonable and circumspect!…

[25] Bacchanalia were a popular Roman festival, based on initiatory rites dedicated to the Roman god Bacchus, a variant of the Greek Dionysus. Bacchus represented the power of ecstasy and intoxication. Later on, the word became synonymous with uninhibited or drunken revelry and corporeal excess. Women held prominent positions in the Dionysian rites as maenads (female followers of Dionysus, priestesses of the Dionysian cult) or Bacchae (Bacchantes) and the ritual activities endowed them with significant agency.

Poor Mirdja!

Mirdja pressed her feverish head against the windowpane and a soft sigh rose from her breast like a prayer... How wonderful you must be, Life, with your abundance of rich joys and great sorrows, with your frantic horror of emptiness! — So wonderful is life's smarting inscription on the human heart!

But it was Sunday, and in thousands of churches the minister sang: 'Lift up your hearts to the Lord' — and the devout congregation responded 'We lift them up...'[26]

Poor Mirdja!

---

[26] These phrases are from the Eucharist prayer in the Lutheran Mass, as outlined in 1549 by Mikael Agricola (1510–1557), the first Lutheran bishop in Finland, considered the founder of literary Finnish.

MADRIGAL TALES[27]

RECITATIVE[28]

Come hither, all ye great fires of life, and burn! Sparks flying and flames billowing, burn like racing wildfires! Cast upon me your joys and sorrows, like blazing stars falling from the autumn sky, like yellow leaves dropping in the autumn woods. For it is autumn I love most of all, that time when everything withers and dies, blossoms and wilts, glows and pales in the same blink of an eye. When you've lived through autumn you've lived through life.

Ignite in my heart, love, though you may be no more than the dawn of a single morning, the shooting star of a single night, the fading odour of a single flower, because that's all you ever are anyway. Take me in your arms, great, deep-sinewed life, just as I press you in my ardent embrace!

And then, may darkly eloquent laurels and mystically fragrant myrtles rain upon my head, forming ephemeral garlands on my brow. For I wish to be crowned like a queen, for I have been born a queen. And may altars spring from the earth and sacrificial smoke waft in my wake: you worship fate when you worship me. Because I can tell you I am your fate, but you cannot tell me who is mine... Therefore, I am wiser than you, and stronger too, because I dare to place everything in doubt, though my soul is like a lone corpuscle pulsating with melody and colour. I exist, that you may feed this corpuscle with the very pith of your lives... While you are to become desiccated and

---

[27] A madrigal is a short poem, often about love, 'with a secular text and featuring elaborate counterpoint' (*OED*). It is also the name of a polyphonic musical form originally intended for two or three unaccompanied voices, developed in Italy from the late thirteenth century. Etymologically, the word *madrigal* derives from the Italian *madrigale* (of uncertain origin; probably from Venetian dialect *madregal*, 'simple, ingenuous', from Late Latin *matricalis*, 'invented, original'; literally 'of or from the womb', from *matrix*, 'womb' (see *OED* and etymoline.org)). The connotation of mother and the maternal is present on several levels. The title of this chapter also evokes Baudelaire's 'Madrigal triste' ('Gloomy madrigal', 1857), a poem in which the lyrical subject addresses a woman, 'slave and queen', of whom he demands beauty and who can never claim to be his equal.

[28] A recitative (*recitativo* in Italian) is a kind of declamatory singing, combining ordinary speech with musical performance. It is used in oratorios, operas, and cantatas. In operas, a recitative serves to express action or passion, sometimes to tell a story, or to connect scenes and situations. The German composer Richard Wagner's (1813–1873) use of recitative is particularly famous. Like many of her contemporaries, Onerva was interested in Wagner and his music.

sallow and wasted with hunger, for I am nothing more than a will-o'-the-wisp… But you have the superstitious faith of a gold-digger, you imagine bottomless hoards of treasure under the wisp, all ye doomed to destruction, ye happy unfortunates in the hands of fate! Come to me, ye who dream of treasures! I will wink and wave and beckon you toward me, because thanks to you, life will find me. And I wish to know life, and know myself.

ALLEGRO APASSIONATO[29]

~

Mauri Etso is strong, sure and sound, hot-blooded and passionate in love.

Mirdja is lithe and nimble, ardent and twining like a wild oriental vine. She wants to take pleasure and pleasure she takes. She wants to experience life in love's sweet breath, and she surrenders to it. She craves the ecstasy of the moment and allows it to clasp her trembling soul, thirsty for life, in its wild embrace. But Mirdja is a woman and adores strength. Oh, how she loves being hoisted up by the mighty arms of a giant, being guided, being led by the hand like a child, being carried like an unwitting cheap mistress, and in that moment, feeling how physical enfeeblement seeps to the very tips of her fingers, in delightful languor.

And Mauri Etso tells Mirdja: 'you will come here this evening, and go there tomorrow...' and the girl bends like a sapling. Mirdja is transported by the hypnotic power of a man's iron will, she complies with her eyes shut, the sensual rapture of feminine weakness has gone to her head. Her soul, intoxicated by unhealthy desire, raves in madness:

'Abuse me, kick me, wear me to death. Eat me piece by piece! Behave as one who defiles temples, who slanders saints, be a looter. Be cruel and strong and selfish and rob me of everything, so that I can feel I have been in the path of a storm.'

In response Mauri Etso caresses Mirdja with his hot, commanding gaze, and Mirdja is happy. Life alongside Mauri Etso is a delirium, a dream banquet. But Etso is no dreamer, and the lavish banquets of dreams are always short-lived. — This is a brief account of exiting a delirium:

'So you are mine, mine for evermore?' Etso asks with the familiar confidence of a commander.

A cloud forms on Mirdja's brow: was this the end of their spontaneous emotional euphoria, free of questions about yesterday and tomorrow? This almost sounded like an invitation to semantic debate, like a call to arms... And suddenly there is a shift in Mirdja's soul, and her ears are pained by the cold, merciless ultimatum of love behind his words. Stalling, she answers:

'I am yours for now...'

---

[29] 'Allegro appassionato' is a musical term that translates as 'fast and passionately' (the Italian word *allegro* means 'joyful', *appassionato* means 'passionate'). It is a common tempo marking, *appassionato* being used also as a mood marking, i.e. 'to be played passionately'.

'I know that, but I would like to know more' — Etso's eyes look at her piercingly.

'So would I, but that's all I know,' Mirdja replies, offended.

'Why such caution? Why do you start at the prospect of our evermore?'

There it was again, that terrible, hollow 'evermore'. The party line of the bourgeois soul, of all those who don't appreciate the emotional evermore of fleeting seconds, the glorious musical beauty of the blink of an eye! — Mauri Etso's tall, handsome figure dwindled instantly in Mirdja's eyes, into a run-of-the-mill bargain-basement soul, a tight-fisted miser as far as happiness was concerned, and as if by magic, Mirdja's former self awakens, the real Mirdja, proud and strong, who governs men with light, contemptuous disdain, as one governs the weak. Etso is just an ordinary man, one of those weaklings, Mirdja recalls, as she draws herself up and adds:

'I don't care to play with the truth.'

And Etso starts at the hard, decisive inflection of her voice: he was not used to it. Mirdja was an ardent wild vine, thorny and capricious it's true, but nonetheless compliant as a child, the most feminine of women, the meekest of the meek, as if born for man's sake. And now a perfect stranger stared at him, from behind her stone armour... But surely it was all a mistake, surely... He must get her back by caressing her, kiss her back into a woman... And taking Mirdja in his arms, Etso says:

'You don't care to play with the truth, but you're happy to play with me, you blessed kitten. But there is one word of advice I will still give you: don't play with the evermore either! Don't make piecemeal of your life, don't turn it into a wretched mosaic, Mirdja. My Mirdja! Surely you're not afraid to make your life whole with one great love. It is the salvation of all torn souls.'

'But perhaps I am not destined to be one of the saved,' Mirdja quips as she pushes Etso away. — And she stares ahead as a whit of irony flits across her cold lips.

To this Etso reacted with fervour:

'Your fatalism is intolerable. It's not even believable. It's an excuse you bring up in order to avoid having to confess that you don't love me. You don't love me, Mirdja. Your love is so tiny that it doesn't even know if it will last until tomorrow, if it will make it through the night. It's a frail, mad, spent sentiment you have thrown me, and yet you have dared to say you love me! You have no knowledge of love and the greatness of love, you have no idea what it is...'

Etso had spoken vehemently, with an almost spiteful tone in his voice, clenching his fists... But Mirdja just looked at him as if from afar, remote. True, his reproaches had incited her pride to occasional flushes of intense anger, but they had died down just as quickly, and now she merely felt the wonderful, soothing frostiness of scorn. So this was what a strong man looked like, one who accuses woman, one who despises woman, with brutal words on his lips, brutal sentiments in his heart, brutal pressure in his arm. So this was what a sound character looked like... Blessed, blessed be the broken and the frail!

Now Mirdja felt quite liberated from this man, quite a stranger to him, quite indifferent to his happiness or unhappiness. Now she was able to lampoon him, deceive him, lash out at him in her thoughts, test him... And unadulterated joy pulsed through her veins: what a pleasure it would be to turn this big man's head like a schoolboy's! — Mirdja began talking quietly, with perfect calm and dispassion:

'You say I do not know what the greatness of love is. This is what I believe: the greatness of love lies above all, in its truth. But truth is a kaleidoscope of sparks fired by the gods, and it is only in the fleeting, present moment that we mortals can see it and identify it. And no one knows when the second will strike, in which one moment's truth turns into another's lie. And you, however, have the temerity to ask of me that I should conjure up hidden shadow images of the future. How can you believe what you can't see, when you can't even believe what is under your nose? So don't talk about tomorrow, talk rather about this day we are living in, or even better, don't talk at all, because sophistry kills feelings. But what right have you to doubt the greatness of my love, if I say that I love you more than anyone else in the world?'

As she said all this, Mirdja spoke in a shrouded, steel-grey voice. Etso hadn't the strength to see through it into her soul.

'You speak with fluency. No doubt you have spoken those same words to others before me... And where are your great loves now? They were just trifles, and you throw me your scraps,' Etso said in a hoarse, bitter voice.

Mirdja laughed.

'Do you measure love's greatness by its length, and life's worth in numbers of years? Cannot one day be greater than ten years and one true moment of love be fuller than thousands of false ones...?'

'I believe in the reality of love only on the basis of ten years' experience.'

Mirdja smiled to herself. She saw herself as a ten-year experiment in the hands of this man... as a guinea pig... And many tens of similar couples drifted past her mind's eye: the man stout, exuberant, exuding a certain brute force; the woman with the look of a startled pigeon, pale and long-suffering, old and worn by too many years of childbearing, by too great displays of love. Truly the image of a model wife: obedient, humbled, tamed, raped, with nothing left but the timorous dependency of the weaker marital partner. Truly the image of a model wife! And they too were once fine, feminine ladies who, fearing they may break by virtue of their own fragility, had craved a buttress and had clung to a physical point of strength, to nature's violent and cruel love. They had run into a trap, just as she had almost done. Mirdja shivered in disgust. So much for the ten-year love experiment. — She said almost sternly:

'In that case you have never believed in love, nor ever seen it, for the greater the love, the briefer it is. The best moments in life only last a split-second, and the deepest love is dead as soon as it is born...'

'I don't understand you. As I see it love is great precisely when it has the power to withstand and last for evermore.'

'Oh that is a small love. It has the power to withstand, because there is so little to withstand, and it lasts simply because it is adaptable and flexible in seeking its own comfort.'

'But isn't it possible to withstand a lot and still last, to give a lot and forever...?'

'I am not trying to play the psychological prophet. The human soul is many and varied. I'm simply saying: let's not compile statutes and provisions for the evermore in any area, lest we be disappointed and lose faith in ourselves and others.'

'But constancy, Mirdja, constancy! Is the concept unfamiliar to you, does it mean nothing to you?'

Mirdja felt as if someone was shouting at her: my dog, my dear dog, what has happened to your canine instinct! But the sophistry had begun, and she knew that it did not respect the boundaries of logic, but never mind the subject, attitude was paramount, the dialogue had to continue, so she answered:

'It means everything to me. But one is only truly constant, to oneself and one's environment, if one has the courage at every moment, day in day out, year in year out, to live and recognize the truth in every instant. Remaining constant to the course that life runs is the highest act of constancy.'

'Mirdja, you are changing and confusing issues. Constancy is when something remains the same forever, inconstancy is when something vanishes with the moment.'

'Those are short-sighted assumptions, false patterns, that people have come to revere only by relinquishing their own self-respect and robbing life of its meaning; as if eternity were not merely a continuum of vanishing moments, and as if a moment couldn't contain a whole eternity! But people are so blind and stupid, what do they do? In the expectation of eternity, they throw away one moment after another, seeing them as worthless fractions, until they have thrown away their whole lives, their whole human eternity, and replaced it with a meaningless void. Or then they embrace the moment and its meaning, but fail to give it the value of eternity, and by doing that they cut to pieces those beautiful threads, from which eternity is woven. This is because they don't understand that eternity and the moment are one and the same.'

'It really is difficult to make head or tail of your verbal outpouring, but this is not a criticism, quite the contrary, it merely proves that you are a woman and...'

'It merely proves that you are an idiot.'

'Right, well there is no point in arguing with you any further. But with regard to your last metaphor, I would just like to say one thing, notably that life's fabric can never be a patchwork of colourful threads taken from here and there, it must be woven from one continuous thread in order to be worth anything. But as I just said, let us not for heaven's sake carry on this conversation. All abstract discussion with women is completely against my principles. Es geht nicht![30] Woman has not been made to think, but to feel. It is only on the level of feeling and sensuality that man and woman can melt into one. Forget philosophizing. What use is it? Let's go back to the way we were, you go back to the way you were: my own precious wild vine, all right? And I promise you, darling, that I want to create my whole life from your strands, from you alone and for you. You will have everything, everything, but I also want to possess everything, do you hear, everything. My love requires that you too weave your life of me, always and only me... Do you feel love: all or nothing!'

'I will have everything, you say... But have you then something more to offer me than the familiar advances and familiar phrases?' Mirdja said with bleak irony. 'But of course you think that any old rubbish can be tossed at a so-called woman, and she will accept it as God's gift just because it comes from a man. That's how you have treated me too. It's the "woman" in me you have nurtured, the "woman" in me you have loved. You really are astonishing, you men who promise to weave your whole life out of one single imperfect woman who is nevertheless only to be met outside the bounds of reason and thought! You really are astonishing, you men who forget that she is also a human being! That suits you better of course. It is your love which has the right to command and demand, while woman is granted the dubious happiness of obeying you. And that is how you gradually kill the human being in her. But my human being wants to live, and do you have any idea what it would take on your part, for me to be able to live only through you: first you would have to forget that you are a rutting male and be a human being, and the kind of human being who is a genius encompassing all the spirituality of the world, its wisdom, wealth, and power, in a word, encompassing life itself, because it is only in the heart of the wide world and roaring life that my human being can live... but you are crude and stupid...'

'All that is a *backfisch* girl's fantasy of men![31] Some women remain children throughout their lives. All this is understandable and also forgivable precisely because you are a "woman", even though you denounce the word so unfairly.'

'There is nothing for which you have to forgive me and you will never

---

[30] German for 'It is not possible', 'It does not work'.
[31] *Backfisch* (from the German, literally meaning 'fish for baking') was a popular expression in English as in Finnish at the beginning of the twentieth century, denoting an immature teenage girl. The *Backfischroman*, or 'teenage girl novel', was a genre in German literature, originating in the nineteenth century with Clementine Helm's *Backfischchens Leiden und Freuden* (1863).

understand me. Go join those you can grace with your understanding and forgiveness… The world is full of broodmares!'

'Mirdja, Mirdja, have you gone mad, you…'

'Oh give it up, and I too will give it up. It was all just a game, but you don't like games… So I think it would be best to finish here.'

'Yes, I have to admit I am not fond of tempestuous scenes with women. So I think it best for me to withdraw until the worst of your storm has abated.'

'Don't wait in vain.'

'That would be a shame. But I'm not going to take this so seriously. As I say, I don't care about all this and I am trying to defend you. As a sign that everything is back to normal, you can come and find me.

'Don't wait in vain.'

'I'll be waiting.'

And Mauri Etso withdrew with a slight bow, as one bows before a separation that is to last one day.

*

They stood in wait for a long time, too long did they stand waiting for one another, as if at either end of a bridge. — And then finally one day, when her pique had subsided and Mirdja at last looked out at the road before her, she noticed the bridge had been raised, and a strange, terrible gulf lay between them. And so she understood that everything was over between them, and she began to grieve for Etso as one grieves for one's dead, with subdued, heavy thoughts… She tried to fathom the strange connection between life and death, what it had all meant and how it had all happened…

She had wanted to experience life… She had thought it was possible to enjoy ardent souls and ardent embraces like one enjoys fine dinners and then forgets about them. Fool that she was, though clearly life did not comprehend sport… And so, she had surrendered herself to an adventure with Mauri Etso. Why him, exactly? He was something new, and he was masculine, and Mirdja was sick to death of Eino's effeminate lamenting and pining for love… And also sick of philosophizing with Rolf… which was never more than just that… And above all she was sick of standing on the respective pedestals they had created for her, and so she had gladly embraced the other extreme: she had wanted to imagine herself as Etso's footboard. But even that was a lie, a mere lie; even their final scene was a lie… She had reprimanded Etso for using well-worn phrases, as if she herself had invented any of her own! She had not one original thought! It was spite and sophistry that had driven her that evening, her weapons for parrying his offensive had been recitations of Rolf's ideas. No more than that. And deep inside her heart she knew that she too expected an eternal quality in that sentiment she called love. No, it all came down to the fact that she didn't love Etso. Why else would she have made an issue of one carelessly spoken word? Was it not the right of emotions to employ all the words in the world! And she supposed that love must after all be the centre of life, the greatest part of it. Etso had never been that to her. It had all just been frivolity, the desire for amusement, a whim. And nevertheless, now Mirdja heard her heart calling out with the pain of regret and longing. Her life felt empty. Why was that…? What if, after all… But wasn't it so that often people dwell on the memory of someone they don't love, and even long for those harmful influences back? From force of habit. And in this case? Perhaps it was just female desire for a man in general. Could it not just as easily have been some other man, in Etso's place, why not? And to call that love! Mirdja swore never to let such a thought enter her heart again, never to utter that word again, her life would sidestep the whole matter and — spare others! But surprisingly, Mirdja could not erase Etso's image from her mind. It stared at her long and hard, and she closed her eyes thirsting for his lips, his voice, his powerful arms! Oh, how this new experience had tainted her, marked her… This new loveless experience…! Dear God, dear God, am I likely thus to throw myself at anyone, on a moment's impulse, for a moment's pleasure, and then they, those men, would be able to boast that they had had possession of Mirdja…

Mirdja would have liked to hate Mauri Etso in order to free herself from her self-hatred, but she couldn't. Her heart simply wept and sobbed with a vast emptiness, with life's brevity and insignificance, with the pointlessness of simply everything, everything. And her thoughts gradually softened and quietened, as they do when one grieves over loss.

In the end, she remembered no more than that she had known love and cast it aside. And now and then, when this came to mind, she would be moved to tears.

And so it was that one winter's evening she was moved in this way. She stood and stared out of the window with longing in her heart. All the sophistry was long since forgotten and her imagination put a new gloss on all the old memories. In Mirdja's own view, the proud, cold flirt that she had been turned into a woman unfortunate in love.

And she stood and etched strange words to Etso's ghost into the silver frost on the windowpane. Words that one can only address to those who no longer hold one to account.

I love you, I love you…

Ah, it was only an epitaph!

But even much later, it still seemed as if the deceased was not quite at rest. The spectres of the graveyard murmured many restless fairy tales into her grieving ears for a long time. But eventually even they began to fade, until finally they subsided into total silence.

And Mirdja no longer had a bad conscience. She had at last given the deceased her blessing.

ANDANTE CON DOLORE[32]

~

Who is that pale young man sitting every evening, regular as clockwork, in front of his tall glass of absinthe on the terrace of the pavilion restaurant?

A semi-glazed, semi-dazed look in his eye, he is rarely inclined to engage in conversation.

Mirdja sets her sights on him, finds herself staring at him... and soon she only has eyes for the pale young stranger. The pale young stranger is a silhouette etched onto her brain, a dream branded onto her soul. She is familiar with every detail of his appearance, she could spot him in a crowd of thousands. Two dark furrows have settled on his brow, his eyelashes are slightly heavy, as if following a sleepless, feverish night, and at the corners of his mouth sit two little devils, barely discernible and very quiet. His head is slightly bowed, his demeanour slightly slouched, but every gesture is that of a born dandy, every tiny fault merely accentuates the overall effect, giving him the gentle appeal of modern jadedness.

Such is the man Mirdja holds in her gaze day in and day out.

She sees him often, increasingly often, and she tries to read his face, though surprisingly, his expression is never the same. Sometimes those two furrows on his brow are sharp and black, sometimes they blend almost imperceptibly into the overall greyness of his face, sometimes there is a thick blue cloud floating under his eyes, sometimes it covers his whole face like a sinister blood spot... Sometimes the devils in the corner of his mouth skip forth shamelessly displaying their horns, sometimes all is slumber... It is all so strange. And the man looks at Mirdja with the eyes of a blind man, unseeing. Why do those eyes look at her so? Do they look at everyone in the same way? Why do they look at her so? Mirdja watches this person before her with acute impatience. She craves this soul, whose mystery is not revealed in his eyes. These eyes are not merely veiled, they are the eyes of the blind. Why would one force blindness onto the eyes of one's own soul?

'Who is he?'

And Mirdja is told:

'Eero Selinä, he's a failed student.[33] When he completed his bachelor's, he was still terribly young and terribly talented. Then he started working on his

---

[32] 'Andante con dolore' is another musical term. *Andante* means at a walking pace, moderately slow; *con dolore* means with grief.
[33] The character's surname is typically a female first name.

doctorate, and started drinking absinthe, and now he doesn't do anything, except deteriorate from day to day of course. It's a real shame. Such talent…!'

'I would like to meet him,' says Mirdja.

'I wouldn't recommend it, miss, he's a terrible misogynist, quite impossible.'

'So terrible at everything!'

And Mirdja becomes obsessed with one idea: to possess the soul of Eero Selinä.

I want to look into those eyes that play the blind man, I want to look into that terrible soul, which denies everyone, and I want to govern that man, who hates women. — And this thought burned in Mirdja's soul day and night, and spurred her on like the vanity of deluded grandeur, like the thirst for supremacy, the thirst for power, the thirst for love.

*

Finally, Mirdja had progressed to the point where Selinä had started to talk about himself.

Mirdja had certainly had her work cut out for her, just getting him to open his mouth! No man before Selinä had ever behaved with such impervious insolence towards her. This was definitely her most challenging conquest to date.

At first, Selinä hadn't even acknowledged her presence. Then he had tossed her a casual word the way one tosses a conciliatory coin to a beggar. It was almost an insult but Mirdja paid no heed; she was determined to get to the bottom of him. She studied her subject in secret, from a distance, every minute, every second. She knew she was the active party, but her primary tactic was this: to go as unnoticed as possible, and to avoid making the first move.

Gradually, Mirdja learned to see ever more clearly into the soul of this silent knight. It scared her, and thrilled her. It was like an infinite, black gold-mine, the entrance of which was inscribed with an order of silence and stillness: all is vain. And Mirdja knew that there would be a high price to pay for the key to this soul. She couldn't be tight-fisted, she would have to hawk her own soul in the process. And Mirdja gradually excavated from within her all that she guessed to be in the soul of her silent friend: all the pain and disappointment of her life, all her sincere and insincere experiences, all the pessimism of her view of the world. And she began to talk about herself, almost imperceptibly, candidly as if to her closest friend, with no desire to influence, with no probing of trust and understanding, with no expectation of reciprocal confession. Mirdja asked no questions and Selinä gave no answers. But every now and then Selinä would forget his glass of absinthe and follow what she was saying… he began to observe her… Who was that girl? Was she a girl? Yet with the bold, broken outlook and life experience of a man… Surely there was nothing a man and a woman could have in common? And nevertheless, there she was telling the tale of his own soul? And then he would look on her with suspicion: was she after something perhaps? No, that wasn't possible. But she was laying herself bare before him... Did she sense a kindred spirit? Could this woman be a friend? No, that wasn't possible either.

A hundred similar questions arose in Selinä's mind, and he could not stop thinking about Mirdja. And sometimes he too would add some passing comment to Mirdja's analysis of their souls...

Then at last, Selinä spoke about himself, just one sentence: 'je suis perdu'![34] But he had discharged it with such terribly bitter, fatalistic emotion, that it was almost a revelation. 'And nothing nor no one can save me,' he had added with a sharp laugh, as if to fend off any possible attempt to comfort him on Mirdja's part.

But a cry of joy filled Mirdja's soul: happy, so happy am I that your casual laugh is just a lie and that beneath it your heart still pumps the life-blood, happy, so happy am I that I discovered you in your woe, because I and I alone can save you. I have been given all the power of heaven and earth and I want to give you back your life, my friend, my friend!

But Mirdja said nothing, because if she had revealed the great triumphant elation in her soul, her friend would have left never to return — and that must not happen, not yet. Because Mirdja had decided to play the miracle-worker... she had decided to melt their souls into one, thus to strengthen his with the power of hers, to channel her life's sap into his withered cells... But he must never know anything of it, must never notice anything until he was quite well again... And then, then Mirdja's job would be done. — And Mirdja felt her breast fill with vital courage and fortitude as never before. She was like an apostle secretly appointed by God, a martyr at the altar of quiet good deeds, a Hercules who bore the wondrous clue to righteous feats.[35]

*

'So many beauties swimming past you and you wish to run away... Don't you feel some strange, arresting, melting something, like a ray of sunshine flitting across your temples when they smile, or are you by chance a woman-hater... ?' Mirdja asked Selinä as if in passing, in jest, when he was insisting on taking a side road to avoid the crowded thoroughfare.

'How can one hate something one holds in contempt?' quipped Selinä.

'Ooh, you connoisseur, as if I didn't know that contempt is the finest form

---

[34] French for 'I am lost'.

[35] The word Onerva uses in place of 'Hercules' is *voimaihminen*. The notion of *voimaihminen* or *voima-ihminen* ('powerful human being') is composed of the words *voima* ('power', 'force', 'strength') and *ihminen* ('human being'). It was used to denote people of special strength of spirit and will, and in the literature of the *fin de siècle* it appeared in conjunction with the Nietzschean ideal of the *Übermensch*, which is introduced later in the novel (see note 72, p. 125). The Finnish *fin-de-siècle* woman writer Ain'Elisabet Pennanen (1881–1945) gave the title *Voimaihmisiä* ('Powerful human beings') to a novel published two years before *Mirdja*. In that novel the 'powerful people' appear in a rather negative light. See Introduction, p. 19.

of lust. That's exactly the position I would take if I wanted to maintain my guard at the same time.'

'But you Mirdja, what are you? A man in a woman's body? A woman concealing a man's soul? Why do you live beyond the confines of your sex? I know all about your sex. And do you know what they're like, the women I know? There are two kinds: either common hussies, good-natured for the most part, but animals nevertheless, bare, undisguised animals, whose only remaining trace of genuine humanity is their unbridled lust for money; or the so-called girls of good families, who have been given a remarkable upbringing, placed in gilded cages and required to bear the heavy shield of virtue, as well as to lower their eyes and faint when called for. In fact, the only difference between the two is that the latter are much more stupid and unnatural than the former. And consider us men, who are introduced to life, to society and all its virtues in the form of the dumb, hypocritical woman. What can she possibly offer us? Nothing, a thousand times nothing! If we say: we are sick, make us healthy, they answer us with a smile: we thank you God, for not making us in the likeness of such decadents and lost souls, who are the mockery and scourge of the earth! And what's more — philanthropy being the first item on their hypocritical agenda — they send us pamphlets recommending as a cure the widely accepted, morally enhancing qualities of hard work and advising an ideologically appropriate, healthy lifestyle...

But we incurable decadents, we're a proud lot, we grow a hard and spiky carapace, like all those who must suffice unto themselves, because we are unwilling to receive the alms of abhorrent compassion from the masses, from those who see our inner standards as an eternal enigma. And since it is not within our power to silence their constant outcry, we withdraw in dignified contempt. This is what I have always done, without exception, I have pushed everyone away. You see, even I have had their pity and compassion pressed upon me. Ah, how different you are Mirdja, from all the others — you proffered me neither, which is why I don't find your presence offensive, unlike theirs. Without debasing or deriding myself I can admit to you what I have never admitted before, I can reveal the real me beneath the carapace. Yes, I am just a sensitive, trembling soul, wandering in the dark, sick and feverish, temples pounding, walking in a delirium, bitterly stumbling past the castle gates, a lonely heart, misunderstood and drowning in the bottomless void of life. Oh Mirdja, I may be a decadent, but to such a degree where innocence is depravity and depravity is innocence and there is no wisdom nor morality in the world that has the power to do anything about it!'

Selinä had spoken in halting, tense, muted tones, as one who listens to the strange echo of his own words for the first time, at once hesitant and entranced.

But I have more power than all the world's wisdom and morality, and you are just beginning to find that out... so spoke Mirdja's haughty soul, but she suppressed its voice and said aloud:

'How well I recognize myself in you! It's a sickness, a sickness indeed, but of what kind? Does it not strike precisely when one's soul's evolution somehow enters unfavourable conditions, and thus becomes deformed, over-developed? And does it not affect precisely those souls whose fabric has more beauty, more sensitivity, more delicacy and more potential than others! But this they fail to understand, those who wish to mend that fine mosaic patchwork, that splendour so beautifully wrought that it hurts, with their coarse plebeian ideas. They just don't understand…'

'There is no way of mending us. Some may find release in certain words and phrases, but not us. We don't believe in anything anymore.'

'I too have experienced the deception of the imagination, I have seen beliefs crumble into emptiness and self-deceit, I have been helplessly, oppressively engulfed by the weight of pessimism and I still believe…'

'Beliefs and religious faith, they are feeble-minded inventions for women and children! Even you cannot escape your sex.'

'I still believe that every stage of development, whatever it may be, has its own ideal, or at least its own purpose, which makes sense of life. A full-blooded pessimist is more ideologically aware than any idealist. By recognizing sickness and evil, one gives recognition to the inverse too. Full-blooded decadents, who stand at the very cusp of their fatally doomed development, can surely only live with joy because they are exactly where they should be in their evolutionary course, born to fall, knowing that the life to follow will have matured enough to discover new, better forms of development! There is no concept without its counter-concept. And that is all one needs to be able to live.'

'People cannot live on concepts alone.'

'Faith in goodness is living doom; striving for goodness is life in health.'

'Why should we struggle and strive, we prisoners of fate and of our development. Life may strive through us towards somewhere, God may strive… but we, we…?'

'Your cynicism is laughing at my neo-idealism, but as you know I'm not exactly in the first naïve flush of life… And the further we progress on our course, the more unclear, ghostly, and ethereal our goal becomes. A single-minded people united behind its flag flows toward the hills, it's the lonely and the noble who reach the summits, and at unpredictable intervals the universe gives them a sign, at least a sign…'

Mirdja had suddenly improvised an ideology for herself, a cause, with images, a whole charming fairy tale, and she had spoken persuasively, warmly, as if she herself believed in what she said. Or perhaps she wanted to persuade both their doubting souls of the truth of her words…

But Selinä shook his head in disbelief:

'You have to be a fantasist to reach for the unexplored universe… an eager fantasist at that, and that's something I don't believe in.'

'Believe in work!'

'In work, what for?'

'In work for work's sake, for existential relief!'

'I can't take up work simply for eudemonic purposes, I've tried it, it amounts to nothing… and I cannot find an ideology for which it would be worth doing anything at all. What's the point? Who would find joy or happiness through my work, through my life? Not me anyway.'

'Me.'

'You?'

They took the measure of one another like a pair of duellers.

If I were to believe in anything, I would believe in you, but I don't wish to be disappointed again, to believe again, Selinä's soul spoke.

If there were anything to save you, it would be your love for me, but then I would have to love you too, Mirdja's soul sighed.

I could live for you, Selinä's gaze said.

I would never leave you, my ailing knight, Mirdja's eyes assured him firmly.

'Are you saying you care if I live?' said Selinä, 'tell me the truth!'

'I do,' answered Mirdja.

And Selinä took hold of Mirdja's hands and kissed her still lips.

It was as if the air were filled with sanctity and holy incense… Mirdja trembled like a silent spirit in a high temple… It had to be done. It was the only way to start the healing.

*

From that day on, their real relationship began: Selinä was the ailing knight, who lay weak and bruised, at the mercy of the gentle day; Mirdja was the sun, bringing warmth, creativity and recovery. And these were their most wonderful moments, they both felt it. For is there any sweeter sensation in the world than being brought back to life, and is there any spiritual state more delightful, more sensual in its gentle solicitousness and sense of omnipotence than that of the attentive nurse? Every day was a new flower opening to the sun, a new faith lifting its head, a new wish taking to the air, a new imagining taking form. Every day was a catalogue of surprises, secret joys, inexplicable ecstasies for the biologist.

Selinä was now as open and sincere as a child. It was a relief to surrender his tired soul to the arbitrary impulses of his own repose. And on quiet nights, he unburdened his soul by telling about his life, its small futile joys, its great lonely anguish.

'There was much bitterness in me,' Selinä recounted, 'much doubt and, above all, boredom and sombre scorn, but all that has melted away beneath your gaze. You have won. "Life is faith in goodness," you once said. You are the goodness I can have faith in, you are the life I can live. Everything that came before you is a shadow; everything after you is death.'

But at moments like these Mirdja couldn't help feeling a secret stab in her chest… like a false note, a cloud, an omen. Would she really have the strength to play the eternal nursemaid, to bear this heavy charge of someone else's

life… never to falter, never to rest, never to give in to her own whims in a
moment of apathy? Because that would be the end of both of them. But it was
after all very beautiful, this sacrifice for a sick friend; this friendship was
Mirdja's finest action. Because on one hand she had a natural aversion to
all that was decaying and worm-infested, but she had overcome her loathing
in order to reach out and help a sick man. And she had her reward: at her
touch the patient's darkly oozing drops of blood turned into pearls and crystals,
his wounds shone with gold… never before, never in her dreams had Mirdja
seen so much beauty as in the aching soul of this man. But it was a constant
sufferance at the same time, and with increasing frequency, Mirdja was plagued
by shattering fatigue. It was like saving a drowning man, with the slimy seaweed
wrapping its ugly tentacles around her white limbs and trying to drag its prey
down, to smother it in its stale breath, to strangle it in its sticky embrace… I
must be allowed to be weak, I can't take any more! Mirdja's soul would lament
at times like these. And it often happened that then they would both be staring
gloomily at the floor in silence. But when Mirdja noticed the restless, unhappy
expression on her friend's face, she would pull herself together and hasten to
dispel the phantoms with good cheer.

Once Selinä said:

'I've always been told that a woman can only love through pity, which is
why I had shut myself off from the love of a woman. A pity-kiss is worse than
a bought one. A curse, a curse on every kiss which is not given in selfish, all-
consuming and burning passion! True love is always powerful and gay,
sensuous and vital to oneself, and it is the only right way to love. Tell me
Mirdja, that you love me for your own sake…?'

And the stab in Mirdja's chest hurt so hard it almost paralysed her. She
could neither refute nor admit the charge so she answered:

'You know that I hate pity just as much as you do.'

'Thank you Mirdja, you have taught me to respect woman,' said Selinä.

But Mirdja was left under the pressure of her conscience, brooding terrible
thoughts. No, she didn't love Selinä for her own sake… and yet she still wanted
to keep him. What did she want from this man? Why was she sacrificing
herself for him? Was it simply altruistic love, pity, then? Both the pitied and
the pitier were pitiable creatures. Why had she not walked by, once she had
seen what the pale fellow was made of? Why had she not coldly gone on her
way, why had she allowed her heart to melt, her mind to yield, she, the egoist,
the glutton for the froth of life, why, oh why? She cursed woman's fatalistic
tendency to sacrifice herself for those she did not even recognize as the object
of her selfish love…! What kind of man would he be, the one Mirdja would
claim for herself in the heat of love? She always had the same dream about
him: tall, powerful, a ruler, whose twin spirit would be Mirdja, the weaker
twin spirit. And yet she would be everything to this man: his inspiration and
his muse, his friend and his companion, his champion and his critic, like life
itself. And not just in parts, as up to now, sometimes a companion, sometimes

a friend, sometimes a sister of mercy, sometimes an exciting vixen, sometimes an abstract intellect, sometimes… just morsels, shards! Their bond would be fearless, intellectual, and joyous! But this incessant languishing under the shadow of death, this moral support which sapped her strength, this wrestling with herself in secret… it was unendurable! She had to get away from this debilitating existence, from this incessant smell of infirmity, away, away! But how? —

Mirdja had badly miscalculated. First, she had resolved to cure the patient, and to this end she had loaned the shadow of her love. After that, so she had reasoned, the healthy subject would be sustained by work and ambition, and she, Mirdja, could step aside… But this man would never be healthy, never enjoy work or ambition without love, without Mirdja's love, this she knew now. And Mirdja was not in love. Was she even his friend! Why had she deceived him, why on earth had she loaned herself to him, fed him lies like a doctor? She would have to rip herself free in the end anyway. What terrible game had she been playing! Healing and claiming a soul for herself, only to kill him a thousand times more surely and painfully, giving him everything only to crush him in a trice by stealing it all back. And the end was drawing horribly and steadily nigh. The horrifying alternatives were: saving Selinä by maintaining the lie of love to the end of their days, or telling the truth and killing him on the spot.

Mirdja's soul moaned and groaned at the cruel inevitability of it all, and her anguish grew more dreadful and unbearable every day. But it became clear to her that the relationship could not go on. It was impossible. She had to admit the truth. It was not within her power to cure her friend.

*

This evening, Selinä was due to visit Mirdja. They were in the habit of spending the evening singing together. It had to take place tonight, that great, awful act of putting things right.

Selinä turned up a little late. Mirdja had been waiting in anguish and suspense.

'How beautiful and pale you are this evening,' Selinä said to Mirdja. 'But there is also something great and terrifying about you, like sorrow, or like the sea outside the window…'

They sang some Grieg.[36] The wild Nordic gloom of Grieg's mountain troll mysticism seemed strangely suited to the darkening evening and the sea. It was as if a new, eternal spirit were born.

The sea glinted and swelled. The sun went down and the dusk set in.

---

[36] Edvard Grieg (1843–1907) was a Norwegian composer of the Romantic era. The 'mountain troll mysticism' points to one of Grieg's most famous works, *Peer Gynt* (1874–75), after Henrik Ibsen's play of the same title from 1867. Though encompassing a wide range of stylistic and philosophical aspects and predating the literature and art of

And still they sang.

The sea was vast and magnificent.

'There is a lot of selfishness in Grieg,' said Mirdja, putting Grieg's music aside.

'As must be with all things of beauty,' said Selinä.

The stars came out and lit up the balmy autumn sky. And they sang further. Selinä sang to Mirdja:

> 'Fylgia, Fylgia, flee me not,
> when I'm drawn down by all that is trite,
> timid one, lofty one, shun me not,
> when with dark intentions I blight
> your figure so pure,
> which hovers before me in beauty
> and starshine and dreams of light...'[37]

The melody quivered with more beauty and splendour than ever. Selinä was more soulful than the music itself. He was on fire, newly aglow with love and faith, he, who had risen from his deep doubt, hate, and fever, he burned with a sacred fire.

Ah, the bitter delusion of all beauty!

Mirdja burst into vehement tears. This was it, the awful moment of truth.

She shut her eyes, covered her ears with her hands so that she would not see, would not hear anything... and she expelled from her lungs a harsh, dreadful cry with explosive force.

'I don't love you! Can you ever forgive me...?'

Selinä froze, he thought he would suffocate.

They fell into a terrible, fateful silence.

Finally Selinä said hoarsely:

'And this, what has all this been? A lie? Pity, tell me, was it pity?'

'No, no, friendship.'

Decadence in the Nordic countries, the play has been associated with Decadence due to the irresolute character of its protagonist and his abortive search for his self.

[37] 'Fylgia' (1893–1897) is a song composed by the Swedish composer C. W. E. Stenhammar (1871–1927), an admirer of Wagner, identified by Nietzsche with decadence and sickness in *Der Fall Wagner* ('The case of Wagner', 1888). The song, originally a poem by the Swedish neo-Romantic poet Gustav Fröding (1860–1911), whom Onerva read and translated, and whose poems she recited, is a plea to an ideal, ethereal beauty called Fylgia. The word *fylgia* points to a guardian spirit figure in Norse mythology, accompanying a person and connected to their fortune, life-force, and fate. In Fröding's poem, the lyrical subject implores his Fylgia not to leave him, because she is a 'consolation for the day's distress'. The original Swedish is as follows: 'Fylgia Fylgia, fly mig ej | när jag drags av det låga mot dyn, | du skygga, förnäma, sky mig ej, | när med lumpna tankar jag skymmer din | rena gestalt | som svävar i skönhet och stjärnglans | och drömmar av ljus för min syn.'

'Does a friend betray a friend? But of course you are a woman, a half-wit who thinks she can acquire a human soul with a handful of pity, ha ha ha!'

'Oh God, don't laugh at me, don't despise me, try to understand me! You are very precious to me, dear to me as my dearest friend!'

'Friend, isn't that always a woman's trump card, the one she throws out when she's had enough of betraying her lover and is ready to move on. But for you to do this Mirdja, you, Mirdja!... You were supposed to be above your sex... And what a fool I've been, even though I knew all about women... Poor Mirdja! — Oh yes, we were supposed to sing, that's right. I'll carry on... with your permission, mademoiselle —

> Bah, are you not a man?
> You are Pagliaccio!
>
> ———
>
> Laugh Pagliaccio,
> Your love is broken!
> Laugh of the pain, that poisons your heart!'[38]

Selinä's voice resonated with supernatural force and bitterness, as if in the face of death. It contained all the disappointment and pain of his entire life, relived a thousandfold, relived in such a way that there was nothing more to be done.

It was the death wail of the incurable.

But Mirdja had crumpled into a heap... She sat motionless, her lips pressed tight, as if in the shadow of the final judgement... This was her work, this... and she was supposed to have sacrificed at the altar of good works.

A curse, a curse on everything except selfish egotism.

*

Mirdja sat still as a statue. She had hardly noticed when Selinä left. Everything was quiet and black...

There was just the sound of a maggot gnawing at the old wall. It was like the sound of eternity ticking away.

Suddenly Mirdja started. She jumped to her feet. It was surely past midnight. There was a strange noise in the corridor and the door opened. It was Selinä, so drunk he could hardly stand. Mirdja had never seen him like this before.

'This may well be an inconvenient time, but so what! Love doesn't ask when

---

[38] Selinä sings a part of the aria 'Vesti la giubba' ('Put on the costume') from the opera or melodrama *Pagliacci* ('The Clowns', first performed in 1892), written and composed by Ruggero Leoncavallo (1857–1919). The famous aria is sung by the 'tragic clown' Canio after he discovers his wife's infidelity, but still has to deliver his comic performance. The character who says of himself that he is 'not a man, but a clown', has to put on his costume and powder his face, smiling on the outside but crying inside. The Italian original is: 'Bah! Sei tu forse un uom? | Tu se' Pagliaccio! [...] | Ridi, Pagliaccio, | sul tuo amore infranto! | Ridi del duol, che t'avvelena il cor!'

to come and when to go — like death; they are lords and masters; I keep noble company… The thing is, I didn't answer you just now, I was distracted. You begged forgiveness. — You needn't ask forgiveness for failing to cure me and save me and hoist me to my feet… I mean, it wasn't your fault, and you really did go to so much trouble… Oh my, what hard work it is to be a sister of mercy. Not everyone is cut out for it… Not you anyway… You see, you made a few tiny errors, things to watch out for next time… Let me tell you what they are: firstly, a sister of mercy should be holy, a white cross on a blue breast… she is not to kiss her patients — no — no! — That's rule number one. Followed by rule number two: a sister of mercy never lies nor deceives, not with her eyes, not with her lips nor in her heart. It's a sin. Thirdly: a sister of mercy should know her limits, she shouldn't pick sinners off the streets and alleyways — she should leave that to the police — she shouldn't pick and choose the souls she intends to save — she should leave that to God… And furthermore, she shouldn't encourage a man to write his doctorate if she is not willing to be the Doctor's proud wife. What the hell am I to do with such a title![39] It's only good for decorating women, a man acquires it for his woman, like money, like all the pomp and circumstance in this world —

> What good, in the dark night of the grave,
> are treasure troves I cannot save,
> verses and chronicles that sing my praise,
> and epitaphs containing heroic phrase…?'

Mirdja sat and sobbed in silence. Never before had anyone insulted her so. But she understood that this was the inevitable consequence… She too had insulted that man every minute she had been with him without loving him. But her tenderness towards him had grown over time, she couldn't help that, and now she would have gladly given her life if she could have saved him in any way, other than by pledging him her love. She sobbed quietly.

'Go ahead and cry my lovely Mirdja, cry, but not for my sake! I couldn't stand it. A person who grieves over someone they don't love offends them… But don't let that stop you, my lovely Mirdja, they say crying makes a woman's eyes shine like the sun… and your eyes were already so beautiful! You will surely blind many a sailor yet with the light in those eyes… Remember to cry then, you lovely witch, cry every time the boat capsizes! Not for the drowned, but for your own sake, Mirdja, for your own sake… Oh you unhappy girl, you almost make me want to cry for you, and I would have the right to, because I do love you, my tears are like a prayer reaching out to God.'

This was followed by a long silence in the darkness.

---

[39] In late nineteenth-century Finland, men's professional titles were also attributed to their wives, often by the addition of a feminine suffix, e.g. *tohtorinna* (doctor's wife), *rovastinna* or *ruustinna* (provost's wife), *kapteenska* (captain's wife), *apteekkarska* (apothecary's wife); the suffix *-ska* is adopted from Swedish.

'Forgive me for this night,' said Selinä, sober at last. 'I don't think badly of you. And I'm sure you understand me, my outburst... You know everything I've been through, and it all came back to me, the bitter and devastating... And if there is a side to you I don't understand, I suppose it's because you're a woman, and can any man ever understand any woman? Especially you, who are so astonishing!... I never did understand how you could possibly love me, just as no one ever understands their luck; now I understand a little better, how you couldn't possibly love me.'

'Not for my own sake.'

'No, not for your own sake — my friend. — But I was so close to death, that only the great love of the greatest woman could save me.'

'My ailing knight!'

'My tortured friend; my dearest! But don't say anything more to me, not a word. Your soft, merciful voice robs me of my resolve, and I must leave — for your sake. It has been hard for you, living with me.'

'Harder to separate...'

'Don't speak, don't speak...!'

Selinä silently picked up his hat and clasped Mirdja's hand in his, clasped it so hard she quietly yelped...

That was their goodbye.

*

The next morning, Mirdja lay on her sofa with a bunch of orchids in her hands. Strange flowers! It is hard to say what they look like, what colour they are, whether cheerful or sad.

They were like her soul. It was both light and heavy. With Selinä she had been through the nightmare of self-sacrifice, and she could breathe freely again... But the sister of mercy within her grieved for her ailing knight, grieved and insisted that they were bound together forever. And this voice was so love-sick, so convincing, that Mirdja was compelled to seek out her lost friend...

Selinä had gone away, she was told.

Mirdja returned home. For the rest of the day, she sat holding the dying orchids, which resembled her inexplicable, tortured soul.

ALLEGRETTO CAPRICCIOSO[40]

~

The great hall was aglow with glorious chandeliers and dancing flames. Eyes flit past, burning bright or darkly smouldering. Myriad pairs of eyes, thirsty, pleading, eloquent eyes, timid as a gazelle's or sharp as an eagle's, piercing eyes drawing blood like an adder. — Myriad souls, and even more shadows of souls, pale, grey, masked souls, ragged, shrunken and bowed... All brilliant and aflame now...

Mirdja is dancing and dancing... she dances with everyone, and they all dance with her. But Yrjö Särkkä only dances with Mirdja.

Mirdja is the brightest of the bright, her soul and eyes on fire, she is the lightest, and the most fathomless of all.

Yrjö Särkkä is the unwashed gold of Sturm und Drang.[41] He wants to be a black-fisted miner of precious stones. 'Slag, fool's gold,' he says of the whole room, 'except her, that one.'

'Your body feels softer, your soul burns more ardently and astoundingly than anyone's,' he whispers to the one.

'What if I'm not hard nor soft, not hot nor cold, just dark and empty.'

'Not dark, at any rate, for you are brilliant and radiant, but perhaps you're just a will-o'-the-wisp...'

'If you knew the blaze in my life you wouldn't come near me. It's dangerous.'

'Oh I knew it before I had even seen it, just as I knew you before I had even seen you.'

'Others don't know me even after they've seen me.'

'I felt the searing touch of your flame years before you got here. And those years were like one great long yearning, like an endless, relentless, fervent desire for that searing touch.'

'But my life's flame is the flame of destruction.'

'Let it loose, you owe it to yourself.'

'But its course runs over expiring souls and bloody hearts.'

'Let it run. You don't know the meaning of fear.'

[40] A musical tempo and mood marker meaning 'in a lively style' or 'moderately fast'. The Italian word *capriccioso* literally means whimsical, naughty, or unpredictable.

[41] The German expression *Sturm und Drang* is generally translated into English as 'storm and stress' (other meanings of *Drang* would be urgency, pressure, or drive). It refers to a proto-Romantic movement in German literature and culture characterized by the portrayal of turbulent emotion and unrest. It was named after F. M. von Klinger's (1752–1831) 1777 play of the same name, and its characteristics can be seen in the early work of J. W. Goethe and Friedrich Schiller.

'If only I also didn't know the meaning of pity.'

'Consider me your equal then, Mirdja, so you don't avoid me out of pity.'

'Though you may perish?'

'Though I may perish.'

'If only you were as beautifully strong as you are beautifully proud.'

'My love will be my strength.'

'Love is weakness, it only guarantees your defeat.'

'What are we fighting over?'

'The upper hand.'

'And if I lose?'

'Then I look down on you and send you away.'

'And what is my reward if I win?'

'My love.'

'Is it a reward you've often bestowed?'

'I can only bestow it on someone stronger than me, and so far I have always been the strongest.'

'Have you been happy, my victorious one?'

'My hopeless prayer has been: dear God, grant me the grace of defeat, so I can look up and love.'

'Is that true?'

'I have never yet said anything or done anything that was not a lie in the very next instant.'

'Are you perhaps a plotter of intrigues?'

Mirdja folded her white arms in a charming gesture, and quipped with light audacity:

'Es ist so süss zu scherzen mit Liedern und mit Herzen.'[42]

The music starts up again, a melancholy, intense, and seductive waltz.

Yrjö bows lightly before Mirdja. The blood is surging and searing through his veins. He feels like he is holding the huge, red heart of his life in his hands, and a great joy is dancing, swaying, and rollicking on the surface of its great sorrow. — What were those flippantly cast snatches of thought? Chance, light music, madness, emptiness. Above all, words, just words. And yet...

And Yrjö's soul speaks wordlessly to his chosen one:

'If you were simple, straight-forward, transparent, unscathed, noble, and pure, you would not be as captivating. But because you are complicated, inexplicable, caught up in your own web, contradictory, unnatural, unusual, rare,

---

[42] 'It is so sweet, to play | with songs and with hearts' (trans. by Emily Ezust, 'Spanish Songs of Robert Schumann and Maurice Ravel', <http://www.jamescsliu.com/classical/Schumann_Ravel.html>). These are the first lines from 'Der Hidalgo' ('The Gallant') by the German poet and playwright Emmanuel von Geibel (to be sung 'in a somewhat flirty manner', 'Etwas kokett'). The text, representing a stereotypical image of a knight whose 'zither is for ladies' and whose sword is for his rival, was set to music by Robert Schumann in 1840 (*Drei Gedichte von Emanuel Geibel*, Op. 30, No. 3). Onerva sang Schumann's songs in her youth.

possibly insane and criminal, you drive people mad with your wonderful dissonance…'

And Mirdja's soul answers:

'I am full of those self-assured, self-centred devils of derision. I know I will achieve recognition. My pride requires it…'

'You demonfly, you demonfly,' Yrjö whispers.

'I am restlessness, pain, and suffering… Leave me be, if you sail under the flag of peace!'

'No, it's the war of all against all!'[43]

Yrjö looks at Mirdja. His eyes are ablaze, his soul is ablaze.

Mirdja smiles back, enjoying it all.

*

Mirdja and Yrjö meet every night when the stars come out, and go their separate ways when the stars fade into the morning sunrise. A firework display of ideas in the dark, a quiet, undulating union of souls in the soft, downy night, an infinite cosmic symphony of emotions, such is the nature of their co-existence.

Then there came the final night.

They had been out for a long walk, treading the fresh-smelling, frozen April turf. Their thoughts were tinged with tender sadness, as often happens in spring.

Now they sat in the twilight of Mirdja's room. In darkness and silence.

'Blessed be the night, which breaks down barriers and removes people's masks, which frees their souls and connects their hearts,' said Yrjö.

'Blessed be the daylight, which releases their chains.'

'It's impossible to see through you the way one can see through others, naughty, capricious, enigmatic Mirdja. You've been as harsh as daylight and as tender as the night to me. You are a strange creature, Mirdja, a miracle and a mystery. I can't say it often enough. — So inviting and so spurning, so seductive and so impervious at the same time! I have never yet met a woman whose arm's arc was so voluptuous, whose movement was so fluid and exciting as yours, Mirdja. When you curve your am in a light caress around my neck, my whole being sinks inexorably into your momentary ecstasy, into the gentle rhythm of your wonderfully supple body and its feminine desire. And yet you do nothing, you feel nothing, and so my feverish rapture always awakens with a start at your icy reception, because it longs to burn with a mutually uplifting flame. You are a woman, and yet not a woman. You are depraved, and yet innocent.'

---

[43] A reference to the famous phrase about human existence as *bellum omnium contra omnes* by the English philosopher Thomas Hobbes (1588–1679), considered one of the founders of modern political philosophy. Onerva cites the sentence also elsewhere in her work.

Mirdja stared ahead into the dark and smiled a strange smile, as if to herself. She said nothing.

'Perhaps you misunderstand me. I'm telling you this because I have no choice. I have to tell you everything I've been thinking. I no longer have the strength to wrestle alone with my thoughts. Or perhaps I can no longer wrestle with your presence, you sphinx.[44] The thing is, I know, I can sense that you are an unusual, exotic, and tropical bloom, sensual and sensitive, but why is it that I only see your cool, collected veneer? Why at my touch do you turn hard as crystal, like a frozen bud? I don't understand you. If you love me, why don't you ever burst into bloom, into that florid red, queen of the night lily, that I know grows within you? For whom, for whom will it flourish if not for the one you love! Or then — if you don't love me — I can't understand you. Your contradictions are flagrant disdain. If you don't love me, why do you behave the way you do, why do you twine your arm around my neck, why do you imprison me with your eyes, why do you intoxicate me with your kisses, why don't you let me go, do you hear me, if you don't love me? — But you do love me, don't you, else you would be like those flighty wretches, else you would be — an immoral woman.'

Mirdja's eyes flashed like lightning. The queen of the night opened her petals for an instant, but it was fury she glowed with, fury, lifelong fury at this deathly insult. — Quietly, with dignity, she raised her head, now a perfect stranger. Her expression was hard and imperial.

'Go,' she said quietly and deliberately, 'since I am nothing to you but an immoral woman.'

'Mirdja my goddess, my idol, you are the most beautiful, noblest, and purest of mortals, a beauteous dream amongst women, you know how much you mean to me...

'I don't love you... I'm just an immoral woman.'

'My goddess, I have mortally wounded you, can you ever forgive me? No, you can't, I can see that. Begging you is as futile as giving you orders. I have sentenced our relationship to death. — I failed to understand you, I tried to make you fit the mould of bourgeois convention. And at that moment I died in your soul, I could see it and I could have choked on my anguish. And now I must go, I can tell.'

'Yes,' said Mirdja quietly, deeply forlorn, 'something is broken forever. This was just a dream that singed its wings.'

'The most wonderful, beautiful dream of my life! — Do you remember that evening we played with grand words? You were stronger than I. I couldn't match you. It's time for me to go. The Grim Reaper stands between us.'

[44] The sphinx is a mythical creature, famous mostly from the ancient Greek and Egyptian traditions. It has the head of a human, the body of a lion (squatting on its hind legs), and the wings of a bird. The rich *fin-de-siècle* sphinx imagery alludes mostly to the Greek sphinx, depicting her as a mysterious, merciless, and treacherous female creature.

*

Yrjö Särkkä treads the frosty April ground alone, he walks all night, and his aching, love-sick heart breaks as it sobs its mournful swansong to Mirdja:

'Your white arms wrapped me in their lure like the foaming whirlpools of a strong current, and I stare after them now and would gladly dive into them even at the risk of losing my life. But you are drifting on, drifting on like the water in the current, and I know that like the water, you and your love will never return. But I will turn to silent stone on my rocky shore. I will not call after you in vain. I fear the cold disdain or murky pity in your eyes more than death. I want to think of your eyes as the light on the water, as the gleam in the current. I want to remember them as the silky green, seductive eyes of a siren, even if they have already forgotten me.'

But Mirdja is sitting in tears in the darkness. He was stronger after all, that man, for withdrawing when he was beaten by his own, self-inflicted blow. He spoke the truth, a truth that Mirdja's own soul had repeated to her in quiet moments, a truth that everyone thought, of course, but no one had dared to speak out loud. Now it was out there at last, that word, large as life! But to love the victor who pulls her into his arms with the words: immoral woman! Never! Poor philistine Mirdja! But Yrjö didn't even believe the truth of his own words because he loved her. What infinite male stupidity, what fainthearted romantic gallantry! No, no! What understanding, what sensitivity, what fortitude in being able to walk away! And he will never return. He was proud. So he was a man, after all. But not the man for Mirdja.

Mirdja's soul sobs: I love you, I do love you! And her emotions pick at her heart like birds of prey. But if you came back, I would hate you, I would despise you. I love you, I love you now!

Irreparably, the last evening.

BARCAROLA[45]

∿

The night in June, over the water, the seashore, the islands... The mystical June night full of the earth's nectars, its moist, sultry atmosphere, its demurely wafting mists... The still June night — interrupted only by the occasional silver castanets of the nightingale.

A boat skims the water's surface. The reeds rustle, a frightened pike shoots off into the distance... then everything is still again.

The boat comes to a halt, and the two people sitting in it remain silent... two complete strangers, two people thrown together by chance, two friends of one night — young Torild and Mirdja.[46]

How very strange! This is how it all came about:

They had been introduced at a concert given by young Torild. What twist of fate had brought Mirdja to this small town, for this very concert! — They had stopped to stare at each other as if struck dumb. 'So this is who you are,' echoed through their otherwise unremarkable first exchange of greetings. — And then the young artist's friends and admirers had invited him to spend the evening with them as a last farewell, because he was due to travel abroad the next day. And the artist himself had invited Mirdja to join them. And thus Mirdja chanced to spend Torild's last night in the country with him.

They had approached one another with the lightness and fizz of the bubbles in their champagne glasses. And now in the middle of the night, they sat together in the boat, just the two of them, floating quietly and aimlessly on the dark waves.

'You're such a woman of the world, and to think you have wandered into a tiny backwater like this!' said Torild in a warm, soft voice. 'Having met you, no woman's charms will ever hold any surprises for me again — not even out there, in the wide world. There is something about you which is so... so... I can't explain it. But I immediately guessed you would be like this — something of a contradiction, at once enduring and evanescent, like a moment's bliss, like someone to encounter only once, at the height of one's life course, and who remains thereafter unforgettable, untarnished, unattainable...'

[45] The musical term *barcarola* alludes to a folk song sung by Venetian gondoliers or to a piece of music composed in that style. At the turn of the twentieth century, *barcarola* was associated with love themes, mostly thanks to Jacques Offenbach's (1819–1880) 'Barcarolle', famous also under the name 'Belle nuit, ô nuit d'amour'. The latter are the opening verses of the aria from Offenbach's *Les contes d'Hoffmann* (*The Tales of Hoffmann*, first performed in 1881).

[46] Torild is a Nordic (Norwegian) name, used as both a female and a male name.

You really are an artist, thought Mirdja, to be able to understand the fleeting quality of beauty — as I do. But she said nothing, merely answered him with the most radiant gaze she could muster. And for Torild that look was like love.

Then they both stared at the water for a long time, in silence.

'The water is like the stuff of clouds, like a dream,' Torild spoke again. 'Are you looking for water lilies?'

'The water lilies are sleeping.'

'They will awaken at your gaze, bloom anew and happier than ever, the amazing, wondrous Victoria regia will rise and fade with its cheeks flushed purple... at one glance from you.[47] But the ordinary yellow water lily is not for you. Your flower must have a scent, the scent of the night... Listen, let me go and find you the scent of the night. I would like to bring you a fragrant white fringed orchid. That would be so beautiful.'

They stepped out of the boat onto the shore. Torild offered Mirdja his arm.

The dewy leaves hung heavily over them... The sultriness of the earth's nectars swelled powerfully in the atmosphere... But everything was vast and silent, infinite as space. Just two souls, two poems.

'You are a marvel of nature: a shooting star in the white night. And I am happy that I will not see you again tomorrow, nor the day after. The first day would be a fading, the second — an extinguishment. The breath of a single night is love, the most beautiful love.'

Torild looked passionately into Mirdja's eyes.

And Mirdja remembered what she had said to Mauri Etso. 'You resemble me,' she thought then.

'Beauty worshipper,' she whispered quietly.

They smiled at each other in mutual understanding.

Suddenly there was fire in Torild's eyes and Mirdja's eyes grew dark. She felt herself lying limp in his arms and her lips were seared by a long kiss.

Torild was quick to let go of her.

She stood silent as a statue, looking away from him.

And why exactly should she have taken offence, or screamed or fainted! Why play the blushing rose when there had been so many before... But nevertheless... What right did this man have to...? Love, perhaps? But what right did he have to assume Mirdja loved him? Or perhaps he didn't even assume so, perhaps he had just fallen into the trap of his own love. But the love of a single night... that's just words...! Mirdja stood frozen to the spot by her thoughts.

Torild said quietly:

'It was the fragrant essence of this night. I don't have to apologize, do I?

---

[47] *Victoria regia* is a giant water lily found in the Amazon river and surrounding areas, named after Queen Victoria.

You too are a worshipper of beauty, and the breath of a single night is love —
of the most beautiful kind.'

But Mirdja held her tongue and looked away.

What was this man to her, this man who came along by chance and then
deigned to claim her for the night, for just one night, in all frankness? What
was this man to her? And yet she had given herself up for use, and now this
man wished to reward her by giving this night a testimonial: love — of the
most beautiful kind. Just words! The same way one visits a streetwalker,
swearing to one night of love… And yet Mirdja recognized her own words on
this man's tongue. Well maybe it was possible to suggest such ideas to a man,
but for a man to suggest the same back to a woman, never. A man should
approach a woman with dignity, bearing sacred incense, swearing eternal
bonds of love, he should approach her as if she were the only woman in the
universe… Such are the needs of a woman's soul, even a flighty woman's. It
may all be lies, but one shouldn't say so, one shouldn't say so! Mirdja was
offended. It was as if she yearned for her own sanctity. The beauty had gone…

She stood like a statue and looked away. Her expression turned blank and
hard.

The night lilies exuded their scent in the moist air. A grey mist rested like a
cool, fleecy bridge between the two strangers, who had loved each other just a
moment ago.

'May I bring you your white fringed orchid now, though I can see you don't
love me anymore? — You shooting star!'

'You don't regret it?'

'Don't you regret it either. It was certainly beautiful. But a moment ago you
would have pressed the flower to your breast. Now you will perhaps throw it
away. You're not the same anymore…'

Mirdja was silent. Not the same by a long shot. It seemed she was not, after
all, that free spirit they had agreed on. — This man thought either too highly
of Mirdja or… too basely. But Mirdja was evidently just a perfectly ordinary
young lady who, in keeping with propriety, condemned as sinful the freedom
of summer-night fantasies.

Mirdja laughed aloud at herself.

Torild looked at her questioningly.

'Shall I walk you home?'

'The night is over… the "most beautiful" is over. Are you happy now?'

'I am, very content. This night was beautiful. You are tired now. But you'll
feel the same way later on…'

They walked in silence, apart.

The morning dawned slowly. The first rays of sun were already lending a
rosy tint to the horizon.

Mirdja glanced over at her companion. Pale, wan, unkempt after the night,
a tired pinch to his lips and a hungover glaze in his eyes.

How disgusting!

How in heaven's name did she end up with this complete stranger? What was she, Mirdja? Available to be kissed at the drop of hat! And this man was unknown to her... Mirdja felt ashamed... Then she was ashamed of feeling ashamed, which was such a shallow, bourgeois attitude. But in her soul, there was no trace left of the wonderful romance of the night, it had been completely washed away.

The sun rose red and vivid...

Like an evil-doer, a sinful wife, a sleepwalker discovered naked in the street, so stood Mirdja in the broadening daylight, afraid to look it in the eye. An invidious position!

'Would you deign to receive this night lily from me?' asked the man.

'I'm cold,' said the girl, shivering ashen-faced and weary in the sunrise.

'It was the dream of a single night, blanched by the sun. — Don't be glum... over a single dream.'

'I'm cold,' repeated the girl, already at her door and unable to pronounce the vituperative words that were on the tip of her tongue. — What if it was all just her fault for not being able to see the beauty in it...

'Thank you Mirdja, goodbye.'

'Goodbye!'

Mirdja threw herself face down on her bed. She thought and thought and thought... One embrace on a beautiful summer night... what on earth did it matter to her anymore! But what about him? Was he really the person he wanted to project: a child, a naïve and beautifully wanton believer in the mood of the moment, or was he an arrogant, cold-blooded, corrupt libertine out for thrills? On that night, who between the two of them had been the betrayer and who the betrayed? Who the philistine...? And Mirdja repeated the man's words to herself: I am happy that I will not see you again...

But Mirdja could not sleep. Something strange had happened. She tossed and turned. She felt hurt, humiliated, tormented, tormented because of the inexplicable, confused state of her own soul. And she suffered, as one suffers who has been hoisted by their own petard.

NOCTURNO[48]

~

T
he winter night glistens in the biting cold... Another winter, another
night...! Who can keep track of their constant rotation! Time plays conjur-
ing tricks...

The winter night glistens in the biting cold, but Mirdja is feverish. Her
thoughts gnaw at her brain like jagged flames and her heart beats irregularly.
We people... How curious is the way we cross each other's paths, each of us
crouched in the grip of our own shivering cold. The pain of loneliness... Or if
we join together then that causes pain too, the terrible pain of coming close
and tearing away... We people... Or more specifically you men and we
women... No, only I, I... Who are those others? Happier people? Perhaps...

Mirdja cannot take the sedate, stifling atmosphere of her room any longer.
She has to get out... into the winter night!

She looks out of the window. That big city lying under its black shroud...
So deceptive, it doesn't sleep, it hustles and hungers, it burns. If anyone knows
this, it's Mirdja. For many years now it has scorched her every day and every
night. Is that how it is... life?

She rushes down the steps as if to escape her own visions, she runs, lecturing
herself as she goes:

I must become stronger than I am, I must abrade my languishing memories
and foolish dreams until they are hard as stone, cast out my tender heart,
there, onto the cold blanket of snow...

And she walks and walks, knowing not whither, noticing no one. Gradually,
her thoughts begin to grow numb. She senses only the mechanical pace of her

---

[48] The title alludes, once again, to a musical composition, usually referred to as a *nocturne*.
It conveys a variety of moods and is often associated with ambivalence of feeling, oscillating
from lyricism and tranquillity to sorrow and gloom. *Nocturne* means evocative of or
inspired by the night, but it can also refer to a night-time performance. In poetry, the
term *nocturne* has a long tradition of evoking musical qualities as well as various moods
of the night. In this period, the word *nocturne* also became associated with the inter-
mingling of different art forms — music, literature, visual arts — as exemplified in the
work of the American painter James McNeill Whistler (1834–1903). 'Nocturne' is also
the title of one of the most famous poems ever composed in the Finnish language (1903),
by Onerva's close friend and (for some time) partner Eino Leino. Leino was one of the
most versatile, visible, and later also canonical figures of Finland's *fin-de-siècle* literature.
Onerva met Leino in 1907. He has been considered a model for the character of Mirdja's
mentor Rolf. See Introduction, p. 18.

steps… How many steps does one take in life, and how many of them are steps leading astray…

It is already late. The gaslight flickers faintly, drowsily…

Suddenly Mirdja was roused from her sleepwalk. There was boisterous talk behind her. She turned around. Black silhouettes could be seen moving in the faint electric glow emitting from the doorway of a large hotel.

'Are you going home?'

'I'm not going home, I don't have a home.'

Mirdja jumped. She recognized the voice… She stood and listened. She could hear her heart pounding…

That voice from long ago… 'Where are you, little Mirdja?' A voice she would have followed through thick and thin, had it beckoned to her. — Rolf Tanne! Beloved Rolf, is it you, is it you? Yes, it couldn't be anyone else!

Mirdja walked towards the voices.

Rolf, it is Rolf, it is… And another familiar voice: Eero Selinä, the rest were unknown.

She approached slowly. The gentlemen had already noticed her.

'What a beauty!'

Rolf threw a long look at the approaching young girl.

Mirdja stepped right up to him, slipped her arm into his and whispered quietly:

'Rolf!'

Rolf trembled. That voice, that intonation belonged to… whom? One person alone… only one. Was it a mirage? No doubt it was. But his lips answered silently:

'Mirdja.'

'Will you come home with me?' said the mirage.

'I will.'

Rolf forgot all else.

They drove away.

The rest of the party stood staring at one another, dumbfounded.

*

Rolf and Mirdja drive towards Mirdja's house. Neither says a word.

Rolf senses that this isn't the moment to talk, not yet… This isn't a meeting between casual acquaintances… This is something meaningful, like a spiritual journey, like a hallucination.

They both sit deep in thought.

Many images of their mutual past run through Mirdja's mind. With this man too, she had a history, and more than a history… Even nowadays, after all this time, she caught herself constantly repeating this man's views and barroom philosophies, much to her annoyance… Mirdja took a veiled look at her companion's face. It had a strangely crushed, insular look. But otherwise it was the same, the same ironic smirk on his lips, the same worn furrow in his cheek, which had deepened if anything... he was the same, the same! This was the man Mirdja had known, this was the man she had chosen as her friend.

The driver stopped.

They went silently up to Mirdja's lodgings.

'Make yourself at home, like old times,' said Mirdja, once she had closed the door.

'At home at last! You have no idea how homeless I have been in today's world without you, Mirdja,' said Rolf. 'I am an outsider and a reject everywhere except in your company. Do you remember what I said last time we parted? God only knows what kind of old crab I will be when we next meet, I said. — But how have you not forgotten me, how can you be just the same towards me, how can you...?'

Rolf searched for Mirdja's hand in the dark, and his voice trembled strangely.

'Perhaps I am not quite the same,' said Mirdja quietly. — 'The bridge connecting our fates has broken. A lot has happened since. I was a child back then.'

'Yes, and now you are a woman, fully mature and self-aware, a queen, who commands men with a single glance, who disarms them with a single gesture. You think I don't know all that? You see even out there, invisible, I have been keeping an eye on you. I couldn't give you up completely you know, I couldn't. I have been following in the wake of your conquests with envy...'

Rolf's voice broke unexpectedly into tears.

'You are my old, dear friend,' Mirdja said tenderly, stroking Rolf's large, trembling hand — and her soul confessed to his soul: you are the only one who knows me, you knew me long ago before anyone else. Bless you, and your great, understanding soul.

'How soft is your touch, my benevolent sprite. Let me put my head in your lap, so. And now we can talk again like we used to throughout this night. — After that perhaps — never again — who knows! This one night only.'

'Why only this one night? Your words are as strange as your behaviour. You disappeared on me like smoke before, like the wind, you left me without the slightest indication, like someone taken by death. It feels like an age since I last saw you. And immediately you talk of separating. What is it that takes you away, separates you from me? Why didn't you look for me? Chance was kinder than you. Could you not have sought me out, my old friend?'

'I want to learn to be just that, your old friend — nothing more. But the world asks a lot of a friend these days, and what it asks of me is to leave you...'

'Why?'

'Because my company was poisoning your soul, which needed to find its own life, not to live off shoddy theories. Do you think I don't remember all the harm I did you?'

'You just taught me to see myself and others more clearly.'

'No, no, it was poison, poison you got from me — and from others too, because of me. And you suffered a lot.'

'No I didn't, I took pride in it.'

'Yes but at the same time as your pride mounted, you suffered, you became hard and cynical. What a terrible crime it was against your sweet tender soul, which was like a dream, like gossamer and wax. Because of me. Do you see now, why I had to leave? You must have a lot of awful, unbearable memories related to me...'

'It's you I prefer to remember, best of all.'

'Best of all! And there have been so many...'

Rolf fell silent for an instant, then slowly continued:

'You are a strange girl, Mirdja. I don't really know what to say about you. You retain a lot — and yet you have the ability to forget, to forget more than any other mortal soul. I'm not sure whether to call that a greatness or a weakness. Others buy their memories with their suffering. How much they have given, to whom they have sacrificed, this knowledge they retain for themselves. They find it impossible to forget that they have ripped shreds from their soul, signed for their debts with their heart-blood, because they love themselves. But you Mirdja, you can give it all away, suffer everything, cast yourself aside — and yet remember nothing after the fact. You don't keep a ledger of all the treasures and honours you have bestowed on others, of all the little apportionments of your soul, of all the cruel vivisections. You are a strange girl, in your egotistic altruism, your shattered wholeness,[49] your care- lessly proud self-esteem. I've often wondered about it. And there are other strange aspects to you too. You have the courage of a man and the gentle, multi-subtle soul of a woman, you are as intellectual as a man and as feminine as the most feminine woman in the world. That is what is so irresistible, so enchanting, Mirdja! You dare to look at the world through men's eyes and yet feel it with the finely tuned sensitivity of a woman. That is possibly why you are so extremely rich and unable to count the alms and gifts you proffer, as others do, as the poor do, because by counting their expenses they estimate death, predict the moment when it is all over, when there is but emptiness left. That is why they cannot forget the sand in the hourglass, they count the grains with feverish suspense. — You Mirdja, have no end, no diminishing, no shrinking of life. It is in everything you give away that your life acquires renewal and recovery. How could you possibly waste your life counting your expenses, waste your memories keeping an account book of your past. The evolution of your present moment is the judgement and confession, great and

---

[49] The striving for 'wholeness' was a recurrent motif in Finnish *fin-de-siècle* literature; wholeness was seen as an (unattainable) ideal, opposite to Decadent fragmentation. Given the importance of Goethe for Onerva and her generation of writers, it is likely that this passage alludes to Goethe's often quoted praise for *Ganzeit* (wholeness, unity, integrity), as in Goethe's notorious dictum 'Im Ganzen, Guten, Schönen resolut zu leben' ('To live resolutely in the whole, the good, the true'; from the poem 'Generalbeichte' ('General Confession') from *Gessellige Lieder*, 'Convivial Songs', 1827).

intact, of your past... Mirdja, my wondrous friend, you cannot be measured or assessed like the rest of us mortals...'

The instantly excitable master of paradox that Mirdja recognized so well, had once again awoken in Rolf. This was Rolf's eulogy, produced by his agitated brain, to the woman he most respected and loved.

But Mirdja felt her soul fracture at the caress of this familiar exultation, and her soul whispered to his, very quietly and very sadly: So it seems you didn't know me either, then! A stranger, a stranger to me you are, a man, same as all men, all men...

She laughed sadly:

'No, my friend. Measure me up with the broken and wretched, the rootless, and the aimless.'

'Like me, you mean. No Mirdja, as far as heaven is from earth... but let us leave the word of God in peace... But do you know me, and do you know yourself? — You are wise, Mirdja, wiser than any other woman... The biggest wisdom is self-knowledge. Do you know yourself better than I do?'

'I am bad, very bad, very unstable, very complicated...'

'Because you are wise: it is all part of your wisdom.'

'Are all bad people wise then?'

'No, but all good people are stupid.'

'Oh, what a philosopher you are!'

'Me! All people are philosophers one way or another. Because it is a path to salvation, one which in its wretchedness human nature has invented for itself: to philosophize away all our grief and joy into glorious indifference and a theory about fate. It shelters us from too much envy and malevolence, it comforts us when we end up in the ditch, it enables us to contemplate with a smile the slow demise of our beauty and strength, and life's utter degeneration. With philosophy on our lips, we can live without a wife or lover, and — why not, live with them too. But,' he added, in a more subdued tone, 'it doesn't provide a living. They will soon put me out to pasture; my usual quips are starting to be old hat, and my dull brain hasn't the energy to invent new bait for fresh times... I am already old and worn — alas —'

'Your eternal youth is alive and well only in front of a glass or two.'

'Well, what the hell! At least it releases from bondage both my brain and my tongue. The source of eternal youth, it's true, it's the only chance of eternal youth! Everyone's your friend and brother, and the sorriest among us, the most downtrodden, are given the divine halo of martyrdom, given the higher position they deserve... In a humane Realm of a Thousand Years...[50] You know whose company I was just in? Eero Selinä and Mauri Etso... I understand them well.'

---

[50] Revelation 20. 6: 'Blessed and holy is he that hath part in the first resurrection: on such the second death hath no power, but they shall be priests of God and of Christ, and shall reign with him a thousand years.'

'What are you telling me for? What's it got to do with me?' snapped Mirdja angrily, but she calmed herself immediately. 'So what?'

'They are still in love with you.'

'I don't like you spying on me,' said Mirdja, but at the same time she felt a great flush of warmth in her soul, thankful for Rolf's loyal heart. 'Drunks are in love with the whole world,' she added.

'Drunks speak the truth,' said Rolf seriously. 'I'm just saying that he who once falls in love with you, loves you forever. You see, I understand that this is the way to love you, the only way, and only you, it has to be… a one-way affair… That's the way it has to be, and it's good that way… better one-way than two-way love.'

'Why?'

'Because then it lasts forever, the love of a lonely heart… "Chagrin d'amour dure toute la vie."'[51]

'Yes I remember that…'

'Yes of course, I've mentioned it before. You see how worn out I am, I can't think of anything new to say. Always quoting and plagiarizing.'

'And I plagiarize you. A double honour!'

'You, you…! You don't know me anymore, what I've become… I am not the person you see before you now, in this instant, in the infinite, secure silence of the night, before the duchess of my dreams. Oh Mirdja, Mirdja, life also has its dreary, grey, ordinary weekdays, those shabby, shameful hours without dreams or faith.'

'What have you been doing then, during those dreary, grey, ordinary weekdays without dreams or faith…?'

'Ha ha ha, hanging myself from the noose of my very meagre daily ryebread,[52] and now my legs are kicking in the air to everyone's glee.'

'A slow death… why didn't you just string yourself up by the air vent pull instead?'[53]

'Good grief, do you really think we are looking for death, we people who joke about the hangman's noose? Not on your life! Everything and anything we do, we do out of a robust lust for life… We really are a fantastic species, we humans!'

---

[51] Here, again, Rolf is alluding to the song 'Plaisir d'amour' by Jean-Pierre Claris de Florian (see note 17, p. 69).

[52] The Finnish word in the text (*reikäleipä*) refers to a traditional rye flatbread with a hole in the middle. The hole was used to hang the bread from the ceiling.

[53] An air vent pull, made of decorative cloth, resembled a Victorian bellpull. Newspaper reports of the period indicate that it was not an uncommon choice as a device for suicide by hanging. Onerva's use of the expression may also be an intertextual reference to Joel Lehtonen's novel *Villi* ('Wild'), published in 1905, in which a similar conversation takes place between a cynical, hard-drinking journalist and a depressed young boy called Villi, about the nature of society and the compulsion to live.

Rolf had spoken loud and bitterly. He fell silent for a moment. Then he uttered in a tired, low voice:

'Admit it, I'm just an old crock...'

'No, because you are the grey enemy of the grey mundanity of your days.'

'My own worst enemy...'

'Like me...'

'Just a dreamer...'

'Like me...'

'My friend!'

'My only friend!'

They held each other by the hand, and sat together in silence for a long time.

The first grey light presaged the new morning.

'Another grey day, the day we must separate...!' sighed Rolf.

'Why must we separate?'

'Life requires it, our lives, your life.'

'But we are kindred spirits.'

'Doomed to be apart.'

'Why apart, why?'

'Don't ask any more questions, I have said everything there is to say... or perhaps... there is one thing.'

They are both silent.

'Have you ever missed anyone?' Rolf asks timidly.

'Never, no one... except perhaps myself sometimes...' Mirdja jokes, though her laughter sounds hollow and unnatural.

'Right, never, no one... but tomorrow you will cry over me... I know you.'

'Yes, you know me,' Mirdja whispers, suddenly tender, 'but not well enough... I will cry over you even after tomorrow.'

They are silent once more... The night is gradually receding... Two pairs of eyes, wide with pain, burn into each other.

Suddenly Rolf rises.

'Goodbye.'

'Why goodbye? For God's sake, why, why?'

'It has to be, my friend.'

'My friend, my friend!' Mirdja squeezes Rolf's wrist in deathly anguish. 'You are so like me.'

'You are so like me, why not! So like anyone you meet, like all of us, but there is no one like you... That's the way it is... goodbye!'

'Plaisir d'amour ne dure qu'un moment,' Mirdja's voice trembles quietly, as she holds her hand out to say farewell.

'Chagrin d'amour dure toute la vie,' answers Rolf in the same mode.

One handshake, one look, one smile, and then... the door closes.

Mirdja collapses under the weight of her loneliness.

Why did you leave my side to go out into the world again? her heart complains. You, you who carry my soul with you... I will cry over you tomorrow, and the day after that, and always...

——

But the next day, there were floods of glorious sunshine, there were glistening snowbanks and bells a-jingle, and sparks of gaiety in everyone's eyes... So Mirdja forgot to cry.

GAUDEAMUS IGITUR[54]

❧

How goes the feast of Walpurgis or more precisely, of Walpurgis Night,[55] in the main dining hall of a familiar hotel?[56]

There are white caps bobbing through the hall like restless rings of surf on a sea of light,[57] there are roses and confetti cascading like floral showers on the happy mortals, and high above the general babble, the wine glasses are singing like nightingales.

Artificial light, artificial summer, artificial birdsong in the air, an artificial dew over everything… that hot, moist glow brought on by fortified wine.

For we are a species which thrives on artificial forces.

'Gaudeamus igitur
juvenes dum sumus…'[58]

The room is alive with the unfettered sprites of joy, with the laughter of vivacious Walpurgis.

But do you know, dear friends, which table hosts the real spirit of Walpurgis, the traditional spirit? Only the table at which Rolf Tanne is seated. He alone holds those Walpurgis aces in his fist, he alone knows how to fly the flag of tradition.

Even now he is surrounded in his corner of the restaurant by the usual bunch of regulars, a long tableful of revellers, young and old, the very best of

[54] 'Gaudeamus igitur' ('Let us rejoice') is the first line of a popular goliard song. Goliard songs were secular songs in Latin, disseminated mostly by the goliards, i.e. wandering students and clerics in Europe of the twelfth and thirteenth centuries. 'Gaudeamus igitur' (in Latin also 'De Brevitate Vitae', 'On the brevity of life') was often sung at graduation ceremonies and other academic festivities or student gatherings. Thanks to its light and humorous content, it also became a student beer-drinking song.

[55] The feast of Walpurgis falls on 30 April, and Walpurgis Night (*vappuyö* or *vappuaatto* in Finnish) stretches into the early hours of 1 May. The eve of May Day and the day itself traditionally mark important student celebrations in various European countries, including Finland.

[56] This refers most probably to the Hotel Kämp in Helsinki, which in the 1890s served as the gathering point for the Symposium Circle, composed of male artists (writers, painters, composers, and other musicians) and intellectuals. They met in order to debate issues of philosophy, aesthetics, and politics. The favourite restaurant of Eino Leino and his friends was Kappeli in Helsinki.

[57] Student caps worn during the Walpurgis festivities, not only by current university students but by everybody who has passed their *Matura* or matriculation examination.

[58] Latin for 'Let us rejoice while we are young'.

collegiate cohorts. But aside from 'Onkel',[59] as Rolf is known among his cronies, the indispensable members of this well-assembled boozers' table include that inevitable trio: 'Morre', 'Morpheus', and 'Orpheus'.[60] That is to say Etso, who takes care of the beginning and the end, namely the orders and the bill; pale Selinä, who is always tired; and little ruddy-faced Riku Tapela, the party's ever-jolly improvisor, who is never tired.

On Walpurgis Night no one misses Onkel's plenary session. Even Yrjö Särkkä, who rarely takes part in student life, has chanced upon the gathering in the company of a couple of old friends. The mood is already high.

> 'Vivat omnes virgines
> faciles formosae...'[61]

'Last year Mirdja was here too. She's left us now,' someone commented in a loud voice. This turned the tide of the conversation.

'Naturally, she's bored of playing the regiment's daughter to a bunch of students.[62] She is moving up in the world. Today she was sitting like a prima donna in the company of artists.'

'Nothing like variety,' a third piped in.

'Especially for her. But anyway, she would be quite at home as the artist's lady. She has the hue and the temperament.'

'She is quite an artist herself. She may even amount to something.'

'Oh the world is full of budding talent.'

Each phrase engendered another and soon the whole party had joined in the discussion.

'Today Mirdja was riding in a carriage with that half-lunatic painter Bengt Iro,' someone tendered.

'Don't call Iro a half-lunatic; he's our only impressionist.[63] Artists are always a bit odd.'

---

[59] German for 'uncle'.

[60] Morre is a nickname for Mauri, based on Mauri Etso's first name. In Greco-Roman mythology, Morpheus was the god of sleep and dreams. Orpheus, another figure from Greco-Roman mythology, was a musician, Thracian bard, poet and prophet. In modern times he has stood as an example for the legendary figures of bards in various national mythologies. The figure of Orpheus inspired the character of the semi-god shaman-bard Väinämöinen, which appears in the *Kalevala* (1835, final version 1849), an epic compiled of 50 poems of Karelian, Ingrian, and Finnish origin by the public educator and patriot Elias Lönnrot (1802–1884). See Introduction.

[61] Latin for 'Long live all girls easy, beautiful!'.

[62] A probable reference to an opera by Gaetano Donizetti (1797–1848), *La fille du regiment* (1840), in which the main character is a young woman who, as an orphaned baby, was rescued and raised by a regiment of soldiers.

[63] Impressionism, sometimes called the first modern movement in painting, developed in late nineteenth-century France. The impressionists developed a new style and techniques, which emphasized subjective impressions and transient effects of light and colour. The exponents of the movement were attacked by conservative critics who characterized their

'Talking of a bit odd, have any of you seen Mirdja's new summer hat? It must be an example of Iro's latest impressionism. Mirdja has decided to dismiss the bourgeois notion that Walpurgis is about white caps.'

'Hats and caps are petty stuff, but hell and damnation, those dashed wastrels and braggarts are stealing our Mirdja.'

'The water's never fresher
as in a wetland spring
Nor never a girl more tender
as after a jilter's sting,'[64]

trilled out unevenly from down the other end of the table. It was some young whipper-snapper, who had already imbibed rather too much of Walpurgis Night and who wanted to add his own witty seasoning to the conversation.

Yrjö Särkkä was sitting next to the young lad and suddenly, before anyone could comprehend what was happening, he stood up, grabbed the young boy by the scruff of his neck and pushed him under the table.

'Your kind shouldn't even try to be witty!'

'There's room enough for my song to air!' cried the angry voice from under the table.

'There's no room for crudity.'

'The dog yelps when the stick bites.'

There was a general commotion. The crowd was laughing, speaking and arguing over one another.

'Yrjö, don't take it so seriously,' someone cried.

'It's not worth playing the knight in shining armour to that woman.'

'I will be that woman's knight till the last drop of my blood!' shouted Yrjö.

'He's a gentleman, even if he is a jilted lover.'

'It's not worth it, if you ask me.'

The *digestif* continued its popular rounds. Inspiration flowed ever more spontaneously. But the sophistry had already sunk its teeth into Mirdja and, with characteristic drunken stubbornness, it wouldn't let go.

'Mirdja Ast, Mirdja Ast
Graced him with a kiss at last,'

someone hummed between clenched teeth to the tune of a familiar variety song.

---

works as sketchy and unfinished. Impressionism flourished in Finnish art at the turn of the century. Finnish critics used the word impressionism rather vaguely and mostly negatively, often applying it loosely to other *fin-de-siècle* styles and movements.

[64] The lines come from the Finnish folk song 'Matalan torpan balladi' ('The ballad of a small croft'). The lyrics tell, in a light and careless tone, the story of a boy who seduces a girl from a small croft and subsequently leaves her.

Rolf, who contrary to habit, had up till now remained silent and limited himself to listening and drinking, drinking and listening, now spoke up:

'Boys, may I say a few words?'

'Quiet everyone, Onkel is speaking!'

'I am an old veteran in these circles. I've spent every Walpurgis Night in your company for as long as I can remember, no matter how far I have had to travel to get here. But Walpurgis Night is my anniversary, the anniversary of my youth. And, my good friends, you all know me. You know I'm not one to balk at any subject of conversation. But there's one thing I will ask, if we are to be singing variety songs… skål för Wein, Weib, und Gesang![65]… Yes, if we are to sing variety songs, and why not, let's leave Mirdja's name out of it. That's all I ask; if it's not too much? She is one of us and — she is my friend… She is the only woman in the world who can rise to being a man's friend, and that's no small achievement. Which is why I say, like Yrjö here: we should remain her knights to the very last drop of our blood. When you slander her, it is only jealousy or hurt pride which is speaking through you. That's right. Each one of you has been in love with the girl and some of you perhaps still are. But you are not meant for her, and she is not meant for you. You'll have to set your sights elsewhere if you want to find yourselves a woman, and yet I say to you that all the others are not worthy enough to kiss the dust beneath her feet. She is no saint, by any means, thank God, but she is of a different blood. I know her. A toast to our absent friend! A toast to Mirdja!'

They all clinked glasses enthusiastically. Rolf's eyes were moist.

'That's all I wanted to get off my chest. Don't let me disturb you any further, fellows!'

'That's right, Onkel, that's right!' shouted Yrjö.

But a solemn silence still rested on the company's lips for a moment. So tender-hearted and easily moved are the children of Bacchus.

But the night and wine form a spontaneous and double-winged genie. A genie as deceptive as it is plain-spoken, as white as it is black, as heavy as it is light, as vulgar as it is chaste. It is a strange genie; it laughs and cries all at once, and in the next moment it has forgotten why.

'A toast to Mirdja!' cried Mauri Etso. 'A double toast to Mirdja, because it was Mirdja who taught me to drink. That's the truth. She left me with a terrible thirst. I've never said this before, but I'm saying it now. I'm not saying a bad word about her, no-o! But ever since she left me, I keep drinking and cannot quench my thirst.'

---

[65] 'Skål' stands for 'cheers!' in Swedish, the exclamation made while clinking glasses and drinking at festivities. 'Wein, Weib, und Gesang' (German for 'wine, women, and song') is used to indicate an attitude of hedonistic lifestyle. It is also the title of a Viennese waltz written by the Austrian composer Johann Strauss Jr (1825–1899) in 1869, and of the book of translation of medieval Latin students' songs into English by John Addington Symonds (1840–1893).

'How can you even admit you started drinking because of a woman? Are you a child that you can't get over Mirdja?'

'Well, perhaps I drink for the sake of drinking then, but this much I will say, that ever since her, I have not been able to quench my thirst. A toast to you, my good sirs!'

'Hey, you there young Bellman,[66] the Orpheus of the Opera's underground corridors, are you ready?[67] You better sing Morre here one hell of an instructive and cautionary verse. He's badly in need of it.'

Little Riku smirked.

They gathered reinforcements... The glasses clinked again.

The improvisor winked meaningfully at Morre and raised his guitar, which he always brought faithfully with him like a lapdog. He started strumming it gently and crooned:

'Tell me my dear brothers,
And learned philosophers
How can a fellow be
So drunk and disorderly
O'er a woman, a woman dear me,
For all the world to see,
When the world is hardly short
Of women of every sort.'

Everyone is laughing by now, tapping their glasses in rhythm and joining in the chorus. Only Selinä sits silently staring at his glass of absinthe, an aloof and weary expression on his face.

'No, sing that Persian serenade of yours!'

'No, no, a drinking song!'

'Or the one about the paid hussies.'

'The paid hussies are so cheap
With doors unlocked they sleep.'

'Why always the same old story?' Särkkä raised his voice. 'Disparaging women like that is both ignorant and crude!'

'What the devil is eating you today Särkkä! You're turning into a right little madam... And as for disparaging women, it may well be crude but it is far from ignorant, because you mark my words, if you want to respect yourself, then disparage women!' — This was said by one of the older cohorts with such comic gravity and pathos, that even Särkkä could not help laughing.

[66] Carl Michael Bellman (1740–1795) was an eighteenth-century Swedish poet and musician famous for his drinking songs and for songs celebrating the elusive qualities of the present moment and sexual pleasure.

[67] In Greek mythology, Orpheus (see note 60, p. 120) descended into the underworld in order to meet again his beloved deceased wife Eurydice. Several operas draw on this theme.

'Hey, Tapela, get on with your Persian serenade.'

'Did you hear me coming,
My sweet fire-eye darling,
My desire's jewel and favour,
my sweet, sweetest Zuleima.

I have a chalice so deep,
you have a dagger so steep,
may the blood of our love linger
My sweet, sweetest Zuleima.'[68]

'Why are you so quiet tonight?' Rolf addresses Selinä as the song continues.

'That's a question you mean for yourself, you really are odd tonight. When have I ever been talkative! I stare at that glass of absinthe before me like a foretaste of Nirvana.[69] Everything else is so petty. See how it changes colour and winks its impervious eye, and no one else here understands its spell, only we two.'

'We two separatists, and individualists,' said Rolf sarcastically.

'What is that rubbish the others are drinking?' Selinä fumed, 'no, I'll tell you this much, even if I were a millionaire, I would never swap my absinthe for champagne.

"Car nous voulons la nuance encore,
Pas la couleur, rien que la nuance,
La nuance seule fiance
Le rêve au rêve et la flûte au cor."'[70]

'Verlaine himself couldn't have recited it better! When you die we can all sing: "La Finlande a perdu son Morphée."'[71]

'I have you to thank for that name.' Selinä laughed.

---

[68] The 'Persian serenade' might be a light-hearted variation on or an allusion to Heinrich Heine's (1797–1856) tragedy *Almansor* (1823), a story of the doomed lovers Almansor and Zuleima against the backdrop of the end of Moorish civilization in Spain. Heine, considered one of the most distinguished German poets of the nineteenth century, was well known to Onerva, who also quoted him in her letters.

[69] Nirvana is the final goal of Buddhist philosophical tradition, suggesting a state of peace, in which there is no sense of self anymore. The subject does not feel desire nor suffering, having been released from the cycle of life and rebirth. In late nineteenth-century Western philosophy, it was not uncommon to turn to Buddhism for inspiration. Nietzsche, for instance, used some Buddhist ideas for his own purposes.

[70] 'For Nuance, not Color absolute, | Is your goal; subtle and shaded hue! | Nuance! It alone is what lets you | Marry dream to dream, and horn to flute!' The lines form the fourth stanza of 'Art poétique' (1874) by the French Decadent poet Paul Verlaine (1844–1896), whom Onerva translated (see Introduction, p. 24). English translation by Norman R. Shapiro (in *One Hundred and One Poems by Paul Verlaine: A Bilingual Edition* (University of Chicago Press, 1999)).

[71] 'Finland has lost its Morpheus' (French).

'Listen, don't you laugh, the name does not bode well, there's something terrible and fatalistic about it. I could tell you a thing or two about it, I'm older than you, and we have Verlaine and absinthe in common... But oh how I hope you don't end up like me... Yes you are younger than me, so it is, so it is... Listen, may I speak my mind?'

'Go ahead and speak your mind. My mind's beginning to disintegrate into oblivion... after which there'll be peace.'

'Hold on, hold on my boy, you've a while yet... you're younger than me... But I'll say this to you, a man who starts talking about colour nuances is no longer a real man, and a man who stares into the blue tint of his glass of absinthe, even if he had a million dollars in his pocket, is no longer a well man. So — you're not a well man and not a real man! When a man starts to think in nuances or a woman in maxims, things are not what they should be. It means that the madhouses have a future in this world. Do you understand? A man can tolerate his view of the world precisely because he does not get his feelings mixed up in it, and a woman can maintain her emotional values because she understands nothing... But if you put them together!... No, that's when you get the *Übergang* and *Untergang* that Nietzsche talks of... The *Übermensch* is close, but we'll be beaten before that.[72] You and Mirdja for example, you'd better be careful... and me... well anyway... I'm not a real man either, because I can cry like an old woman, but at least I am old... We're of the same weak and sickly stock, you and me, we lack any great drive, but instead we have a nervous life rich in a myriad subtle sensations, in a given instance we can fluctuate between murderous anguish and stifling joy all at once. Ours is a depleted strength, is it not...? But Mirdja, Mirdja, she's both weak and strong, both man and woman.'

The Persian serenade had long since abated, and most of the party had started listening to what Rolf was saying without him noticing, including the little ruddy-faced Bellman.

'Listen Onkel,' he said slapping him on shoulder. 'You said Mirdja is both man and woman. Now that's not a very clever observation, I have at some point fooled myself into thinking the same. I have to recount a little episode I have never told anyone. It's about Mirdja and me. The thing is, I too was once in love with Mirdja, really head over heels in love...'

'In love!' There was laughter, 'now you're telling fibs again, you rascal!'

'It's the holy truth, every word! As I say, I was in love and completely

---

[72] *Übergang* and *Untergang* are terms used by Friedrich Nietzsche in *Also Sprach Zarathustra* (*Thus Spoke Zarathustra*, 1883–85). They are famous for having various, often contradictory, meanings. When coupled with *Übergang* (transition, crossing), *Untergang* (understood as decline, downfall, and destruction) points both to descent and transition. *Übermensch*, a term coined by Nietzsche in *Also Sprach Zarathustra* and developed throughout his work, is usually translated into English as Superman or Overman. It points to the Nietzschean ideal of a 'higher' kind of individual who has transcended the limits imposed upon the rest of humanity. Nietzsche's work is an important intertext in *Mirdja* in terms of both style and direct quotations. See Introduction.

governed by the laws of human nature. I became feeble-minded, started singing morose love songs and generally behaving like a fool, in the manner of all Amor's loyal worshippers. Mirdja was of course ultimately extremely fed up with my whimpering and finally snapped at me sardonically: "Must a man really behave like a woman in order to be a great poet?" … Can you imagine a more poisonous object of one's love! Naturally, I immediately retreated into my shell, my whole malady was wiped away in an instant, and I boldly retorted: "Must a woman really behave like a man in order to be a great woman?"'

'Bravo, bravo!'

'Yes, but it wasn't a pertinent joke. That's my point. Because, whatever you say Onkel, Mirdja is a woman, she's all woman through and through.'

'Was that the end of the affair?'

'That was the end of the affair… but we became good friends.'

'That's a lie if ever there was one,' cried Morre. 'If a woman is all woman through and through, you can never become friends!'

'Have you really only ever been Mirdja's friend, nothing but a friend, if you know what I mean?' Selinä asked Rolf.

'I swear it! Hand on heart!'

Selinä fell silent again, staring his verdigris stare.

The voices were already beginning to slur. Some forgot their questions, others started flagging mid-way through their stories. They were all getting close to Selinä's Nirvana.

'The night and wine are the genies of forgetfulness…'

But Selinä himself, Nirvana's pale apostle, cannot forget… He remembers two things: the phrase 'if you want to respect yourself, then disparage women!', and the fact that, to Selinä woman still meant Mirdja, in spite of everything, woman still meant Mirdja, and probably always would… How he has struggled these last two years between two contradictory ideas, two contradictory instincts…! Yes, that was it, woman was Mirdja… But why should he disparage Mirdja? For being a sphinx? Rather disparage himself, for being ridiculous… Woman had made him ridiculous… Woman is Mirdja. But Mirdja isn't a woman, she is a divine white shining miracle, who carries his soul with her… Thief, traitor!… Hush, hush, little devils! Mirdja isn't a woman. Mirdja is Mirdja… And what does any of it matter, disparagement or love or anything at all! Nothing… before the great, liberating release of mental oblivion…

POST JUCUNDAM JUVENTUTEM[73]

～

That same Walpurgis Night, Mirdja is walking through the streets alone.

She feels like an outsider among the throng of people around her, all shouting and hollering and brandishing their paper garlands.

Once a year, the chance to wave your worthless party toys in each other's faces, you lucky people!

As she walks on, Mirdja becomes increasingly irked by the ebullient, carnival mood, by the bursts of laughter and the smug, jubilant eyes of the passers-by.

She can almost feel the distant pull of the dance tunes of old... No, no, it no longer has the same attraction... Mirdja has had her fill of dancing... Mirdja is old now... Hasn't she lived for at least a hundred years?

Mirdja walks faster. She has promised to spend the evening with her friend Bengt Iro... Her friend! Strange, strange! If she had said that word aloud, everyone would have shrugged their shoulders and smirked a knowing smirk. True, they both had a reputation for erotic freedom... That couldn't be denied... But that didn't mean... Or maybe it did... How else would they have stood each other's company for so long...?

They had met somewhere in the wide world quite by chance, or perhaps by calculation, why not, as one generally meets people in the wide world. Their first brush had been frosty and exciting, venomous and scintillating, simultaneously polite and curt.

Mirdja well remembers the swordplay of their first encounter.

'You have a poor reputation, Miss Ast: they say you are not one to spare souls, but I suppose that is because you are as wise as you are beguiling...'

'And they say you don't even spare bodies, but I suppose that is because you are — an artist...'

'I swear I have never taken a body without its soul.'

'And never a soul without its body! How very wholesome, simply too hale and hearty to be true!'

'But as you can see, my lovely lady, so far I haven't died of love.'

'You flatter yourself! There are many who survive on morsels!'

'They may survive; but with a ball and chain, in ill health... I do hate a ball and chain.'

'I think it would do your soul a world of good to have a desire unfulfilled.'

---

[73] 'Post jucundam juventutem' ('After the pleasant youth') is the third line of the popular goliard song 'De Brevitate Vitae', mentioned earlier in note 54, p. 119.

'Maybe yours too... But don't try and convince me that you count among those who survive on morsels.'

This had carried on for quite a while, but in an increasingly serene and serious tone. Why are we fighting it? they both suddenly realized, and as if by mutual consent they had discarded all wordplay and bared their souls to one another with dignity and devotion...

But then Iro had, in a moment of madness, grabbed her by the wrist and cried:

'But we have clearly been friends since the crib, you have the temperament of a rare artist, Mirdja, Mirdja...!'

At that point Mirdja was almost vexed. In that old chestnut of a phrase, she thought she espied the self-adulation of an arrogant drawing-room dandy, and regaining her haughty, sardonic poise, she answered:

'You aspire to be so gallant, you men. What do you ask of woman? Nothing, or at most a reflection of yourselves, so you can add her to your list of achievements! Men bestow their own professional titles on their wives with such touching ease, but you, Sir Rare Artist, are a little too bold in tossing yours away to the first passing stranger!'

'You certainly have your pride,' Iro had answered. 'Should I have first held out my soul to you in silence for ten years, and only then opened my mouth? You know very well that sometimes the first passing stranger can happen to be someone you've known all your life... And anyway, you have to believe what I say because I'm talking to you as a comrade, not as a woman, and I take my hat off to you when I say: Artist, who shines in her own light!'

And then they had become very good friends.

Lost in thought, Mirdja arrived at the atelier door... She found herself there almost unexpectedly. She looked around absently, as she felt the need to put her thoughts in some sort of order. She stepped into the dark corridor and sat down on the steps, just inside the door. How often she had come here, as if coming home!... Thousands of memories lay hidden in the shadows of this dark stairwell... beautiful memories at that... Memories of moments when her soul was full of bold artistic conviction, when her brain was boiling over with self-assured motivation, and her imagination floated blissfully in the lofty gardens of the *Übermensch*[74]... memories of her dreams of greatness... These two, Bengt and Mirdja, had known how to inspire one another to titanic heights. They had told each other about all the odd caprices of their souls and all their bizarre experiences, and in this way they had gradually become exceptionally close... exceptionally close. At times, Mirdja asked herself whether it was not possible to call this beautiful, sturdy relationship love, but then she had pushed the thought away and reproached herself for being impossible: she really did not have the right to be naïve anymore... And anyway she had no reason to wish to end the relationship as it was. She wanted to be just a

[74] See note 72, p. 105.

comrade in art, a friend… And yet she knew full well that, all too often, she would remind Bengt that she was a woman, she would arouse him on purpose and enjoy seeing how his eyes drank in the fine red curve of her lips, without daring to kiss them, nonetheless.

Once, on one of the early occasions when they found themselves alone together in the atelier, Bengt had asked:

'Aren't you scared?'

'I'm never scared,' Mirdja had answered with slight provocation.

And Bengt had taken her hand, stroked it, and said:

'You make power respect its own strength, and it heeds your will proudly, like it heeds its own sense of chivalry, you strange, strange creature…'

Yes, Bengt had always been chivalrous, absolutely always, but Mirdja had noticed that he was suffering… In recent weeks he had even grown oddly pale and sickly.

She could hear nervous steps pacing in the atelier. Bengt was waiting for her… And waiting is the hardest of all torments… But Bengt would always have to wait…

Wait for me, wait for me, love me, love me! shouted Mirdja's soul and she pressed her head against the door, writhing in secret, cruel pleasure.

How wonderful it is to hold someone's soul in your hands without them knowing it, how wonderful, wonderful!…

Aargh! — Was she Bengt's friend! Wasn't it all just a lie from beginning to end, this time too, just like all the others…? Bengt was a man…

Mirdja laughed quietly, opened the door noiselessly and looked inside. Bengt was no longer pacing. He was standing with his back to her. His dark, motionless silhouette glimmered in the half-light.

What a beautiful figure of a man Bengt was! How sublime was the line that connected his head to his shoulder. He was too beautiful! It always made one suspicious of a man's intellect… Anyway, while Bengt's intellect might well have been a bit so-so, he was at least perfectly cultured, there was no unculti-vated corner in him, no untilled soil…

Bengt suddenly turned to look behind him, as if drawn by a hypnotic force.

'Was it your eyes drawing me?'

'You are much too beautiful a man, Bengt Iro,' Mirdja said almost solemnly as she stood by the door. 'The Greek canon no longer suits the modern era. The physical image should not supersede the spiritual: its beauty is too facile.'

'Well you should be satisfied with yourself then, because your beauty is the most difficult thing to fathom under the sun. Every point on your body reflects your soul, and yet it is impossible to grasp it. It can drive a person mad. It allures and arouses, dismisses and depresses, all at once. I'm thinking of myself primarily as an artist here. And guess what I was thinking just now, when you walked in? The same as many times before: if only I were the man to paint you, I mean really paint you! It would make me the greatest master of contem-porary art! I would paint only you. You would be to me what Mona Lisa was to Leonardo, Hélène Fourment to Rubens, Saskia to Rembrandt, or Mrs Siddal to Rosetti.[75] But what are their women compared to you! You are a sybarite and a Madonna,[76] you are everything at once and nothing at all, you are something new every day! You have no idea what fantasies you stimulated in me again today, when we were riding through town. Your dress glowing red, your broad-brimmed hat, they brought out something new in you again — something unpredictable, something so strangely beautiful and striking. "My princess, my Polish queen," I was muttering to myself. You looked at me, every cell in your body was pulsating in one unified, gently undulating motion.[77] "My lithe-footed panther, my silky pawed wild cub!" I whispered again, and every minute I had to create a new interpretation of you. Good God, is it even possible to paint something like that, to commit this unity of endless transformation onto a single canvas. It would be the prime essence of all artworks. And yet it is the most fervent of my ambitious dreams. But why just a dream, a dream...? Why couldn't I...? With hyacinths beside you, pungent lilies on your knees... But that wouldn't be enough... You yourself should exude all the split-second moods of today's rippling nerve-life, its over-taut sensorial impressions, its opium delirium, its absinthe madness, the fragile mysticism of all those painful sensory stimuli, its unhealthy, beauty-seeking emotional fever and... the opposite of all that. Because your eyes, those fascinating, changeling eyes, are more stone than fire. The tearful swelter of the ruby, the pale capriciousness of the opal, the captivating green of the

---

[75] The Renaissance master Leonardo da Vinci (1452–1519) painted a Florentine lady (most probably Lisa Gherardini) in the painting known as *La Gioconda* or *Mona Lisa*. The Baroque artist Peter Paul Rubens (1577–1640) painted his second wife Helena or Hélène Fourment. The key figure of the Dutch Golden Age, Rembrandt van Rijn (1606–1669) painted his wife Saskia van Uylenburgh, a wealthy burgermeister's daughter and the cousin of a successful art dealer. Dante Gabriel Rossetti (1828–1882) was an English poet, painter, and translator. Together with William Holman Hunt and John Everett Millais, he was one of the founders of the Pre-Raphaelite Brotherhood, inspired by fifteenth-century Italian art. The Brotherhood was a precursor of the Aesthetic Movement and a major source of inspiration for the European Symbolists. Elizabeth Eleanor Siddal (1829–1862) was a poet and an artists' model. For a long time, she was relegated to the role of the male painters' muse, shaping and embodying their ideals of beauty.

[76] A sybarite is a hedonist, a voluptuary, a sensualist, a person fond of luxury.

[77] The exclamation 'My princess, my Polish queen' might be a reference to Catherine Jagiellon (1526–1583), a princess of the Polish-Lithuanian ruling family. She became Queen of Sweden, exercising influence over state affairs as the first wife of King John III. John III of Sweden was the ruler of Finland as Duke John, later assuming also the title Grand Prince of Finland. He was the only holder of the title to reside in Finland and to hold court at the castle in the city of Turku (Åbo in Swedish) in south-western Finland. The dramatic events of John's and Catherine's lives have provided inspiration for both historians and writers. Eino Leino was interested in the life story of John and Catherine and, in 1919, published a collection of poems called *Juhana Herttuan ja Catharina Jagellonican lauluja* ('The Songs of Duke John and Catherine Jagiellon').

emerald, they all dance on the surface of your eyes, sometimes stinging like a flying spark, sometimes as numbing as the unyielding density of an ice crystal… Oh Mirdja why do you turn my words into lies! Why do you stand and look at me like that… so soft and engulfing and mysterious? Not stone, no, your eyes are everglades, patches of hazel moss, soft as white sedge, treacherous as grassy swampland. So enticing, alluring, inviting…!'

The twilight darkened, the blaze in the fireplace grew brighter. Two figures could be seen motionless, caught in the same poses as when they began…

Finally Mirdja stirred. Laughing clear as a bell, she walked over to Bengt and slapped him on the shoulder:

'You mad fellow, I'm to be your model now, am I?' she said.

'One imagines all sorts of things in the half-light… That was my poem to you. And I haven't composed very many, you have to admit, my friend. I've been a perfectly good comrade, haven't I? — Thank you for coming. I was beginning to worry you had been led astray…'

'I prefer it here, *chez toi*[78]… And how nice everything looks here, with only the light of the fire…'

Bengt smiled.

'I've organized a feast for you. See, there's punch? Do you believe it's good?'

'I know you're a master of many trades.'

They fell silent and stared into the fire.

'We've known each other for two years now…'

'Has it really been two years?' Mirdja sighed.

'Is that too long for you?'

'I have never yet got along with anyone for that long… you know how it is…'

'I know… Same as me.'

'So have we lived beyond eroticism and met one another on the other side of it, or how can we explain the long, harmonious duration of our relationship?'

'On the other side of eroticism… no, my friend, that's not it… Neither of us has been neutered. If we have lived as comrades, it's because we've been pulling the wool over Eros's eyes. I have carried you in my arms, once when we came across a steep ridge in the forest, carried you like only a brother could. I have studied every line of your wonderful body from top to bottom and in close-up, studied you like only a pure artist can, but nevertheless the deepest and darkest part of my soul, of my eyes, has longed for you, lusted for you, your lips, your arms, your whole being, and… you've certainly noticed it…'

'I have noticed it…'

[78] *Chez toi* means 'at your place' in French.

'You have felt how my arm has trembled with suppressed desire when carrying you...'

'I have felt that...'

'And you've understood it...'

'I have understood it...'

They fell silent again... Then Bengt spoke very quietly, in quite an untypical voice:

'Perhaps you haven't quite understood everything... Many times I've asked myself why I don't just kiss you, friend or whatever you may be. Don't friends kiss each other! Or don't they kiss too, those who love each other...? And who can guarantee that we don't love each other...? But I haven't done anything because I've been reluctant to kill the relationship we have. Because it wouldn't be like this anymore. Perhaps it would be love for a while at first, perhaps not even that... And this has been so beautiful. I have been a miserly, self-interested speculator... This reminds me of a novel by Bourget, called "Flirting Club".[79] It's about a club formed by a few old libertines who had had their share of loose living, and who, even though they'd had their fill, still yearned for some excitement. They wanted to experience unrequited pleasure for once, to maintain a continuous sensation of mounting ecstasy, without the descent, a continuous tickle of excitement without reaching its breaking climax. So they formed a club in which they could flirt with wonderful, spirited women, enjoy their irresistible charms, but without crossing the line of physical contact: they could fall in love, but they could not be lovers. But you have to be a real decadent to love the aroma of liqueur more than the liqueur itself, as Bourget says. Anyway, you have been that aroma to me, that continuously mounting thrill, full of desire and love. You have been the most decadent and delectable erotic sensation to me Mirdja, by being a comrade, a friend. Now you understand...'

'It seems we have been stronger than our own will... Or you have been.'

'And yet you don't see me that way. Remember, you once said you could love someone who was strong and the fact is — you don't love me...'

Bengt had said this in a matter-of-fact voice, even and sure; without the slightest trace of timidity, without a hint of reproach or even a questioning tone. Like the most natural thing in the world: you don't love me... And yes, of course, he was right, of course he was... Or perhaps Mirdja did love him after all, this fine strong spirit who even had the strength to keep Mirdja's soul in harmonic balance... Madness! There was always a certain beauty

[79] In his short story 'Flirting-Club' (1885), French writer Paul Bourget elaborates on the idea that the most refined and sophisticated pleasure is brought about not through sexual fulfilment but by an art of abstention: 'Il ne s'agissait de rien moins que d'un art à apprendre, l'initiation à cette sorte de dilettantisme: la volupté interrompue' ('It consisted of nothing less than an art to be learned, the initiation into this kind of dilettantism: sensual pleasure cut short'). Paul Bourget, *Cruelle Enigme. Profils Perdus* (Modern-Bibliothèque, Arthème Fayard et Cie Éditeurs, 1885), p. 106.

before a rupture, so it had been in the past too. Of course Bengt was right, of course. But he shouldn't have said it; this felt just as awful as if he had said the opposite. Or was this some kind of trap...

Mirdja pressed her lips tight together, and then with an indifferent laugh she said:

'No, I don't!'

But then violently, as if she'd been struck by thunder, she fell at his feet in a flood of tears, and she pressed her head firmly against his knees. What a terrible fate she had just condemned herself to! What high court of justice within her heart forced her to deny her love and her happiness! Why, why? Crushed, she sobbed at the feet of the one she loved.

Bengt lifted Mirdja up like a child, stroked her head fondly and reassured her:

'My dear friend, my dear friend, I wasn't asking you for anything, there's nothing I want... everything is fine just as it is...'

Then Mirdja's heart sobbed even harder: everything is not fine, everything is not fine... We love each other, that's the truth of it, we two, doomed to damnation and loss... But because we dare not lose each other, we try and trick ourselves into believing we don't love. Because we both know that our love is the thing of a moment, after which there is nothing. That's the truth of it, that's the truth of it! But this cannot go on either, this ruinous strain on the nerves. No my friend, I cannot keep you ransom at that price, and I could not bear to witness the end of our love, my friend, my friend, now it's my turn to be strong...

And suddenly a great calm came over Mirdja's soul, and the noble, blissful tranquillity of having conquered herself settled on her brow. She had decided that one of them would have to withdraw.

She placed her hand on the chimney breast for support, this motionless, silent, pale girl... The flames were reflected in her cheeks, her eyes, her lips and she was still pale.

The painter stared and stared... He swallowed, savoured, and sucked those light reflections into his soul, which soon seemed to fill with the clear music of oboes and violins...

Everything really is fine as it is. You have given me the finest, sensual ecstasy, you strange, pale creature, he said to himself.

'I trust it doesn't offend you,' he said aloud, 'if the artist within me loves you, dreams of you. Your beauty is supernatural. You are like the apotheosis of contemporary concepts of beauty. That's what I feel, seeing you standing there in front of me: a wonderful, waxen figure of a woman, whose Grecian passions have been exhausted, a drowsy narcissus on a silk stem, your wan lips, your suffering soul, which, having partaken of all there is to offer, still tremors with inextinguishable, hopeless desire, but the whole scene is shrouded in a sombre mantle of silent melancholy, a mood which is conciliatory, mollifying, misty, and mysterious... You don't believe you will ever again find nectar for your lips!... You don't believe it.'

And with a sudden movement of fatal passion, he raised his arms to close Mirdja in his embrace.

Mirdja turned, agile and forceful, and slipped out of his grasp like a playful kitten. Then she stopped in the middle of the floor and stared at the painter with slight mockery on her lips and a hint of sadness in her eyes... There were many voices in her head, speaking sense to her... There was Selinä's voice shouting: 'A curse, a curse on every kiss which is not given in selfish, all-consuming and burning passion.' She heard Bengt's voice explaining that her 'Grecian passions have been exhausted... your wan lips, your suffering soul... You don't believe you will ever again find nectar for your lips!... You don't believe it.' And there was her own voice: 'You have no passion, that is why you cannot find the nectar: you are a pale, wan, weary doubter, and if you give yourself up nevertheless, then you will cease to exist, because your passion is all lies, lies, lies.'

'Mirdja,' said the painter, 'your body escapes me, just as your soul does... Just as your soul does,' he repeated slowly. 'Whenever I think I have grasped some part of you, and I try to feel it, touch it, possess it, you slip away like a deceptive image in a dream, and I am left empty-handed and disappointed. I hold nothing, nothing of you, though I have so much... And then I am struck by a mad impulse to shout at you: "give me your body at least, as a sign that you would like to give me your soul, which I can't have..." Please understand these moments of mine, Mirdja my friend...'

I understand that such a thing can be asked and granted only by a passionate love, which is blinded in the face of its beloved. How you deceive yourself, or try to! 'My love, my love,' is what you should be shouting, if you were to be honest. But that word would only reach my soul by slithering along the long antennae of thought, which is why I couldn't accept it, if I were to be honest. Now it's time for me to leave, thought Mirdja. And slowly she spoke, as if to herself:

'I don't have that capacity for total submission which erases everything else and makes one forget to keep hold of oneself, and I never will have, that much I know. I always want to keep myself for myself. I am not even looking for that experience, though it might mean happiness, because submission would mean losing myself...'

'It would mean finding yourself, as sure as you are a woman. Don't you understand yourself, you who understands everyone else? Or do you keep your innermost self a mystery on purpose! But I'm no stranger to you, explain to me the riddle of your being. You have given so much of yourself to me, and yet I feel as if I have nothing to hold on to. There's something very puzzling about this, and for two long years I have been trying to solve the puzzle without success. In the daytime it is like a fog between me and the sun, at night it sits on my chest like a nightmare, and — I still don't have the answer. Are you so rich, that even your greatest gifts are like insignificant fractions of your infinite being, or are you nothing at all? Just a silhouette, a wonderful, deceptive, surface image, or is it because you are so profound that I simply can't fathom you? Are you unfathomable depths or crest foam, are you the weight or the lightness of life? When I see all the white giddy spindrift that dances and sings within you, playful and pearl-like, light and delicate, senseless and charmingly child-like, I think you are completely devoid of any depths, those torrents of primeval chaos and confusion that God controls and in which humanity's faith and doubt meet as mortal enemies. But then I look into your eyes and I take it all back: there they are, those chaotic torrents of the gods; if I stare at them for any length of time, my faith and doubt become confused in your eyes, they fight, they tear each other to pieces, they kill each other, and I am left as ignorant as before. You can make me believe anything with those eyes. In the middle of their brightest laughter I can suddenly start at their holy solemnity, and I whisper: you are destined to be sad sirens, you deep, beautiful eyes... Driven by passion, I have tried to become close to you, and I always remain as distant from you as when we first met. Is it because you have too much content or too much form, I don't know. This has all been very delightful, but at times, I have to admit, it has taken a very severe toll on me and then I've thought that no degree of violence toward you would be too great. I've felt I could squeeze you until your blood would stop flowing, if I could then command you: tell me what you are!'

All this time Mirdja had stood still as a picture, leaning on the chimney with her head bowed against her crossed arms.

And she reminded Bengt of a broken carnation, a beautiful broken carnation.

While Bengt was talking, Mirdja had developed only one thought. Now it was ready, uncompromising in its just resolve. Mirdja had to leave. His outburst was a natural consequence of all the long-sustained, concealed pressure. But things had come to a head, they could not go on as before. Bengt would not be able to cope with Mirdja's half-hearted commitment and — Mirdja could not give herself up. She had to leave. But as she considered this, her heart was crushed by the anguish of it and a boundless, strange tenderness that resembled love filled her soul, and she felt weak. How was she to tear herself away! — And her voice trembled with barely supressed emotion as she whispered:

'Don't ask me what I am, I hardly know myself... or... I'm everything you believe me to be... But don't think about me anymore, let the spindrift fly light and delicate, let the fathoms rest, wherever they rest, dark and untouched, wise in their sorrow, and everything will be as it should... don't think of me...'

Mirdja's voice started to falter. Bengt listened anxiously, almost fearfully to its mournful, bereft tone. He thought he had offended her.

'I'm an ass,' he cried, 'torturing the most beautiful woman in the world with my idiocies! Why don't I just let her be the miracle that she is, after God's six days of labour![80] Well be with you, Mirdja! Looking into your face is like looking into life. But we people, we torment God, we torment life, we torment the one we… everything we hold great and good we torment…'

But Bengt's words gave Mirdja a sense of déjà-vu, of something long ago… A bad omen, a bad omen! Then something else happened, which was also like a déjà-vu of course. No — not that! Where would she get the strength to leave in time!

'Mirdja,' Bengt went on in a gentle voice, 'you cannot give yourself up, you said, and for two people to live together and share something, one of them always has to yield: I give myself up to you…'

You wretch, you wretch! Mirdja screamed in her soul. Now it's that same old routine again. And it's your fault. Life in its harshness can yield, they say even God in heaven once yielded, you, you who dare to take it all, you don't have the courage to give it all up, you who think you know everything, you don't know how to give yourself up. You believe you understand everything, but you don't understand your own being.

And suddenly Mirdja's eyes were black and smouldering like the craters of a volcano, and a spark of defiance set her soul on fire… For a second or two she trembled at being the odalisque of her own heart, then she wrapped her arms around Bengt's neck and pulled his lips against hers.

Their bodies pressed against one another with the all-engulfing passion of two years' denial.

'So you loved me all along,' whispered Bengt at last.

It awoke the real Mirdja. 'So you loved me all along.' Behind the tender elation in his words, she sensed something ruthless, akin to the glee of victory… you were the same as other women; now I can pass you by. It was to come at least, soon, very soon. This is what Bengt had been fighting against for two years. Mirdja herself had destroyed everything. Now it was up to her to salvage the end at least.

'That was just my farewell,' she declared with feigned bluntness.

'Farewell… now…! Oh Mirdja, why do you play games?'

'I'm not playing games, I have to go.'

'How can you be so cruel? What's the meaning of this?'

'Don't call me cruel, not when I'm giving you something invaluable for once…'

'I don't understand…'

'You reproached me for never having given you anything proper. Now I am giving you back my self — and leaving you.'

'Mirdja, don't tease… I love you.'

'No, you said earlier that the artist in you loves me. If I were to stay, your faith would soon be broken. If I leave you now, I am at least leaving you with

---

[80] A reference to God's six days of creation in Genesis 1.

your beautiful dream. And as sure as you are an artist, you will find yourself in that dream.'

Mirdja started to yield again, she could feel herself becoming weak... She had to leave, right now. Now they could no longer pull the wool over Eros's eyes. If she stayed, she would only have to face the gradual waning of everything, and she was too proud to accept, even for one second, the kind of treatment a man, whose love has grown cold, usually concedes to the woman who kissed him first... Now she had forced herself to separate from him.

Hastily, with trembling fingers, Mirdja placed her hat on her head. Bengt stared at her, stiff and motionless. He thought of them both... He was crushed, limp and lifeless as if a great rock had fallen on him.

Mirdja glanced at him briefly, as if in passing, and disappeared through the door.

The painter's head slumped into his hands like that of a dead man. He sat like that for the whole night and he didn't even notice the fire dying slowly or the dawn coming up, because all he could see before him was his soul's infinite night and loneliness.

But Mirdja spent most of the night sitting on a damp rock on the far side of town. How had she come to be there? She hardly knew herself. She had run down the stairs like a madwoman, like a madwoman she had run further, as if running for her life, without knowing where she was going. Finally she was drawn by the sound of distant singing, and she ended up in the gardens of a large summer restaurant, and stayed there to listen to the last songs of Walpurgis Night.

Everything seemed so nonsensical. To force oneself to separate — without saying goodbye! But she couldn't have spoken; she would have collapsed on the spot, melted into tears, clung to Bengt's knees... And even now she wanted to go back, to go back to Bengt. Poor Bengt. He was surely unhappy. Why shouldn't she go to him, as she had done hundreds of times before? No, now it was impossible. She herself had made it impossible. Fool that she was, fool!

The cold and the loneliness made Mirdja shiver, not to mention her extreme tiredness; she was tired of life, tired of this city, tired of everything and especially tired of herself. She had come here to work, but life had swallowed her up, her monotonous and colourful, her conflict-ridden and empty life. But how to escape it, when she herself was the source of it? How to escape oneself? At any rate she had to get away from here, without delay, otherwise tomorrow she might find herself crawling once more to the door of the man she kissed today. And that was never to happen, never.

It was time to move on from all this pointless turmoil and torment and strife. She would go off to see her old uncle in the quiet of the countryside, in Lumiluoto![81] — This thought made her feel better.

---

[81] Lumiluoto, the word literally meaning 'snow skerry', is a fictional place, though the name may have been taken from a tiny island in the south-eastern area of the Gulf of Finland.

Mirdja got to her feet slowly. Icy rime had gathered on her clothes.

At this rate she could easily fall ill and — die. How would it feel to die here alone now, in the wet April snow, by the backyard of a tavern? No, she rather preferred a visit to her uncle in wonderful Lumiluoto.

And Mirdja set off slowly towards town.

LUMILUOTO

I

~

Arnold Ast is an old man.
Arnold Ast is a dreamer and a recluse.

On the cold and rocky seashore looms the lonely realm of Lumiluoto.

It belongs to the dreamer, it is built on dreams and dedicated to dreams. Because people are happy only in dreams and Arnold Ast is happy.

At least this is what the waves believe, for they have followed the course of his life from his youth unto manhood, and from manhood unto old age. They know him well, for Ast has always been a friend of the waves. His arms have often rested fondly on the white manes of their foal-like forms, he has stroked and caressed them, and sometimes told the creatures his remarkable secrets… And he is full of secrets, this hermit, he is a wise man and a shaman.[82] A good shaman. How could he not be happy!

This is also what those in the neighbourhood believe. They could tell many a fantastic tale about the preposterous 'Snowman', as Arnold Ast came to be known locally from the moment he arrived. It happened thirty years ago and it was a terrible, infamous year for the fishing community, marked by all the worst signs of the heavens: storms, shipwrecks, abundant snowfall which all but submerged the entire impoverished community. And then on top of all that, that same year, there appeared as if by magic a peculiar human abode on a section of the rocky embankment, like a cross between a polar bear's cave and a bird's nest, and an even more peculiar human started showing up in the area. A very eccentric individual, with hair as white as a snowdrift and lips as silent as a ghost's. 'It doesn't bode well,' said the elderly folk 'he's the bogey behind this snowfall.' But over the last thirty years everyone has had time to calm themselves. There had been no further significant snowstorms or floods. The Snowman no longer attracted much attention. They all knew his ways. He had done nothing during his thirty years in the area, he never fished, never went bird-shooting, never ploughed the land, nothing. He was a little off his head of course. But to be so wealthy as to do nothing for thirty years! How happy he must be!

---

[82] The figure of the hermit sage, known from various mystical traditions and sometimes fused with the character of the Decadent recluse who despises bourgeois society, also appears in other works by Onerva. In some prose works, the figure merges with that of the seeker, i.e. a person looking for alternatives to traditional forms of religion, new forms of faith, widespread in *fin-de-siècle* literature and art.

It is spring once again. The wind is playing its kantele of white foam,[83] the sound of the sea soaring high.

A restless flag is flying on the roof of Lumiluoto castle.

A flag is festive raiment, a messenger announcing merry company, a beacon to honourable procession. — There it flies and flaps, whipping the wind and floating wide, but no one comes. Only loneliness stares at it with its fossil-like eyes. Perhaps that is what the flag is here to honour, hoisted as the very emblem of seclusion?

But the waves approach proud and snorting, a long, dauntless succession of waves, they know many splendid secrets...

'The child is here again,' splutters an old, white-bearded wave.

'She's not a child anymore, she's a fully-fledged woman, but what would you know about it, you ancient thousand-year-old goblin,' laps a lighter wavelet by the old-timer's shoulder.

'Which one is wiser, the man or the woman?' inquires a young green-eyed ripple out of curiosity.

'The woman, the woman! She comes from afar and has learned about life. A woman is always wiser than a man, life is always wiser than seclusion...'

'The man, the man of course! In seclusion speaks the voice of God! The old man has learned from God!'

'Is that why he has gone so grey? God charges a high price for enlightenment.'

'And fells them early. Humans are no thousand-year-old goblins....'

The waves witter away endlessly. They draw near but pull back again and sink to the depths. They are never too noisy with their questions...

'After all we know so many splendid secrets,' they murmur as they go.

[83] A *kantele* is a traditional musical instrument known mostly in Finland and Karelia, a plucked string instrument similar to the zither. It belongs to the Baltic psaltery (the southeast Baltic box zither family). The old traditional kantele had five or six strings; the modern concert kantele can have up to 40 strings. A kantele plays an important role in the epic *Kalevala*, mentioned above (note 17), where it acquires magical and mythical qualities. The music played on the kantele by the semi-god, sage, and bard Väinämöinen, modelled partly on Orpheus (see note 60, p. 120), enchants all creatures and draws them nearby to admire its beauty.

II

~

The first weeks Mirdja spent at Lumiluoto, she simply rested, rested without thinking or feeling, enjoying the peace and the solitude. — They were two old recluses…

Then Mirdja said to herself: but I'm not a hundred years old yet after all, I'm almost born yesterday!

She felt as if she were a child whose eyes had opened for the first time to take in God's great and magnificent nature. She behaved like a child. She could sit for hours by the sea splashing barefoot in the water or stepping from stone to stone along the shallow cove of red sand, until she reached the outermost rock. And when on occasion she happened to fall in up to her waist, she would often stay there laughing at her own distorted image in the water, and over and over again she was driven to breathe the vast salty sea air deep into her lungs, now that it was so close, so close. Or then she would climb onto the high rocks along the shoreline, hooting like a bird into the woods, hooting out to the sea or hooting to her uncle… All Mirdja wanted was to be a small, foolish child, and for this man to be her old, wise and kind uncle, nothing more. She was constantly dragging him with her, constantly asking him about the air, the earth, and the sea, everything under the sun, not because she didn't know the things she asked, and not even because she would have wanted proper explanations but because it felt so nice and safe to slip her hand into her uncle's big, weighty hand and ask: 'why, uncle?' And besides, Mirdja knew that this game was one of her uncle's few pleasures in this world, it was comforting for him to see that someone needed him too. And she understood her uncle, which was something Mirdja secretly took great pride in. For Mirdja knew a lot about her uncle's splendid secrets, she alone could have explained many a curious matter that remained an eternal riddle to everyone else. A lot of superstition had become attached to the old recluse over the years. The local folk had never completely overcome their fears concerning him. One particular bone of contention was the little tower rising above the far side of the house at Lumiluoto, which the local people had christened the Devil's Lighthouse. No normal person required such a structure, seven rooms one above the other, like the seven deadly sins. And always on stormy nights, they could hear music coming from the tower, no light, nothing visible in the windows, only singing and wailing and whimpering like the lament of a hundred voices. More than likely it was the Devil himself howling away. So the rumour said. And children who had been berry-picking nearby had seen the Snowman walking around muttering to himself in tongues, and after every word he had taken a scrap of paper and thrown it into the wind. 'He's practising black magic,' some believed, but many others didn't think that far, and simply laughed at his antics: 'the feeble-minded fellow knows what he is doing, and to think he's so rich he could be throwing gold nuggets into the woods, but he's clearly still too sane for that!' This is the kind of talk Mirdja had overheard. Oh, she alone could have told them the truth behind the strange music in the Devil's Lighthouse and the scraps of paper thrown into the wind.[84] And sometimes she felt like climbing to the highest ramparts of the Devil's Lighthouse and proclaiming to the whole world: revere this tower, children, for no madman nor devil lives here, only a wise man and thinker, a great philosopher, whose only madness lies in that he has dismantled his philosophy, a great musician, whose only devilry lies in that he has only ever played for the ocean winds! But then she thought that no amount of respect and reverence would have brought her as much pride and joy as her singular right to tend and understand the great mystique of a great human spirit. And this wonderful privilege had brought with it a thousand fine obligations towards her dear, reclusive uncle. Their relationship had developed on both sides into something very special, something inexplicable.

And so, while in her uncle's sphere of influence, Mirdja had all but forgotten the many sad ruptures that lay behind her. This wonderful place made her soul wish only for all that was beautiful, delicate, and sweet. And Mirdja put an end to all self-reflection with a single phrase: I feel so good here with you, uncle, I feel so good...

But after a while, even that wasn't enough. Inevitably, all her old thoughts and memories reared their heads again, all the draining cross-examinations, which only had her up against herself every time she tried to air them. They pressed against her like a thousand-pronged iron snarl, pushing her down, squeezing her. All the life that was behind her, all that was ahead, teased and tormented her and whispered: you craved me and now you slander me, you found me and still don't think you have. You fool, as though I could ever be anything other than a reflection of yourself. When you slander me, you slander yourself. Empty, contradictory, debauched, ha ha ha! You'll never find me until you find yourself. What are you looking for, who are you, you, you?

Yes, who was she, why was she the way she was? Was it her fault? Was she not simply subject to the unshakeable laws of nature, had she not, unknowingly and unintentionally, simply lived out and replayed the family legacy passed down by previous generations? Even Rolf had said that her sins were inherited.

---

[84] The ancient belief in the relationship between the Devil and music, especially violin music, well known from the Romantic period, was very popular in Symbolist and Decadent literature. It is present also in Finnish Decadent writing, most visibly in Joel Lehtonen's *Paholaisen viulu* ('The Devil's violin', 1904).

Was Mirdja's line tainted by madness? She remembered having once heard someone whispering behind her, there goes the daughter of that madman Ast. Or perhaps they had only been referring to her uncle then too… And her uncle had never uttered a word about it.

The secret of her origins began to weigh upon Mirdja more than ever before. How had she never thought of examining her personality from that point of view? She had grown up like a mushroom springing from the ground, she was like a seed of her own making, with roots of her own making, like a lonely shellfish, like a creature fallen from the sky or a miracle formed from nothing, an impossibility… For heaven's sake, even she must have been born out of the love between two human beings. What had they been like, those two people…?

Mirdja was suddenly struck dumb. She could think of only one thing, and yet it was something too hard to speak of. For uncle and niece had one peculiarity, which was that they never asked anything about one another. They knew that each would always instinctively bring up whatever might be of help to the other. And if one remained silent, so would the other. In their extreme individualism, they approached each other's souls with discretion, dignity, and respect. They spoke about all kinds of things, but rarely about themselves. But they knew each other so well, that they were able to sense one another's heartbeats no matter how objective the discussion. — Yes, Mirdja knew that her uncle had told her all he wished to without being asked. But why, why had he never spoken more about his brother?

For several days, Mirdja wandered about in a dark and silent mood. Then she finally asked:

'Uncle, tell me, was my father much like you?'

'No, or who would be so bold as to say for sure,' answered her uncle quietly.

'Was he much like me?'

Her uncle was silent.

'Oh uncle, you don't wish to tell me anything. For heaven's sake, why, why? He was my father after all. Do you understand what this means to me, being as rootless as a shellfish in the sea or a star in the sky? Tell me one thing at least, did my father die a madman?'

'Perhaps he did, I can't say,' answered her uncle slowly.

'Do you really not know anything more than I do? Father was a restless soul, a wanderer, mother was a foreigner who died in childbirth, that's all you've told me. So what, is that enough, it's my father and mother we're talking about. They must have had their own souls, their own lives, their own fates, moment to moment, day to day. And I, I am a continuation of them now: their souls follow me everywhere, and I don't even know them. I'm so unhappy, so unhappy!'

Mirdja burst into tears.

Her uncle rose slowly to his feet. He stood and looked at the girl for a long time. Then he went over to an old cabinet, opened a drawer and fiddled around inside it for a while. When he returned, he was holding an old letter. With a heavy heart he placed his hand on Mirdja's head, held the letter out to her:

'This is the only thing I have known in addition to what you already know. It is your father's last and only letter to me.'

'My father's letter! Why have you never given this to me before?' asked Mirdja, taking the letter between her trembling fingers.

'You had to find yourself first, children are prone to believe in ghosts… Read it and decide for yourself, Mirdja. You're not a child anymore.'

'I want to read it alone,' said the girl.

Mirdja rushed to her room as if she were being chased. The ground beneath her feet was burning, the letter in her hand was burning, her whole soul was burning, the whole world was burning… And she had to double lock the door in order to feel that she was truly, truly alone with him, undisturbed, on this, the first day they were to meet… Her soul was burning but she trembled as if she were freezing to death when she slowly unfolded the old sheets of paper, and started reading…

III

~

'Do you ever think back, brother dear, to your life that was, do you remember the people you've met in passing? I generally don't. I've looked someone in the eye, not to mention the soul, then separated, and — forgotten them. But you, my brother, I can't forget, so deeply have we looked into each other's eyes, even though it was a long time ago. We spent unnaturally little time together, considering that we are brothers. A year or two as children, a few years at university, and that is all. And yet I think we managed in that time to win each other over, we managed to surprise each other and understand the vast distances that our different natures had put between us. Because we have always been different. From the start, do you remember? Even as children. I went ahead and lived out my feelings, you followed behind, rationalized the same feelings and didn't think they were worth acting on. I was a fantasist and a poet, whole-hearted in my commitment, indiscriminate, excitable, and sickly. And I never feared anything as much as deliberation, because I believed it would kill the wonderful lust for life that coursed through my veins so powerfully. You were a fantasist too, but you were also a man of thought, always ready to deliberate, and so you placed your fantasy in the balance, and lost your lust for life. Which is why you never fulfilled your dreams. You were blasé without experience, tired of life without having lived. And you suffered for it, and felt half-baked...

And I played with life, and it with me, and we broke each other in the process. I became an adventurer, a wanderer... and you became a recluse. And we've both stuck to our place, haven't we? I know all this and you know all this, even though we haven't been in touch for — a hundred years — I was about to say. But who would be able to tell the tales of the wanderer and the recluse? They are both lost to the world. And anyway, we knew our fates long ago, back in those years of burgeoning self-awareness, when we tortured ourselves incessantly by trying to analyse our souls and asking ourselves and each other: quo vadis...?[85]

And of course we went our separate ways because our personalities were clamouring for a rift. Yes, we parted company even though we knew that it

---

[85] Latin for 'where are you going?'. In the Christian tradition the phrase has been attributed to Peter, who asked the resuscitated Jesus 'Quo vadis, Domine?' ('Lord, where are you going?'). Jesus answered, 'Romam eo iterum crucifigi' ('I am going to Rome to be crucified again'). In popular usage the phrase *Quo vadis?* has become a means to inquire about the deeper meaning of somebody's actions, decisions, or goals.

was only together that we formed a whole, a perfect human being. We were twin souls, who completed each other and who would always come to miss each other. And I have indeed missed you very much over these long years, in both my moments of clarity and my moments of darkness, but my individualism always carried me further from you and kept me out in the wide world, and now I die without seeing you, I write my last will and testament without seeing you. It is a hard legacy I have left you, but it is all I have, the only, best, most precious thing I have, and you are the only person in the world to whom I can entrust it.

Yes, death awaits me. I die a stranger in a strange land, as I have lived, a pagan without a priest. It is only you I wish to hear my beliefs, my sins, and my final confession. I wish to fill the empty void created by our long separation.

Back then I went away, as you recall. I considered myself a poet, an artist, as indeed I came to be called. For my soul burned with a searing pain, and tall, untameable *ignes fatui* leapt within me,[86] and I believed in them — at first. I began to search for the treasures they augured. I searched in many places, too many. Morsels, morsels! This was followed, typically, by huge disappointment. I threw all the tiny jewels of my dreams onto the scrap heap. And then I became the incurable doubter that you have always been, and I realized that there is no creature under the sun more tragic or pathetic than a dilettante. And that is what even a born artist can turn into, if strength, integrity, and confidence are lacking. Because then the artist also lacks the energy to work, to create art in which to take pride and joy, and without that no artist can survive… And the greatest misfortune is that such an artist also lacks the strength to put out the increasing flames of misfortune; it still burns and smoulders. Such is a full-blooded dilettante, and such was I. The fire would not die in me, and neither would my lust for life, it was more dominant than ever. But I no longer believed in anything, and I began purposely to exhaust, shatter, and destroy myself. A victim of my uncontrollable desire to consume, I wandered the world as a vagabond with no name and no ties. Who can even describe a life like that! From one profession to another, from poverty to luxury, tossed here and there by chance. I joined travelling theatre troupes, gaining occasional laurels if my inspiration happened to coincide with the evening's performance, which, for the most part, it did not. And I was indolent, I didn't try hard, I didn't push myself, I didn't approach anything I did as proper work, least of all art… This lasted several years. But then my lust for life disappeared — and I was so tired that I simply wanted to die, to disappear. And first I wanted to visit you. But why didn't I achieve either thing? You see my life story is just a story of mediocrity. Even my death-wish was that of a dilettante, and what happened to me then was what happens in

---

[86] Medieval Latin meaning literally 'foolish fire' or 'foolish flame' (here used in the plural), denoting a will-o'-the-wisp or deceptive hope.

the everyday chronicles of all ordinary folk. A woman came along... No, brother dear, don't imagine it was the first time I'd seen a woman. I had seen them all, and I had seen them to be flighty. And I held them in contempt, in the manner of all men who have gone to seed. But now that my self-contempt was at its highest, I suffered from a strange visual impairment and once again looked up to woman, that pure, innocent, inexperienced creature... Such a cliché! And in fact, say what you will, but those women are precisely the greatest danger to men. It is useless slapping the word "man-eater" on the foreheads of philandering women. Those who can really suck a man's soul dry and make his life empty, unbearable, deceitful, bestial, and base are the women who have no experience of life, who have never seen anything or done anything and therefore understand nothing. — I found a woman like that. She was a petite bourgeois girl, an orphan from the countryside, and can you imagine anything more absurd, I married her, me, a philanderer, a world-traveller, and a stage-player. She had large, understanding eyes, like the eyes of a cat on a hearthrug, trusting, a nice smile, a gentle touch. It was all so beautiful and happened so effortlessly. I married her...

But I ended up alone. And that was really the first time in my life I felt truly alone, and unhappy on behalf of both of us. Anna, that was her name, was too stupid to be completely unhappy on her own behalf and too good to show even her mild discontent. But I knew she could hardly be content, because even the most stupid woman has her intuition, her invaluable animal instinct...

But I left my good, faithful domestic cat. A long rest had improved my health and I was drawn to the road again. Domestic cats always find a good home and if they end up as stray cats, so what... I left her.

Romantic desire burned wilder than ever in my soul. I spread my wings like an eagle escaping from a cage, for such a period of rest in the crass, smug environment of well-adjusted philistines was so alien to me that it required a reverse remedy, a veritably rousing revolution. I assure you I endured it as long as I possibly could: domestic life with all its palpable virtues is anathema to me, anathema. I took to the open road again, and fool that I was, I started searching again, I started searching for a wild flower to tint my romantic dreams. Why did I find her! If only I hadn't found her, I could have lived out my longing, I could have perished basking in my beautiful fantasy. Finding what you seek is always like having your dreams shipwrecked, it is the encroachment of persistent grey day on a fading starlit sky. But why do I slander the best thing I ever had, wretch that I am! I found so much, I found something so extraordinary and thrilling, so free and wild as nature, a potent burst of life instantly brushing away all memory of the narrow, dusty, shrunken existence to which my brief marital idyll had bound me. And later — I found even more than I could ever have dreamed of. I found Mirdja.

What? Who? you are thinking.

Take note: I found Mirdja.

I didn't know where she came from or who she was. A stranger, a wanderer, a travelling singer. But I loved her. Haha, my dear fellow, there it is again, that old word, love, so worn, so very worn but there is no other word for it. We lit a bonfire together and spent the nights playing with wild flames that reached the sky, free as gypsies, free as birds. She was not stupid, neither coarse nor bourgeois. She was born rich and the life she lived made her richer still. She wasn't, strange to say, one of those whose existence relies on theft. Even though she had nothing but herself and her life.

And then I started to want something else, something more fulsome, more complex in form, more cryptic in content... something which could unite nature and culture, unite the opposites of raw originality and sophistication. Thus, my great notion started to take shape, my dream of perfection for which I am even now considered mad...

My sins are many. Mirdja died... But now I have another Mirdja... I am getting to the point at last now, because it is this Mirdja I am sending to you.

I have been so long in explaining this in order for you to have a better chance of understanding me and — above all — understanding the child. Because in her my ambition now lies, my dream, my faith, my madness, in a word, everything... At last, I have found something to come back to, no matter what I am searching for in the wide world. And now it's easy for me to say what I am looking for, what dreams I see when I sleep. Woman, I am still dreaming of woman, but she has to be an all-encompassing spirit, as resilient as reason, as ingenuous as instinct, profound and light, everything at once, and above all, human, a human being who can declare: I hold no facet of humanity alien to me![87] Isn't that what I have always been yearning for, without knowing it? Oh, I have travelled the world in search of one thing. One woman, a woman who would also be a human being, and a human being who also contained every facet of life. Do you understand now? I am going away, and you must carry on my search, that is my last wish, and I will put you on the right path: you must look for this in Mirdja, only in Mirdja must you look. You will not find this human being elsewhere, of that I bear witness, I who have grown poor and weary in my long pilgrimage and found nothing. But now I can feel the breath of humanity, residing here close to me, but I cannot find it yet. It possibly lives in my Mirdja. I look upon her as upon a holy child in a manger and I bow before her as I bring myrrh and incense.[88] They say I'm mad. But what do I care of society's views of madmen and wise men! I see one single calling before me, ever since my art turned to dilettantism, only one calling: to find a woman who could be an all-encompassing spirit. And I worship my own child now. This may well be

[87] A paraphrase of the famous sentence by the Roman playwright and poet Publius Terentius: 'Homo sum; humani nil (nihil) a me alienum puto'.

[88] A reference to Matthew 2. 11, in which wise men bearing gifts (of gold, frankincense, and myrrh) visit the infant Jesus to pay him homage.

an unhealthy exaggeration of fatherly feeling, late awoken, or so I tell myself, but that does not prevent it from being my obsession. She is now the greatest of my many grand and deluded dreams. She is now the world I wish to explore in order to make unprecedented discoveries. I am forever observing her, even when my eyes are turned elsewhere. I already feel I can read such secrets in her dark child's eyes, as have never before existed in a human soul. And I believe that if she could speak, every word would ring out like birdsong, like the music of jubilations never before seen.

I have not been granted the privilege of witnessing the development of my dreams. I am to die. But I am sending Mirdja to you. My dream will thus shatter yours: you always wished to be alone. Don't hold it against me. You understand me. She is my madness and my wisdom, my love and my every-thing… I cannot abandon her to the world. Perhaps she will become that perfect human being, you and me combined, and something more than that. You can fulfil my dream… Now you know enough. The rest you may concoct for yourself… My life cannot be written down, it must be lived…

I am writing this now, as my life flits past in pictures and my thoughts struggle to organize and explain everything that has gone before, in the face of this new unknown. I grew old as a young man, now I can grow young again… But to have to die now, now when I do so desire to live! Perhaps that is why my love for Mirdja is so fervid and eager, because it is so hopeless. I entrust the unfinished threads of my life to you… I have always been mad and unreliable… It's up to you to judge how mad exactly.

I bless you both in farewell.

Ervin.'

Such a father, such a dream, and such love!

Mirdja's brain was throbbing with fever and delirium.

Now I know my roots! Her heart cries, filled with joy and anguish. I belong to a fantastic bloodline of eternal dreamers, budding artists, and madness. I can recognize my own now, and my own recognize me, and all mad souls belong to my limitless realm! I govern you, I govern you all by virtue of my father's soul! You have all come bearing myrrh and incense as you approached me, you have all bowed before me. One could almost think that there are none but the mad in this world… But that would make me the greatest ruler of all. Ha ha ha…

Mirdja is horrified by her own frenzied laugh.

Terrible was the letter before her, great and terrifying. Oh, Nemesis, Nemesis![89]

The predictions of past generations pursue me, the souls of past generations are living in me, all the world's pagan dead have risen in my flesh. I am living your life, I rule with your wasted powers, I defend and champion your slan-

[89] In ancient Greek religion Nemesis was the goddess of retribution and just punishment, namely for hubris, i.e. arrogance vis-à-vis the gods.

dered tribe. Ah, imbue the air around me with good wishes, all ye in the unmarked graves of unknown travellers and lunatics!

Mirdja steams back and forth across the floor, speaking with spirits, visions and souls, and her eyes glow inward with a sightless fire.

This is me, Mirdja, a minute ago I was an orphan, now I am heir to a great line, and a ruler!

But in the early hours she begins to see normally again… The spirits have evaporated and Mirdja is sitting deep in thought…

Her thoughts are focused on one thing only, her stare directed at one single spot…

*

Her uncle is also sitting and staring. He has been waiting all night for Mirdja to come and ask him something, say something… But she hasn't come and her uncle has grown increasingly worried by the minute. Oh, what a lot he has had time to think over during this one night, he has taken stock of his whole life… Then again he remembers Mirdja and the letter. Maybe he shouldn't have given it to her after all. Madness can be contagious. He had to admit that his deceased brother's dream had transferred itself to him… How would it affect Mirdja…? There was so much truth in that letter…

And the old man started to think over the letter he had read countless times… There was so much truth in it… But about the two of them being so different, the two brothers… well, much of that statement could be argued away… especially lately, when everything was clear to him too. It's true that once upon a time he had thought himself wiser than his brother, because at least he didn't drag his dreams and ideas into the real world. But he had only deceived himself. Because when as a young man he had retired into solitude, it hadn't been his intention that no one would ever hear of him. Quite the contrary, in those days he dreamed of being world famous. He was going to write some sort of philosophical encyclopaedia. But he never completed the philosophy. His original maxims he had long since cast to the four winds, and he had admitted to himself that he had never invented any new or more durable theory than thousands before him, and what was even more depressing: he had overturned his own theories in the way he lived. Or he had been distracted by the mad dreams of his mad brother. The child who had, by an accidental twist, turned up on his doorstep, had changed his destiny and usurped the sovereignty of abstract illusions. Philosophy and the philosopher in him were dealt a death blow. But that was something Mirdja must never know… And now it was unimportant: the child had simply become his destiny… At first she was something of a disappointment, like a miscalculation… Then she grew into a wonderful necessity. Whenever his cloudland turned everything upside down, it all fell into place again on this new life-affirming soil. He could easily dedicate his many years of intellectual work and wisdom to this child. It was like throwing abstract concepts into the hellfire of living life… It was a test of faith for a seeker of truth…

And that is how he evolved from a proud theoretician into a humble and remarkable educator, who suddenly and unexpectedly shared his mad brother's dream of a new, mysteriously wonderful creature, a perfect human being. And the more this child prodigy seemed to understand and adopt her brilliant master's ideas, the more he became crazed with faith and pride. This person was to be the great proof of his life's work. And together they pondered all the various stages of humanity's development and thought, and Mirdja's uncle worked doubly hard to ensure there was always something new and beautiful to offer his ward. But he never imposed his ideas on her, never lectured his pupil, allowing for knowledge to mature within her, for her own sacred individuality to blossom into a flower so rare, grand and exquisite as possible.

This is how they lived, strangely together and apart, for many years. They nurtured each other's souls. And when Mirdja went to take her matriculation exams, she was much more sophisticated than any other student her age. But that is when the two colleagues parted ways. Mirdja remained in town, and her uncle understood that he must make way for life.

It was only then, when he was once again alone in his Lumiluoto retreat, like in the beginning, that he noticed how much he had changed. His intellectual work no longer brought him pleasure, quite the opposite. It was all for Mirdja, and Mirdja was gone. And Mirdja was his happiness, his life's purpose, his everything, he realized this now. His thoughts were constantly about Mirdja. What was she to do with her life, and life with her? Now she really did possess both their souls, her father's and her uncle's. Or rather, what difference was there between them! They were both made of the same stuff, they were dreamers, sleepwalkers, dilettantes the pair of them. So what if he hadn't taken his dilettantism onto the stage of the wide world, as his brother had. Mirdja had hindered his philosophy, and philosophy had hindered his violin. Ah, the violin, the violin! The great love of his youth! It has been left to slumber for a long while, and no one knows its story. No one knows that often, even now, when the night is lonely, when Mirdja is far away roaming the world, the recluse sits in his tower, crying with his violin on his knee… Crying because in his youth he hadn't done as his brother. Why hadn't he just tucked his violin under his arm and gone out into the world? Perhaps he would be something else today! But then he remembers his brother and laughs sceptically at his thoughts. He was just an old fool! But he missed Mirdja! And he sits in secret in his dark tower, and his violin sobs as if mourning a life gone to waste. No one needs him anymore, now that life itself had taken over Mirdja's education… Oh Mirdja, Mirdja, never must she know the sacrifices that have been made for her… Without Mirdja, long, dark, and sad are her lonely uncle's days in Lumiluoto.

But whenever Mirdja returns, there is light and laughter, and the flag flies on the Lumiluoto tower and the old violin sings of a new spring.

Mirdja's uncle sits alone in silence waiting for Mirdja and wondering: perhaps I shouldn't have given her the letter, it's like the writing in the stars. It may rob her of her senses. Mirdja is very wise, but she has both our souls, the soul of madmen…

He sits and waits… Mirdja doesn't come. On that night her father stands between them.

*

The next morning Mirdja knocks on her uncle's door very early.

'Uncle, how did you come by father's letter? It's strange. There is no postmark, no place nor date, nothing at all. It's as if it were sent from the lap of eternity. How did you receive it?'

'I received it together with you.'

'How is that possible?'

'There was a nursemaid who brought you, someone your father had entrusted with both you and the letter.'

'Where is she now?'

'She lives in the neighbouring parish.'

'Uncle, I will go and see her.'

IV

~

Mirdja is in unfamiliar territory, going from one rural shack to another, asking for Loviisa Kuutanainen. This is the village in which she was supposed to live.

'So, it's Loviisa you're after is it, madam, for the laundry I suppose? I'm afraid she's no longer up to the work, she's already so poorly. Not sure she'll ever get up again. She's been bed-ridden since the beginning of the year.'

From the cottage where she hears this news, Mirdja is pointed to a small run-down hovel at the base of a little hillock covered in pines, near the seashore.

So there, under that roof lies the secret of her birth!

Mirdja stepped into the impoverished house. She was met at the door by a gust of stale, grimy air. It was so unpleasant that Mirdja instinctively stopped in her tracks. But she overcame her distaste immediately, and closed the door behind her, although she would rather have left it open. The sick woman was on her death bed, they had said. The woman was to draw her last breath in the same awful, stifling atmosphere she had lived in. Such conditions, Mirdja could never have imagined anything like it…

She approached the bed. An almost insufferable, putrid smell emanated from the filthy sheets. — How was it possible for a human being to be left in such a state of neglect, alone, with no help! Was there not even one kind soul living nearby! A great sense of pity erased all Mirdja's other emotions. She bowed… The old lady was lying motionless with her eyes closed, whisps of her white hair lay untidily around her head, her bony hands were crossed on her chest…

Those hands had carried Mirdja, that horrible, ugly, wrinkled mouth had kissed her perhaps… Mirdja trembled… But one feeling dominated: now it was her turn to help, to look after someone… it was as if all this reflected the sins of her neglect…

'Loviisa, are you very sick?' Mirdja managed to choke out the words.

The woman opened her eyes and stared in glazed amazement at the young lady before her…

'It's me, Mirdja…'

'Jesus Christ,' muttered the sick woman, 'is it possible… Mirdja, Mirdja, God bless you, you were always an angel…'

'Is there anything you need?'

'Me, no, what could I possibly need,' gasped the patient. 'I'm not long for this world and everything's as good as it can be now… That Tiltu Mannu, bless her, even came and took the snivelling children away. May God have mercy on the poor orphan devils. At least the Lord in heaven doesn't give us an eternal cross to bear. Soon be saved from all my years of hell on earth. May heaven protect you from anything like it, Mirdja. You aren't married yet are you — or you must be by now. But it's different for you gentlefolk. There aren't such beasts among you. Alas, only those who are made to live like me with a drunken wastrel, cursed and hungry, beaten like a dog, know the price you pay in this world. God punishes us sinners in all kinds of ways. The prouder the child, the harder the whip. It's better that way. Punishment here, salvation there! It all comes to an end eventually, even the world will come to an end. A person lives barely a hundred years. I'll soon be gone from this vale of tears.'

Mirdja listened in horror to this unnaturally lengthy outpouring, which was soon due to be followed by eternal silence. — Yes, such was life! Always the same tune, its arrangement sometimes coarser, sometimes subtler! What was all the suffering Mirdja had seen or felt up till now, compared to this? Child's play, sheer amusement. No, no! protested her bitter and callous thoughts, we are more sensitive, we suffer more; this persecuted creature doesn't know how to suffer, she is content, she is at peace... She has the gift of resignation. Yes, that's true, a person lives barely a hundred years. Good God, a hundred years wasted on purposeless, humiliating torture! And that's nothing yet! — This woman's humble resignation to her inevitable, abject fate troubled Mirdja.

Was it religious faith that crushed the human soul so? No, not faith, but priests... No, not even priests... Even they didn't have such terrible power. The abject wretchedness of life came first, then the priests with their talk, their words drizzling over autumn's great decay. It makes everything worse of course but so what, the decay has already set in, set in deep... But those words of comfort: 'never mind, it's nothing, a person lives barely a hundred years', that's them, the priests! Her one and only life — nothing! No, not the one and only, for thereafter comes the real, blissful life... Mirdja laughed. And gave herself a start. Why was she staring like a madwoman and laughing by the bedside of this dying woman? But life's wretchedness was indeed too great for her to have cried. Mirdja felt herself grow numb before it. The smell of decay and devastation stifled her nostrils, and on the other hand the terrible, unknown darkness of death stared out at her...

A minute ago, Mirdja had felt that she should help this dying woman, but now the idea seemed childish. It seemed natural to her now that Loviisa should lie in her filthy, putrid hovel and die alone. What good could her help do, or anyone's help, in the face of this wasted life, which had never even had the chance to blossom into life, to aim any further than basic physical needs, to mature into a human being...?

Mirdja shivered as if from the cold. Was she still too great an idealist, was the light of idealism so bright that it cast such a sudden, black shadow over this life? Why was she so moved before this hideous old woman? Had she herself been sleeping on too downy a bed? But her heart pounded with just one thought: gone to waste, gone to waste, everything just gone to waste, this woman's life, her uncle's life, her father's life, and now — her own. There is a power greater than that of a human being. — But who was it who taught that it was a power for good! And was it called God! Oh what a terrible, violent force of nature was God, punishing human weaklings and yet seeking godliness within them...

Mirdja stood by the side of the bed with her head hung. She had been transformed in an instant... She had come here looking for the secret to her own soul... from this miserable creature... Was that not a sin?

'You looked after me when I was little... and you knew my father... do you remember him?'

'Oh you precious child, what are you asking! Do I remember — I remember everything like it was yesterday. He was a sweet man, your father, there'll never be another like him. How he doted on you! To think he had to die so young! I doubt I would have ended up in this state if your father had lived, he never raised a hand or cast a dirty look, not even to the worst of them. But it was my own fault for marrying that husband of mine. He was like the prince of darkness himself, ripped from the back end of hell. But who would have guessed at the start? Didn't dare show little Liisa to the gentleman of Lumiluoto, he was always so serious looking, and a mother's heart is what it is... Yes, he was thin-blooded your father, would never have guessed him to be brothers with the gentleman of Lumiluoto, and he had to go and die in foreign parts. But you Mirdja, have grown into such a comely, pretty thing...'

A coughing fit interrupted her speech. The old woman was sweating and panting and now suddenly her body stiffened unnaturally, and her tongue became stuck...

Mirdja felt frightened... Was this it now, the...? This was surely a sin. Loviisa surely had more personal things to think of as she approached the great unknown. Her final moments should be reserved for herself...

'Loviisa, I will send you a nurse,' said Mirdja.

'Oh, bless you Mirdja, what do I care for nurses anymore. Send me the pastor! I still have a few matters to settle with God...'

Mirdja felt as if she'd received a slap in the face. — Yes of course, the pastor! How little she understood what people really needed! How little she understood the longing for eternity in this person's heart! She, who had believed humanity to be on a par with God, its own intercessor, its own supplicant and priest!

Ah Mirdja, kneel you arrogant creature, you who recently boasted of your ancestors dying as pagans! You hadn't ever seen how people really die. Ah, kneel and learn what others have been taught: 'For dust you are! It is by grace you have been saved, not by your own doing'...[90]

---

[90] These sentences are paraphrases from the Bible, Genesis 3. 19, 'for dust thou art, and

'You will have what you need, Loviisa. Goodbye!'

Mirdja held out her hand.

The old woman squeezed it tight with her bony, yellow fingers.

'You're an angel Mirdja, like your father... May God bless you with a long and happy life.'

Mirdja stepped outside. The bright sun of early summer was blinding, and the fresh air almost made her faint.

It seems one can even get used to such stale air...

So she had come here looking for herself... Always looking for herself, herself... She was leaving empty-handed because she had come empty-handed, in order to take... She should have come in order to give...

Mirdja walked slowly. Her thoughts were persistent, reproving...

She repeated to herself the sick woman's last words: 'bless you with a long life'... A person lives barely a hundred years...

Oh God, oh God, she sighed.

unto dust shalt thou return', and Ephesians 2. 8, 'For by grace are ye saved through faith; and that not of yourselves'.

V

~

The local folk festival was just beginning when Mirdja reached the field at Kannisto.[91]

This is what she had walked five kilometres for. Why exactly? She couldn't even explain it to herself. But ever since she had been sitting in the home of dying Loviisa, ever since then a certain strangeness had inhabited her heart. Some bizarre sensation which would not give her peace, which made her restless, unsure, and dissatisfied with herself. Mirdja stood at the threshold of a new, unfamiliar form of humanity, one which was great and terrifying, of which she had had no inkling before, she who had always boasted of her knowledge of humanity.

What exactly was that entity known as the 'folk'?[92]

From her bird's eye view, she had always assessed it superficially and in passing, like people who only look skin-deep and assume the worst, and so she had always largely ignored it. But now she felt it coming to meet her there and then, tall and deep as a tidal wave, unavoidable, exacting, and as beady-eyed as the unresolved question of life…

Mirdja slowed her footsteps. Before her and behind her surged the folk, giggling young girls in colourful party dresses, garrulous young men with foul-smelling papirosas between their teeth.[93] Mirdja found it all rather repulsive, and she turned off the country road onto a small, quiet, woodland pathway. — But hardly had she done this when that strangeness started to worry and disturb her again. That was something you shouldn't have done; how can you ever expect to dig deep if you recoil at the very topsoil, Mirdja, Mirdja, Mirdja…? — And the impact of her reflections drew Mirdja up short…

But she began to hear hymnsong coming from the field. It rose loud and earnest, with the conviction of a thousand souls coming together and speaking with the same tongue for the same cause… And at that moment, there was nothing else in the whole wide world! Just the great word and the infinite silence around it…

[91] As a place name, Kannisto could point to different areas or villages, some of them close to Helsinki, others further (the Kannisto village in the region of Halikko or in Häme), but still in the southern or south-western part of Finland.
[92] The Finnish word *kansa* used in the source text denotes 'folk', 'people', and 'nation' (see Introduction, p. 23). Throughout the nineteenth century, Finnish national identity was constructed on the identity of Finnish-speaking country folk.
[93] See note 14, p. 68.

God's glory, God's glory! sighed Mirdja.

And suddenly in the grip of powerful emotion, she fell to her knees as if in prayer and warm tears ran down her cheeks... It was devotion and it was suffering... It was a harrowing, aching yearning to be part of this great folk, this God, this divine worship... It was a yen for friendship and understanding, a desperate, infinite yen for something to fill her life and her heart.

What if this folk, this folk struggling in pursuit of its great primordial needs, had something to offer Mirdja...? What if therein lay that everlasting life force she had been craving...? and that wholeness? She would go toward the crowd... and suddenly become great and good and selfless... she would sacrifice everything, give up her soul... And the folk too would grow warmer and greater at her touch, it would rise higher, shine brighter, and its thousands of eyes would glow towards her in blessing, like the perpetual glow of the sun... This would be the most impersonal of all personal relationships, free of all forms of the self-enslavement attached to sacrificial dreams. It would be like a mysterious, infinitely close connection with the infinitely distant soul of the universe or God or...

Mirdja rose quickly. She almost ran towards the festival gates, and she bought a ticket with as much haste as if her life depended on it... But as soon as she stepped within the fenced area, she was back to her normal self. She found it all repulsive again...

The thick, grimy air penetrated her eyes, her nostrils and her throat, that common characteristic smell of the folk which revealed in the blink of an eye the panorama of their existence, their rough, sparse conditions of life: the sweat of labour, dirty clothes, tobacco, children...

People gathered curiously around the fine young lady walking alone, some of them timidly, others elbowing purposely closer and jostling.

'Now, now, don't be so bold, can't you see the good lady,' one woman whispered to her husband just next to Mirdja.

'Down gentlemen!' barked one fellow with a brazen laugh.

Mirdja had turned her back on the speakers and was about to go on her way, when a small drama made her stop.

The sergeant-at-arms had noticed a couple of fellows hiding flat under a bush in order to make use of their ample hip-flask. — 'You've no permission to drink here.' — 'We don't need no one's permission.' — 'Don't squabble or you'll end up behind bars, there's no drinking allowed in public places.' — 'Who has the right to stop me from eating and drinking what I like and where I like, or d'you think I haven't earned as much with my own labour, eh? Look at these hands, not the palms of a thief are they, but I suppose an honest working man's hand is not good enough to shake...' — 'No, the constable means we should have our own club for wining and dining like the gentry. But this is a new age and the whole world's a working men's club from now on, and this festival's a working men's festival, and you, you copper, you're our public servant, because it's us as pays your wages, us too. Whose blood and sweat d'you think has gone into polishing those buttons of yours, if not ours, and all the grandeur of the gentry, whose labour has paid for that, if not ours, and that missy there too, in her finery…'

The voices disappeared under the general hub. The drunks were carted off. But Mirdja felt as if the focus of the whole scene had suddenly shifted onto her, and as if a hundred envious and accusing gazes had turned to fall upon her, and then yet a hundred more, again and again. They fell like burning cinders on her all too delicate skin, her all too lily-white and tiny hands, they brazenly and malevolently fingered the luxuriant colour of her dress, they ripped the expensive feather from her hat, there was not one spot that they left untouched… And they all screamed: 'Pale and pretty lady of Lumiluoto, how have you earned your cushioned lifestyle, your riches and luxuries? You don't have the hands of a working man, but the palms of a thief you have. It's we who deserve your fortune, your beauty, your delicate figure, your fine skin…'

Mirdja glanced around in panic, oppressed by her thoughts. The voracious, cannibalistic gazes swallowed her up on every side. They craved her material well-being, they wanted it all, there was not one of them who would have needed her soul… And fool that she was, it was her soul she had intended to give away…

Mirdja turned rapidly around, pressed her purse into the hand of the nearest bystander and hurried away without looking back.

Away, away from here! Her soul cried out. You who need so little for your happiness have no need of me. And what could I have to offer those of you who still possess the wonderful gifts of faith and imagination! You are at least the only people who have the strength to live. My soul would be poison to you, you whose souls are healthy! I could never, never offer you anything or take anything from you, and your instinct is correct when it ignites blind hate in your heart for the likes of me. Because we are, inescapably, born enemies. My approach just now was a lie, my faith in you was a lie, and equally a lie was my altruistic attempt to offer help, just as was my egotistical attempt to seek help from you, all lies, lies! I am not here for you and neither are you here for me. We are each sick in our own way. We cannot help nor understand one another.

A patriotic song could now be heard, coming from the distant field. Mirdja stopped and listened. Then she laughed loud and bitterly to contain her anguish. It had been madness, her desire to connect deep in her heart with that song, that folk, that ideology. Madness it had been, and unnatural. Because she was a stranger, she, the pale and pretty lady of Lumiluoto. They were not her folk, not her people, taunting her sick mind, this was not her homeland, this ground under her feet, not her God under the flag of this festival. The pale and pretty lady of Lumiluoto was a stranger here, sick and homeless. Where was she born? Where were her roots? Where were her blood relations, her kindred spirits? These people here were neither.

And Mirdja set off on her way again. Her heart was heavy and bitter, and her proud lonely soul swelled with the emptiness of exile.

VI

The summer was drawing to a close, that perplexing summer in which life had disturbed the bedrock of Mirdja's soul in many new respects.

The first devastating quake had been her father's letter, the second her visit to Loviisa. After that, the impressions left by both experiences had been wrestling within her, until the doomed attempt to unite with the folk at the festival cured her of any further helpless, sacrificial plans. But this only served to fuel her eagerness for self-examination. Because, amazingly, the more she studied the letter, the more inexplicable and important she became to herself. And the more she studied herself, the more complicated the questions before her became.

Sometimes she would sit motionless for hours, staring into her soul, puzzling over the riddle of herself, exerting herself to the extreme over every smallest trace of an idea that could produce a result and give her some peace, but without success... Equally often, however, the opposite would happen, she wouldn't want to think at all, and in moments like this she would avoid the slightest shadow of an idea, as if in fear of her own reason. At times like this, she would become unnaturally vivacious, almost agitated, seeking out company, laughing and singing and joking with everyone, trying to bury her private concerns in her rambunctious behaviour. But this didn't help either. She was somehow bewitched into always returning to the same questions about herself.

Or, to be precise, it wasn't Mirdja asking the questions, but rather certain secret voices in her soul, independent of her will.

They would hold the following kind of speeches:

'Mirdja, Mirdja, every minute you linger here is blasphemy to the gods. You were made to live your life swiftly and leave immortal fame in your wake. You must hurry, hurry; your life is crumbling! You are destined to realize the great dream of your lineage, to cross the bridge that cracked beneath the feet of your forefathers. You were born to dazzle the world. You must put everything else aside so your life can begin, your artistic calling is awaiting, the shadows of the dead are watching over you...'

'Ah, you mad girl, do not cling like a lunatic to the beliefs of the dead! It's a trap. If you were born to be something, made to be something, then you are not free to be your own creator. It means your path has been preordained from the crib, thanks to a certain combination of germinations, forces, and influences.[94] How can you be sure that the dilettantism and madness that

---

[94] The theme of fate and fatality evokes the interest in predestination shared by the

crippled your ancestors is not also written into your future? And if you cannot be sure of reaching heights of greatness, then avoid the slippery slope!'

'Only your incessant doubts are obstacles in the path of your greatness. Why is it that your thoughts are forever plagued by doubt?'

'It is the work of reason against madness.'

'You are a divine and wonderful creation, you deserve your throne. You've seen how others grovel at your feet…'

'Don't you remember how tired you are of all that praise you've had to listen to throughout your life? You've even taken to yawning at it all.'

'You are sick to the teeth of your own plenitude. You have to find something greater than yourself, whose strength and brilliance can eclipse your own ego.'

'Go out into the world!'

'Go seek out your calling, Mirdja!'

*

One day towards the end of summer, Mirdja finally made up her mind.

'Uncle,' said Mirdja, 'allow me to go abroad, I want to learn to work. This life is not for me. This is not a country where freedom, intellect, and art can prosper. I'm a prisoner here. Let me travel!'

'Go ahead,' said her uncle.

That was all that was said about it.

But that same week, Mirdja was ready to leave. She had purposely hurried her departure, so that nothing could come in the way of her decision. And indeed, no further inner conflicts presented themselves.

Only when her uncle handed over her travel allowance did that strangeness slip into her heart again. Was it not wrong to use all this just for her own sake?

No! No one person can help another.

And Mirdja smothered the strangeness in valiant defiance.

And it was in autumn, on a day that was warm and chilly, airy and close, a day of vivid ripening and lacklustre wilting, that Mirdja went out into the world.

Decadents and the Naturalists. In the Nordic countries, including Finland, French Decadence and Naturalism were received and debated more or less simultaneously (see Introduction). Onerva was very familiar with the works of French Naturalism, namely those of Émile Zola, whose theories she used in her newspaper reviews when analysing contemporary paintings. In *Mirdja*, she engages especially with Zola's ideas about hereditary degeneration and determinism.

SOLILOQUIES ABROAD

~

Now I have it all, everything to which I have aspired: solitude and freedom, and life in all its intensity and incandescence around me.[95]

But it all amounts to nothing. Because the world is only a reflection of oneself. What we imagine to be life's vibrant embrace is just the beating of our own restless heart. And so long as I remain who I am, the world remains in my likeness. — That is the long and the short of it.

There it lies before me, beckoning to me as I speak: the great, the magnificent, the mysterious… And I reach my hand out towards it: yes, I'm coming! But because I am who I am, I don't move, I remain rooted to the spot as if to say: why are your joys so old and worn, your agonies so mundane, have you nothing to offer me, you pointless, lacklustre life?

The problem is that life wears a mask in my image. Well so be it, may it don the mask of the Devil for all I care; I am bored with *les sensations*, all I long for now is work.

Alone at last, just as I desired. In solitude, it turns out, lies the only true perfection, the only true freedom. One is safe in the knowledge that society's beasts of prey cannot come breathing down one's neck unexpectedly, not even in the guise of one's best friend. If only I could bark 'go to hell!' at them all whenever circumstance required! But to what end…? Or perhaps it would have been for the best. For when I look back, I cannot help but cry out: such infinite substance in the world yet only emptiness surrounds me, such infinite love yet here I walk through life trembling and alone! And moreover, I am supposed to feel remorse? — oh you men, you porcelain playthings, is it really my fault that you are so very fragile! A single bodily movement can cause you anguish, a single vocal inflection can drive you to distraction… Why should I always be the one to tread carefully, why don't you watch your own step! And yet you are the only ones I can live with.

The last words I heard as I walked away were: is it a pleasure to have them all fainting and fawning at your feet?

Slanderer, slanderer!

So now I want to be alone.

*

[95] This is the only section of the novel written in the first person; all the rest is written as a third-person narrative.

The bright lights of colossal cities burn like the coloured lanterns of several thousand secret infernos, and several thousand more human souls flit towards them like flies, some scorching their wings, some fully combusting.[96]

I see this happening over and over again, and I have come to reflect that it is perhaps humanity's lot merely to fly towards the flames and be consumed by them.

Any flame-resistant human being surely exceeds purpose!

See how sweet life is for those who nurse their suppurating burns, who tread with anguish in their hearts and cry themselves to sleep. And see how beautiful death was for those who, on the impulse of a single sentiment, had the courage to discard themselves and leap into the flames. Humanity at its best!

And not so long ago I hated them. I reached out towards the cold and rational, such people they say the world is full of, though I had never met any. And I prayed:

Your stalwart indifference, your staunch inviolability, these are the things I desire. How exquisite to be as cold as ice, no — even ice melts, to be as hard and beautiful as a diamond glinting in the hollow of a rock, how exquisite to be able to endure oneself. I pray to destiny to make me hard, as hard as destiny itself. And if needs must that I should spill a few drops of my heart's blood on the white snow, may these drops turn to stone, piercing the eye of anyone who passes, cutting the air with their ruby rays, because heaven forbid anyone should ever see the steaming flood of my anguish!

This was my prayer and it was a terrible prayer.

For there is nothing in the world more gratifying than bursting into a deluge of great anguish. This I learned in the moment my prayer was heard and all feeling within me was extinguished. Or at most I may still be capable of feeling envy — envy of those who are capable of great feeling!

I am as but a memory to myself, and I cannot understand the change that has taken place inside of me.

All my inner passions and external cravings, the eroticism, the delightfully capricious flightiness which once constituted the very core of my being, now seem like false shadows and fantasies whose day has long since passed. Quiet indifference has slowly penetrated my whole being like a deadly poison. And

---

[96] Onerva spent several periods abroad, mostly in Paris, Rome, and Berlin. The description of 'colossal cities' in *Mirdja* is similar to the way she describes Paris in her unpublished manuscript 'Myöhästyneitä Pariisin kirjeitä marraskuun alulta. Katkelmia' ('Belated Paris letters from the beginning of November: Fragments, 1905–07', Suomalaisen Kirjallisuuden Seuran arkisto, kirjallisuuden ja kulttuurihistorian kokoelma, Archive of the Finnish Literature Society, Literary and Cultural History Collection). A description of her real-life experience is to be found in her letters. In the novel, the mixture of Schopenhauerian pessimism, Decadent rhetoric, and Nietzschean ecstasy overshadows the material reality of the city and the whole journey: everything essential happens in the mind of the subject, in the fashion of Des Esseintes's journey to London in J.-K. Huysmans's *À rebours* (1884).

I am often overcome by moments of dread, stricken by a dullness which leaves me fumbling dimly in the void. My train of thought escapes me, my words remain half spoken, and my numbed brain drifts into unconsciousness. It is terrible and makes me fear the worst. Why is this happening to me? Is it over-exertion? How little we humans can endure.

Sometimes I reason that in fact I no longer exist. I am like an atom in nature, a power point which has lost its power. But what good are such pseudo-philosophical theories!

What was the point of being so good at burning the candle at both ends if I was incapable of discarding the wick!

I am weary, weary of my own weariness even.

Why dear God, did I try to live beyond my capacity?

'You are your own worst enemy.' This is true. I remember this from the days I spent reading Nietzsche with Rolf. Back then, I was especially fond of the quote: 'Verbrennen musst du dich wollen mit deinen eignen Flammen. Wie wolltest du neu werden, wenn du nicht erst Asche geworden bist.'[97]

I didn't understand it then as well as I do now. Now both of us have been reduced to ashes by the blue flame of our own souls.[98] But it is unlikely that anything will rise from these ashes...

Ugh, why am I still thinking other people's thoughts? Is it because I'm a woman, or because I'm a mediocrity? It seems to me even my emotions have always been other people's emotions, an emotional dabbler, that's me. Is it only geniuses who can think and feel for themselves...? Not that I've ever encountered a genius.[99]

*

I am going to be an artist after all, a first-class artist. It is only now that I am finally mature enough to work as an artist. It was foolish of me to lament my lack of emotional life. On the contrary, I possess precisely those rare and

[97] The quotation is from the chapter 'Vom Wege des Schaffenden' ('The way of the creator') in Nietzsche's *Also Sprach Zarathustra*: 'Ready must thou be to burn thyself in thine own flame; how couldst thou become new if thou have not first become ashes!' (trans. by Thomas Common in Friedrich Nietzsche, *Thus Spake Zarathustra: A Book for All and None* (T. N. Foulis, 1909).

[98] The symbolism of blue flames (here juxtaposed with the phoenix imagery, connoting the colour red), known from folklore and mythology, is typical of Finnish Symbolism. It is a recurrent image in the poetry of Eino Leino. In Onerva's work, the image of blue fire or flames appears mostly in prose (e. g. the novel *Yksinäisiä*, 'The lonely ones', from 1917). Read within a biographical frame of reference, this passage in *Mirdja* points to Onerva's and Leino's dramatic and tragic relationship, as well as to the two writers' struggle with mental health.

[99] As elsewhere in Europe and Russia, the debate around the concept of genius and the gendered nature of creative forces was a hot topic in Finland. Onerva treated the topic both with a huge portion of irony and with serious dedication, engaging in a direct or indirect dialogue with other women writers who also dealt with this issue.

chosen qualities that are necessary to make a great artist. I boast both conceit and ambition. I know it won't be long before I will be holding in the palm of my hand the many souls that fill the glorious opera houses of the great cities of the world, and this thought fills me with an eagerness to work that is akin to passion. Work is my perfect happiness. Or who knows? Who knows what happiness really is?

> 'Höchstes Glück der Erdenkinder
> Ist nur die Persönlichkeit.'[100]

Do I qualify as a *Persönlichkeit*? In any event, one should not be so hell-bent on seeking one's personality as I have been. Better to capture 'happiness' such as it is, but it is something I have never cared for. I am still on a quest to discover myself, even though self-discovery is precisely what has shattered my existence. Am I to blame if I have never been able to look into my soul with humility and faith, as a silent supplicant before the image of God? I have only ever taken the scientific approach, spreading the contents of my inner being onto the surgical table and mercilessly dissecting every aspect, every cell, crushing every sentiment and mood, every expression of will and act of intent, every belief and desire. And I have gone even further than that, with almost suicidal precision. Every self-analytical thought has been like a cross-cut bullet which explodes in my soul and rips everything to smithereens.

This is the kind of person I am. And when I think about it, it seems to me that everything I believed to be life's burning passion, was in fact nothing more than a longing for death, a silent, unconscious yearning for the grave.

What am I really?

*

I have often heard others castigating me for having unhealthy foibles. But it is only now that I find I actually have one… Or what else should I call my sudden passion for a particular image…

Because now I have found myself a chapel containing a holy image that I adore.

My God, what a beautiful creature is woman! I almost wish I could be a man for a while, that I might take better pleasure in woman, and for that matter, in myself. After all, the role of the pleasure taker is better than the role of the pleasure giver.

But my Madonna, whom I adore, is not a real Madonna nor even a real woman.

---

[100] 'The utmost happiness of human creatures | is nothing but personality'; from J. W. Goethe's *West-östlicher Divan* ('Book of Zuleika', West-Eastern Divan, 1819). In the original, these lines are indirect speech which is rendered in German with the verb in the subjunctive I 'sei'. As is common practice when these two lines are quoted independently as a statement, Onerva has replaced 'sei' here with the indicative 'ist'.

I found her quite by chance in the darkest corner of a major gallery. Quite by chance, I lifted my eyes in her direction. Everyone has their own Medusa,[101] and she was mine. I turned to stone then and there. And ever since, I have done nothing but watch and worship her, this cold, motionless false idol.

Because she is as cold and motionless as stone, although she has the comportment of a passer-by, and she lives in a large gold frame.

Her long, fine, opaque fingers glow like opal... And who knows what her gaze once was? Sunstroke or teardrop? Now at least, it is just a tiny mysterious precious bead... For everything about her must be precious; every single dot on her surface is an impenetrable jewel...

If I were in her place, this noble phantom whose hysterical beauty haunts us from her gold-rimmed stage even after death,[102] I could never make a more dignified appearance than she.

Ah, you pale daffodil, inviolably frozen on your silken stalk!

You really are a saint!

Or have others never, like me, admired Crivelli's magnificent medieval saintly woman...?[103]

But contemplating her is not enough. I have become obsessed with the idea of possessing her. And I have begun stealing her, forging her, taking her home with me piece by piece day after day. Every morning I go and stare at her and every evening I try to recreate her gemstone perfection on my canvas. I am no painter and my work is feverish. But I have managed to capture a little part of her...

---

[101] For the mythical figure of Medusa, see note 20, p. 72.

[102] Hysteria, widely discussed in *fin-de-siècle* medicine and literature, is alluded to often in Onerva's works, where it assumes a range of different guises, from Max Nordau's 'degenerative hysteria' to an explicitly gendered 'female hysteria'. This latter diagnosis was developed mostly by Jean-Martin Charcot (1825–1893), whose work inspired Sigmund Freud. Onerva's Madonna-Medusa transgresses the boundary between mysticism on one hand, and hysteria and perversion on the other. This framework recalls the way that Decadent writers (especially Huysmans) fused elements of religious and psychological discourse in order to define their own Decadent aesthetics; see Ellis Hanson, *Decadence and Catholicism* (Harward University Press, 1997), p. 109. The notion of 'hysterical beauty' also evokes the idea of 'Medusean beauty' or 'tainted beauty' (see note 20, p. 72).

[103] Carlo Crivelli (*c.* 1435–*c.* 1495) was a Venetian Renaissance painter. Crivelli might have appealed to Onerva as an artist of a transitional period. She connected him with rococo art, in which she specialized in her university studies, and hence to Decadence and her 'own' period. She characterized Crivelli as a 'euphuistic mannerist', a 'perverse epicurean, a cold aesthetical hedonist', drawing — most probably — on Richard Muther's 1893 *Geschichte der Malerei* ('History of painting'). See Kortelainen, *Naisen tie*, pp. 356–57. The novel does not specify which of Crivelli's paintings Mirdja is referring to. Art historian Anna Kortelainen speculates that the painting is a fiction, inspired by various of Crivelli's Madonna figures, and possibly by his Mary Magdalene. However, the description of the woman in the painting contains features that are strikingly similar to Crivelli's *Sainte Lucie*, hanging in the Louvre.

And perhaps I could have captured more but now it's all hopelessly lost.

The one time in my life that I have admired a woman and even now a man has come between us.

Yes, a man has robbed me of my Madonna and I don't even know who he is.

All I know is that he wraps himself in a worn black cape, and there is no moustache adorning his delicate lips, only spiteful words.

I had been sitting in peace gazing at my Madonna for five days in a row. Then he arrived.

That was the first time I noticed him.

The next day he came again and stayed in the gallery until I left. I could feel him standing behind me all that time, but I was loath to turn around.

On the third day, the same thing happened. By then I could not resist stealing a glance at him. And at that very moment he spoke: 'You must be an extremely conceited person, to spend so much time sitting and admiring your own portrait...' I was taken aback, but my facial expression gave nothing away. I was a foreigner after all, so there was no reason for him to assume I understood him. But on that day, I thought of him more than I thought of my Madonna and I couldn't paint a single stroke.

On the fourth day I didn't go to the gallery at the usual time, only much later. He was already there, sitting in front of my masterpiece, this time with his paint box open and brush in hand.

'Oh you thief, stealing the source of my obsession!' I addressed him in my heart, and I was so disquieted that my whole body shook. I decided to walk past him, but when he saw me he rose quickly from his chair, came toward me and said: 'My dear young lady, whoever you are, please allow me to paint you!'

And when I failed to respond he continued, as if to himself but without taking his eyes off me: 'It is truly unusual to meet a woman suffering from malaria.[104] God was even more decadent than Crivelli in creating you...'

I looked at him as though I hadn't understood a word and left.

'You can understand me very well, stop pretending!' he shouted as he pursued me.

And just then I was suddenly overcome by panic. I blushed crimson like a schoolgirl and tears filled my eyes. I flung my hand out in a gesture of repudiation and bolted like a madwoman.

I still don't really understand it all, but this much I know: at that moment I was terrified of that man. Because never before, in my whole life, had I ever felt such desire to remain by a man's side as at the very moment I fled from him as if fleeing for my life.

---

[104] Onerva translated into Finnish Paul Verlaine's short piece 'Mal'aria' (from *Les Mémoires d'un veuf*, 1886), in which the narrator celebrates the beauty of sickness, and sick and convalescent women, disparaging healthy looks as ugly and vulgar. The translation was published in the weekly *Päivä* in 1909.

This was the first time I had ever fled from a man...
Since then something in me has changed....
And I don't want to see my Madonna anymore...
She is a Medusa...

*

I don't know whether to cry or laugh.

How terribly justified I felt when I named you my Medusa, you ruthless, stony-hearted saint! What diabolical twist of fate was it that threw me under your gaze! Ha ha ha! Is there ever any escape from one's destiny! Like a terrible, fatal flaw passed on by my ravaged forebears, there you stood before me, insistent and inscrutable. And all the while, as your visionary eyes gazed at me, the Fates on high prepared a banquet over my head,[105] they jangled their chains and tendered their traps, spreading opiate madness with every swish of their skirt-hems; and in the underworld, jubilant little demons cast their dice over the last member of a derelict family line... When I finally managed to tear myself away from under your beady eyes, I was already crippled, mad, and blind, sedated by treacherous potions, and I humbly set off in pursuit of my misfortune.

And I have no one else to blame but myself. Or in truth I had little to do with it... It was simply fate...

Because I can think of no other explanation for what happened to me... Something drove me on... It was simply fate...

When, after those two weeks of insanity, I finally returned to my singing lessons, I was perfectly prepared to be reprimanded because I had been absent without leaving word. It was madness, I knew that.

But the old man thought I had been ill, and although he was offended by my lack of courtesy, this was nonetheless a relatively fortuitous outcome. Then I was overcome by a devilish urge to tell the truth, and I threw the whole business in his face: I simply hadn't bothered to attend my lessons because I was devoid of inspiration and my attention was drawn to other things.

This I really should not have said, because my benevolent teacher was immediately outraged.[106] And he gave me a piece of his mind. A student has no right to speak of inspiration or indisposition. A student should have no interests other than studying, no freedom beyond the teacher's instructions.

---

[105] The Fates, or Moirai, deities from ancient Greek mythology and religion, were the incarnations of fate, dictating and directing human destinies.

[106] The figure of the old, slightly edgy, but good and committed music teacher evokes the character of Maestro Porpora from George Sand's *Consuelo* (1842–43), which is, together with Sand's *Lélia* (1833), a notable intertextual presence in *Mirdja*. Onerva repeatedly mentioned Sand in her 1905 master's thesis 'Musset'n naisluonteet' ('Musset's female characters').

And because my temperament displayed such destructive impulses, he was henceforth obliged to be extremely strict with me and I was blindly to obey his every command if I had any intention of making progress. He concluded:

'I wouldn't be so stern with you if you were not my best pupil and if your future were not so precious to me. If you display such tendencies, how will anyone ever dare to trust you with an important engagement? Suddenly mademoiselle might be gripped by a lack of inspiration and choose not to attend! No, my young lady, I am forced to say this once and for all, if this ever happens again, I will not be able to keep you on as my pupil, because I cannot bear to see such potential go to waste before my very eyes.'

I stood there and listened and was aware that he was making sense. But the stricter and more rational he became, the more it stirred the devil in me... And in the end I was only half listening, and in my darkly growing defiance I thought dark and arrogant thoughts.

Am I to suffocate my whole being at your say-so, and by this suffocation supposedly bring forth some great artist that possibly lurks within me? Never, never in the world will I submit to pressure from someone else. And if it is true that within me there lurks a great artist then who are you to be placing me behind bars! Surely our freedom is limitless and you baton-waving old wigs merely our stepping-stones to success!

And so playing the minion to my evil spirits, I rebuked his wise rhetoric:

'Forgive me but I cannot accept these conditions, I cannot commit myself in advance to such rigid regimentation. It may indeed be that I shall find myself once again afflicted by a lack of inspiration... I hope you manage to replace me with an equally talented but more tractable student.'

And with that, I set off on the path I still find myself wandering today. Once again without work, without purpose, without a future. But I can no longer turn back. I almost did once, but then I remembered my father, who also never learned to apply himself or to control his moods and therefore failed to become a great artist... What use is a stern teacher to me! Is there any discipline in the world which could tame the dilettantism which runs in this family...?

It was simply fate....

I am once again plagued by increasingly morose thoughts. Disappointment, despair...

And there is one thing I cannot deny: I dearly miss that great singer whom, for the sake of a single caprice, I cast aside.

*

I wander alone down dark, tawdry streets.

Searching for God, and a church in which to kneel.

It is strange to think that everything within me seems to startle me, and that I cannot get a grip on godliness, on wholeness, on life's purpose or even on myself.

I walk around muttering to myself: your time is ill-used, your talent thrown to the wind!

What is the use of being born an artist without a point of focus, that is to say, without an art? Does there exist anything more pitiful? I am just an idle fool, feasting on the shrapnel of my own spiritual capital, which I have dispersed and squandered into nothingness. An unproductive onlooker, whose creativity has been extinguished by inertia and lack of courage. A Lazarus, a directionless drifter, a mixed bag of pathetic scraps — was there ever any chance of me being something whole? Hardly. I am my father's daughter.

So it is, father! Our kind will never be appreciated by the average boor. And yet we are condemned to live by his grubby rules and his blinkered judgement.

Your life must have been an awful torture, father, carrying as you did a divine spark within you and yet forced to listen to a voice that berated you for it: what did you do with your life? 'Wasted, wasted!' you replied.

Oh how that feeling weighs heavy! Because I can hear that same voice, although I try to block it out, to drown it or escape it, to conceal it like a coward. But even under a plate of armour, its essence lives, it breathes, it howls in pain and refuses to die. I have the conscience of a murderer. And over and over I feel like picking it up, stroking it and comforting it, even though every caress is like the thrust of a dagger and its slightest resistance like the pain of judgement on my soul.

There is a church before me. I can hear its quiet, sombre, deep organ music:

Crucifixus etiam pro nobis...[107]

They say that Catholicism is a suitable faith for the fallen.[108] I cannot say, but I think it is wonderful that there is one church whose door is never shut to the weary wanderer.

---

[107] 'Crucifixus etiam pro nobis sub Pontio Pilato passus et sepultus est' is Latin for 'He was crucified also for us, under Pontius Pilate, (he) suffered and was buried'. It is an allusion to the work of the Italian composer Antonio Lotti (1665–1740), and one of his most famous works, the *Crucifixus*. It was written in 1718 and is even today regarded as one of the greatest Italian compositions of liturgical music.

[108] In Finland, the dominant religion was the Protestant/Lutheran confession, called also one of the key elements of Nordic identity. Within nationalist discourse, Lutheran virtue was contrasted with Orthodoxy (typical of the Eastern parts of the country and often associated with the Russian element) and Catholicism. In the nineteenth and early twentieth centuries, the Lutheran cult of simplicity and proximity to nature, opposing any idea of refinement and luxury, saw Catholicism (so important to the Decadents) as standing in direct opposition to the essence of the Finnish nation. Onerva's interest in the figure of the Virgin Mary grew stronger in her later works, culminating in her 1918 collection of short prose pieces *Neitsyt Maarian lahja ynnä muita legendoja* ('The Virgin Mary's gift and other legends').

Here I stand in the doorway and stare at the flickering candles and the glittering gold dedicated to God…

I too would like to kneel at the cross and exchange my tears of emptiness for the infinite mysterious meaningfulness of religion… But I cannot.

I stand apart, and I have only one thing I would like to ask the church's silent saints…

Mother of God, have you ever come across my mother among the servants who kneel before you…?

*

So here I am, travelling aimlessly in an aimless world. I've crossed all the great cities, followed the reluctant ebb of all the great currents. What they were and what name they went by is all the same to me. They all live out the same life, reach the same autumn…[109] Yes, it's autumn again. It's strange how of all the seasons I am only ever aware of the autumn. It was autumn when I left Lumiluoto, and it is autumn I have probably been carrying with me ever since…

> Life's pulse runs deepest in the autumn season,
> with berries in clusters of scarlet and crimson,
> dome lights decking the night sky wilderness,
> and revellers hoarse with chills and feverishness.
> Leaves on the four winds lightly frolic and skip.
> The moribund sparrow a last dance does muster.
> Infected is the soul and pallid is the lip
> which chooses to feast on the crimson cluster…

Such are the verses I recite under my breath to the passing landscapes. The lonely dull thud of the train in motion turns my thoughts into rhymes, and quiet songs fill my soul…

But I will not put anything down on paper, I must avoid the temptation to publish….

Because I have read quite enough bad poets to know that they are a sufferance and a scourge on our souls, and I have read quite enough good poets to know that every thought or sentiment that flourishes within me has been expressed before, and has already been sung more beautifully than I ever could, so inevitably I would belong to the former group of poets… And that is pointless; there are enough poor imitations in the world.

And besides, I was not born a poet, but a dramatist. All the relationships I've ever had, have constituted a drama. But it is not my place to turn them into art…

---

[109] In a typically Decadent manner, Onerva frequently explored the topos of autumn both in her prose and in her poetry, beginning with her first collection of poems, *Sekasointuja* ('Disharmonies', 1904). In her letters, she would mention autumn as her 'favourite season'.

People build castles in the air from such inconsequential things, my spirit for instance... I was hailed for having such promise, yet I provoked such disappointment! And I myself contributed to both. But it doesn't stop me from being mean and contemptuous every time I am confronted with some newly repeated eulogy, which has already proved stale and hollow a hundred thousand times.

A few days ago, I ran into a young man I knew. He isn't the sort of fellow a woman can be fond of, but he plays the violin... And quite by chance we found ourselves in the same mood, we rented a studio and started a conversation in music. We were full of enthusiasm, we played together for a whole day. That is to say he played and I sang; he improvised the tune, I improvised the lyrics. It was beautiful. We were possessed. But then, he started talking about me and broke the spell.

He started saying I should publish my improvisations, and all my poems in general. I would be an overnight sensation. He was quite certain of it, because my work was reminiscent of this or that celebrated artist, and he rolled off a dozen names.[110]

I found his remarks so inane and preposterous that all the magic of the music wore off instantly and I was propelled into the harsh light of banal pretentiousness. So I laughed in reply:

'Oh so I remind you of all those great artists? That is the unequivocal mark of a minor artist. Anyone who has something new to offer this world resembles no one else. Don't you know that, you who are to be an artist yourself... You seem to be doing yourself a remarkable disservice. And what is more, in the last half hour you have encouraged one and the same person to take up singing, acting, and writing, as well as guaranteeing her diplomas in every discipline! That is very irresponsible behaviour and idiotic to boot. A person can only be great at one thing at a time, or perhaps you imagine a woman's highest ambition is to be a tenth-rate artist... No, my good sir, say nothing more to me. You do yourself better credit by sticking to your music...'

But the young man wouldn't play anymore. For him too, it was a brutal awakening...

'Don't misunderstand me,' I added, 'just because you speak like a fool doesn't mean you don't play well...'

That's when he stood up and left.

---

[110] Apart from Sand's character of Consuelo, Mirdja's musical ambitions and the 'musical spirit' of the novel strongly evoke the Genevan French political thinker and writer Germaine de Staël (1766–1817) and her novel *Corinne ou l'Italie* (1807). The novel combines ideas about improvisation and female artistry with discussions about national identity, politics, language, and affect. It inspired nineteenth-century women writers throughout Europe. Onerva wrote an essay on de Staël during her university studies and in 1920 she published a booklet called *Madame de Staël*.

And I realized he fled because I had been beastly...

As I always am...

*

There is one faith to which I am slowly drawn, my father's faith.

I was born to be a human being, nothing more... A human being with a life...

Which is why I was born into the wrong era.

You really were mad, father dear, and you never understood your time, when you prayed for me to fulfil your dream.

I should have been born two thousand years ago. Nowadays it is no longer acceptable for a human being simply to live as a human being and nothing more. Such a person is hounded and scorned more than anyone. These days one has to be a *spécialiste*. In other words: as practical and custom-built as possible. In other words: as narrow as possible. There is no room for understanding or developing oneself in more than one pre-determined field, and this field must be mastered so successfully as to be able to compete with a thousand other similar specialists. But of course, only the one who gets first prize is of any use to anyone!

What hope have we, the few of us who have nothing to commend us to today's great marketplace, other than the fact that we have spent our lives trying to achieve a broad and balanced understanding of life!

'What good are you, you wastrels!' scream the specialists, and they run their rattling work carts over us. Because the more completely they lose their humanity, the brighter are their prospects.

There is only one school of specialists whose greatness depends on retaining their humanity. Artists. This is why an artist is the loftiest, most perfect entity in all creation, and why only very few have the strength to become one. Many fall by the wayside exhausted, and are whipped into submission by their own profession... It is a tragic fate. I have seen so many such failures. And what about me? At least I think have escaped the worst of it...

But who needs someone like me, someone who is all and nothing? I am half the woman I could be. Until now, I have devoted everything to this half-self, must I now try and reclaim it all?

Dare I say that I have found myself at last?

*

Sometimes I think I am a martyr unto myself. As if I have renounced all the happiness and glory the world has to offer merely to remain loyal to my star-crossed destiny, to be the apostle of a clear conscience.

At other times I think I have no clear conscience. As if I have desecrated, defiled, and secretly murdered my better self...

There are two Mirdjas in me. One lives, the other haunts.

When one laughs and plays, and is hard and pitiless, like all people committed to life, the other, the ghost, cries helpless tears of sorrow and tenderness…

She is undoubtedly the better Mirdja.

*

Now that I think I know what I am, I have stopped searching for myself. I turn away from myself, and strive towards other, like-minded souls.

At first I thought there were none, but there are thousands and thousands of us. One just has to look in the right places. They are to be found among the gadflies of the night. Their tortuous night flights map my own destiny.

They are excluded, misunderstood, cursed, and damned; because they are all people who have been ready to throw away their future on a sudden impulse, deny their gift on a whim, and gamble away their happiness at the bat of an eye. They are poor; because they are all people who have never bartered so much as a single strand of hair on that great capitalist marketplace run by the specialists, because they know full well that their humanity would have been sold for a pittance, as inferior goods. That is how they have preserved their spirit. And why they are so terribly poor for all their prosperity, why they are so extremely wretched for all their good fortune.

But there was a time when you would have been taken for Olympian Gods, you proud, lonely creatures![111]

You are the ones I now long for and seek out, it is your company I crave and frequent, even in the worst dens of ill-repute, little do I care.

Because for me you are a new and wonderful sector of humanity, for whom I have much to thank.

Because you have helped me transform my conceit into compassion; I could hold you all in my embrace, I love you so much. And when I see that I understand you, and that your sombre gaze lights up when I approach, my soul is filled with such bliss and warmth as I have never felt before. You have given me new purpose in life. — And I recall my old friends that I only understood just well enough to pretend that I understood them…

You have made me a better person, you tempest-tossed, you damned and displaced. And I think I have grasped the secret of this betterment, as taught by your wasted lives:

From joy comes great emptiness, from great emptiness — great sorrow, from great sorrow — great tenderness, and from tenderness — endless pity, the great pity of sorrow, limitless in its pain and love —

*

[111] Olympian Gods, or the Olympians, the principal gods of the Greek pantheon, comprised primarily the third and fourth generation of immortal creatures. Mirdja's exclamation points to the exceptionality of the 'like-minded souls' discussed here. It can be read as a eulogy for Decadent dilettantes who do not sell their art and themselves 'on that great capitalist marketplace' run by the despised 'specialists'.

I admire all you clear-browed, steely-eyed Caesars of this life, you who command fates, who create and efface worlds.[112] You who are like gods in the magnificence of your power, unaccountable for the tyranny of your actions, unassailable by virtue of your stony hearts.

I do, I admire you, you giant, unflinching Caesars of this life.

But those of you whose hearts fail you, life's unflown kites, what should I say of you? You who were made to ride on the air like magic, yet in poor weather plummet head-first into the dirt. You who have such beautiful, fragile spirits that they break at the sound of one false note, and are therefore almost always broken. All you faint, timid and tender souls, you wounded winged creatures and tarnished wonders, you shamans tossed by Chance and painted like butterflies, what should I say of you?

That I admire you?

Ah no, I cannot. But my soul, my soul resides with you.

*

I am on my return journey at last, coming back much older than when I left, because I have left my future behind me...

And I return a much better person too, because I have neither the fervour I had at the beginning nor the bitterness that followed, only peace now.

I think this is what they call *la résignation.*

I feel like expressing my gratitude to the life I have lived, for all its suffering and madness. Why is that? I don't know, and neither do I know whether this is intrinsic to the state of resignation...

But this much I will say: Blessed be the life that encourages suffering! Blessed be the suffering soul, so loftily incorruptible in its solitude!

I am old and weary, my life seems to have ended before it began, but I wouldn't want to be anything other than what I am...

---

[112] The name of the Roman general and statesman Julius Caesar (100 BC–44 BC), who played a key role in the rise of the Roman Empire, has often been used as shorthand for a ruthless way of ruling by force, which relies on the cult of personality and exacerbated egotism.

RUNAR

I

~

Once again, Mirdja finds herself in that familiar small town which is the biggest city of her native country.[113]

Nothing has changed in her absence. The same old way of life, the same dull, boring people, the same grey mundanity hanging over everything.

No, this country had never generated any bohemian souls or bohemian fantasies; and such tendencies were therefore summarily dismissed from Mirdja's mind too. She could hardly conceive that she had entertained such flights of fancy out there in the wide world. It was all nonsense: mad notions about *la résignation* and humanity and specialists and understanding the human psyche. These ideas served perhaps as travel inspiration but here, what was she to do with them here? Nothing at all.

Grey mundanity was the rule of the day. And anyone who wanted to live here was obliged to apply themselves to the daily drudgery…

This Mirdja had always known. But now she knew something more; she knew that her turn to capitulate would come. She was going to have to find some substance to her life, whatever it was to be. She was going to have to strive for something, to do something, and to believe only in the visible fruits of her labour. It was time she became a realist. From now on, she had to pull her childish head out of the clouds! Now that she had made the stupid mistake of coming back to this place…

Petty and foolish she had been, to abandon her work and return home…

At present, what irked her the most was that she was now forced to remain in town for a little while. She would gladly have moved on immediately, moved on to Lumiluoto. But she was bound by a promise she had made. She had promised to perform… And this also vexed her, because it was probably another stupid thing to have done…

But there was no way out of it. All the news sheets already carried the announcement of Mirdja Ast's performance at next week's major fundraising evening: she was to sing and act the leading part in a very promising new work entitled 'Odalisque'.[114]

---

[113] Again, the Finnish capital Helsinki is not mentioned explicitly, but the 'biggest city of her native country' can hardly point to any other place.

[114] The word *odalisque* refers to a female slave, a concubine in a harem. In the visual arts, paintings of odalisques were common from the eighteenth century onwards. Examples range from the highly sexually charged works by the painter François Boucher

176

When the delegation first approached her, she initially refused outright. But gradually, various mitigating factors came to light. Firstly, it was her own student society that was organizing the event,[115] secondly there was currently a veritable dearth of acceptable singers in town, and thirdly the new piece was rumoured to be highly accomplished.

'The famous composer Toivo Salava has written the music, and the even more famous young writer Genius Norkko has written the libretto,' they assured her.

'Who, what?' she said, bewildered.

'That's right, you've been abroad, you don't know all the latest talent.'

'It really is hard to keep track of them all, even though they're in our midst. It's the age we live in, geniuses are simply coming out of the woodwork.'

'No, but seriously, Genius Norkko is worth getting to know. His books I mean. Because only very few people actually know him personally. He is never seen in society. He sends his short stories in from the countryside. Hardly anyone knows exactly where he resides. Just now he happens to be in town though, and will probably turn up to see his piece performed. His name isn't really Genius Norkko of course. That's just an old nickname his friends used to tease him, and then it caught on somehow. So people only ever refer to him as Genius Norkko now, even though he publishes under his real name, Kaarlo Norkko.'

Mirdja accepted the manuscript with a good deal of reluctance. The efforts of some provincial genius! Surely brilliant. And to have come up with a title like 'Odalisque'. He must have picked it out of an encyclopaedia! No doubt the romantic scribblings of a starving village schoolteacher! Very fitting for the audience of a student fundraising event...

But later, Mirdja had nevertheless agreed to take part, and what's more, with secret delight.

There's no explaining the vagaries of the human soul!

Even Mirdja did not quite dare to analyse the impulses that had persuaded her to take part in 'Odalisque'. It was an accomplished piece, true. But that was hardly the only reason...

Perhaps it was a stupid mistake, however. Another of her usual mad foibles.

Mirdja started reading over the manuscript again...

(1703–1770), whom Onerva knew through her interest in rococo art, to works by Eugène Delacroix (1798–1863), Pierre-Auguste Renoir (1841–1919), Frederic Leighton (1830–1896), and many others. In Decadent literature, the most notable work of Orientalist exoticism is Gustave Flaubert's novel *Salammbô* (1862). 'Oriental themes' were intensely explored in Finnish *fin-de-siècle* literature too, as shown for example by Jalmari Hahl's (1869–1929) work *Haoma ja Anahita* ('Haoma and Anahita', 1900).

[115] Student societies or student associations (*osakunta* in Finnish), also referred to as 'nations', draw on a tradition that dates back to the structure of medieval European universities. Students would be grouped in societies according to their region of origin. The societies would organize various social and cultural activities. See Introduction.

The music was very beautiful, there was no denying it, and the scenes were drawn with incomparable, exotic flair.

It was set in a tranquil, oriental paradise replete with harems and black slaves, with fans of palm leaves and pearl-encrusted goblets. All is tranquil... Nothing is stirring... The harem is asleep and the black men stand like statues. The fans seem to hang eternally in the same position, likewise the celestial ball of fire high above them, and the golden goblets seem rooted to their stands. And as in some blissful oriental dream, a sultan reclines still and silent on his divan, the master of all this splendour...

Then the odalisque steps in, and with her, life begins... The palm fans begin to sway, the goblets are raised, there is the flicker and flash of countless mirrors and golden trinkets... The men's glistening black skin reflects the endless sunlight of the odalisque's white limbs...

Mirdja turned the page and read in a half-whisper:

'I am not a slave.'

'You are mistaken, my beautiful girl, a human being is always a slave... a slave to destiny...'

'A human being perhaps, but not a woman, a woman is stronger than a human being...'

'You make a mockery of yourself, my beautiful devil.'

'Do you intend to conquer the devil?'

Mirdja threw the pages down and started pacing nervously.

So she had been right. This was all too close to the bone, more than close: it was her... How did he find her, this man? What power had enabled this country bumpkin to recreate Mirdja? It was incomprehensible...

She stopped in her tracks.

Do you intend to conquer the devil? she repeated to herself.

No! she cried, with a proud, arrogant smile, why this procrastination! Since Chance has gifted me such a marvellous role, play it I will. But don't be surprised then, you who have unwittingly sought to create my image and as unwittingly enlisted me as a partner in your creation, don't be surprised if beneath the form you know so well, there lies an unknown soul! Because from the moment I set foot on that stage, your soul will expire and mine will inspire. For just this once, for the first and last time in my life, I wish to play myself, to dazzle and amaze in my very being, and your odalisque will have no other soul than mine. And I can guarantee you that on the night I reign over your Mohammedan paradise, on that night there will be no one capable of conquering the devil!

II

~

Mirdja's performance was over.
She had electrified hundreds of hearts with a beauty which flowed like magic through her lithe young body, through her voice of myriad colours, through her gaze and through her soul, especially her soul…

The crowd roared…

'An unbeatable performance!'

'A star is born!'

'No one has ever made such a debut!'

And when Mirdja eventually joined the guests, all eyes turned towards her. It had been a complete success. She was the prima donna of the evening…

But Mirdja herself doesn't seem to notice. Or rather, she notices but her soul remains cool and indifferent to the favours of the general public. Not because she no longer feels ambition, but because on this occasion it has acquired a special, personal quality.

For Mirdja can no longer hide the truth from herself…

Her performance had been for one person, and one person alone… For that stranger who had known her without meeting her…

It was he alone who had been in her thoughts from the beginning, from the moment she accepted the role… and ever since. Every surge of ambition, every rush of joy and enthusiasm had been inspired by him. It is for him she rehearsed, for him she adorned herself and set her soul on fire, for him she stepped onto that stage… Yes, on this evening when she burned brighter than ever, it happened because of him. He was the one she had wanted to impress, to stun with her genius, to have bow before her. He was the only one she wished to hear pouring his thrilled adulation on her evening's triumph…

For this reason, Mirdja now walks through the crowd in a remarkable dream, seeing no one and hearing nothing…

The people are like a distant murmur, a background hum in anticipation of the one who will arrive bearing laurels and gifts and heartfelt praise…

But no one comes…

Mirdja wanders distractedly, turning left and right…

The dream starts to fade… A thought pushes through the empty disappointment. And a cold terror begins to smother the dream, the rude awakening of hurt pride and malice…

'What does Mr Norkko look like?' Mirdja shoots the question as if in passing.

'Well, nothing special really. Don't you know him? Has he not introduced himself? When he has you to thank for his success! How scandalous. That man has no manners, really! Where is he now? I saw him talking with Runar Söderberg just a minute ago.[116] And here's Söderberg. May I introduce you: Mr Söderberg, this is Miss Ast.'

Mirdja bows indifferently to a blond man of average height.

'So where is Norkko?'

'He left almost immediately after the performance. He's a little weird and can't bear crowds...'

The answer washes over Mirdja like a murky wave. He left! How was it possible! How was it possible that they had understood each other so little. And he was the man Mirdja had wanted to inspire! How could she have squandered her soul on such a despicable fool! How could she have dedicated her spirit to such contemptible dust! Nevertheless... he was a strange fellow, to have left like that... A riddle, a mystery, an aberration leaving her soul in suspense, and as such so hateful, perfectly hateful...

A very small, malicious smile settles on Mirdja's lips. And she quips as if to herself:

'Well geniuses are weird by trade...'

Runar Söderberg looks at Mirdja for a while and then says:

'Something in your voice tells me that I should defend my absent friend. You seem to be making fun of his nickname and character... To avoid any misunderstanding, I would like to point out that Norkko isn't the type to wear either on his sleeve. He is simply who he is, incorrigibly natural, and for that reason, yes, weird according to the standards of the public at large. But that is undoubtedly the fate of all those who are simply themselves... You probably know something about that, don't you Miss Ast, you yourself are not like all the rest...'

The voice that speaks all this is masculine and resonant, but so calm and controlled that it sounds almost monotonous.

For the first time, Mirdja looks at the man who calls himself Norkko's friend, and who thus launches unknowingly into battle against the secret currents of her mood. He has a fine, quiet gaze, unusually quiet. 'The flames of passion run so very deep in his soul, one has to wonder if they've ever surfaced. An unassailable man!' so Mirdja reflects. But by what right did he come and assail others! 'You yourself are not like all the rest.' What a shrewdly worded introduction!

And as befits a woman of the world in the face of well-worn flattery, she feigns a light, indifferent shrug as she answers:

'Aha, and how would you know?'

[116] Runar is a male first name, used in Nordic countries, mostly in Norway. It is supposed to be derived from the Old Norse, presumably from the elements *rún* (rune, secret lore), and *herr* (warrior or army). In Finland, it was used by the Swedish speaking population and felt unusual in Finnish-language circles.

'You gave your all on stage,' says her companion in his quiet, soft manner.

Mirdja's smile falters. This was sorcery. Since when had she become so transparent? Or had Norkko and this friend of his been put in this world to lead her by the nose?

'Did you not know,' she laughs, 'that actors merely ape the human soul? They give and possess all but themselves, of that you can be sure…'

'But I can be equally sure that artists cannot imbue their art with more than they possess. And there can be no artist without the artist's temperament… But I do not pretend to be someone who can perceive the soul of an artist on the basis of a single work of art… So what I just said about you… was quite ill-advised… don't be offended… Your name was in fact not unknown to me.'

Mirdja takes another look at this man before her. Nothing had changed in his expression. The same soft calm, the same dreamy quiet…

'How is it I've never chanced upon you before!' escapes from Mirdja's lips.

'I have been abroad for several years…'

This makes Mirdja start. The whole thorny process of her quest in the wide world suddenly comes to searing life in her memory… She wondered what drove others over the border. What were they searching for, what did they find and bring back with them? And this man before her, what did he carry in his breast beneath his unflinching composure? Life's sanctity or defilement? That wholeness perhaps…? Or could it be that there stood before her a fellow unfortunate, one of those broken souls with whom she had imagined she could unite out there, forming a new humanity…

Suddenly Mirdja notices that they are alone together.

She notices this because a miracle has taken place within her. The callous, scathing quipster that she is, has turned thoughtful, quiet, almost shy even…

They are sitting together in a small room adjacent to the main hall. The air is filled with the hazy, muffled noise of the crowd, and above all, with the gentle but nonetheless penetrating sound of a heart-breaking, sorrowful waltz…

And Mirdja's soul is deeply moved, moved with the force of a long-withheld sob. Everything is blank and forgotten, both the past and the future, only the present, only this moment is alive! Which is how it should be. And the madness within her once again prays for the grace of unthinking surrender… To cast aside all masks and armour for a moment, to be open and tender and defenceless in front of another being who is equally so… Ah, what bliss! But who would ever believe in her sincerity again, given how well she knows how to act! — And everything about this man ran deep, every move was deliberate and permanent, it was written in every feature of his face… If ever he were to open his heart and his arms, his embrace would be a safe place to rest…

There is an awkward silence between them…

Mirdja has to force herself to swallow her tears and her dreams:

'But then we must have unwittingly met each other before, breathed the same air out there in the wide world, brought back with us the same memories... Or no, what I am saying! No one can have the same memories as me... I was chasing after pipedreams...'

'That's what most people do...'

'Then most people would return with broken wings, empty-handed.'

'You always find something, even if it's not what you're looking for.'

'Something! Well, I thought I had found something in the end, but even that turned out to be a pipedream, perhaps the biggest pipedream of all.'

'You speak with bitterness, and yet you already possess everything I've been looking for in vain...'

'What's that?'

'Your self. Your very being is proof of it.'

'I don't understand what you mean... You almost sound as if you are mocking me. Or then you don't know what you're talking about. At least you cannot possibly have ever searched for the kind of self that I possess, and that I have even found a term for. A person of sentiment who lacks sentiment, a person of reason for whom reason is a trap, a seeker who has nothing left to seek, all rolled into one, and crushed by her own inner void... A splendid discovery indeed! That's me! Save me from myself! It's nothing but misery!'

'That kind of talk only goes to show that you still hold yourself very dear. You still have something to search for and discover in life... something more precious than your self... Therein lies your salvation...'

'You certainly know how to hit where it hurts... But I am already old and jaded...'

Mirdja falls silent again. Her companion is just as quiet...

At last Mirdja adds:

'Listen, tell me the truth, did I really give my all on stage, as you said earlier? Did I really bare my soul just like that, to everyone and anyone who happened to buy a ticket...?'

'Don't worry my dear, you haven't prostituted yourself, not at all. Please forgive me for putting it like that, it was thoughtless of me. Take no notice, really...'

'But I do take notice,' Mirdja almost shrieks, 'because you have stated aloud my most intimate thought. For when I came here tonight, I came here with the intention of giving my all on stage. Exactly, word for word. But not to everyone, only to one person, one who would understand... *für die Wahlverwandschaften*...[117] And now with all my heart I hope that you are the one, the only one,' she repeats earnestly... 'Yes, it's your turn to be astonished and my business to apologize. But you see, during this evening you have touched my soul more than once... At first it annoyed me, but now it

---

[117] An allusion to Goethe's novel *Die Wahlverwandtschaften* (*Elective Affinities*, 1809), famous for its enigmatic stance on marriage.

makes me happy, because I feel I can be honest with you. I instinctively feel you understand me, even if you were to deny it, and I always follow my instincts... Don't let this disturb you, don't feel obliged to be polite, just be yourself, as I am myself with you. You may think of me what you will! You've probably never known what it's like for someone who has always played at dissembling, suddenly to find herself fiercely compelled to be natural... I would take up acting professionally,' she adds in a lighter tone, 'except I can't... Nothing enthrals me and yet my life is in thrall by far too many threads...'

'The threads of Destiny.'

'And who weaves the threads? God, they say. Life, all of us, ourselves, none of us...'

'Yes, life is an eternal mystery...'

'Yet some say it's a mere reflection of something greater... symbolism...'

'Great and objective it is, the world according to religion and metaphysics... But subjectively speaking, considering my own small world, it feels safer and cosier to use another term, impressionism for example. After all it's so change-able, constantly in motion, coloured by a moment's mood...'

'Again you voice an idea that is by no means unfamiliar to me...'

'It's actually you who expressed this idea to me. Because I was just thinking about the play you performed. It was definitely the triumph of impressionism over the human soul if it was anything, and that is what true art is. It glows with such colour and warmth that it brings to the world its own hue and faith. That is what I felt so clearly this evening. While you were acting, my whole world-view was putty in your creative hands. Everything you tendered, I had to accept, believe and experience. It was the strangest of imagined worlds, so distant and irrelevant, and yet thanks to your input it suddenly became a close, marvellous reality...'

'It is so very appealing to play with beautiful lies... It must be the human soul's most intimate, inexplicable longing for unattainable dreams that can never be fulfilled, for beliefs that no longer exist, for all the beauty which is nowhere to be found...'

'But what is more real than our imagination, once it has broken free of its hazy slumber and begun to shine! And the artist is a great god who can bring our imagination to life and make beauty real. You mocked the actor's art just now, but it is probably because you keep a permanent seed of self-mockery in your heart. Because for my part, of all human endeavour, I can think of noth-ing so wonderful and versatile as acting. An actor must have the great soul of a great person, of your soul and my soul and all the hundreds of souls we walk past coldly each day. Actors understand everyone through their art, and every-one understands them. Thus, people find each other in the actor, who bears the creative talent of reincarnation at every moment. And that is why actors strum the strings of the soul to every possible tune, why they are the greatest rulers and educators of human souls... You have the most wonderful gift...'

'I've heard that before, but what good is a wonderful gift if you don't put it to use? As I said, I will never take up acting professionally... I have never had the capacity for regular work and never will. So the very thought of any occupation at all fills me with dread...'

'But there is a vast difference between an occupation and a free vocation. Who in the world has ever heard of an artist creating art for the love of a career or working to the ticking of an office clock! On the contrary, artists are the only ones who have the wisdom and courage to call work and job-seeking a social prejudice. Because that's what it is.'

'My, you are a danger to society,' Mirdja laughs. 'Had I better start teaching you a healthier outlook? Listen to me... But do you even know what society is? It is our career office, a perfectly advanced house of correction set up according to all the latest theories, intended as a penitentiary for all our bad deeds and as a potential source of felicity for all future generations. It thrives on work and offers a living. Offers a fat living, even, and the more labour and restricted freedom one can slap on the table, the fatter the living. It is this estate's gold. And indeed, good order and welfare prevail, while such amorality as a career-free existence is completely out of the question. Luxuries and curios will not be tolerated...'

'Do stop! Do stop, I implore you!' Söderberg cries out in turn, 'spare me, I'm not so thick-skinned. And on your lips, all that sounds infinitely more cruel. Leave such harsh, bitter ruminations to the likes of us who are currently waging war against the penal governors, and who will clearly soon have to submit to forced labour... Most of us have at least very little to lose compared to you. But what have you to do with society? Are you not in a position to be able to live free of its constraints? You have no need of society and society surely considers you far too precious a curio. But individuals need such curios. Humanity cannot live by bread alone. My dear Miss Ast, please don't stop being the comfort and salvation of beautiful souls! That is enough of a job for you.'

'I don't think I've been anyone's salvation yet. I have the conscience of a murderer...'

'You're too sensitive! And as such, even further away from sharing that great common conscience... the conscience of the murdered... No external violence has ever been imposed upon you, I take it, you have always been free...?'

'Therein lies my ruin, perhaps. It may have done me some good to have been held in the clenched fist of fulfilment, or in the iron grip of necessity...'

'And yet many have lost their lives that way...'

'It might have killed my talent, but it would have strengthened my character, made me hard as nails...'

'Would that have given much happiness?'

'I don't know...'

'Or perhaps you are not looking for happiness?'

'Of some kind, yes. Something solid beneath my feet, work that would be worth doing, fulfilment that would make life worth living…'

'Oh Miss Ast, just be there for all the beautiful souls!'

'Where are they?'

'They will always find you. You are a magnet to them. The call of one's kindred can be heard for miles. Have you not found that?'

'I have found myself in all of them, just as I find myself in you now. I have also loved some of them…perhaps… but I have never been able to get along with a single one of them…'

'So very different from me in that sense! Because I have always been able to get along with all kinds… but I have never been able to love a single one of them,' Söderberg quips playfully.

'That's not true, or only half true,' Mirdja draws him up short. 'You are speaking of the shell and I am speaking of the inner core. Because deep inside, you walk among people as lonely and uncomprehending as I do. You get along with them by not playing the game…'

'That's bold of you… What makes you say that?'

'Oh everything. Your quiet, inwardly turned voice for one, with its dark, reserved timbre. You have a lovely voice, like music, but it's not for others. And I know that it is only in an air of persistent, impenetrable doubt that you could have forced its original warm glow to become so cold and indifferent. Now it has a tone of perfect equanimity, capable of neither hate nor love…'

Mirdja falls suddenly silent. Her companion is staring at her so strangely…

For a long time neither speak.

Then Söderberg says:

'Women are usually children, but you're not a child…'

'My Sturm und Drang period is also behind me…'[118]

'You're quite sure it's behind you?'

'Quite sure.'

'It's often considered a turning point in a person's life. When one grows…'

'Old, yes. One can grow old in a day. Having noticed that one has scorched one's wings…'

'Something like that. But personal development does not end with the snap of golden wings…'

'They may only be fool's gold…'

They both fall silent again. Without noticing, they have become quite isolated from the crowd.

'But look at us sitting here on our own, like a pair of lovers!' Söderberg laughs suddenly.

'Or a pair of old pensioners,' Mirdja adds.

[118] See note 41, p. 102.

'You are not enjoying this crowd.'

'No.'

'Would you allow me to walk you home?'

'Gladly.'

They leave discreetly.

They walk along the street in silence.

'It's strange,' Mirdja says at last, 'I feel as though I've always known you, and yet we only met for the first time tonight... Is this the call of one's kindred?'

'I have no doubt this will be one of those evenings I will always remember, like a rare oasis in my life...'

Again they walk on in silence, like two unspoken thoughts side by side. All the way to Mirdja's door.

'This is where I live,' says Mirdja.

But her companion still does not speak. He simply stops before her and looks into her eyes...

'Why are you looking at me like that, what is it you see in my eyes?'

'I see a woman who understands a man,' thinks Runar Söderberg. But he does not say this aloud. — And his thoughts run further: this is the kind of woman I could love and — be her knight for the rest of my life... But he suppresses this thought even more forcibly...

And the young woman before him stands waiting and thinking similar fool-in-the-night thoughts: a man like this, so calm and profound and reassuring, so restrained and refined, I could love with an enduring love... But she quickly adds: childish nonsense! I am what I am, and you are surely just like all the rest of them...

They stare at each other in silence.

And suddenly she remembers: but I don't even know how to love...

And he: but I'm no longer looking for a woman...

They shake hands and part company.

III

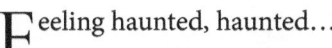

F eeling haunted, haunted...

The wind is blowing and the hinges of hell are squeaking... Witches are riding the air on old broom stumps and little demons are grinding their teeth in the treetops. The air is filled with sighing and whining and lightning.

But none of it is real, don't be fooled!

It is just shadow-play, the bloody masquerade of lost spirits... Full of colour but also tinged with grey desire... Fire and ice, gossamer dreams and leaden nightmares...

Mirdja sees all this in her soul and thinks:

It was not long ago I believed I was a stone statue standing above my own grave. A soulless, formless mass... A black cross sticking up from the burning coals of a lost spirit.

And now all that has changed.

Now I am haunted, truly haunted! The heart within the stone has started beating... Two deep, anguished eyes open in its icy surface, and those eyes fill with real, human tears...

So it's all been a fake death, or the dreamless slumber of one who is over-tired... And wasn't Mirdja very, very tired once... back then, long ago... One Walpurgis Night... when she cried herself beyond her limits... That must be when she succumbed to this slumber... And ever since then, she has been asleep and time has been dancing on her prone body like a shadow...

But now it is time for awakening and rebirth, this moment marks a turning point in life...

So she said to herself...

She would move forwards, but leave something better behind her, she would raise her gaze to the stars once again but to purer, more permanent stars, she would burst into searing flame once more but burn with a deeper, steadier glow than before...

The thousandfold fool that I am! Mirdja cries to herself. Will I never learn? A thousand times have I pushed away the trinity offered by good people and a thousand times have I prayed to have it back. That I may still ask for hope and faith in life, I can understand, but to ask for love — to think I am still wishing for love!...

How tirelessly I snatch at dreams... yes indeed... like a dreamer on the seashore, wasting her life away, risking her life by straining to reach the bellflowers in the watery mirror...

Straining, straining...

Further... further... further...

——

IV

∾

A thick fog lies over the city. The air is heavy, the heart is heavy. It's as if everyone must be repeating the same boring thing to themselves: such fog, such fog. The damp cold insinuates itself into every nook and cranny... eliciting shivers and bleak, sluggish thoughts...

It seems there are only two people in the whole town who have not been overcome by the fog... but those two are plagued by fever...

They sit side by side in the warm glow of the lamp and reach out to one another's soul. For they believe they have found a trusted confidant who can reconcile their contradictions. And their sudden faith in this is like an intoxicating drug. Which is why they feel an eager compulsion to prove it over and over in endless conversation. They are compelled to talk and share...

'You... can't have been as difficult a nature as I: craving everything yet bored with everything; feeling plagued by a lack of work while yet leaving work neglected.'

'Yes, yes...' Runar merely nods.

'And you can't possibly have been as worthless and forgetful a friend as I, a socialite above all, even though it is precisely in society that the loneliness weighs most heavily, that the desire for a true friend feels most urgent... Can you even understand a thing like that? Can you understand that when life rushes over you with the force of rapids, such a force that you can hardly keep your balance, there's no time for friends from the back of beyond... And I've always, always been looking for something new in life...'

'And now? You're still looking for something new, is that right?'

'Yes, I really am looking for something new,' said Mirdja slowly. 'Don't laugh! I know the only person who can never find anything new is someone chasing it... And yet what I really long for now is something I've never had or even known how to hope for: peace... yes, inner, holistic peace is what I long for now, nothing more. Something which would melt all my myriad impulses into one resilient whole... Or really, if I am to be honest with myself, I long for that loyalty I have so often spurned. Loyalty to some cause or mission, to some task or why not, some person... You see, it turns out I am getting old. Signs of weakness can already be discerned. I can't bring myself to make new friends day after day.'

'And what about all the old ones?'

'Oh I've cast them all aside!'

'On a whim?'

'Or out of a desire for freedom, or out of pride — or stupidity perhaps.

God knows. Most probably stupidity. Because I cannot bear to be alone all the same. Everyone needs a confidant. Someone to talk to, if only the dog...'

'In which case the dog is probably better off than the confidant. Because a confidant must swallow all the lies like everyone else but is also obliged, by the status conferred, to believe them...'

'Runar!'

'What? It surely comes as no surprise to you that most people are terrible philistines. No one reveals the secrets of their soul, especially secrets whose virtue may be in doubt. Or if they do, they make a huge confessional performance of it, the great benefit of which is that it demonstrates their capacity for deeply sensitive self-analysis, and for courageous, exceptional and unprejudicial genius in the service of truth... And quite right too, poor folk.'

'But you can't alienate a true friend by playing the wrong cards...'

'Not the One,' Runar adds ironically.

'You don't trust women...'

'I don't know. I don't have any experience in the field.'

'You don't trust me...?'

'You know how to deceive,' Runar says slowly.

'You don't trust me?!'

'There is a dangerous devilry about you, *ma diablesse*!'[119] Runar laughs.

'I've been told I'm careless and impetuous. I know that. But I'm not shallow. I hope you believe that at least?'

'I do...'

'And when I say to you now, do you hear me, that I will never deceive you... never... I can be more honest than anyone under the sun, unconditionally so, frighteningly so... Or does that mean anything to you?' Mirdja continues, barely audibly.

Runar has turned serious. He squeezes Mirdja's hand slowly.

'I see a beautiful dream, too beautiful, of a friend, a companion, a woman...'

'A dream... You still have dreams! It's usually only very immature men who have dreams of a very mature woman they haven't yet learned to know... But you...'

'Me, yes, I'm not very young anymore, am I... But perhaps immature...'

'Are you a poet then, to have remained a child so long...?'

'Only insofar as it helps me to live. I dream because it makes life easier...'

'And there was I thinking that dreams only made life harder...'

'Life is life, and dreams float in the distance, it's true. But if you have one very good dream, it can imbue everything with a strange light and strength... But you have to have real faith in it...'

'And you have such a dream, such faith?'

---

[119] 'My she-devil' (French).

'Yes. I suppose everyone has some kind of ideal of life, some notion of human purpose...'

'Except for me... Give me your dream, Runar. I'm in need of it. Ah, how often do I feel that life is utterly purposeless.'

'I've had such moments too, many such moments. But they always pass. I work in a field that doesn't much tolerate "Weltschmerz"[120] — history... as you know... And through it I've found...'

'I know what you're going to say. "The finger of God" or "the thread of life" or some other such hackneyed phrase... One of those tired old chestnuts...'

'Let's just say then, I've found that everything has its purpose. It's hard to deny. Because human history is full of indications that there is a consistent power at work, we can call it evolution or God or whatever. But when you look back on the astonishing curve drawn by this development, in which every crest marks some shining truth and every valley the start of a new crest, it's impossible not to imagine bright, beautiful progressive dreams about humanity's presence and purpose. And then it's a pleasure to work...'

'Or not work, depending on one's nature.' Mirdja joked again. 'The marvellous thing about your world-view is that it accommodates both the idle and the industrious, both the victims and the heroes. In the Orient they would call it fatalism, laying human will to rest... And I suppose it is of little consequence to the development of humanity whether I lie at the bottom of the valley or ride its crest. Because since the world and its progress is predetermined, to the very slightest of its nuances, by the same purposeful course, then no matter where I am placed on the graph, I am always in the correct spot and fulfilling its eventual purpose. Because who am I with my tiny life to be challenging eternal forces! It doesn't matter how conservative I am, how averse to enlightenment and worthless, I am always, albeit indirectly, fulfilling humanity's purpose...'

'But not your own in that case. An individual must have the same goal as humanity, the purpose of seeking truth and light... And I really am filled with awe, every time I come across one of those ancient great silhouettes which rise up through the mists of history like visionary beacons...'

'And what about the millions of millions who are never to become divine torchbearers?'

'They can embody the same aspiration. They can support the lonely geniuses and stand in the courageous frontlines of their era. Defending newly won truths and paving the way for future ones. The little people in the eyes of history...'

---

[120] *Weltschmerz* is German for 'world-pain', also sometimes translated as 'world-weariness'. It denotes a literary concept coined by the German Romantic Jean Paul (Johann Paul Friedrich Richter, 1763–1825) in his posthumously published work *Selina* (1827), suggesting that actual reality can never meet and satisfy the expectations of the mind, creating a feeling of deep sadness and melancholy.

'You mean the rare few who embody such aspiration! Never! They are cast about this globe, captured by darkness and evil; they cannot possibly serve anyone's frontline, because they are the ones most in need of support. Because they are precisely the ones who are born to crumble. Whose sensitive, truth-seeking spirits are harnessed to the front of the mightiest wagons of prejudice... They are whipped and trampled underfoot and eaten alive!... Ah, once again you seem to have forgotten about society and its victims! And who knows, even you yourself might one day subscribe to compromise, you dreamer of beautiful dreams! So what if an individual, purpose and all, is killed, as long as humanity's purpose is fulfilled!...' Mirdja concludes with some bitterness.

Runar's mood has darkened. He doesn't answer, and for a long while both remain silent. Then Runar speaks, as if to himself:

'Perhaps you are right. A weak man should not indulge in god-like dreams.'

Mirdja looks at him, almost horrified.

'No, no!' she cries, 'That's not true. I am wrong. I'm just the Devil's advocate, possessed by a negative, nihilistic spirit which never rests until it has destroyed everything beautiful and whole, until it has undermined every faith and dispersed every dream... But it should not be so. I would like to give it up, to take refuge in your dreams, Runar... Talk to me, tell me something else. Ah yes, your dream. About a friend, a companion, a woman... That's what you said, wasn't it? Tell me about that! I will shut my eyes and listen to you... Tell me about it Runar...'

'I would lay myself bare then, because it was the dream of a weak soul... but I often have such dreams... Yes, I imagine a lonely, sorry fellow, a potential frontliner, but who has been captured by darkness and evil just as you described. And he is given a secret code by which he can be released. But every time he shouts out the code, he denies himself... And the whole environment makes him feel dull and blind and those who have no code are given no bread... He is doomed... But then he unexpectedly meets a kindred spirit, a companion, like a mirage in the desert, a bright light of a woman, whose unquenchable inner fire burns with tall flames. And the man is reborn, powerful, as if he had never been weak at all. And together they burn with one sacred flame, the flame of love for truth and love for one another, and with flaming wings they soar to impossible heights... The ghastly shadow of their old demoralizing life is barely a memory... Their hearts beat with humanity's great purpose and they leave a golden ring on the chain of progress... They can manage this because there are two of them... That's how I've always imagined a relationship between two souls... in its most perfect, most brilliant form...'

'Is that what you've imagined...? And that a woman can turn a drowning man into a hero?'

'Not every woman, but one who is brighter and more profound than most, one who… yes, someone like you, Mirdja… You can turn a man into anything. With your help a man could rise to the very crest of human development…'

'With my help! The help of a doubter, a blasphemer, a stumbler. Who always destroys everything in others and myself. When I myself need help. When I myself need someone to lift my confidence, to encourage me and make me whole, to give me faith… Perhaps then I too could make something of myself… I too am just a weak soul with a dream…'

'You say that, but in truth you possess faith and infinite strength, which flows all around you like an electrical charge, which irrigates the driest waste-land, which imbues life into death itself. Life's highest purpose must lie within you untouched, otherwise you couldn't be the constantly inspiring and profound creature you are and have always been, you couldn't bring to life the seeker that lies in others… And you yourself know you are one of the first of a new breed among your generation and your sex, and that as a person you are a rare wonder and a revelation! This self-awareness glows in you with conviction, it fascinates, it disarms, and makes all who lack the same conviction powerless before you. That's what makes you so outstanding, so invincible and wonderful…'

'Oh Runar…' Mirdja almost moans.

Suddenly her stomach turns. Here it was, the confession, that unavoidable, recurring evil in her life. It always rose before her like a fence whenever she tried to get close to someone… And it was a fence she couldn't scale. No. She didn't need a worm crawling at her feet; worms couldn't help her. And she didn't need any more praise… But for Runar, even Runar to have spoken so!… She should have noticed the slant of his speech earlier!… For she did so wish to look up to the image of this self-reliant man, so calm and collected… To see him as her support, or perhaps — as the dream of her love.

Mirdja gets up to say goodbye quickly.

'I'm tired,' she says.

'Of me?'

'No, of myself. Never again remind me of myself.'

V

What had happened? What was about to happen?

Was this the same as all the other times? Mirdja was about to win a man's heart and surrender to love... All very familiar so far; and this would be followed by the usual sequel: the rift. A new rupture.

But she could not let that happen again. Mirdja was getting old after all, striving for wholeness and peace. This wasn't how to find it... How could she have forgotten that! And yet the very reason she had so convincingly and bitterly experienced the shame, pain, and numbness of her old polyandrous surrendering, was that she had turned from being a restless intriguer of romantic adventures, into a worshipper of humble, pure souls, a respecter of loyal hearts...

Yes but, said her inner voice, perhaps now you've found the very faithfulness you have been dreaming of... Perhaps you could love Runar with an everlasting love...

Idiot. Who could believe that! Not Mirdja anyway.

Doubt would never ever make room in her soul for flawless love. She could never possess another person just as no one else could ever possess her. The broken splinters of many an embrace.

She had to break it off, break it off. At least if she loved him...

But she had promised to be honest with Runar. Unconditionally, frighteningly honest...

Now the moment had come.

And fired by a sacred flame, she wrote:

'You noble, pure soul, I love you...

I love you so much that I dare not let you into my soul. — I cannot invite a lone, proud prince to visit the market stall that the whole world has frequented, that bears the footprints of the dirty rabble, and the ravages of life...

The dirt and the ravages were the price I paid for my knowledge of humanity. It is also why I can read people's eyes. I see so well how you walk and suffer in solitude, and I know I am the only one who could withstand and temper the darkness in you. And, dear God, how gladly I would sacrifice my life as a trifle for you!

Nevertheless, I am telling you: go away, don't come near me! Continue to suffer in solitude, for I love you too much...

I don't want to add you to that long line of suitors which has all but sucked the life out of me, to that thirsty, grovelling crowd which drop by drop has drained the very depths of my life-source...

I have prostituted my soul. Don't come near it. My realm is the slave kingdom of lost spirits. Every minute I can hear the chains of those slaves rattling in my ears…

I wish you to bear a crown, not chains, and that is why I say: go away, so that you may always remain my darling knight!

For the others too, were noble loners like you at first. Because there was a time when I understood the loners, before I came to possess chained dogs…

Go away, alone and innocent, as you came, and preserve your self and the greatness of your invulnerability. I have lost all that, and I am therefore not worthy of you.

What little substance I have is in a million shards. Impossible to put back together. And if it all vanishes in the wind, it's not such a great loss, my friend… That's what it was meant for…

But my honesty was the beginning of my downfall. Because I have been on the receiving end of so much that I have always given as good as I got. My sorry sense of honour has demanded as much!

Ah, but every new soul sacrificed to my honour only brought new humiliation and shame to my proud inviolability. In every case, my soul turned blacker in the dark, bloody, sacrificial smoke, and now it is a broken old altar whose sanctity was stained over time by the hearts of sinners.

If you are great and noble, do not kneel at the same altar where all others have knelt. Build yourself your own, untainted one, my friend.'

Once she had written the letter, Mirdja felt a strange sense of relief…

She almost felt as if she had saved someone's life… As if for once she had been selfless and seen something more precious in this world than herself…

She sealed the letter as if it were her death sentence. With a heavy heart, but a clear brow and gaze….

The single tear that had welled up didn't even fall, only hung on her lashes…

They would never see each other again, but they could dream of one another for the rest of their lives — good dreams.

VI

~

Evening falls.
Mirdja sits with her head between her hands. And her soul fills with dreams and images and poems, as it always does in the aftershock of a lightning strike...

She addresses her lonely speeches to her one true love... the man she has rejected for fear her own love is not good enough...

'Alone in those tired, frail moments
When my soul is
wanting of steel will,
then will I remember and yearn for you,
crying softly —
years from now, crying still.'

So sings the silent girl to her dream. And at present all she can see of the past and the future are frail moments...

There is a knock at the door.

Mirdja starts. She glances at her bloodshot eyes in the mirror and then answers hesitantly: come in!

'It's you Runar, you came...'

'Yes... I... I have to talk to you Mirdja, I really do. Don't worry! If you want us to part company then so be it...'

Runar pauses —

Mirdja just stands speechless, trembling...

Runar goes on:

'But I cannot walk away from you until I too have had an opportunity to confess, to reveal myself, to cast myself aside, just as all the others. Because I am no greater nor nobler than they, I do not wear a crown and I am not the image of your romantic knight. I am worse than all the others who have thirsted for your life-blood. Because if they have been beggars then I have been a thief. I have worn a mask, hiding my weakness to the very last. But I couldn't stand the idea of you going away with false dreams of me in your heart. I had to come and rid you of such dreams. Because I'm no different from that long list of your suitors, but I wanted to be. It's true. You see, I had heard so much about you beforehand, and so I looked upon you with great prejudice. I had been carefully instructed in exactly who you were: a great seductress of men, a diabolical soul-sucking vampire, a champion of caprice and pretence, who invites and shuns in the same blink of an eye, for whom dazzling intellectual and verbal *esprit* means everything, but people's aching hearts mean nothing, just playthings to toss aside… Yes… and much more… And that's when I swore I would never succumb to being a plaything in your hands. And even though right from the start, your sensitivity and candour stripped me of all my armour and I could tell I felt about you quite the opposite to what I had intended, I didn't want to admit I was conquered. I wanted to maintain caution, the shadow of a doubt, like a *sordino* to counter your ever-gaining influence on me. No drastic moves and, above all, no confessions of love, these were my small precautions! Fool that I was, as if you wouldn't anyway notice that I loved you. And I was such a vain, arrogant coward that, if it hadn't been for your letter, I probably would never have mentioned it. Such low-minded chivalry! Because telling the truth is always the bravest, most noble thing to do. And in that too, you have been strides ahead of me Mirdja…'

'Don't be so sure of that! It's so hard to tell the truth, because it is so hard to know what the truth is…' Mirdja says quietly, struggling with her own thoughts.

'The truth is that I love you, Mirdja, that's the truth. As truly as a man can love the only woman in his life… It is with joy I kneel at the same altar as all the other sinners' hearts seeking comfort. Because I am as sinful and broken and weak as all the others. And you are the one I need and desire to consecrate my life. But I'm not begging you to be mine. I can go away now — and with a lighter heart for knowing that I haven't left a false impression on the one woman I hold in the highest and best regard. Yes, believe me, it is easier for me to go now than it was for me to come. It was a heavy struggle against the dark forces within me, embarking on this mission of self-humiliation and destruction. But all is well now, isn't it, and it will be easier for you to erase me from your fantasies now that you know I'm not the proud, noble, pure person you thought I was…'

'Compared to me you are a thousand times purer, for never having squandered your love along the highway, never having served up your soul for all the world and given your trust to hand-me-down hawkers, for having always played *con sordino*, for…'[121]

'Mirdja, Mirdja, listen to me, that is not true either! Even if I haven't had as many friends as you, or as many trusted companions in my life, that doesn't for a moment mean that I am any purer. On the contrary, there was a time when I would feverishly give my soul to anyone, not caring who they were. Life, you see, has treated me poorly and I have treated it likewise. Only three years ago I was still walking the banks of the river Seine ready to throw myself in at any minute. You don't believe me! Take a look at all this! This is proof that I haven't always played *con sordino*.'

Runar tosses a small pile of manuscripts down before Mirdja.

---

[121] In musical terminology, *con sordino* means with the use of a mute. It is normally used as a direction to string players.

'The Diary of a Sick Man,' Mirdja reads.

'These are from that time. I thought to milk my soul for money, you see. But luckily all this still weighed too heavily on me, I couldn't do it. Eventually the wounds closed but so did a lot of other things. — Anyway. That's all over now. I've already begun making peace with life... Do you want to read one of them? I brought them for you. This was after all a mission of destruction,' he laughs morosely.

'But you may regret such revelations later...'

'No. I've never felt happier than I am now, being who I really am. As before God. If you are willing to accept the worst of me. You dare to understand a man...'

'And you dare to trust a woman.'

'Only you!'

'Me... without even the shadow of a doubt?'

'More than God.'

Mirdja is gripped by a strange sensation, and she cannot tell if it is one of joy or pain... She browses through the manuscripts...

'I've only had one friend before you,' says Runar, 'one friend who has seen those —'

'Who?'

'Norkko.'

'Him!!'

Mirdja almost jumps at the sound of her own exclamation, and she starts talking to cover her confusion.

'What a strange title for a short story.'

'Parisetta, you mean?'

'Yes, it has a strange ring to it... Come and sit by me on the sofa and we can read it together.'

And holding Runar's hand in hers, Mirdja starts reading:

'Parisetta, I loved you once, for one mad, all-consuming split-second of my existence, and I will never forget you, like all the others on whom you squander the lustful aching of your unhappy life...

You must be completely ravaged by now... I like to think so. I like to think that you lived your life for that one moment we had together, that I had the strength to reduce you to ashes, that I had the strength to extinguish the bacchanalian torch of your life. Because I would like to preserve the memory, so cruelly delicious, of the way you were when we first met...

I was very unwell back then. I was tired of life and tired of living. I had dissipated myself into a single, fragile pulsating cell, and my soul was racing at throttling speed. I had no peace, and did not wish for rest. A self-destructive urge still prickled and seared through my veins. I wanted to burn myself out in a single moment, in a single midnight flame, and thus feel the death throes of a soul pushed to the brink, because I craved the pleasure of this sensation.

As I say, I wasn't well. All I looked for in life was its underbelly, its darkness, sinfulness, and sickness, and, above all, death toying with itself. I wanted to shatter the glittery, outer core of deceit, to uncover that deepest, blackest vein, that festering disease-ridden sewer within, and experience its suffocating air. And so I wandered in a daze, chasing pleasure and pain. Looking and waiting for the one who would kill me…

That's when I saw you, Parisetta.

You walked up to me one autumn evening and you were an artificial light under the artificial lamplight. But at least you were a light, for there was fire in you, that hellfire which burns even after death. Because your flame was dead, Parisetta! Your eyes were black and fathomless like the scorched chasms of empty craters, but they still glowed like a reflection of the inferno's last coloured lanterns. It was a persistent reflection, which burned its way in defiance of life and death…

I loved you from the moment I saw you, Parisetta, for you were the one I had been looking for. That wonderful demon of dissipation, a victim of life yourself, sacrificing others, a silent black spider crawling at the Devil's door…

Your hair was vivid red, so vivid that the colour hurt my soul, and your movements ensnared me with their suppressed eroticism.

"Parisetta," I asked, "are you afraid of death?"

A disdainful smile danced across your fine lips.

"Are you rich?" you asked.

"Is it wealth you were expecting in life, from the outset, Parisetta?"

"Oh, from the outset! I was expecting life itself…"

"And it came — was it rich?!"

"Yes, and poor…"

"Parisetta, I'm as rich and poor as life itself, is that good enough for you?"

"You're mad, what do you want?"

"To live myself to death — with your help, Parisetta…"

Your eyes flashed strangely. The flare was a bold cross between love of death and hatred of death. And you answered:

"I have longed for the same thing, but I wonder if you are man enough to be my saviour!…"

And I followed you Parisetta.

It was night-time on the streets of Paris. But your flame-red hair glowed with demonic glory in the haze of the lamplight and your crater-like eyes reflected the last lanterns of the inferno…

I followed you Parisetta…

And when I finally stood beside you in your sweet-smelling alcove of yellow silk, my old morbid desire returned a thousand times stronger.

You could see it and you looked at me with haughty indifference. Your eyes shone, your hair shone, everything about you shone with a life force that suggested you knew nothing of dissipation, nothing of the yearning for death.

But I was already possessed with the intoxicating thrill of knowing I could be the one to put out your light, to reduce you to ashes, to extinguish you — and in doing so, also extinguish myself with you. I had forgotten that an artificial life cannot be extinguished, only the other one — and that was long dead in you.

But I wanted to forget that. I wanted to believe that Parisetta was real, bright, vital life, and I was the great fire that would kill it.

So I took her like a beast takes its prey. I clasped her in my arms with deadly frenzy. I wanted to see her reduced to embers, to see the spark in her eyes disappear, the red in her cheeks fade, to see how this glorious vision would be turned to ruin, into a pale, ugly, tortured shadow, and I wanted to be the one to achieve this. I wanted to kiss her until all the artificial colours were erased, to rip away that shock of hair, everything, to destroy all the sweet artifice.

And I did. Because I was a sick man and all I wanted to see was the dissipation she kept hidden from others. I wanted to see it because I loved it. And I loved Parisetta precisely because she was so wasted and sick and yet bothered to play the game of life with brightness and energy...

And I tortured you, Parisetta. I said: beautiful, celebrated Parisetta, I love all that is ugly and naked and dirty and dissipated about you, and I wish to see the things I love...

And my wish was granted...

And when I left you, you lay there barely conscious...

Your soft, pale body lay tortured and lame. Your wan face bore the fatal marks of dissipation. There was nothing left of your colour but a few spots and shreds here and there. The shining stars of your eyes were now two tired, lifeless, opaque filters... And having robbed you of your beautiful red locks, there was nothing more to cover your head than a few dark, lacklustre curls...

Beautiful Parisetta!

Yes, to me you were shockingly beautiful in all your naked truth, beautiful in sacrificing your beauty for me — probably for the first time in your life. — I had willed it and you had given in to my will, as powerful as you were!

"Am I man enough to be your saviour?" I asked. "I have delivered you from an age-old lie..."

"But you have delivered me into a new one... Can a woman like me sacrifice anything more than her beauty? That would mean the sacrifice of supernatural love — and — I don't love you..."

"Then why did you submit without the slightest protest, if in your heart of hearts you loathed and refuted my ruinous assault...?"

"You asked for ugliness... that makes you the exception — others seek beauty — and what purpose have I, other than the fulfilment of your whims..."

"What about you Parisetta, have you no whims of your own?"

"To please the likes of you…"

"You are a depraved, shallow monster and a beast, Parisetta!"

A scornful, mildly victorious tremor could be heard in Parisetta's weary voice:

"I thought you were supposed to love the ugliness in me. I thought you were supposed to love the truth. You fool! You are an erratic fellow, more stupid and mad than most! As if any of you could love the truth in me! As if I haven't been beyond the reach of love for a long time!"

"Ah, Parisetta, but I did fetch you out from under your veil of lies and I did love you the moment you turned ugly…"

"Has there ever been a hunter who hunts out of love for its prey…! And if he skinned and chopped his victim and studied the pieces under a microscope, would that make his love any greater! Beasts have no souls…"

"You have devoured as many souls as bodies, Parisetta, even if you may have lost your own. Because your wisdom is wiser than one person's wisdom, your sense of truth greater than truth itself and so at least your greatness is greater than your baseness…"

Ah Parisetta, Parisetta, as I leave I am a different man from when I came. You have cured me, so sick yourself, you have drowned my crazed passions in your own endless dissipation; and you have replaced them with a cool, quiet, and saddened faith in your truth… You have saved me…

"But there'll be no saviour for me…"

"I will love the memory of you Parisetta."

Parisetta, Parisetta, sometimes as the sun is setting and its vanishing rays dance against the soft moonlight of electric flicker, I think I can see the glow of your flame-red hair and the vacant stare of your fathomless eyes… But I no longer think of you with desire, I merely swathe your unhappy figure in gentle thoughts. I switch the wonderfully exciting dissembler for that other creature, pale and serious, whose body and soul lay dissipated, but who spoke the truth… And I bless her pained, distorted features.

Parisetta, Parisetta, who knows how many have drowned because of you, but as for me, you were my saviour.

But I can still hear your stifled, broken voice whispering those last words: "There'll be no saviour for me!"

That was the Parisetta who spoke the truth…

You still wander the world, glowing beneath your flame-red halo…

I hadn't the strength to extinguish your fire, I hadn't the strength to save you…'

*

Mirdja has finished reading.

It is dark in the room, and they both sit quietly reflecting. For the air is now thick with that timid, heartfelt solemnity that makes it hard to talk.

'Men were so much more sublime in the old days,' Runar says at last, more

to himself than to Mirdja. 'Those troubadours in the spring dusk.[122] Envelop-
ing their heart's beloved in a shimmering aura of beauty and a delicate flavour
of romance… And now, now we offer her life's ugly truth as a morning-gift,
a crude, harsh, dirty touch first thing…'[123]

'Women were so much more sublime in the old days,' says Mirdja, 'How
ugly we are, we who speak and understand that ugly truth! How ugly we are,
we modern wise women! Ah Parisetta, aren't we all, like you, simply beyond
the reach of love! Can any man ever love a woman as much as in ancient
times, on those misty spring nights, those misty spring maidens…?'

'Perhaps more than before…'

'Oh hardly, hardly! We no longer have the love of beauty nor the beauty of
love that once was. Think of all those people in ancient times, so whole and
perfect compared to us! Strong, brave men, good, kind women… What a
beautiful sight they must have been! — But they thrived, those happy creatures,
because they did not know enough to think! Because thinking is an unhealthy,
crippling activity which has depraved us all. Thought does not make life
whole, only faith does. Look at the people of ancient times! They had no
awareness of either themselves nor others, and knew very little of life, but the
gaps in their knowledge were filled with faith, and this maintained their
beauty and equilibrium. And now, what are we now that endless thinking
has wrought havoc on us? Weak, timid men, capricious, dangerous women,
and everyone tired to death. What has happened to that healthy, unconscious
difference between man and woman, that mysterious source of love and
beauty… I often think of this and always miss the fairy-tale atmosphere of
ancient times, their pearly dreams in the spring night, their childish beliefs,
all that great indecipherable poetry of love wafting on the air between two
sets of eyes… *L'amour sans frases*[124] — Life was more beautiful before. And
it's all because of us, we women. Why can't we be pearly creatures, we who
have been given the task of weaving the pearly dreams of life.'

'You are weaving more solid fabric now.'

'No, no, we are all Parisettas! Or why do I say we, fool that I am? I mean
only me. I am Parisetta! Did I not say right from the start, that you and I
have met before somewhere in the wide world! How did you fail to recognize
me as her twin? And how did you fail to know how to handle your Parisetta?
Never with caution! But quickly and in passing. Approaching her as if by
chance in the thrill of the moment, amid the joyful anticipation of some
great festive cheer, it is easy then to make merry with her for a few moments
of oblivion. You must take all the beauty, depth, joy, or lust she has to offer,
this goddess of the moment, let the torches sputter and the fireworks flare,

---

[122] See note 11, p. 60.

[123] 'Morning-gift' refers to a Scandinavian custom whereby a man provides a gift to his
wife on the morning after their wedding.

[124] 'Love without phrases' (French): the incorrect spelling of 'phrases' is Onerva's.

let blaze all the joy that no one will ask about tomorrow, or wonder where it came from and where it went... And then you must leave her before the party lanterns go out and her own dark night begins... *Une fille-de-joie* is duty bound to provide *joie*;[125] who would care to listen to her woes or breathe the fetid air of her everyday life! But who am I to be lecturing you! You know all this. I just wanted to say that I am doomed to the same fate. I am pleasant, spirited, and exciting company now and then, but no one would want to be with me forever! I am not made for love or friendship, I would be much too hard work for anyone.'

Mirdja's voice betrays her bitterness and anguish...

'You know Mirdja, friends exist precisely to share in the hard times, and someone who loves is willing to share in death itself...'

'But the Parisettas of this world are immortal!' Mirdja cries out fiercely. 'Someone who loves or hates can kill and die too, like normal people, but indifference makes a person immortal! And being with someone like that makes life eternal, but also a living hell: eternal torment. You have no idea how good I am at tormenting another. I no longer know how to love any other way. Leave me Runar! Leave me!'

'Yes, I will go, because that's what you want. And because even if I never mentioned the word love to you again, you would feel it, and it would make you uneasy, being unable to return it...'

'Yes, it would make me uneasy, being unable to return it...'

Mirdja burst into tears.

'My dearest friend, what is it? Have I kept you too long?'

'Yes Runar, much too long, so long that I cannot bear to part from you anymore. And yet I cannot ask you to stay because I have nothing to offer you. I've already lost all I had. Even though I spent my whole life skimping and holding back, I've still managed to deplete myself. And now that I want to give all of me, I find I have nothing left. Oh why have I nothing to give you my darling, darling Runar, when I would so like to give you everything! I beg you, don't leave me after all, I am so tired and lonely and poor...'

'My darling, dearest Mirdja,' Runar whispers. 'We understand each other. We are both depleted. But we can be stronger together. We can heal each other and conquer life together, my precious friend...'

Mirdja presses her head against Runar's breast and he kisses her.

And his large frame trembles with strange, sweet happiness, as if it were the first time he ever kissed a woman.

But Mirdja lies in his arms silently with her eyes closed, as if overcome with exhaustion. She feels better, though her chest still heaves with the occasional sob, and she feels safe. Runar is a good, strong giant carrying her, a small tired child, on his shoulders up a steep hill. Runar will shield her from

[125] A sex worker. The French expression means literally 'girl of joy', as does its equivalent in Finnish, 'ilotyttö'.

everything, from herself even, and the terrible prostitution that life is. — Ah, and Mirdja will be loyal to him unto her last breath... And she will love him always as she loves him now... But is this love then, this quiet, unsensuous glow? This is all as old as... What a wreck she is! — and Mirdja takes fright again...

'I feel,' she begins, 'I feel like I have had no life before now. Yet now, when my life could begin, I feel I'm no longer up to living it. I would like to say all kinds of good, tender, happy things to you, to say I will love you with an everlasting love. But I dare not. Because I doubt everything. My beliefs have always turned out to be lies, but absence of belief is emptiness. You can see what I'm like, and can guess the kind of life I've led. I'm forced to doubt myself. Tell me Runar, do you believe it's possible for me to love?'

'Life has trampled over your ideals, more than is necessary in the pursuit of truth. But if you say you want to give me everything — and you know, there is an amazing truth in giving oneself — then I believe you. And for me, your well-worn love is worth a thousand times more than all the first loves in the world. There is so much more to you than there is to love itself.'

'Your words do me so much good, Runar, I want to believe you, to love you, to be true before you as before God. Perhaps this will make me whole. And you will give me new energy, and that is exactly what I need. I was both tired and sick, nevertheless more sick than tired; now I am more tired than sick. But I don't want to think about the past. And to ease my burden, heaven has granted me the wonderful gift of forgetfulness. — Runar, listen,' Mirdja adds suddenly as if afraid, 'listen, I think there will be friction between us, and pain... They tend to follow me around. What then? Will you cast me aside?'

'Whatever survives friction and pain is always more enduring and genuine. It is through suffering we seek one another's most resilient inner selves.'

'And find them.'

'And that is when we will truly belong to one another.'

'May the friction begin!'

And Mirdja once again lies quietly and blissfully in the arms of the man to whom she had already made her farewells. She wants to love this one man, to follow this one man, and through him to become whole again...

Poor tired Mirdja!

'But I still have doubts...'

'Forget your doubts!'

Mirdja presses her head against him once more.

VII

~

From this moment on, everything feels like a dream. Mirdja cannot understand what has happened, nor what will happen next. But something in the world has changed, that is certain…

And yet, everything seems the same. Life carries on as before. The winter slowly turns to spring, the banks of snow melt, the streams ripple, the pigeons coo on the sun-drenched eaves…

But Mirdja is unaware of all this. She is only aware of one significant thing: she is engaged to be married… And that is something she still can't understand, and she can barely look herself in the eye.

It is only when she finds herself by the seashore on one of her walks that she becomes conscious of spring's arrival. Because the waves are tall… And that is when she remembers that the waves in Lumiluoto are tallest of all. That only in Lumiluoto is spring really spring. That is where she must go…

With these thoughts in mind, she walks on and fails to notice that an acquaintance is walking towards her.

It is Anni Mantere, an old friend, one of those ordinary girls she knew from her student days…

'Good day, Mirdja,' Anni greets her.

Mirdja absent-mindedly lifts her gaze from the ground, and to cover her distractedness she answers with a sweet, blank, civil smile, in the manner of civil people.

'How come you are walking alone… what has happened to your entourage of knights?' the cheeky young girl chaffs.

'Entourage,' Mirdja repeats even more absently.

'Yes. When have you ever settled for one!' the girl went on in the same tone.

'Oh no, one is never enough,' Mirdja answers just as playfully, but her voice betrays a hint of bitter irony…

Her companion notices as much, and afraid of having offended, she changes the subject. But it doesn't help. Mirdja is in a hurry and must get on…

'Goodbye Mirdja, I suppose it's pointless inviting you to drop in sometime…'

'Utterly pointless! I'm leaving for the countryside today. It's spring. — Goodbye, have a good summer!' she answers, breezily curt, an iciness around her mouth.

The impression only lasts a second before she is warm and natural once again... Anni was one of the better ones after all, with an artless, open, and sunny disposition...

Mirdja shakes her hand and adds warmly:

'I wish you a really pleasant and happy summer!'

They go their separate ways.

'What a peculiar girl,' Anni Mantere reflects. 'She's impossible to read. There's no knowing which way the wind is blowing in her presence... No wonder she is so compelling, like a magnet...'

But Mirdja has drifted back into her own thoughts.

She has to take stock. Get away from all the enchantment, at least for a while!

Ah, thank goodness for Lumiluoto!

VIII

∼

It is a dark August evening.

Mirdja sits looking out of the window at the water rippling in the moonlight.

And she counts on her fingers the days she has spent in Lumiluoto. She has spent exactly three months here in this wilderness, analysing her fate and waiting for a sign from heaven. As if such a thing were possible! She had almost managed to forget the whole business during her stay…

But tonight was just the kind of night that young girls need as a backdrop to their dreams and a spur to their imagination… Young girls! How long ago that seemed to be!

And Mirdja remembers another such night over ten years ago. She was already a young girl with dreams back then!

That day she had been standing on the shore when a sailboat passed close by. A young student was sitting in the boat, and he looked at Mirdja and smiled and waved his white cap. And Mirdja had been embarrassed by her short skirt as she watched him sail away… And then evening had come, an evening like this, with the moon brighter than usual. And Mirdja had stood on the outlying coastal path and cried, her arms wrapped around a white birch. She didn't sleep that night, trying to ingrain forever on her memory the white cap's farewell gesture, the passing smile on the sunlit waves, and she vowed eternal love to both.

How well she remembers all that! And yet she has forgotten so much that has taken place since then. Because so much, too much, has taken place since then. And no one remains a young girl forever…! Why was her very first vow to be a false vow!

Yes, and now she was much too old to be having a young girl's dreams in the moonlight. Much too experienced. And anyway — she was engaged. Something she had almost forgotten. But she didn't want to think about that. It had all been decided after all. What did it matter anyway, whom she was to marry. She would never be able to give herself up completely to anyone, nor love anyone completely and think only of him. She could love everyone and forget them all. This she knew from experience. And yet she had to get married. It seemed she could not do without an erotic life. And she had to stop somewhere. This would at least help her keep her youth…

Mirdja shrugged her shoulders at her wicked thoughts.

So now she was to start practising purity and youth! 'Demi-vierges'![126]
She gives a sinister laugh.

Prévost's novel really did seem to cut a bit close to the bone. She would gladly have challenged that poisonous whisperer in her heart to a duel! The slanderer should keep quiet, she really didn't want to listen!

Mirdja shifts nervously. It wasn't healthy to stare at one thing all the time. What else could she look at? The moon? It wasn't even beautiful. Round-cheeked, laughing, and cold... No, the foam crests of the waves were more pleasant to look at...

The wind hoots now and then like a fire siren, long and slow. The sea roars restlessly. The clouds float across the sky in white, misty shreds. Her eyes finally come to rest on them!

Strange images speeding past, up above... Carriages of light, valerian flowers, horses with fiery manes.

The moon was already high. Its pale, silvery sphere now seemed to express silent, sophisticated contempt. A moment ago it was larger and uglier, lower and brighter. Like the broad face of a marketwife. Which Mirdja had found unpleasant. But it had started out as a bloody, passionate, giant flame, glowing on the horizon as it rose like an apocalyptic ball of fire, like the face of a mysterious volcano...

What an odd moon it was!

The clouds wafting past are now stranger than ever. And the images begin to take flight in Mirdja's soul. She quite forgets that it is no longer appropriate for her to be dreaming in the moonlight...

White misty figures riding on white foaming stallions. Rocking and skipping closer and closer. They nod their heads at Mirdja...

> 'Ah, I can't come now, you know
> For my heart is full of woe:
> Preciosa is a prisoner held
> In Rinaldo's citadel!'[127]

---

[126] 'Demi-vierge' (literally, half-virgin) was used to denote a girl or woman engaging in suggestive speech and various forms of erotic and sexual involvement avoiding, however, sexual intercourse and thus retaining her virginity. Here, it also refers to the title of an 1894 novel by the French writer Marcel Prévost (1862–1941), which depicts the effects of Parisian society on the education, interests, and economic needs of young women.

[127] Preciosa is one of the imaginary figures of 'gypsy' female singers and dancers explored in European literature and music at least since the early seventeenth century. With the intensifying of 'gypsy' Romanticism in the nineteenth century, the figure of Preciosa appeared in various textual and musical works. Rinaldo is a character from *Rinaldo Rinaldini, der Rauberhauptmann* ('Rinaldo Rinaldini, the robber captain', 1797), by Christian August Vulpius (1762–1827), often imitated in literature and other media. The quoted lines are from the Finnish translation of the children's theatre play *Rinaldo Rinaldini eller Röfwarebandet* ('Rinaldo Rinaldini, or A band of robbers', 1858) by the nineteenth-century Swedish-language author Zachris Topelius (1818–1898), known mostly for his historical

How strange that song should come to mind now! It was after all a long time since she last played at being a gypsy princess![128]

But that was what she was. Or not even a princess, just a tattered traveller from the long, sombre seashores of the world...

A pale dancer in the moonlight, born to be unattainable, a mirage, a shadow, a deceptive dream...

Ah, but now she was a prisoner!

novels and fairy tales. There, the characters of Rinaldo Rinaldini and Preciosa appear together.

[128] A possible allusion to Mirdja's maternal heritage. Among the manuscript drafts for *Mirdja*, there is a fragment (not included in the novel) in which Mirdja talks to her uncle Arvi (in the printed version, the uncle's name is Arnold), saying: 'Dear uncle, forgive your gypsy girl for loving you so much'. In nineteenth-century literature, the figure of the 'gypsy' was frequently used to symbolize freedom from all social restrictions.

IX

~

Mirdja often has bad days. Today is one of them, and it's worse than usual.

She wanders restlessly along the coastline. She is desperate to evade her foolish, sinister thoughts. But nothing can stop the voices echoing in her ears. Even the sea is like glass. And in the stationary air, Mirdja can hear the hard clangour of her sledgehammer nightmares.

The whole world can hear your cruel words! Be quiet, please be quiet!

But they won't hush.

It is only as dusk falls and Mirdja sits exhausted by the piano, that their evil power fades. Their daggers are sheathed, their cruelty gradually relents and melts — into sorrow.

One chord follows another. Quiet, soulful music like a mysterious enigma...

Mirdja suddenly stops playing.

Wretched, wretched soul that you are! Such is the permanent bass note of your life! Suffer, suffer! That's all you deserve with the life you've led.

No! That's not true! Was it her fault if she was condemned to walk the path of a seeker, of a cursed conscience, like all Don Juans, like all love's eternal Wandering Jews, that no power on earth can rescue.[129] Rolf used to speak of them back then. Now Mirdja would be able to speak of them too, and better, and of one special variation of the type: the female Don Juan...

Oh how they grimaced at her, her long line of victims! Or not her victims. It was she who was their victim. They followed her every step, drained her life, eroded her faith, denied her love, her freedom and all her human rights.

---

[129] The Wandering Jew is a mythical immortal figure from a Christian legend of uncertain origin, which began to spread in Europe in the thirteenth century, and was often used to justify anti-Semitism. In the legend, the character struck or taunted Jesus as he carried the cross, and was then destined to walk the earth until the Second Coming. Specific features of the character vary depending on the version of the legend, as does the rationale of the tale. This is apparent from the names the figure has acquired in different languages, from Wandering Jew to Eternal Jew. In Finnish, he is called 'the cobbler' or 'shoemaker of Jerusalem' (*Jerusaleemin suutari*), which determines his profession; 'shoemaker of Jerusalem' is also the subtitle of an English broadside ballad from the seventeenth century. The Wandering Jew has been the subject of many works of art, from literature to theatre, the visual arts, and music. In Decadence, the figure often assumed the role of the alienated artist and their existential search, destined to failure. Onerva's interest in the character (standing for the figure of the seeker, mentioned earlier) culminates with her collection of prose pieces called *Jerusalemin suutari ynnä muita tarukuvia* ('The cobbler of Jerusalem and other mythical tales', 1921).

Mirdja was just a witch and a man-eater! Everyone warned against her. They even warned Mirdja against herself.

And now she had gone and got engaged!

Why not before, to any one of them? Why not to the first in the long line or why even now? Had she found something — more than before? No. Had she given more? No again. — She had gained much from them, learned much, she had put together her whole person from them crumb by crumb, piece by piece, a little here, a little there. And she herself had chopped her own soul into shreds in order to be able to give something in return... And with each such encounter, two people had parted company a little richer than when they met, but also a little more broken. — Or at least Mirdja was, after sharing mere slithers of herself. The others always gave themselves completely. They had held out their arms and prayed for her to take it all, for her to stop and take everything... And Mirdja had never been able to walk past unmoved. She had always stopped, but only in passing... Because life was waiting for her with new treasures, new souls. They wanted to possess her, Mirdja, and thought they could, ever onward moving Mirdja... But it had become increasingly difficult for Mirdja to walk on, because there were more and more eyes pulling her back, blind eyes in which only her image was reflected...

And there were so many of them. They flew around her like bats in the night with their long, dark wings. They were like chained spirits, magical bewitched creatures. And Mirdja no longer knew how to undo the spells... She had only known the charms of entrapment. She no longer had a soul of her own. She only had theirs, the ones they had left behind. That's why they still kept guard over her... She couldn't just live as if her soul were her own! She couldn't just fall in love and give it away. She couldn't just pledge her soul with loyalty and devotion, because it was only right that she should respect other people's property...

Because Mirdja was carrying contraband, mountains of undeclared goods... And how often this weighed upon her heart!

Perhaps she was now the embodiment of her mad father's dream of a whole humanity. A miserable fairy-tale creature, living somewhere deep inside his daughter's eroded soul. A phantom with a hundred heads and a thousand souls... A microcosmos of the soul of life...

In moments of exhaustion, Mirdja would be filled with the uncontrollably wild, violent hate that only love can generate. But indeed there they lay, all the loves of her life!

Mirdja is a born seer of visions. — Again the spirits take physical form. She recognizes a head here, an eye there, the caress of a voice, the touch of a caress...

Perhaps the very first kiss had been the best, the kiss of a stupid nonentity, Eino Kailo! Because she had taken a secret pride in that kiss. — It had been like holy water... The rest she could hardly remember. And what did they even mean to her anyway. She had simply been obliged to give something in return and such a minor thing seemed to make them all so happy…

But why did all those various people she met follow the same pattern of behaviour! If only there had been one exception! She would have finally loved the exception… No, enough of such ramblings. Enough games. And such thoughts behind Runar's back were a crime, because she had sworn never to betray him.

And once again Mirdja winces with one of her familiar, sudden pangs of conscience.

She abandons the piano and her thoughts and rushes to pen Runar a letter. She writes:

'You shouldn't have tried to make a doubter believe. That's a test that can come with a high price. — I let you lead me, because it was sweet to believe in you and imagine being in love. You assured me that my feelings were worthier than what is normally called love, and contained more love than love itself. I myself have never known what love is, and so I just listened to you in wonder. But I shouldn't have. Because even if I didn't know what love is, I did know, only too well, what the absence of love is. I don't know how to love, not you any better than anyone before you or after you.

Now my soul is healed and tranquil, and I have forgotten all about you. I haven't seen you for three months. You are a complete stranger to me now, like any other chance acquaintance. If you were to die now, or leave me, not a single heart string would tremble. I might just as well be engaged to anyone, I could let another man kiss my lips without your picture rising to haunt me, just as your predecessors haven't haunted the great feelings I have for you. Ha ha ha! That is love. Yes, you said it and I said it myself. But my emotional life was in turmoil then, I was sick and therefore so very dependent on you. I would have walked through fire for you. I remember it well. It wasn't a lie, but it wasn't love either. It was just the result of strained nerves and emotions, and anyone else could have proved just as useful to me, because I always need a personal soul at my disposal. But if this is what they call love, then I could just as well love anyone, any number of men and just as grandly. No man means so much to me that I couldn't live without him. I don't need anyone to be the great fulfilment of my life. The only thing I need is constant variety. And in this whirl of change I only have two choices, both equally dreadful: either to ride the waves of my emotions, give in to each 'love' as it comes, go from man to man, being straight with myself and them, always coming and going as novelty or boredom takes me; or then always to deny my feelings, always to conceal them and remain aloof, always, do you hear, to withdraw from the company of you men so as not to ignite dangerous fires in me or any of you. My better self would choose the latter alternative, but is it really a better way of living? Think about it, always a poor player, always shutting the other out! And for what? So that neither would be consumed or broken by the touch of the other. — Good God! What in the world are we saving ourselves for! Isn't life about being consumed! And isn't the most wonderful consummation the exchange that takes place between two souls, in their hearts? The most wonderful because it enriches, it enriches us and makes us greater, and more profound and understanding. But in the end, there is more consummation than enrichment and that is a person's downfall. Polyamory eventually wears away the purity, the profound sensitivity which preserves nobility of soul, and replaces it with market familiarity, with crude vulgarity, until it takes a drumbeat or a cudgel to stir emotion. And in the end, it is impossible to tell the difference between a gentle and a brutal touch, it all turns into the same dirty, grey, and indifferent numbness. — That is the average harlot's experience. — I have already been through it all.

Must I still speak of my love! Do you not yet believe me when I say I am incapable of love?

And yet I think that if I saw you again my old feelings would awaken, and I would hang on your neck and feel a deathly grip on my heart at the thought of our separation. And I might even swear to follow you to the ends of the earth, if I still believed in my feelings. But I don't believe them anymore. Never ever try to save a doubter again!

And I don't believe in you anymore either. You were supposed to make me feel whole again, to lift and heal me. But now it seems to me you could not manage it. You would try to rein me in. And I could never tolerate that. Four walls and a window do not make a home for Mirdja. Mirdja and the domestic idyll! The irony is too crushing! I must be allowed to fly, to fly freely into the open, and land alone, no one by my side.

Forget me! I am just like Parisetta. There'll be no saviour for me—'

But having written all this down, Mirdja begins to think... Of herself, of Runar and the world...

Whence, whither, why, wherefore all melt into one nerve-shattering mess in her head.

And she doesn't send Runar the letter.

The truth, was that really the sum of it? By the time Runar were to read it, it may well all be a lie many times over...

And even if she pushed Runar away, someone else would come along soon enough...

Why shouldn't her salvation lie in sticking with Runar now, in giving up impulsiveness for fidelity, to find the selflessness within her and relinquish her 'demi-vierge' existence...

She won't back out now, not for anything. She makes this promise to herself, to Runar, and to God.

But the mischievous demons in her mind still whisper: You idiot, you self-deluding half-wit! If anything, this fidelity of yours is precisely selfishness and impulsiveness. Such caprice, such caprice. It will cost you!...

X

Mirdja has finally taken a decisive step: she has told her uncle everything. Now it is impossible for her to back out because she doesn't want to reveal any inner weakness or madness to her uncle. And neither does she want to appear unhappy. So she forces herself to remain calm and cheerful.

She manages this most of the time. Lumiluoto has never before seemed so beautiful and precious to her. And every now and then it seems to fire all her inner strength into a great and glorious symphony of life and vigour, music and rhythm all at once and as never before...

But then she almost always takes fright. This fine-tuned sensitivity of her soul, this strange music and frolic in her heart, what exactly is it an overture to? Death? Or a new, better life? More likely death.

But she wants to be cheerful. For her uncle's sake. Ah, she has long been a bad, neglectful child!

Her uncle also seems reborn to her, very close and dear once again. And she would often talk to him the whole day long from morn till night as she did when she was little. And she would even display uncharacteristic bursts of affection. She would throw her arm around the old man's neck and whisper remarkable words of love and devotion.

And then they would play music together at length, longer than ever before and better than before. And in those moments the silent retreat would burst into one great sea of harmony. The music would capture their souls. They would tell each other fairy tales and move closer together, hold and caress each other's hands, understand each other and have the same thought without speaking, come close again and grasp each other in a lengthy embrace — as in a farewell.

So Mirdja and her uncle speak every evening. Every evening the ghostly Devil's Lighthouse rings out with Tchaikovsky's *Sérénade mélancolique*.[130] It is pitch dark inside and pitch dark outside. The spirits play and the sea answers like before, but every night more faintly than the last. It becomes

---

[130] P. I. Tchaikovsky's (1840–1893) *Sérénade mélancolique* (1875) is, as the title suggests, filled with emotion and melancholy. Stephen Downes points out that recent studies have shown the Decadent and melancholic aspects of Tchaikovsky's music, which provided a 'pessimistic alternative to Nietzschean Dionysianism'; Stephen Downes, *Music and Decadence in European Modernism: The Case of Central and Eastern Europe* (Cambridge University Press, 2010), p. 58.

harder to answer those two. Never before, never before has the sea heard such confessions of deep love.

But with every evening Mirdja feels the anguish in her chest increasing, as if the life is being squeezed out of her. How could she leave! She can't possibly leave behind the beauty of this place, can't possibly live without her violin, Lumiluoto, and her uncle. — What madness, madness!

But when Mirdja feels this mood coming on, she calms herself, puts an abrupt stop to her terrifying imagination and smiles a happy smile at her uncle. So she cries without tears every evening. —

Because there's nothing for it anymore. Mirdja has resolved to go to the stranger, Mirdja has resolved to love the stranger.

So she must say goodbye to Lumiluoto, a sweet, painful farewell.

One evening in late autumn it finally happens.

The sun has set and a thin, unnaturally red line is drawn where earth and sky meet.

It looks like the artery of life itself to Mirdja, and the more she looks at it the redder it grows until it ruptures into a painful, bleeding wound.

Mirdja is pale and startled by the blood-red sting.

Her uncle is pale too. And Mirdja suddenly notices that he has grown curiously old.

And in her soul she cries: you are draining the life from him as you go, you cruel, cruel child. It is wrong of you. He isn't the man he used to be, he needs your understanding and affection. Your place and your vocation are here.

And the sea looks at her reproachfully: your place and your vocation are here…

Mirdja's soul convulses as in death, or madness, or with the bad conscience of the whole world.

But she has to go.

And for the first time in her life, she writes a song about herself. A cruel, heart-breaking song of the pain in her heart straight after parting.

'I was once the hermit's child:
And the hermit sang to me by day;
Now he sings his songs to himself
And I answer from far, far away.

I was once the hermit's angel:
Stones underfoot never slipping;
Now he walks with a stoop, all alone,
While it's a stranger I'm a-kissing…'

WEDLOCK

I

∽

Runar Söderberg teaches at one of the schools in the capital. He is forever pale and silent…

Sir is probably not quite well, his students conjecture.

Newlywed exhaustion, one or two of his colleagues titter.

But the married townswomen all know that Runar Söderberg has an unsuitable wife…

And what an unsuitable wife! Who could possibly be ignorant of her bad reputation of old! Who could possibly be unaware that beneath that surface of yellow silk there beat a selfish, wanton heart of deceit! Who could possibly fail to realize that marriage to such a creature spelled sheer madness and misfortune! And to think that a decent fellow like Söderberg should have ended up being her ultimate victim! How could a wise man be so blind when it comes to choosing a wife! And it wasn't as if he were strapped for choice! He could have won the moon's daughter down from heaven! Such a fine, upstanding man with a solid career ahead of him and a long, respectable lineage behind him! What a dreadful blow this misalliance must be to his parents! Their only son, to boot!

Much astonishment and admonishment and invocation circulates through hundreds of warm-hearted and clean-living homes on account of the newly wedded couple.

But the two of them know nothing of this. They live in their own isolated world.

So what kind of life is it, this life on everyone's lips, that no one has ever seen?

Ah, the rumours are only too accurate. Mirdja is indeed an unsuitable wife.

She spends her days pacing up and down her room and wringing her hands. In their marital home!

Was this it, then — that great spiritual wholeness, that equilibrium of life and love, that wonderful mutual aspiration to human purpose that she had been striving for? Sitting endlessly between four walls, fulfilling only a vague, silent function as her husband's wife! This was apparently substance enough for thousands of women, this fabrication of a career in the service of a single relationship… But what did it mean to Mirdja? The same as it did to her husband it seems. Submission to something greater, being an instrument, not a purpose, an appendix to life, not life itself... And yet she had placed all her eggs in this one basket, thrown herself like a mad fool into the disintegrating webs of her fantasies... Only to find herself so very far in the opposite direction from her objectives...

She had dreamed of a life made whole by fidelity, of a bright, strong male companion, of flying with him to giddying, unattainable heights — and she had gone and hitched herself to a work camel, a pallid schoolteacher, with whom came the stiflingly shallow world of the petty bourgeoisie, the donkey-bits and bridles of society, and everything else she loathed in this worm-ridden world.

It had come to this, poor Mirdja. And so there she stood, the harsh, naked reality of her existence staring her inexorably and callously in the face, now that the last of her dreams were shattered. Worse than ever before did she torment her mind with cruel thoughts, flaying both herself and Runar in the frenzied, uncontrolled passion of her heart... And the more they suffered the more fiercely was she tempted to flay...

Thus their life shrivelled and shrank, that life which was supposed to have been so enlightening and restorative...

These days Mirdja was inhabited by two different souls. One was cold and sardonic, bitter and cruel. It lashed out and bit constantly like a rabid dog. While the other suffered so deeply from having bitten, suffered for both their sakes, but mostly for Runar's sake... Because this other soul was kind and gentle and inclined to make sacrifices...

And so time passed, in endless, senseless battle between her two enemy souls. In particular, the meaner of the two never let up. It was tireless in its outbursts of heartless, stinging remarks, which did not spare their listener. Because Runar had to know everything. It was a matter of frankness. And so it never forgot to include even the tiniest of cruel reflections or mean-spirited asides in order to add conviction to the frankness. This soul knew that Runar was not at fault, but he was nevertheless in the way, an instrument of evil fate, and therefore it could not stand to lay eyes on the man. And the other soul, which loved him, sobbed silently in the wings...

Mirdja's inner life is like an infinitely drawn-out death throe.

And Runar, silent, reticent Runar, grows quieter by the day. Everything that had flourished in him under the radiance of Mirdja's love, once again sinks to its former depths, drawn down by sorrow and solitude. And the more Mirdja speaks, the quieter Runar becomes. But Mirdja sees this as weakness, cruelty, stupidity, everything negative at once, and it infuriates her even more. Yet when Runar tries to speak and comfort her, they both feel it is even greater stupidity...

And so they carry on living day after day, these two neurotic and tedious individuals. Irritating and irritable... But Mirdja is the source of it all, because everything irritates her. She is irritated by Runar's presence and irritated by his absence. She is also irritated by the fact that he works... By the kind of work: career work, breadwinning work, salaried work... But to ask him to give it up for Mirdja's sake, for the sake of a useless, unemployed idler, an eternal dilettante, that would be sheer madness! For most of all, Mirdja is irritated by the fact that she has nothing to apply herself to... But even this she turns against Runar: she could have been an artist if Runar hadn't crossed her path in her moment of weakness... And she could still be an artist if he weren't in her way now... But he is, he is there... Like destiny itself that cannot be avoided, like the very thought of life, which must be thought through till the end and pushes everything else away, like something she can never be free of again, and without which she may not even be able to live...

Ah, this captivity! Ah, this slow death under the gaze of the bourgeoisie! Mirdja's soul cries out constantly.

But even so the winter passes.

Mirdja and Runar have lived through it together, immersed only in one another, like two lovers. And in doing so they have followed their hearts, because even though they cannot live with each other, neither can they live without each other.

A lot of vague rumours about them circulate, but no one really knows anything of their peculiar, secret story.

But Runar and Mirdja both know they have changed a lot over this first winter together.

Runar has turned back into a pessimist, sombre and withdrawn.

And Mirdja has acquired the typical characteristics of a typical bourgeois wife: she has become petty and spiteful...

II

Mirdja and Runar spend the summer in a small villa on an island close to the city.

The heavy winter is long gone, but the wintry nightmare seems reluctant to move out of their home. It has taken up residence…

The long June evening is slowly drawing in. Clouds are hanging low in the sky. The air is heavy with melancholy. And as they sit on their porch drinking tea, Mirdja and Runar speak not one word. The silence is verging on awkwardness.

Mirdja occasionally makes nervous gestures followed by ironic smirks, as if she wished to poke fun at her own nerves, at their boundless stupidity: surely you understand that this is what our normal life is like, this — and this is what it will be forever…!

Then her thoughts would be suspended in a void once again…

Suddenly a tiny worm on the edge of Runar's plate catches her eye. She takes pleasure in it as in an unexpected distraction, thankful for even a moment's diversion… She focuses all her attention on it. It crawls slowly and surely around the rim and then starts climbing onto a piece of bread with the same calm, steady motion… Mirdja simply stares at it and in this moment, there is nothing in the world more absorbing than the worm.

Just then, Runar picks up the bread and is about to take a bite when he notices the worm.

Mirdja gives a cruel little laugh.

'I had spotted it, you know,' she says.

'And you said nothing…'

'I didn't want to disturb this holy silence…'

'How very wicked of you,' Runar quips, with forced playfulness.

'Wicked am I, when I'm finally beginning to acquire your great skill at remaining silent, this eternal eloquence of total quietude…?'

Mirdja's voice is bitter and caustic and the atmosphere is awkward again.

Then the maid enters with the post.

It saves the day. The tension subsides as they both concentrate on their own letters.

'Mirdja,' Runar says after a moment, 'would you read this?'

Mirdja throws a sideways glance at the letter Runar holds out.

'Another missive from Job,' she grunts.[131]

---

[131] The biblical figure of Job is characterized as righteous and devout, even in the face of

'Mother and father will likely pay us a visit next week,' Runar continues.

'Well wouldn't you know! Another round of inspection. Oh, I've turned into a real display item this last year! It's revolting!'

Runar's face flushes deep red.

'Why do you always insist on seeing everything in the worst light! Surely you understand... They love us and...'

A wicked smile on Mirdja's lips cuts him off mid-sentence.

'Yes, of course I understand. What else has there been for me to do but understand, endless understanding ever since we got married. Well, I no longer wish to understand. Understanding kills one's ability to act according to one's nature. Understanding turns a person into a statue... And this solicitousness, this great solicitous love, I'm fed up with understanding that. It is wearing me to death... And anyway, what do I care for the love of all and sundry! What's it got to do with me? It was only one person I married...'

'You've lived your whole life with no social ties. The most natural feelings are alien to you. That's why you say these things. But try and imagine if you had a mother and a father, and they came to visit...' says Runar in a quiet, restrained voice.

'Their visit would be different. They were free gypsies leading a free life, and I was born the same. And that's the very reason I can't stand this anymore, I can't stand it!'

Mirdja has worked herself into a frenzy.

'But Mirdja... darling Mirdja, what is wrong with you today?'

Runar tries to approach her, but she pushes him away fiercely.

'Today!' she gives a bitter laugh, 'the same as yesterday and tomorrow, the same as every single day... Or are you blind, can't you see that I'm suffocating? Oh, in what terrible emptiness and captivity have I languished this whole long year with you! And you still can't see it, not now any better than at the beginning, you happy, sightless man! You who didn't even notice my blushes of shame during that dreadful ceremony referred to as nuptials, into which you coerced me...'

Runar is indignant:

'Coerced you! How can you possibly say that? How can you possibly claim that I coerced you to marry me? You are your own witness against you. You have always said there is no chance of coercing you in this life. You have always called coercion a form of degradation that marks the moment a person dies, a death which is only for the weak, not for you...'

'For me too... I am weak now. I've lost everything in your sphere of influence: my pride, my independence, my strength, my self-respect; I have only one thing left of my former comforts: my ability to speak the truth. And this

---

great adversity. The Book of Job, in the Old Testament, examines the problem of divine justice.

is the truth: I was forced into marriage under duress, and with duress came degradation, and that moment marked the beginning of my death…'

Long silence.

Then Runar spoke in sotto voice:

'Those are terrible words to speak to someone who has loved you more than anything, and for whom the sacred autonomy of your person has meant more than divine worship… But perhaps you are right. I have been blind, totally blind… And at that dreadful moment you speak of, I could see nothing but you, I felt nothing but my infinite love, and fool that I was then, I believed you cared for me a little too…'

Runar's face betrays his infinite suffering… Mirdja can see this and it pierces her heart, but it merely aggravates the savagery in her soul… And feigning the hard, invulnerable cruelty of indifference, she continues against her heart's inclination:

'Yes, I cared for you a little, but too little, and I sacrificed too much for so little. And as for the wedding and all the formalities of our relationship, we talked them through and I agreed, it's true, but that's just it. You don't see any trace of duress there. As if, in this day and age, duress still only signifies physical force! Rarely is it so! No, it is something much more elusive, damaging, and fatal. It is murderous combat between a couple's differing values, raging within the human heart, where the outcome, whichever way it falls, means certain destruction of the human spirit… But you knew me so well; you should never have pushed my back against the wall. Yes I agreed to everything, but I agreed against a thousand inward voices, against my very self. Why? Because I wanted to be good to the man I believed I loved. Ah, one should never appeal to another's goodness! Because of all the sins that stem from weakness, goodness is the most widespread and the most in need of forgiveness. But it's still a cardinal sin, for which there is no mercy and nor should there be. Because in this world, more evil has been done in the name of goodness than anything else. In the name of goodness, natural self-love has been denied and replaced by a commandment to love all of humanity, which is the most cruel and idiotic of commandments. It has rallied all the stupid, mean, small-minded, and ostensibly well-meaning people, and with their help placed world-wide hypocrisy on its everlasting throne. Yes, yes, just think about it, where on earth did this scourge of humanity come from, this moral depravity, this great community of self-righteous, spineless para-sites, of narrow-minded prophets and cowardly philistines who have no respect for individual freedom, who write the gospel according to prejudice, drawing up laws and punishments, who send their missionaries to convert people against their true nature!… Anyway — now I too have obeyed the laws of humankind's nightmarish enemies of progress. Can you understand the significance of such a sin, the sin against one's nature, the single most deadly sin? There is no salvation for those who commit such a sin. All my struggles this last year have been for nothing. My sin is too great…'

Mirdja looks at Runar through the twilight...

He is bent with his head between his hands, and Mirdja thinks she can see his shoulders quiver in anguish. And she feels how infinitely monstrous is her cruelty towards this good man. This good man! The most forgivable and hateful phenomenon under the sun! Because a man should not be weak, and therefore neither should he be good, because goodness is the mark of a blood-line steeped in weakness. But that her husband should be one those mild-mannered innocents, that he should be part of humanity's spongy layers of swamp that constantly exude their stultifying atmosphere and engulf in their soft embrace all those who trample angrily over them! Ah, no power in the world could stand up to their quiet weakness! And Mirdja too was powerless against Runar. His permanently controlled temper and incessant goodness hurt her more than any amount of wrestling. That's what she would have wanted, it would have made her big and strong, it would have made her confidence and exuberance soar to new heights. But to be the lone aggressor, against someone who never strikes back! It was so exhausting it was killing her. And yet she had to strike, and even to keep on striking for that very reason. And sometimes the feeling grew so intolerable, it would swell into a tearing rage against this quiet man who remained so meek, who submitted to his fate and suffered Mirdja's insults with such infuriating serenity. Why didn't he grab her, pummel her with his fists, kick her with the metal tip of his boot! For Mirdja was a bad wife... Even now, such fantasies of brutal love, as if she would ever put up with anything of the kind in reality! Runar's love was deep and noble... But Mirdja was a bad wife... Why not be kind and understanding, she too, and make peace...? Ah, no more of that. She had just done that earlier, and it had merely led to this terrible self-loathing, this terrible bitterness...

Still looking at Runar, Mirdja feels as if the contours of his figure deepen and soften under her gaze — like sorrow. And she is suddenly overcome with infinite tenderness. With pity for them both, but especially for him, her companion in misfortune, who was suffering because of her... At that moment she would even have been willing to atone for her sins by pain of death.

'Darling, darling Runar,' Mirdja whispers as she hangs on his neck. 'Darling, darling Runar.'

A strange, prickly smile crosses his face.

'Mirdja...'

'Yes, Mirdja is so wicked, so bad, but she still loves her Runar. And she is killing the one she loves...'

'Is it true Mirdja? You still love me... is it true? Then I'm happy to give you everything, take my life, my sanity, it all belongs to you, for the expiation of my sins... I should never have crossed your path... Tell me, do you want me to go — now?'

'No, I don't, I don't, but I am driven by a strange, fatal force... I am born to be your tormentor and I do so suffer from being this way. Let us understand each other, my friend… Oh how well aware I am of your suffering… It would be better for you to leave me, but I have no one else but you in this world. You are everything to me…'

Mirdja chokes on her sobs.

And with the full passion of his anguish, Runar clasps her in his arms.

The night envelops the two of them. Briefly, their eyes are dark to the gnawing terror that stalks them at every turn. They wish to forget, they wish to believe, these two unbelievers, albeit in the awareness of their own lie. They are now powerfully drawn to one another by their secret, fatal sickness, the same sickness that in the morning dawn is just as likely to turn them into enemies a thousand times over.

And they know this… But what of it!…

The June moon grows faint… Its pale and translucent dusk hangs sublime and still, like a melancholia over all of creation…

Mirdja and Runar cling to their cool, lucid mysticism to the very last, with the unrelenting avidity of morbid hedonists…

They carry on sitting there… Tired, but peaceful in the soothing semi-obscurity of the night. A spontaneous harmony has settled in their souls for a moment…

'Runar,' Mirdja says in a quiet, comforting voice, 'did you know beforehand that I could be more wicked than anyone in the whole world?'

'I did, Mirdja, and I also knew that no one in the whole world could be as good and kind as you. You are everything all at once… like the dream of life itself…'

'Dreams should remain dreams, remote and unattainable. What a thorough disappointment it is to try and hold them close. As you can see now.'

'Well, dreams eventually turn into something essential: destiny… You have become my destiny, Mirdja.'

'A poor destiny, and a poor man, who speaks so. A woman cannot be a man's destiny. You have to be able to win me, tether me, tame me, lead me, you have to be stronger than I am, then everything will be all right…'

'One's destiny cannot be tethered, Mirdja, and neither can you. Duress is a poison to you…'

'But so is acquiescence, it just provokes me. You have to rule over me without duress…'

'There are natures that are simply not made to be ruled over, and they never submit to it. Like yours.'

'But man was made to rule over woman…'

'And you were made to rule over all men.'

'But I'm still a woman… Well, I must say it is very curious… The human being in me loathes all forms of submission and force, but the woman in me craves it. It is very curious… indeed… I suppose marriage is just not suited to someone like me…'

'No…'

They are silent.

'But I should have realized it from the start,' Mirdja, deep in thought, went on as if to herself, 'and of course I did. I have behaved badly towards you, my poor friend. You could never have guessed the half of it… Listen Runar, all year long there's been something unclear between us, something mysterious and terrible, don't you agree? Something forbidding and chilling to the soul… something that can't be put into words… It is only during my fits of rage that you have managed to reach my wilful soul… I could not be open and calm before now, before this dim, cool summer evening, this is the first time since we were married. It's all been too close until now… It's only now I feel I can look dispassionately upon our mutual unhappiness, this evening I can almost be kind. I would like to tell you the story of my soul from the moment this wall descended between us… It happened when the cold frost of formalities set in… And ever since, there has been something harsh and inhospitable in the air… But before then, do you remember, we used to dream together… about how together we would find strength and freedom, how we would be the pioneers of a new order, leaving behind everything shallow, sinister, and false… Or that was your dream anyway, and I adopted it because I too hoped to become whole and committed, with a wholesome love…'

'But you were unable to become whole and committed…'

'And you were unable to take me out of myself, and away from that sinister and shallow and false life that we both hated… Quite the opposite! Before, it was only a concept, a distant, contemptible shadow, now it weighed down upon me like a mountain, so real, crushing, and overpowering… And it came together with you… It was the tedious side of your life… You had warned me about it earlier, but I didn't fully understand it then. Only now… from experience. Now I know the right words to describe that abstract evil I have instinctively loathed all my life: financial constraint, making ends meet, livelihood, career prospects, propriety in all things — behaviour, thought, dress, morality, and love… Yes, where love is concerned, the word for propriety is marriage. And so my emotional life had to become a matter of propriety, it required the presence of a prelate dressed in black, with his biblical chapter and verse, that self-satisfied agent of church and society, exclusive purveyors of bliss, stroking his long, white beard, and bestowing his blessings over me. Oh! When that thought first entered my head I jumped as if I had been bitten by a snake, and I pushed it away in disgust, it was a shameful and base notion. How was such a thing even possible! How could we ever allow an external, alien presence to touch the fine, tender mysticism of our souls! Never. It was offensive. What did we care about the common rabble's blessings and curses! If I had matters to discuss with God, I didn't need someone interceding on my behalf… And as far as love was concerned — and indeed — you… You had never before asked permission of anyone, neither councillor nor clergy, but now, when the matter involved me, now was the moment, that shameful and public transfer of goods… And it really did happen. That Beast of

Armageddon was awakened, society, which I had hated all my life but never known.[132] There it was. — In the form of your parents. And that made it all the more bitter. I wouldn't have wished this on either of us. Please understand me correctly! You know my bohemian background, the unprejudicial freedom I have grown up in. An undisciplined outsider, I have always smiled derisively at society, and at all those who submit like slaves to its hypocritical rules, or at least I smiled like a spoiled child with no knowledge of what it means to scuffle with it, to fight for life or death. And now, that necessary evil I had avoided suddenly rose before me as a new authority, now of all times, just as I was at the most sensitive turning point in my life… You loved your parents dearly, I could see that, and they loved you, and I found it beautiful. But they were old school, members of the clergy — the very estate I had, despite myself, always loathed, for being representative of all the falsehood on earth. And they were good people, I could see that too — and who would dream of fighting the good — and they were old… It would have broken their hearts to know that you, a free man, had taken up with a free woman, they would have cursed you for breaking the seventh commandment.[133] And I felt I didn't have the right to come between you, as an orphan I found your relationship strange and wonderful and sacred… And that's when I started fighting against myself. I tried to talk sense to the rebel in me, along these lines: just go through with the formalities! These bureaucratic conventions are necessary while society is still so morally abject. The names of married couples are recorded to protect the position of the children. And it makes no difference who officiates over such practices, a priest or whoever. That person disappears from view and is never seen again. — These were wise words, I know that. What did a brief, formal litany matter if it helped avoid an irreparable rift, for your sake and theirs… But from the moment of that first quiet act of weighing things in the balance, the first night-owl flew screeching into my soul, and it's been there screeching ever since… But it was only when we were standing there before your father like two custodial half-wits that I noticed it… He in his black vestment reading the rites of matrimony, that revolting nonsense, with such ridiculous solemnity, and people weeping around us. I was boiling and fuming inside, I felt like flinging every word back at him like a filthy rag… At that moment my anger mounted like the raging sea, and contempt floated on its surface like green bile, but in its hidden depths lay the worst of all: self-loathing… Yes, Runar, that was the

[132] Revelation 13 mentions a beast from the sea and a beast from the earth, both of which are present at the battle of Armageddon at the end of time. The 'beast from the earth' is also called a false prophet.
[133] The commandment is 'Thou shalt not commit adultery', which is the sixth commandment in Finnish tradition, as Onerva states in the original, but it is commonly referred to as the seventh commandment in English interpretations of the Bible's Exodus 20. The Finnish word 'adultery' (*aviorikos*, literally 'marital crime') covers both extra-marital and pre-marital relations.

worst, and ever since I have been lost. I am no longer as lofty as I was, because I have sold out to the bourgeoisie for a pittance, in order to fit in with the rest of society and in order not to "offend one of these little ones"…[134] Oh, I can still hear those terrible words with which your father blessed — no, cursed us… Why did it have to be your father! Because ever since then I've nursed a secret hatred of him, an unrelenting resentment, and of you too… Oh Runar, forgive me, I can't help it! I almost hate you simply for the fact that you are not an orphaned vagabond, not free as a bird. You shouldn't have anything dear, anything to lose but me. You should be unattached, fallen to earth all alone as I am, alone and free. Then I could follow you to the ends of the earth, faithful and obedient as a slave, but with the same majestic pride in my breast. That would suit me, the restless princess of the travellers' camp-sites. That would be the kind of life and love for me! Then I would really be able to love with a wholesome love. I would be different and you would be different, and it would only be our deep longing for each other that would maintain our eternal love… But now that the laws of an alien bureaucracy have come between us, ostensibly strengthening our relationship, I simply feel like breaking things all the time. "Remember that your marriage is sacred and binding. What God has joined together, let no one put asunder!"[135] Ha ha ha! How often God joins together and blesses the cursed, how often God curses the blessed, by allowing the clergy to do his work. But I will add this: I recognize no concept of marriage. I am yours for every day that you still rally to conquer me, and for every night that I can still choose you freely for my lover over all others. You have to win me with the undying flame of your love, with the endless art and ingenuity of your wit, Runar, do you hear me, so that no one else can get close to my soul. Because I am under a curse now, do you see, which is resolutely pulling me away from you. I can't help it. I can only be kind and faithful within the limits of freedom… Oh Runar, I can see you suffering… I've hurt you again… Why did I even speak!'

'No, no, speak, you must speak Mirdja! Tell me everything, all the weight you have been carrying in your heart all year… Then everything hard and unsurmountable between us will disappear. It's not enough to sense things about each other, we must be able to hear them too, only then can we be true friends to one another. Yes, I have been aware that you hate the people that I love through the bond of blood, my parents… But neither of us can help it! That too is our fate…'

It is beginning to dawn. The contours of objects are becoming clear and concrete once more… And Mirdja's features seem hard again, almost sharp…

---

[134] Matthew 18. 6: 'But whoso shall offend one of these little ones which believe in me, it were better for him that a millstone were hanged about his neck, and that he were drowned in the depth of the sea.'

[135] Matthew 19. 6: 'Wherefore they are no more twain, but one flesh. What therefore God hath joined together, let not man put asunder.'

Runar makes an effort to carry on speaking:

'Their visit annoys you. Shall I write and tell them not to come?'

'They are coming to see you, you miss and need them, what's it got to do with me, as long as I can keep out of it…'

'I don't want them here now. I'll tell them not to come.'

'On what grounds?'

'On whatever…'

'You see. Always lies, always pretexts. What a murky cloud you have perpetually immersed them in! Not a spark of truth ever penetrates it. And now you've dragged me into it as well. You have lied for both of us, play-acted for both of us, pretended we are completely different from the people we really are. I can't do this anymore. This charade is a crime against the sacred path of progress. Let your parents come! You keep on lying if you want to! I want to speak the truth now.'

'Listen Mirdja, I have never asked you to lie, only to show them some understanding and sensitivity. It is much easier for us to understand them, than for them to understand us. They are half a century behind us. There is no need to offend them on purpose, to stir up all the contradictions in their presence. It is pointless and heartless towards the love that has put us on this enlightened path. It's our place to be understanding…'

'Understanding, oh, is that all!' Mirdja interrupts him bitterly, her impatience twisting the corners of her mouth. 'So little to ask! They are most welcome, I know my part: a little rehearsal in the usage of courtesies, a delightful little masquerade ball on our toes, a little resumé of last Sunday's sermon for him, a little list of name-day cake flavourings for her,[136] all in all just a pretty little fairy tale, a little conventionality, a little sensitivity so their hearts won't break, that's all! But I'm the one who has to play this little performance of understanding, me! And my pain, my self-loathing, the slow poisoning of my soul, does that count for nothing? No, no! I have no right to ask for understanding, for sensitivity, for the right to my life!'

Mirdja bursts into tears of hysteria.

'Darling, darling Mirdja, calm down my dear friend! I understand you only too well. I didn't mean anything like that. But what are we to do, we are both so terribly unhappy…'

'But how can you lecture me on sensitivity, me, as if I wasn't already delicate enough on behalf of both others and myself. Is it not for the sake of others that I have been squirming and grovelling and smiling while the anguish gripped me, keeping silent while the anger washed over me, been a deceitful, duplicitous coward denying myself for their sake, to spare them, to

---

[136] A name-day is the day of the year associated with a person's baptismal name, usually that of a biblical character or saint. Name-day celebrations are particularly widespread in countries where Catholicism and Orthodoxy prevail. In the Nordic countries, the Lutheran Church has kept some Catholic traditions, including the celebration of name-days.

pity them, to be good like you! I know what it's like, and what price I have paid for it. That is why I now dare to say: may goodness and pity be damned! I want to be wicked, wicked and callous to the bottom of my heart, only then will I have the strength to be true to myself and regain my self-respect. Oh bless you, bright-eyed hatred which breaks us free from unnatural bonds, which dares to trample even over the bodies of its loved ones! Oh, bless you, gentle contempt, which follows in the wake of its brother and helps a poor abandoned, burnt-out soul to smile again!... There is no middle way. Why do you keep looking for one Runar? Oh that's right, you're part of that lineage, the middle-way lineage, in whose veins flows the blood of compromise, the ancient, meek blood of philistines. Your extensive family tree cannot boast one single honest, plain-spoken devil. So how could you possibly recognize its colours of black and red! All your artlessness, all your strength and rectitude is a dodge, an acquired wisdom, a replica. We two are made of different blood, hopelessly different blood.'

In her excitement Mirdja has been pacing up and down the floor. She disappears suddenly without bidding goodnight.

For a long time she lies motionless in bed, staring at the heavy clouds of the early hours. For the first time, she is seriously contemplating separation...

Runar is thinking the same. They both lie awake... Thinking and suffering again...

III

~

The night is chequered as a carnival, and long as eternity, for one who lies awake.

Mirdja's sleep grew shorter and her waking darkness longer, just like the nights in late summer around her...

Lately, she rarely slept at all. She would lie for hours with her eyes open, staring at some point in the corner of the room... Staring for hours at some specific point... until the darkness would come alive, bursting into strange images and waves of colour...

It seemed to Mirdja that she had once experienced something very similar long ago. In early childhood — yes — that was it... When the autumn nights would turn pitch black, her soul would fill with a strange festive light — Christmas. She would lie awake then too, wide-eyed and motionless like now, staring into the dark until it dissolved into her eyes... And then stars would shower down... Bright, red, yellow, green drops of light like a cascade of fire... It was so beautiful and delightful!

This is the only thing Mirdja remembers of her early childhood. A shower of stars on Christmas night! And all dark nights were Christmas nights back then...

What it really was, blurred vision or an over-active imagination, Mirdja could not explain. But once upon a time she had lived under a shower of stars, of that she was certain...

It felt a little the same now as back then. Mirdja lay in her bed and waited... But those familiar old stars simply would not fall, no matter how much she wished it. She tried every trick she could think of, forcing her eyes to stay wide open until they hurt, keeping them only slightly ajar, using unnatural points of focus to help create light effects, stars... Nothing worked!

She kept on staring relentlessly at the corner of her room. There was something uncanny there after all! The contours of an evil-looking head started to form...

No, not such images! No, only stars...!

This began to disturb her. Peeved, she closed her eyes tight. But she couldn't fall asleep. The chequered carnival in her soul went into full swing...

It was the same old stuff... Thoughts, memories taking shape in loneliness, distant dreams which turned into mirages in the silent darkness...

All this was most unhealthy, she knew that. It only led to her bad temper during the daytime, to her incurable nervous agitation... But in spite of this! — Or perhaps precisely because of this, she always longed to escape the day for night and her night visions. She pined passionately for their quiet, comfort-ing presence, their lofty, delicate intangibility. For they were wonderfully intangible, those beautiful, frail dream-roses, which did not flower for anyone else, which could not stand even the remote presence of another, not even Runar. Runar understood this and knew to keep his distance. But he suffered, oh how he suffered to see how the glow of this wonderful tropical loneliness faded and shrank at his touch, and to know that he, even he was doomed to remain an outsider for all time, a mere onlooker to that 'noli mi tangere' soul...[137]

And this made Mirdja suffer too. Because it was Runar, if anyone, with whom she would have liked to share her mystic fantasies. Her single, great, understanding companion. But she couldn't. And it was all her fault. Runar was perfect, or so she often felt. He had surrounded her with all that was good and beautiful... Ah, not entirely...

And Mirdja recalled the one difficult, painful issue in their lives: Runar's parents. They came as part of the bargain, the most incongruous of incon-gruous intrusions, threatening to smother everything within her, everything except her bitterness...

Of course they didn't keep their distance, and neither could they have been expected to. They had the right to be close, the eternal right of blood-love, but the right bestowed by mutual understanding, by the natural union of souls, this they did not have. But they knew nothing of this, and it wasn't something they could be told without offending their most profound sensibilities...

Mirdja understood only too well Runar's terrible position as go-between, his fine but useless efforts to protect both parties, both his nearest and dearest, from getting hurt... He had really done everything in his power to shield Mirdja's proud, sensitive soul. But he had not succeeded. And why? Because Runar had also tried to shield those others. It was this endless treading the middle ground, this endless need to negotiate and compromise, that made their situation so painfully hopeless. It was this that brought out Mirdja's cruel streak: exaggerating her hardships, twisting the knife in the wound... As if all she understood was herself... Because it was so horribly clear to her that she was a prisoner, that her life would never again be free of falsehood... that mundane, deadly, little falsehood...

And all this simply because of that stupid woman, Anna the pastor's wife, and the pastor himself. Why were they not smitten from her path by the fire of God, why was justice not done! True justice, spiritually brighter and greater justice, her justice! Or was the goodness of unseeing souls something eternal, invincible, the final apocalyptic destruction, and were all the Annas of this world the saints of our last days? An Anna had crossed

---

[137] Latin for 'touch me not', the words spoken by Jesus to Mary Magdalene, according to the Bible, John 20. 17.

her father's path — And now another had crossed his daughter's. Ah, accursed…!

Ssh… quiet! The goodness of unseeing souls is invincible after all. Even the curses rebound…

A memory flashes like lightning in front of Mirdja's eyes, a strange memory, oddly moving and humbling. She remains staring straight ahead, cowed and silenced by it…

It was something that had happened quite recently. Only two months ago. Just when she had braced her soul for the most diabolical encounter… But it was she, Mirdja, who was smitten by the fire of God, and nothing had gone as expected…

The memory persists…

Mirdja lying sick, very sick. Her head burning with a dry, persistent fever, her brain audibly whirring… but Anna sits by her bedside morn and night, morn and night… She puffs up her pillow and changes her compress… Whenever Mirdja opens her eyes she sees the old woman's fond gaze and her ever industrious fingers busy with her old-fashioned crochet…

But Mirdja is seriously ill. The idea of death enters her consciousness every now and then. She trembles at the thought, but she no longer has the will to live… But Anna is stronger than Mirdja now, she is determined to cure her, and Mirdja is cured…

But the more her physical illness subsides, the more acute is the secret pain in her soul. For Mirdja now understands what is going on around her. Sacrifices are being made for her sake, others are exposing themselves to the danger of infection, others are suffering and growing pale. And not even in the most secret chambers of their hearts do they harbour the slightest complaint or reproach… And now Mirdja understands that stupid Anna is the most perfect sister of mercy… and that she is at her service right now.

And this affects Mirdja. She would like to thank her, it would be the proper thing to do, but she cannot. Her stubborn tongue catches in her throat. But sometimes it happens that the pain is so acute that Mirdja cannot control herself. She suddenly grabs hold of the old woman's hand and feverishly whispers: my dear woman, don't worry about me, don't grow pale because of me, it's too much, too much!… And her agitation erupts into violent tears…

But this just makes the old woman a thousand times more solicitous. Her show of affection knows no bounds. Over and over, she assures Mirdja how dear she is, how very dear…

And Mirdja can see that she is telling the truth.

Mirdja's head falls back on her pillow, tired and heavy. Nothing will ever change…

Mirdja's chest and shoulders still tremble with suppressed sobs, but Mirdja swallows her distress and shuts her eyes. She pretends to sleep. Pretence was always the only way out! And even now it has the desired effect. Anna tip-toes out of the room…

Ah, what bliss it was for Mirdja's overwrought nerves to be alone at last! What bliss to release her pent-up frustration, to feel the mask's weight lift from her face…

For Anna was only familiar with Mirdja's disguise, not Mirdja herself. It was the disguise Anna cared for, not Mirdja herself. She had never even seen the real Mirdja, the Mirdja who was her mortal enemy.

Why did Mirdja have neither the right nor the heart to express her own truth! Why was it so? In her soul she could have cried it out like a dying beast, in terror and pain… at any time.

She was a poisonous flower cultivated in an unnatural habitat, sick to breaking point, helpless and incurable. Sick in that every caress and smile on her nurse's lips inflamed her and made her worse. Such was her sickness…

But Anna had no idea. Ignorance is bliss, thankfully! For some people it is even a lifeline! But this infuriated Mirdja. Why was it that those who had been taught since the cradle to be wary of a wolf in sheep's clothing, why was it they were incapable of seeing deeper than the fleece, why was it they even lacked the wisdom of herd instinct? It was nothing but stupidity!

How was it that Anna could not see that even now it was chiefly Mirdja's soul that was in pain, her soul that was writhing as if in death, wailing and crying and trembling under the heavy weight of her silence! No, Anna's grey child-like eyes had never looked into a soul which burned with the fires of hell itself. A child's eyes are for heaven alone! 'Except ye become as little children, ye shall not enter into the kingdom of heaven.'[138] That was the thrust of their teachings. True perhaps but a base and stupid lesson none-theless!

And yet here she was, Mirdja, the great blasphemer and rebel, behaving like a humble disciple herself, promoting the coming of the kingdom of heaven on earth. Lying and despising herself for it yet lying again, in order to allow the good child that Anna was to enter the gates of heaven unscathed. No, indeed, it was not her own mercy Mirdja was seeking…

What an altruist you are, evil, selfish Mirdja!

How stupid you are, unable to find a better answer, wise, self-sufficient Mirdja!

How weak you are, slain by a fly, strong, commanding Mirdja!

Strange thoughts!

Mirdja laughs out loud.

And the hellfires laugh with her…

Should she still believe in fate and purpose? Or in herself? What use was faith to someone in shackles? But who, who applied the shackles…?

---

[138] Matthew 18. 3.

It was all a riddle, nothing but riddles...

The night is long as eternity, and heavy as the universe, for one who lies awake plagued by thoughts...

And no sign of an answer...

IV

Autumn has truly arrived, in all its glorious carnal colour.
Here and there, the treetops are already singed with the red and yellow of decline, and the rugged stretch of the coast shimmers with the pale purple hue of heather.

But the windows of the Söderberg villa look onto the bluff, which glows blood-red in the sunshine. The leaves of the blueberry bushes flimmer like thousands of vibrant butterfly wings spread ready for flight at any moment...

Mirdja sets off on her usual solitary walk in the forest. 'I am off to talk with the spirits,' she laughs to Runar as she leaves. So has she done every day throughout the summer...

For Mirdja still possesses those play-acting inclinations she had in childhood. She still amuses herself by assuming different roles, even now donning the soul of the mad bride. Because she knows how beautiful she is, she knows that her gestures are like music in the eyes of every mortal... Ah, how she enjoys being herself, alone in the empty forest — with a clear conscience... She has after all committed so much evil...

Mirdja saunters aimlessly through the autumn woods. The cool, intoxicating smell of the damp moss fills her nostrils, and the wind shudders through the dense spruces...

Mirdja hums to herself... And how sweetly the soft, distant echo of her voice on the horizon soothes her ears.

But suddenly she is answered by another voice.

Startled, Mirdja stops in her tracks. A man's voice, broken and babbling...

Mirdja's cheeks flush red in vexation. What scoundrel dared to approach her?

But in the same instant the answer arrives: a middle-aged man with a knapsack on his back, wearing bright-coloured socks.

He has a madcap look in his grey eyes which dart every which way, and large freckles adorn his shiny face like bright buttons.

What an odd fellow, thinks Mirdja.

'Ah, good day there, ha-ha-haa-sh,' says the oncomer, mixing his laugh with strange, soft sibilant sounds.

'Good day,' Mirdja answers, laughing as well despite herself.

'Such a beauty you are and not proud at all,' says the stranger, scratching the ground with his foot and bowing gawkily. 'I'm a former gentleman, but who may you be?'

Mirdja realizes the fellow must be something of a half-wit, but the encounter amuses her, and she answers in the same tone:

'They call me Mirdja… But where do you spring from?'

'Wherever I lay my head is my home, m'lady,' answers the vagabond, offering few words but more ridiculous gestures…

'So who are you then?'

'Just some mama's boy, ha-ha-haa-sh.'

'Don't you have a name of your own, or your father's name?'

'Father's name, ha-ha-haa-sh! My father once came to my mother by night and by night he left, and one morning my mother led me to the open road, and that's where I've been ever since, tchah,' explained this 'mama's boy' almost solemnly. But his eyes laughed with sweet joy and his ugly mouth twisted into a good-natured grin…

'And you've been wandering the world ever since…?'

'Tchah, along the very shore of the wide world. Have you ever heard of it, m'lady? It's where necklaces, like the one you have, tarnish badly and there's a lot of thievery… Have you ever seen a thief? — But anyway m'lady, shall we get down to business, I have sewing pins, hairpins, darning needles, all kinds of pins and needles…'

Mirdja is increasingly amused by this funny fellow. This was what life made of those who were ready to throw themselves in its lap, no questions asked. It took everything, and left just one thought, one obsession, as in her father's case… But was there ever any greater wisdom than the wisdom uttered by the minds of the mad…?

'Come and spend the night in my home. The shore of the wide world must offer scant warmth…'

'Ah, m'lady, it offers warmth as it offers cold… The freedom to feel warm and to freeze…'

My dream, my dream! Mirdja sighs heavily in her heart.

And Mirdja takes the 'mama's boy' home with her…

'This a distant relative of mine, from the wide world,' she says to Runar.

'You have the weirdest notions,' Runar, who is in a bad mood, gives a short laugh…

'We both seem to suffer from the same fault,' Mirdja scoffs. 'We dislike each other's relatives. Though this fellow is a very pleasant guest. There's no need hide your true colours with him, no need to pretend or lie. He has already seen the truth in the world. Looked it in the eye till his soul fractured… He is mad…'

'The mad are always unpleasant…'

'You clearly speak from experience, my poor wise friend. For my part, being mad myself, I find nothing unpleasant under the sun except for the lies and obligations that this world's wise promote. If you were as orphaned and free and mad as that wanderer, I would be much happier…'

Runar doesn't answer her… 'Mama's boy' stays overnight.

But the whole night long, Runar cannot sleep. He is plagued by restless thoughts and anger, and something more, which he dare not even admit to himself — jealousy.

V

~

The last day in the countryside.

Yellow leaves are falling constantly, and Mirdja and Runar sit by the window watching this great downpour of decay around them. The blaze in the fireplace crackles unevenly. Half-packed trunks lie on the floor, forlorn and sorry looking. Ruin lies in every direction...

But Mirdja and Runar are silent; and in their silence they share the same thought...

They both remember the previous, difficult winter in town. And their wordlessness expresses their secret fear and anticipation — on the cusp of a new winter. Was it going to be the same as last winter?

They instinctively look at each other at the same time...

'Would you like anything now?' Mirdja asks suddenly.

'I don't know. Why do you ask?'

'I just wish you could feel good, now and then at least, feel good in my company for once. Tell me the truth, do you feel good now?'

'No... Do you?'

'No...'

They fall silent again. The darkness draws in. The leaves carry on falling...

Then Runar speaks quietly, sadly:

'Tell me Mirdja, when did you last feel good?'

'It's an alien concept to me. I have never in my life felt good...'

'But when did you last feel the best you could?'

'Don't ask. Who can choose between shadow and light! I always feel good and bad at the same time... It's always been like that... I don't remember any other way... But when might be the last time you felt good...? It must surely be in the days... before I came along.'

'I've never felt good either... The best I've ever felt was with you though, Mirdja... It's different for you... You expected more and were disappointed, and the darkness around you has simply grown denser...'

'Do you know who experiences disappointment? Not one who imagines, but one who believes. I have never been able to believe in anything, but all the possible lives I could lead I have already lived out in my imagination. So my disappointments have always been slight, this time too... But the pain of imagining has been terrible... It was an act of violence against myself, the moment I came to you, because I foresaw all of this and common sense cried out to me: don't be mad! And my feelings too... But I've never told you this...'

'And do you think my conscience was calm when I welcomed you in? My common sense screamed all kinds of things to me, much worse than yours. But back then I wouldn't listen to anything that would keep us apart. Because you were so wonderful, and already so close... My love was weak and selfish... I kept quiet and allowed you to come...'

'And would you allow me to go now?'

'Be it for your own sake, if you go. My love has grown strong enough to withstand even separation...'

'Yes of course, now that the agony of being together has grown insufferable... That is called disappointment... Naturally it can withstand separation...'

'You refuse to believe I love you. Believe me I do, believe me!'

'Impossible... I sap the life out of you and cause you pain. But I wish you no harm, my friend. I will go, forget about me as if I had never existed...'

'You will live in my heart for all eternity Mirdja, I can never forget you...'

'So the pain I cause you has scarred you for life...?'

'You still behave as if you are talking to someone who doesn't love you. I even love the scars you have left on me, Mirdja. It's my love for you which has marked me for life...'

'Then you are an *Übermensch*. Whenever has anyone loved their own unhappiness? Because it's here now.'

'What is?'

'The friction.'

'Do you remember what you said about that once?'

'May the friction begin... It was the arrogance of inexperience.'

'Yes, destiny needs no bidding.'

'You are wiser than I. Because it's true we are one another's destiny. We cannot evade each other anymore. It's too late for that. I can never leave you Runar, even though I should, I can't do it... And I would love you, if it weren't for the fact you are my destiny. Can you understand that it's hard to love one's destiny?'

'One can't beat one's destiny, and it's never a friend...'

'Why can't one beat one's destiny? And why can't it be a friend?'

'Because destiny is nothing more than one's own spirit fighting itself...'

'That's true... That's exactly it, the answer, the whole answer to the riddle. Where did you get that idea from, Runar?'

'It's the only way I can explain why we haven't already parted company a thousand times, why we're still together, even though being together is constant, debilitating torture to both our spirits. We are fighting against ourselves through each other. Everything hateful and harmful in ourselves we also see in the other.'

'What unusual things you are saying this evening, Runar. It puts everything in a strange new light... One's destiny makes one face oneself... So it is conceit that draws a person to his or her destiny...'

'People seek until they find something that resembles them. And then they think that they have found their equilibrium, but that's precisely when the fight begins...'

'Yes, at first I too thought you resembled me, but when the fight began, I thought I was mistaken. But I suppose you're right, we are simply too similar. Too emotionally sensitive, too immersed in thought. Wherever we go, we turn our life into a sufferance. I understand everything now in the light of this idea, and feel as though I have always known it. It's why sometimes I hate you twice over, detest you, get bored with you as with something so unchangingly familiar, as one can only get bored with one's own relentless perspective. Yet we expect of each other new stimulus, new values and impulses. And when we don't get them, we turn cold with irony and pride, as if faced with emptiness and stupidity. Because we mistake each other for our mirror image and disdain one another for our mimicry and lack of independence. And all the while we want something new, which differs from our self. As if that were even possible for us, we who understand ourselves and each other only in the light of our own individuality. Because our whole lives have been a process of raising the exponential power of our own egos, at least mine has. And that's how it will always be. There's no getting away from it. We hate each other but love each other even more. That is also why we cannot leave each other. Even if we were to separate, our own conceit would be so great that it would drive us back into each other's arms, to face our own image. But when we stay together, our hate often grows greater than love, and the hatred is followed by dispassionate, icy disdain, which is even greater than hatred. Or if we manage to stay calm and look upon each other kindly for a moment, we may soften into gentle tenderness, but only because at that point we feel such pity for our own poor tormented soul, a pity that briefly conquers the hatred and disdain. But I still prefer hatred to pity because I am proud. I always want to believe I shape my own destiny, and when I discover that my own hidden enemy is concealed in my own conflicted personality, I could almost die from the proud fury I feel over my own inertia and helplessness. It's the kind of fury that is felt only by someone who is too strong to obey anyone else, but too weak to be a god...'

Mirdja falls silent. Then she soon continues:

'You have brought me to an astonishing new way of thinking, Runar. I have always felt that even death cannot break us apart, but I have never understood why. Now I know. It is the faith in our own fateful, unhappy union that keeps us together. That's what it is — nothing else, not love, not passion, not lust, not even friendship, with its capacity for limitless sacrifice — nothing other than a fateful force of nature... At least that's how it is for me... What about you? No, you are different. Sometimes you seem so simply perfect that I am almost afraid of you, and then I am almost forced to believe in the unbelievable, that you do love me after all, Runar...'

'I do love you...'

'My poor darling friend, my hapless sweetheart, how dreadfully I have violated our life, our only life, which is disintegrating into madness because of me.'

'And your life has been destroyed by my hand. I am a doomed man…'

'You have the gentlest hands in the world…'

'But in the service of dark forces…'

'I myself have been the dark force…'

'Don't say that, never…!'

Mirdja is quiet. The coals glow in the hearth. The wind blows outside.

'And that's why I should go away from you,' she continues quietly.

'Yes, you have to break free of me. I am a ball and chain to you.'

'But even if I were to go to the ends of the earth, you would never stop living in my heart, never, never… Our destiny is upon us… So what! We understand each other. We have raised our own self-indulgence to the power of two. We have to endure one another. Don't you think? And as truly as I love myself, so do I also love you. Just as much, do you understand, I love you with just as much torment and scorn and reproach and rage. My darling, my darling…'

'We will wear each other to the bone… You should have a finer end, Mirdja, Mirdja.'

'I want my flame to die with you Runar. I will never have anything more beautiful than you on this earth. You have something no one else has: your love for me, for me…'

'You finally believe me…?'

'I've always believed you. I've had to, against my will… And it feels so good… Listen to the autumn drawing in… In the howl of the wind… Everything will disappear Runar, except your love for me… Let me lie in your arms, so. — This is good. I will close my eyes and listen only to your heartbeat, nothing else. I am happy now, Runar…'

The coals gradually turn black.

But in those two hearts, love burns again, great and whole.

And in that moment, neither are afraid of the winter. Even though the autumn howls, grim and baleful, outside. Even though the ruinous downpour has begun…

VI

~

They were back in town now, both with more willing and determined mindsets than usual.

Having been unable to abandon their common existence, it had become imperative to take control of it... Imperative... One needed something to fight for, after all...

And Mirdja had in mind many effective laws of equilibrium, much calm and collected reasoning — in the event of any possible conflict.

She had analysed her current position with a cool, clear head.

She was married. So be it. It was no great good fortune. But neither need it be any great misfortune. And if she really was going to subjugate herself to the confines of such a trivial, common event, one which tended to affect almost everyone in this life, she only had herself to blame. She had to be able to live her life beyond the scope of common events. Besides, she had always known that whom she married was inconsequent. Marriage had its own specific disagreeable characteristics, but there was no reason to allow the disagreeable side of it to affect her. What was it they did in France? Every year thousands of marriages took place, all devoid of even the slightest trace of personal inclination, and there were very few unhappy unions among them. And why should there be? It was an exchange of polite formalities; the whole business was resolved with a little social skill. In the morning a small friendly greeting at the breakfast table: 'bonjour ma chère' — 'bonjour mon ami',[139] a polite peck on the hand, a pretty smile in response, and all is well. Because the French take such matters the right way. Marriage, one of society's many hollow obligations! Under such crude conditions, only the mad would try to imbue the practice with an ideal of perfection. Mirdja too had been mad. She had been ridiculous and doomed in her northern European, earnestly serious view of life, which refuses to recognize form without content yet fails to create any other form for its content than that which is rule-abiding and widely approved. She had lived in the pursuit of perfection as defined by ordinary run-of-the-mill folk, and thus, like they, she had allowed her bitterness and disappointment to engulf her dearest one. She had lived tactlessly. She had been petty and mean, believing she was a slave...

What foolish beliefs, as if one were not enslaved or free only insofar as one submitted to enslavement or kept oneself free.

From now on, she was going to be free. To live as if there were no such

---

[139] 'Hello my dear' and 'Hello my friend' (French).

things in the world as circumstances or marriage or mitigating factors or other people, only herself. She was to fulfil only her own will, nothing else. Then she would be free. And others could rejoice or suffer, love or hate her. What did it matter to her! Never again would she be inclined to defend faint hearts at the expense of her own, as she once did. Those who could not endure her could move aside or be crushed. And anyway, living in a world full of insufferable people was a torment no one could escape.

But there were also other kinds of people in this world, people in whose company life was beautiful and a joy. This was something Mirdja had almost forgotten. She had lived for so long buried in their inward relationship as a couple. Twisting and turning it every which way. Not even God would have survived such purgatory unscathed.

She had been mad to spend so long weaving the sharp threads of her lonely fantasies around and about herself! It cannot have been at all healthy.

But now she was ready to mingle among people as she once did.

Each would go his and her own way, husband and wife. And they would return to one another richer than before, their souls brimming with mysterious, stimulating fragrances and strange, breathtaking impressions absorbed in the company of strangers... The scene would be filled with the sweet, sensuous attraction of newness...

Their previous lifestyle had been all wrong. Constantly, giddily grasping at each other. Such boring convention...

This was the most unfortunate of unfortunate tendencies between two people who are supposed to endure each other for a long time!

A life of half-insights and half-confessions! Half-understanding, half-faith, and plenty of infinite obscurity between them, unfathomable and never-ending...

All these things went through Mirdja's mind, coolly and clearly. And she felt her soul surging with gentle *joie de vivre* once more, for the first time in many years. She craved variety, new experiences, new conflicts, and the wide world around her.

Was it still the same? She wanted to find out. And all the many souls out there? Had any woman been able to fill any of those places she had left empty? Was she not still the most wonderful and astonishing of all women, the sovereign of souls?

Ah, after two years of inner restraint and repression, she once again yearned to see herself where she belonged, on a pedestal, admired, the object of a thousand futile desires...

Ah, after two years of inner despair she needed to regain her self-confidence and her pride. Then, then maybe she could still make something of herself, an artist, why not...

But first, she had to see souls bowing at her feet once again.

That would make everything better.

VII

And Mirdja did feel better...
In fact, she was a different person entirely.

She went out a lot these days, moving in a variety of circles as she used to. And everywhere she went, she attracted attention with her charm and spirit as only she knew how.

She seemed completely and miraculously recovered from her long, difficult nervous exhaustion. Even at home, she was always bright and smiling, jovial even. No more dramatic scenes. Runar too was a new person in this new atmosphere and the whole world seemed new to her.

And that well-worn thought she could still discern in men's eyes over and over again as they hovered around her, that 'madame, ich liebe Sie',[140] seemed almost amusing to her now.

But what sort of reception might she receive from some of her former conquests? Mirdja hadn't yet come across a single one. And her secret, newly awakened longing for power sought their presence.

Then she ran into Rolf. But it was an unfortunate meeting...

It happened late one evening. The first white winter evening. The snow was falling gently. It covered the autumn silt with its shimmeringly new, downy coat.

The streets were almost empty. Mirdja was walking slowly home, enjoying the deserted white landscape which had so suddenly taken the place of the usual herds of bobbing heads...

All was quiet, clean, empty... There was just one figure, one lone pedestrian walking up ahead. A single black dot in the white wilderness. A blot on the landscape! If it wasn't for that dot, she could almost imagine she was alone in the world...

Mirdja takes another step...

The black dot grows bigger. How come it wasn't moving? So it wasn't a person after all...

Mirdja is startled. Anything unexplained can turn into a ghost in the human imagination.

But no, it was a person. It was... and Mirdja is startled again...

Was it possible? Mirdja recognized that figure... It was her old surprise encounter on a winter night all over again: Rolf. His hands in his pockets, his head tilted into his collar, just like before. This is how she remembered him

---

[140] 'Madam, I love you' (German).

the best. She had no summer images of him in mind, she would hardly have recognized him in summertime.

Mirdja's heart starts to beat with unexpected emotion and excitement…

They hadn't seen each other for so many important years. — What would they say to one another now?

At that moment Rolf disappears behind the corner, turning into a side-street. Mirdja starts to run after him.

A passer-by laughs at her and calls out…But Mirdja doesn't stop to listen, she just runs on.

Now she is right behind him. She is sure she wasn't mistaken.

But she does not dare catch up to him. She can hardly catch her breath, her knees are shaking and her fingertips tingle at the excitement of seeing him again.

So Mirdja begins walking in pace with him, to conceal her proximity. — This is what a timorous lover must feel like, she thinks.

At last Rolf glances behind him.

Only then does Mirdja dare to take a step forward.

'I've been running after you, Rolf, for some time,' she manages to gasp.

Rolf looked almost too surprised to grasp the situation…

'Mirdja, you…'

They held out their hands to each other and there were a few of moments of awkward silence.

Mirdja stole a veiled look at Rolf and in the dim lamplight it seemed to her as if he had substantially aged since their last meeting.

She sighed…

Neither knew where to begin…

'What are you doing here, where have you been all this time, I haven't seen you at all, and what are you doing with yourself these days?' Mirdja blurted out as a nervous start.

Rolf looked at Mirdja strangely and then said, with some emphasis:

'And what about you Mirdja, what are you doing with yourself these days, since you know to ask such questions…? In the old days you never asked me what I was doing — but perhaps a question like that belongs to your new position in the world… If what I've heard is not inaccurate, you are now the honourable lady wife of a professor in a state-funded educational establishment. So you've learned to pay attention to whether people are doing their duty to society…'

All the blood in Mirdja's heart rose to her cheeks. She was almost choking with indignation and outrage.

If the insult had come from anyone other than Rolf, her pride would have had her fling it back a hundred times over. But now such unbearable sorrow and despondency welled up in her soul that all she could say between her tears was:

'Oh Rolf, Rolf, how can you be so unkind, so unkind to me?'

'And there was I thinking,' said Rolf as he stared ahead blankly, 'there was I thinking that it was you who had been unkind to yourself, so unkind as to make my black hair turn grey with grief these past two years. It's strange,' he went on almost to himself, 'how all my friends have gone to the dogs, just like me... Some ruined by drink, some broken by love, others by turning their backs on their gods and selling themselves for the tinkle of gold and — yet others by getting married. But for you, Mirdja, to have chosen this very last, most profane and wicked method of going to seed, that is something I would never have guessed — and I still cannot fathom it. Did you really need the assistance of a priest in order to feel loved!'

And Rolf gave a short laugh.

Mirdja's whole being seethed against Rolf. To behave like a stranger and yet come closer than even a friend might venture!

And Mirdja answered in a caustic tone:

'You have no way of knowing whether I have "gone to seed", and least of all in what manner. But you were always one to fixate on life's outward factors. You stumble over its little pebbles and are always ready to rant about ministers and priests and police officers as if they meant something... You rage against them like a schoolboy.'

'Now you have it all wrong. If I mentioned a priest just now, it was not in rage. You see, people change. The schoolboy phase is a passing one. I have long since given up charging against solid rocks and banging my fists against little stones. It's not good for the health. Hard on the fists, you see. What is, is. Anyone who isn't Don Quixote himself must ultimately acknowledge this sooner or later.[141] There are priests, there are police officers, there is madness, there is falsehood. That's the truth, and the only truth. And if you can't bring yourself to take this one truth too seriously, then there's nothing for it but to laugh, to laugh and never stop laughing. To laugh when you see how deftly life lies, cultured society lies, people lie... And laugh at the few fools who haven't the skill to lie, and are left empty-handed! There are several positions which actually require a very sophisticated standard of lie. And when it comes to priests, they are in a class of their own! I have had many an amusing moment at the expense of their immortal social soul. They are the perfect prototype of contemporary mores. And some idiots have had the nerve to call them stupid. As if the swindled were not more feeble-minded than the

---

[141] Don Quixote is the principal character of the novel *El ingenioso hidalgo Don Quijote de la Mancha* (originally published in two parts, 1605 and 1615) by the Spanish writer Miguel de Cervantes (assumed 1547–1616). It is considered the first modern novel and one of the greatest works of European literature. The tragicomic character of Don Quixote, a member of the lower gentry, lives in an imaginary world of chivalric virtues, which he tries to revive with his actions. In popular usage, Don Quixote denotes an idealist, proud, and honest person who tries to realize, at any cost, their noble though unrealistic ideals which clash with the realities of the mundane world.

swindler. And anyway, priests pass on many professional wisdoms from generation to generation. They have a lot of useful knowledge. They know it is wiser to possess a round belly than an eternal soul, and they know where best to acquire the round belly. Every Sunday they recite a prayer of gratitude to that false idol, that great double dunce, the state and the church, and every weekday they put together smaller units of double dunces, man and wife: may you both be as perfect as your great mentors, the state and the church, are perfect. There is satire in this. Ha ha ha! A wise lot, there's no denying it... Yes, yes, in order to live the good life, there's nothing in this world one needs except the ability to lie, but one must learn to lie so well that it becomes a deep moral conviction. It is the most positive morality in the world because it is based on the laws of necessity and material advantage. And it is also the morality of the church... But it's not your morality Mirdja...'

Mirdja laughed in spite of herself...

'You incurable old sophist. You can't resist talking in paradoxes. The church and the state indeed. When we run into each other on a snowy street once in a hundred years. What do I care if they stand or fall...! So that's all you have to say to me...'

'I was talking about lies,' said Rolf heavily, 'I always talk too much rubbish... But I just meant to ask about one thing I don't understand about you. Why are you trying to lie to life? Because even though you are the finest actress in the world, you don't have the morality of a liar... You don't know how to lie...'

'In what way have I lied to you?'

'Not to me, to yourself and to life...'

'What? What do you know?'

'I don't.'

Rolf turned away from Mirdja.

The snowfall was becoming increasingly dense and heavy...

'It'll soon be impossible to trudge through this thick snow,' Mirdja remarked.

'I would gladly invite you over but I'm currently homeless...'

'Well, what if I wouldn't come, even if you had a home...'

Rolf looked at Mirdja sharply.

'It wouldn't do anymore?'

'Looks that way.'

They walked on for a moment in silence.

'Do you think,' shouted Mirdja suddenly, 'I enjoy seeing you like this? You have become distant and harsh towards me, Rolf. One could almost think you hated me...'

'Or rather that... No, Mirdja, that's not true. I'm the same as ever with you. You know how to see into people's souls... So don't you cling to outward factors either! Listen Mirdja, let's say I do have somewhere to go. And you come sit with me for a while like you used to. Don't refuse, Mirdja, you can see it's impossible to talk out here. The snow numbs the mind. We could go and take a private room somewhere. Couldn't we…?'

Rolf's voice was completely different now. It had a strange tremor of helpless tenderness. It was only now that Mirdja recognized her old friend for the first time. She was instantly won over.

'I'll come with you,' she said.

But as they walked towards the hotel, Mirdja felt secretly ashamed and troubled by the fact that she couldn't invite her old friend to her place as she used to, because she didn't really have a home of her own either, now that she officially owned one. A third soul would be in the way there… And Mirdja felt strangely oppressed and subjugated, as if she were a prisoner…

'This is a bit like old times,' Rolf laughed, when they were finally sitting on the small sofa of their private room.

'Yes,' answered Mirdja sadly, 'Everything is as it used to be except you, Rolf. Why are you so changed? I always imagined things very differently… That we would be constant friends, that we would always encounter each other as only two instinctively compatible souls can — and that we would part as mutually sympathetic friends do, a little less depressed than before. And now everything is so different. How could you be so unkind to me,' Mirdja asked beseechingly, 'the first time you see me again after such a long time?'

'I will always be your friend, but whoever taught you that friends are always good and kind…! You know me… The barrooms have ruined me, I've learned everything except the most important thing: how to lie — that's why I can be a bit of a brute sometimes… Listen, I am your friend Mirdja, and — many's the time I've cried for you…'

'Why?'

'You ask why? You know why. Are you forcing me to be unkind to you again… I already told you. Did you not obtain enough love without getting married…?'

'Who said I was looking for love…?'

'Whatever you were looking for. No amount of searching should have so misguided you. — You must have been very tired at the time Mirdja, how sad…'

'You're wrong, there is no need to feel sorry for me. What can you possibly know about the relationship between two individuals you hardly know?'

'God help me, nothing at all. I'm not talking about that, only about marriage…'

'Which is just an abstract concept to you, an acquired prejudice…'

'Forgive me but it's a very concrete concept, and unpleasantly so. Do you really imagine a person can reach my age without ever having run into that so very concrete construct of society? And in my case, it has happened much too often, unfortunately. It's not possible to live in the clouds… So yes, I know quite enough about that side of life. It's the graveside of life, one should not succumb to it too soon. No, only when there is nothing left in life, no work, no love, no hope, no joy, only then may one bury oneself in marriage. By then it's not so great a sin. But while life and life's purpose still lie ahead, while youth and its fire are still burning, while pride and self-worth still beat in one's heart, to tie oneself to the ball and chain of marriage is unforgivable. Because that's when the bird is in a cage, when the individual is finished, reduced to being only a man's wife or a woman's husband. All paths are closed except those that lead to the cares of family life and Sunday visits. Everything lofty and elevated in the human soul turns into the vice of banality. As if I didn't know all this through and through! Do you remember our old friend Nietzsche's words on the subject…? "Ach diese Armuth der Seele zu Zweien, ach dieser Schmutz der Seele zu Zweien, ach dies erbärmliche Behagen zu Zweien"…'[142]

The closer Rolf touched on the truth, the more Mirdja wished to take cover and defend herself.

'That you may have had your fair share of sordid experiences and that you still remember to quote your Nietzsche by heart, all this I can well believe. But none of it gives you license to draw conclusions about me.'

'You're married…'

'So what. Everybody has relationships…'

'That's different — you are married.'

'It's just a word, a term. It's up to you what you care to call my relation-ship.'

'It's a term that doesn't suit you. You are a woman with more talent than most. And now? What will become of your talent?'

'What do you know about woman and the soil in which her talent can flourish!'

'A talented woman can cultivate her skills in two types of soil, either as a man's comrade, in which case she achieves her greatest possible spiritual brilliance, or as a man's lover, in which case she is the most enchanting of earthly creatures… The rest have two fates: either they remain without a man and turn into dried up, lifeless mummies, or they take shelter in the bawdy prison of Christian marriage, and it is this group, to which most women belong, that is the most pitiable… but it's their vocation, they are not good for anything else. You, by contrast…'

'Leave me alone. You have no right to pity me!'

'You've flown into a trap.'

'That's not true…'

'You've lost your inner values…'

<hr/>

[142] A quote from the chapter entitled 'Von Kind und Ehe' ('Child and marriage') in Nietzsche's *Also sprach Zarathustra*: 'Ah, the poverty of soul in the twain! Ah, the filth of soul in the twain! Ah, the pitiable self-complacency in the twain!' (trans. by Thomas Common).

'On the contrary. I have found values of which I had no inkling before. Or do you think women develop their inner values by listening to the fawning adulations of passing men, as I used to? They certainly knew how to sap my fragrance and fading beauty, but not one of them would have had the stamina to follow me to the point where the darkness and loneliness of my soul begins… You fly-by-nights, what have you ever given me…!'

'The same as what you gave us. You don't remember. Our hearts were generous back then. But when you start penny-pinching you may as well go hang yourself. Because life always repays measure for measure. And what sort of life is it, that no longer cares to squander?'

'You are so strange tonight, Rolf. Everything you say is bitter, full of blame, suspicion, or whatever… Good God, what do you want of me?'

'What one wants of a friend: the truth! Why do you insist on being so haughty with me, when I know you so well? Why don't you just admit that you've done something foolish, you impulsive creature? For all its charm, impulsiveness can sometimes have dire consequences…'

'Why don't you believe me for that matter? Why must you make everything sound so shabby! And how can you be so stubborn and stupid as to insist that I should simply assume all your wild conjectures are right? Well I cannot. I am not the right object of your pity. And as far as my marriage is concerned, it was merely the natural selection of two souls!'

Mirdja was incensed.

'You're right, of course… But do you also know how your soul makes its natural selection? In the same way as geniuses, rulers, as all powerful souls in general: they choose someone lesser than themselves. Because when they choose, they choose a realm for themselves, only that. Subjects and servants are what they need, but they cannot bear a rival sun…'

Mirdja felt her heart jump. This was dangerous poison…

'A wise person never enjoys the company of a fool. I don't recognize the breed of person you speak of. And anyway, I have known many kinds of men…'

'If you said "owned", you would be using the right word. But I don't think you've ever known a single one of them, not really. You've always turned them into women, frail and faithful, which is quite against man's true nature. And you cannot possibly have loved them, because a woman can never love the woman in a man… You have known men in a different way from other women. Other women have suffered betrayal, blows and insults, but they have known how to love, which you have not. You have spent your whole life on the outside of love's mystery…'

'You think you know everything right now, my terrible friend.'

'Why wouldn't I know! Or am I wrong? Tell me! Tell me, Mirdja, have you ever surrendered to a man blindly, blissfully, weak and conquered?'

'No — it's not in my nature.'

'No, because they've loved you, but you haven't loved them. They have been weak and you have been strong. But there is also another kind of greatness, in conceding defeat and being vanquished. That's what love is. That's how you recognize it, you invincible creature. You have never loved and you are not in love now…'

Rolf had spoken quietly, but with singular intensity and emotion, as if on behalf of all the conquered, forgotten souls.

Mirdja began to relent again. She couldn't resist the warm, candid tone of his words. This was like old times.

Why do your poisonous words contain so much truth I cannot bring myself to admit! she sighed in her heart.

And suddenly the tension was gone. Mirdja collapsed in tears. It was hurt pride, weakness, remorse, anguish, and shame all at once.

'Mirdja, dear friend, don't cry,' Rolf comforted her, 'I was only speaking my mind: just saying that you are not made for wifely duty… You have no children, after all…'

Mirdja felt her indignation rise again. Her tears turned to stone. She was gripped with a strange fury. She could have killed this man. He had no right to brush so close.

Her silence was dark and foreboding.

'It would have saved you from your present predicament,' continued Rolf. 'It's the only thing that can tie a woman like you down.'

'You are quite mad! You interfere in everything and twist everything. Nothing and no one can tie me down, nor ever will!' she shouted in fury.

'It would set you free at the same time. You would become the most perfect professor's wife without even noticing. At present you're just tortured by it…'

'You are doing your best to torture me,' said Mirdja calmly, but her lips still trembled with anger and pride.

'Are you really offended Mirdja? Then you've misunderstood me… I speak as your old friend…'

'Once upon a time. Now I have no friends but my husband.'

Mirdja got up to leave.

Rolf started to panic…

'Don't leave like this! I beg you. Sit for a moment longer! I confess it's all my fault. I'm just a scoundrel. The barrooms have driven me to the dogs. I don't know how to behave with decent people anymore. Mirdja, try to forgive me, try to understand me! You still hold the same place in my heart as before, as always. Sit here please, I'll tell you everything. I'll tell you why I'm so mean… It's hard for me to admit… I have been jealous of him, of your husband, you see, jealous… It makes a person base… But I had been so sure you were unattainable, I had judged myself and all men to be unworthy of you, I couldn't and I still can't believe that he, this man, has the measure of life, the brilliance, the stature, the strength to bring you fulfilment… And this is what has made me unkind. I have thought many harsh thoughts about you. I even began to think I was wrong about you and you were just as much a fake as all the rest of them... But be whatever you are, even the smallest sign of life in you is your own, is the essence of you... And if I don't understand you, it's simply because it's the nature of your being to remain a mystery to all men's reason. People can't help admiring what they cannot explain... Be whatever you want, I will always admire you. You cannot and must not try to break out of yourself. You cannot do anything that is not essentially you. You have to remain incomprehensible to others, a beautiful illusion which is meant to charm us like poetry. You are a poem in the cold mundanity of real life. What would it be without its poem, and what would the poem be without the golden wings of falsehood! You are as real as you are false.'

'And you hate falsehood...'

'But you Mirdja — I love.'

They both fell silent.

The bitterness between them was gone. 'There is something false about me,' said Mirdja quietly, 'and I have tried to escape it...'

'That is unfortunate, you deceive yourself, don't try to escape yourself. You have to embody everything, otherwise you wouldn't be who you are. You were born to be a marvellous poem, and even your falsehood is beautiful, and beauty deserves to be loved more than truth. You must have struggled against your purpose many a time, my friend. For you are too beautiful to be true, too wise to believe your own falsehood, too generous to avoid self-reproach... I can only hope it hasn't broken you...'

'You say so much Rolf, and contradict your own words at every turn. It's hard to know what you really mean! You are willing to walk through fire for both truth and falsehood at the same time, my poor friend,' Mirdja laughed sadly.

'But this is about your soul Mirdja... It's too complex to be defined by a single maxim... And it's the only thing I'd be willing to walk through fire for... Mirdja, can you forgive me for offending you?'

But Mirdja had already mellowed.

And when she looked into those great, pleading, child-like eyes, which seemed so at odds with Rolf's world-weary features, a strange lump formed in her throat. Why are people inclined to be so hard on one another, even when their hearts ache? They too... How could she take offence at Rolf for being the most astute of mortals, when it was she herself who had given him the keys to her soul? Cowardly self-preservation, ridiculous arrogance! They were close friends after all...

As if a heavy, harrowing hand were pressing upon her, Mirdja started crying again, hard and uncontrollably...

'I'm so unhappy! my dear Rolf. Everything you say is true,' her muffled words came through the tears.

And even Rolf shed a tear.

But then Mirdja remembered Runar sitting at home, all alone. She was startled by the prick of her bad conscience, and this made her feel even worse.

'I must go now,' she said softly. 'This isn't quite the same as the old days…'

Rolf said nothing…

They left.

They walked in silence.

'I am your friend,' said Rolf as they parted. 'But I am who I am. It can't be helped. Everyone has their own tragedy.'

'I was born a *tragédienne*,' Mirdja joked, 'that's no one's fault either… I didn't play well tonight,' she added with a smile.

'And I behaved like a rat. Try and forget it…'

Rolf kissed her hand and left.

VIII

But after that, Mirdja's equanimity was gone.
It was the first time she felt Rolf had been poison to her.

She could no longer look at her husband with the calm, cheerful indifference that she had begun to find customary. Runar was once again the first and last thought in her head. Every remark, every mood culminated to breaking point in him.

And once again she began asking herself: Why am I married to him? Why, why, why? — He lacks strength, genius, wealth. Why am I married to him?

And Rolf's words echoed incessantly in Mirdja's ears: 'They choose someone lesser than themselves.'

Was Runar lesser than she in some way? Whether he was or not, others thought so. And that was unacceptable. Runar should be the kind of man who could never inspire such a thought, never...

And Mirdja started looking at him as one looks at a stranger... What sort of first impression does Runar make?

His features were perhaps too ordinary, and his expression revealed nothing. His eyes were lovely and gentle, but not so very unusual. And his whole deportment definitely suggested under-achievement, sluggishness, awkwardness... And he certainly was an under-achiever, how was it he had never made anything of himself, with his talent... he had merely sunk to the same level as the talentless! As a type, the pedagogue was after all one of the dullest. Who could believe that beneath that exterior there lay anything individual and exceptional!

And Mirdja noticed that there was indeed something of the periwig about Runar these days... something quietly cautious and precise, which would have no doubt made a pitiful and ridiculous impression in any artist's eyes. His teaching post had inevitably given him an air of bourgeois virtue, safe and reliable. He was a man for whom it was now impossible to soar or plummet... But what good was such a fellow to Mirdja and she to him? Mirdja was not made for men who tread the middle ground...

These thoughts gave Mirdja no peace. She found herself walking down the street and staring at people, assessing their outward appearances and inward behaviours, comparing them with Runar...

In this way she catalogued, day by day, characteristics that Runar lacked and needed in order to reach perfection. Thus, she slowly developed a strange, schoolgirl fantasy of the man best suited to her. And astonishingly, the image didn't resemble Runar at all.

Mirdja herself found this all very vexing, but she could not resist the inevitable spiral of her thoughts. She could not change the way she was.

And so there was a recurrence of the old scenes, swinging between cruellest harshness and wildest tenderness.

They would flare up out of nowhere or something petty... Like one peaceful and pretty Sunday evening, in the glow of the fireplace, at a time when people are generally least inclined to tempestuous behaviour...

This was one such evening.

Runar was sitting at his desk as usual, correcting notebooks...

Mirdja was sitting in the corner by the fire, staring at Runar, her hands on her knees.

Mirdja never did anything herself. And Runar's work provoked her.

He was always doing something for someone else's sake, nothing of his own. Even now he had the stooped posture of a daily breadwinner! He looked wretched, heartbreaking! It was a pale fruit, past its best, that she had picked for herself in the fog of her feelings, amidst her profound pity for herself and for him that autumn. What a mistake, what a mistake! And now there they were, shivering and partaking of each other's shrivelled flower, which no longer bore the powerful fragrance of life in vigour...

Mirdja closed her eyes. She was tired of everything... Runar's pen scraped monotonously —

No one spoke... And Mirdja had a strange dream in the brief moment her eyes were shut...

There was a curious melody in her ears, faint at first, then louder and more enthralling. A great song of life, a joyous song of love, reaching up to the heavens... It was calling to Mirdja. And it was so close, it had never been this close before... And Mirdja understood that it was her hero's victory fanfare calling to her, and that this was her moment, that all-engulfing split-second between life and death... She was blinded by the light. She rose to leave... Every cell in her body was pushing forth, was forcefully compelled towards the unknown... And now... She became the sun's rose-blossom, opening wide, reaching, rising towards the heavenly fire, higher, higher, towards that burning, fatal kiss... Mirdja stretched and tensed herself, tensed herself to the very tips of her toes in deathly agony, until every blood vessel swelled, her tendons snapped, life's juices drained down to earth, leaving her withered skeleton in its outstretched position...

The sun is not for you Mirdja...

Look, you fool, at your withered skeleton! Look, look... and listen to the music play...

Mirdja was startled by the brazenness of her dream.

She rolled herself into a ball and covered her eyes.

Again her imagination had run wild and life ahead seemed even more grey and ignoble.

She looked over at Runar...

No change there. Everything was the same. And as if possessed she rushed up to Runar and — started hitting him…

'Mirdja, what is wrong with you?' Runar cried out, taking hold of her.

Nothing like this had ever happened before.

'What is wrong with me!' Mirdja gasped, 'how can you even ask. You, you are, and our life! Can't you see, this would drive anyone mad. Everything is downhill from here, we are growing old and everything around us too, nothing more will ever happen. And it's horrible! And the work you do is horrible, can't you see that for yourself?'

'How would we live without it…'

'So your only *raison d'être* is your daily bread. You must be living very well. You have turned into the perfect bourgeois. You don't even have the will to aim higher anymore…'

'One has to know one's limitations…'

'But the man I acknowledge as my husband cannot have limitations. Do you hear me!' And Mirdja stamped her foot. 'Do you hear me! I need reason to be proud of you! I crave to see you more accomplished than myself, stronger, wiser. And the whole world must see it too, especially the world. You have to be the master of your life, the hard-eyed prince of your destiny, so hard that the world beneath you trembles at your power and glory. My love demands it, do you hear…'

Runar looked out of the dark window without moving or saying a word.

'Why don't you say something you dreadful, insufferable dolt,' Mirdja raged again. 'This is a game out of hell, this life of ours. We're playing for each other's souls, don't you see? You have to win me in whatever way you can, or we will become morally abject… Do whatever you can, as long as you win! A human being has to be like a god, who can create and rule. Create something new for me and rule over me!'

'You would have me be an artist. But that's impossible. It's enough for me that I understand them. I do not belong with them. And my pride has always prevented me from aspiring only half-way up the ladder.'

'Yes, yes, I understand that, that's where I am, me… But that's why I need to see you at the top. I can't help it if that's what I want…! Even though I know it's all pointless. Nothing ever changes, nothing!'

Mirdja grew sad all of a sudden. She felt sorry… and remorse and pity… She went on, more gently:

'It's just for the sake of beauty in our lives… Of course I understand… But it's so unfortunate that we are of the same measure… If our talents don't give rise to genius, they make us captive, instead of free. I know your talents, I despise them and they cannot help you rule over me. But you are a man, and a man's arsenal is different from a woman's. Where is your arsenal? Rule over us both…!'

Runar glanced at his watch. It was getting late.

'Darling you are too excitable this evening. Wouldn't it be better to go to bed… Or tomorrow will be lost.'

'What of it, our whole life is being lost!' And Mirdja started to cry.

'Go and get some rest, darling, it will do you good.'

'Your words are madness! Don't you realize there are times when being rested doesn't depend on the position of your body, or having your eyes open or closed. You can't order someone to rest, but your sprit is impervious to everything…'

And the evening was followed by a very difficult, sleepless night.

Of course Mirdja knew that Runar's spirit was not impervious to everything, and she secretly admired the beautiful tranquillity of his soul. He can control himself, she thought, so he is stronger than me after all. And she finally fell asleep crying bitter tears of self-reproach…

But this was the beginning of all evil. It was as if the Devil had entered into their lives again.

There could be entire weeks when they didn't speak to one another and suffered in silence without being able to open their mouths. This was interrupted by Mirdja's occasional outbursts of either furious temper or stifled tears. Followed by bouts of extreme, exasperating lassitude and silence. They could not restore the equilibrium to their lives.

And yet Mirdja still had her tender, effusively loving phases. But they too were unctuous and unnatural, crawling on her knees and begging forgiveness, endless self-admonishment, and profuse demonstrations of affection towards Runar. An unnatural compensation for unnatural savagery, the former as tedious as the latter in its mawkishness and exaggeration. — Runar maintained his admirable composure throughout his neurotic wife's endless performances.

But Mirdja found Runar too hard and impervious in the face of her divided soul's many questions on life.

Thus they lived their lives from now on. For the most part it was unhappy, occasionally punctuated by wild happiness, but in both cases extremely draining.

Mirdja's wise, cool-headed reasoning had completely eluded her.

IX

~

After the long dark winter, there was at last a beautiful spring day. The blindingly bright sun peeked through the restless clouds flitting by, and the snow was audibly melting, with the gutters and drainpipes rippling in rivalry... And the smell of spring brought a curious sparkle to people's eyes...

The streets were full of joy and life. Everyone seemed to be having a good day today. Everyone — except the Söderbergs — who were never like other people. And of course, it was Mirdja's doing as usual...

They too had gone out for a stroll. And they walked and walked, though the sun's playful radiance failed to elicit even the tiniest reflection of similar joy in their faces.

Mirdja walked lost in thought. And Runar knew from experience that any attempt to strike up conversation would merely be counter-productive. They had spent the previous evening at a soirée, and Runar suspected that Mirdja's bad mood stemmed from that occasion.

And he was right. Mirdja had met an old friend there, and the meeting seemed to have had a poisonous effect on her.

Bengt Iro had been nasty to Mirdja, quite nasty indeed. Not only addressing her like a stranger but with the same condescending dismissiveness that one reserves for the bourgeoisie. And to think Bengt had been the finest, most equal of all her relationships...

Mirdja was still livid at the memory of last night...

The whole soirée had seemed unpleasant and oppressive from the start.

There were more artists than usual present and once the official programme ended, they gathered around the same table. If things had been as before, Mirdja would naturally have taken her place among them, and the most prominent place, this she knew. And even now she felt like joining them. But she was with Runar. And she was perturbed by a sense that her husband did not have it in him to clear a path for his wife like a crown prince and place her on the throne, on the contrary Mirdja would have to leave him in a corner like shameful cargo in order to win free passage for herself. Because artists are an arrogant lot. It's awful to be an outsider in their midst. And yet, as artists Mirdja and Runar were really on equal footing. What difference was there between them? Of course, Mirdja was a woman... She sneered. Everything annoyed her and she would gladly have left if it hadn't been for the proximity of Bengt Iro.

She looked for an opportunity to meet with him alone.

It was after all something, to see him after so many years.

She was always drawn to misfortune… Because it turned out to be a dreadful encounter… It was a mixture of everything — remoteness and familiarity, irony and tenderness, misunderstanding and heart-searching — all at once… as indeed so often before — but this time it put Mirdja in an indescribably contrary mood.

She would not have wished to remember it, but the evening's conversation kept resurfacing in her mind.

What was the last thing Bengt had said? Yes, that was it:

'What a shame that a genius like you went and threw it all away for the sake of such an unremarkable fellow! Even the wisest of women sometimes do unbelievably stupid things. You are a baffling lot. Anyway, I simply cannot understand how you can bring yourself to live outside the circle of artists to which you so intrinsically belong. Artists are the only people who could ever understand and inspire you, just as you them. And why have you abandoned your so promising career? Why have you deprived the world of your art, your wonderful soul and voice, whose chime is more magical than all the sirens of myth? It's a downright sin to swap a brilliant artist's career for the part of an ordinary housewife, and to sacrifice such a fine, sensitive soul to the bourgeoisie, which has no use for it. — It's a sin, a sin.'

'I never commit sins,' Mirdja had answered defiantly.

And her proud, wounded soul compelled her to defend herself fiercely. She continued:

'The pride you take in your profession makes you blind. You are full of prejudice, imagining that life stops at the boundaries of your artists' enclave. I have spent most of my life on the outside of that enclave. And the reason for that, then and now, is because I belong to a different breed. I am not one of you, as you still seem to believe. What do you know of the depths from which my soul springs and to which it must return? What do you know of the people I left to be with you and to whom I once again returned when I vanished? Nothing at all. You call them bourgeois. But that's not what they are, any more than I am. They are simply people who lack an occupational title with which to shield their naked souls. That's why no one knows anything about them and never will, and their conscience is free of seeking anyone's approval. Maybe one is a poet, or a painter, a philosopher, or a minstrel. So what! No one in the world will ever come to know the limitless creativity of their souls, because they are only dreamers. They wander the world full of ideas, images and tunes, dreams that will never come to fruition. And they are doomed to lie under the most forgotten earth, like any petty bourgeois. Is that justice? Must all our souls be industrial goods to be sold for a good price before their worth can be recognized? You artists, that's for you, your kind rely on your outward trappings: work and the fruits of your work, reputation and market value; but they, the ones I'm talking about, they have nothing but themselves. That's my lineage. That's where I come from. I belong to them and they belong to me, inseparably. But it's not something you would understand.'

But Bengt had simply listened to this outburst with the politest smile of a man of the world and then replied:

'Those magnificent eyes of yours could even bring a rock's soul to life. They haven't changed... But you might be mistaking those dreamers' souls for yours...'

'Like you artists mistake my soul for yours...'

'Even artists require a particular soil and climate... Or they get lost. It's an incorrigible shame that you are killing the artist in you, Mirdja.'

These words in particular stuck in Mirdja's mind and they echoed in her ears even now. And the more she thought about them, the more natural they seemed. Of course she would have been a singer without Runar. But now, because of Runar, she had been ripped from her soil and her climate. And perhaps the same was true of Runar... Or hardly... Runar's whole family line had always died of their daily bread... Runar was of philistine blood...

But she had described their position to Bengt in rather grandiose terms. Even she could not really bring herself to hold naked, professional anonymity in high regard. She herself kept trying to distance herself from the idea, seeking some tangible, visible form for her and Runar's spiritual beauty, and by extension seeking recognition, reputation, a name... oh, all the things others wished for too...

Mirdja walked with these thoughts in mind, and therefore could not take pleasure in the healing fragrance of spring. People began to disappear as they went off to dine... The streets were growing empty. The joyous sun was already waning. But Mirdja and Runar just kept walking.

'Mirdja, isn't it about time we went to dinner?' Runar asked at last in the most casual and contented tone, hoping it would dispel the tension.

Mirdja remained stubbornly quiet.

And they continued their stroll.

'Listen,' Runar finally said after a moment, 'aren't you getting tired? Why don't we stop somewhere and have dinner in town, to celebrate the arrival of spring. Aren't you hungry? What do you think?'

'The best time for dining out is already over,' Mirdja snapped briefly.

She felt tired, unhappy and irritable and didn't have the will to escape this altogether consistent mood.

'Would you prefer to go home?'

'No.'

'Where would you like to go then? Surely we can't go on walking forever?'

They stopped and looked away from one another — standing still...

Mirdja kicked her foot nervously:

'This is so dull! Let's keep going. Anywhere. It's all the same to me.'

Her words were hard and bitter. Runar winced. He was aware of standing at the brink of another severe nervous fit.

They started walking…

Mirdja noticed they were heading home. But she also remembered that it was still a very long way, and she was absolutely exhausted and perhaps — hungry.

'Perhaps you'd rather eat in town,' Mirdja said, a little timidly.

'Now I really do think we've missed the moment for dining out,' Runar answered.

'It amuses you to mimic me,' Mirdja now retorted, extremely angry. 'You're always mimicking me!'

Runar bent his cane nervously. It broke. He broke it into many pieces.

Mirdja, walking beside him, looked on and laughed — for the first time that day — coldly and cruelly. She enjoyed seeing how the anguish dug its nails into Runar's soul, little by little, one word at a time. Then her mind went suddenly blank, and a strange, cool serenity came over her. She laughed.

'At least you are more tactful than one gallant gentleman last week,' Mirdja said, 'he bent my umbrella in two…'

'Such a small detail and yet you remember it well, how he must have touched your heart,' Runar spoke darkly.

'All one's possessions touch one's heart — even an umbrella, why not!'

They stopped. Runar threw the remains of his cane on the ground…

'Do you think that makes you interesting?' Mirdja sneered scornfully.

'That is not my intention…'

'Breaking your cane seems to have put you out of sorts…haha!'

Runar gave no answer.

'Pointless taking your anger out on innocent objects…'

'It was accidental.'

'Of course, my respect for you deepens.'

'Can it really deepen any further, who would have thought?'

The harsh, bitter tone of the conversation was chilling.

Mirdja laughed out loud:

'Tell me, don't you just hate me now?'

'Not a jot as much as you hate me.'

'Good heavens, but I love you, we agreed on that ages ago! Have you forgotten? — I love you…'

'But right now your voice is saying: I hate you…'

'Well I am an actress, or have you forgotten that too…'

Silence…

'Mirdja,' said Runar suddenly, 'would it not be better if I didn't exist…'

'No doubt. And probably even better if I didn't exist…'

'Mirdja — it's easy enough to arrange…'

But as soon as he had said it, Runar was ashamed of himself. These were not matters to concur on… Why had he allowed Mirdja to over-excite herself…! Her behaviour was a sickness after all…

But Mirdja was suddenly in a very good mood, and joked as they climbed the steps.

'Don't go suggesting suicide now, it's the most ridiculous thing a man can say to a woman… But if you are feeling vengeful, then I can assure you it is the meanest way of repaying me for my bad deeds. And I do understand that you must often feel a pressing urge to escape me. And since you know there is no way on earth that we could ever be separated, no way at all, well, I can see how such a thought might spring to mind…'

And when they had shut the door behind them, Mirdja wrapped her arm around Runar's neck and kissed him.

As if they had just returned from the happiest little evening stroll.

X

~

L ife is so old. Which is why its pace is so even. Everything is governed by
due process. The seasons always follow one another in the same order.
Flowers bloom and fruit falls, people are born and die. And what happens in
between is short and scant…

Mirdja's life with Runar was inclining towards its afternoon. It acquired
good habits, became more settled and subdued. The seasons passed at almost
the same even pace as in other people's lives. Little by little…

And Mirdja began to love the silence, she felt she had been kicking and
screaming long enough, and that she was getting too old to be reaching for
the sky. What she had seen and done, she had seen and done. There were no
more changes on the horizon anyway. Mirdja had retreated from the outside
world once more. Her nerves could not take it, she had said. And indeed, her
nerves had little to commend them. At least they consistently ensured that
the couple's domestic bliss was as substantially infused with drama as it was
with poetry.

But it was all part of their own particular domestic bliss, and the main
thing was that such bliss existed, no matter in what form.

Nothing untoward was to happen again, nothing new…

Yet there was still one incident that shifted them slightly off their now
customary even keel.

And even that was nothing very significant. Only the fact that Mirdja
became acquainted with Genius Norkko.

It was summertime.

The day was beautiful and cloudless. Nothing on the horizon indicated a
wind of change…

But it began with a dream…

This is how it all happened.

Mirdja had spent the whole morning sitting in a field of clover. It was
always one of her greatest pleasures in the countryside…

Sleepy honeybees were buzzing benevolently around her, there was a sweet
smell which gently stupefied the senses, and so she eventually fell asleep.
And that's when she had this amazing dream…

She was sitting on a gigantic welwitschia leaf.[143] And at a short distance,

[143] *Welwitschia mirabilis* is an African plant, often described as fascinating (indeed,
'mirabilis' means wonderful in Latin), but also peculiar and strange. The plant is very low
and is formed by two leaves which, while growing, split into multiple leaves, each a metre
long. *Welwitschia* can survive for hundreds of years in the arid environment of the desert.

on another leaf, sat a large, hairy faun watching Mirdja.[144] There was a vast gulf between them. But suddenly the hairy creature stood up, leaped into the air and landed in front of Mirdja. It bowed and wagged its tail and asked her to dance. And in the same instant, the tree beneath them started to grow and lifted them at great speed into the void above. Mirdja was filled with dread. She looked at the faun's long hair and the more she looked the longer it grew. And the surface of the leaf gleamed like a dance parquet... And Mirdja dared not refuse nor acquiesce... But then the faun started to stamp its hooves and wiggle its ears, and its horns began to fork in anger. Mirdja felt her last moment had come... she tried to get up but found she could not move... she had become one with the welwitschia leaf... She cried out feebly and awoke. She rubbed her eyes. Everything was as before. The clover smelled sweet, the bees were buzzing, and Runar was standing in front of her laughing.

'I must have startled you,' he said. 'We have a guest... I came to tell you... Guess who it is: Genius Norkko... Do you remember hearing that name?'

Mirdja started and all the blood rushed to her head...

'Ah, you mean that writer who was once in fashion... Some play one evening, aeons ago...'

Mirdja tried to appear casual.

'Yes, you were playing in "Odalisque" when we met. Do you remember? And you said something mean about Norkko and I defended him. I remember it all so clearly. And to think that ever since then, I haven't seen the man! I must have mentioned that we used to be the best of friends. But it was mostly thanks to my dear sister, may she rest in peace. He stayed with us for a full four years back then. Which is quite out of character for him,' Runar babbled eagerly.

But Mirdja said nothing, she just walked by his side and tried to appear casual.

For she remembered the evening of the odalisque all too well — and she really would have preferred to forget the whole affair, including all the emotional upheaval.

But she could not help entertaining the mad idea that perhaps after all she had settled for the servant, and now the master was come — that Norkko was here for her, at last...

But if Mirdja had been disappointed on the night of the odalisque for failing to meet him, she felt twice as much disappointment on finally encountering him.

For in spite of everything, Mirdja had secretly formed a picture of him in

---

[144] Fauns were half-human, half-goat creatures in Greek and Roman mythology. In Greek art and literature, the faun would conjure wild, instinctual, ecstatic sexuality. Fauns often symbolized animal masculinity and virility, though their gender attributes could also be rather ambivalent. In Symbolist and Decadent literature, the major representation of the faun figure is to be found in Stéphane Mallarmé's (1842–1898) poem 'L'après-midi d'un faune' (1876), where the border between reality and dream is constantly being erased.

her mind's eye. She imagined him tall and limber with a pale complexion, his brow furrowed, his intelligent gaze dangerously aflame, and his lips twisted in a permanently disdainful smile, miraculously resembling the ideal man Mirdja had once drawn for herself on the basis of Runar's shortcomings... And above all, he would look very individual.

But the man did not live up to any of these conceptions. First of all, he was ugly. That was unimportant... But he bore none of the signs of a strong personality, not one. And he was so short as to barely reach Mirdja's shoulders, and his manners were clumsy and brutish like a peasant's... Only his grey, squinting, close-set eyes revealed backbone and character.

All the way home, Mirdja had tried to guess what would be the first thing they would say to each other, given that they had in a way met before, on a spiritual level.

But all her anticipation evaporated as soon as she set eyes on Norkko.

The man greeted her with gruff indifference as if all his life he had frequented families in which there was no call to pay any heed to the lady of the house...

And having greeted her, he turned at once to converse with Runar as if Mirdja were not even there.

What a crude, uneducated man... His company would be insufferable, Mirdja assured herself. And she did not emerge for the rest of the day.

She felt strangely out of sorts.

But Norkko didn't leave the next day, as Mirdja had hoped in her initial vexation.

They seemed to be getting on so well, Runar and Norkko... They spent all day together, laughing and chatting. Runar was positively rejuvenated... And neither of them seemed to miss Mirdja's presence.

How could Runar enjoy the company of such a dunce! What an unpleasant pair they were together! And Mirdja avoided them on purpose. She wished to appear visibly indifferent...

But inside she was sorely dismayed and helplessly miserable. It was the first time in her life she felt overlooked and discarded. She, who was used to conquering men at first glance, and bringing them to their knees with a second...! No new acquaintance had ever crossed her path without immediately recognizing how exceptional she was. But this Norkko fellow! What did she care about him, he was a brute! But how was it that he had come to write 'Odalisque'?

And Mirdja maintained her calm, cool exterior, but for some inexplicable reason she was in fact jealous... Of which of the two men, she was unsure.

On the third evening, Mirdja said to Runar:

'Listen I can't help it, but I hate that fellow Norkko... I hate him as much as I love you...'

And Mirdja cried...

On the fourth evening she said:

'Runar, you've never talked about your late sister. Tell me about her. What was she like? Was she beautiful?'

'Beautiful? Perhaps in her own way. She was the opposite of you. As fair as you are dark, as fragile as you are strong, as simple as you are complicated. The kind of person whose life was governed by a single thought, whose heart by a single feeling… A real woman, so to speak…'

'Is that what a real woman is like? How lovely,' Mirdja said softly, 'how very lovely. It's a shame your sister is no longer living… I have never known a real woman, not once… I have only seen myself, and my own blood reflected in others. I have been blind to the rest. Listen Runar, perhaps you would have found it easier to love a real woman, whose heart is made of even silk, and carries only one man's picture for life… I am much uglier, Runar. Can you really love me?'

Runar clasped Mirdja in his arms.

But on the fifth night Mirdja was peevish.

'It's very strange,' she said, 'the way you and Norkko are such extremely good friends. Doesn't it smack of femininity?'

'Friendship can only exist between men, never women… And Norkko has a heart of gold in that respect. He isn't the least bit fickle…'

'How very monotonous… Is he still in love with your sister?'

'Well she has passed away, so… Although I don't suppose he will ever love anyone else… He's that type… The type that believes in one love.'

'Ah, like real women…'

Norkko stayed with them for the whole week, and the next one.

Mirdja began to get used to him, her anger relented and now and then they exchanged a couple of words, but always only at Mirdja's instigation.

Once however, they did have a longer conversation. Runar had left them alone together, either by chance or design.

At first they were silent.

Then, in order to say something Mirdja asked:

'Why haven't you published anything in such a long time?'

'I haven't had the financial need to.'

Mirdja was shocked. She had expected the conversation to turn to 'Odalisque' or to Mirdja herself.

'Is that the basis for your entire literary activity? How unworthy.'

'Well, what is publishing other than a financial contract, and of the nastiest kind. As truly as I hold my soul in greater regard than my body, so truly do I hold publishing to be a greater sin than slavery… Selling oneself for money, hah!'

'But is it not a sin to hide your candle under a bushel? One should give one's soul to others too.'

'Give but not sell, there's a difference. One should have the right to choose to whom one gives — to those most cherished, most loved, most precious.'

'Why not be like the sun that God created, shining on both the sinful and the righteous.'

'I don't wish to be good to everyone, only the few.'

'How ungenerous of you.'

'I have been known to squander too…'

He's talking about 'Odalisque', Mirdja inferred, and said:

'Do you always regret your financial commissions after the fact? With that attitude it's astonishing that you have ever put your soul into your books, even under pressure of hunger.'

'Indeed I never have.'

'But you have published.'

'Only works which are external to me.'

'What about "Odalisque",' Mirdja could not resist pointing out, 'that was certainly drawn with depth and feeling?'

Norkko laughed oddly and coughed, then laughed again. — Then he added:

'I see, so you really know nothing about that. Typical of Runar… "Odalisque" was something we created together on a whim, on the basis of one of Runar's diary entries. It was even based on true events, in Paris or somewhere.'

Mirdja was speechless.

'So the man hasn't even told his wife! That's loyalty for you. Probably afraid my reputation would suffer. The whole thing was really Runar's work. Well there you go… What a fine man he is. There's someone who has never sold himself, even though he could have, and for a very high price indeed… He too has only given to those he wished to…'

Norkko peered intently at Mirdja with his narrow eyes.

Mirdja dropped her gaze. She was confused, but also extremely happy and grateful to Norkko for what he had told her about Runar. At last, here was someone who could see how well she had chosen her husband. But she could not bring herself to stare back at those barely visible, deep-set eyes. As if she had a bad conscience…

And she heard his voice go on:

'He has given you so much, much more than any man ought to give a woman.'

'How so?'

'I have witnessed many cases of perfectly fine men going to waste because of some woman. Women never understand things that aren't glaringly obvious. They only like fancy clothes.'

'Is that an accusation?'

'No, but I am Runar's friend, and I can see he loves you enormously. It's not right to make unhappy someone whose love you've already accepted.'

'Has Runar said he is unhappy?'

'That's woman for you. No, you just don't understand a man's mind, not in the least. You have no understanding of your position as that man's wife…'

The greater the love one receives, the greater the responsibility. I would never have the courage to accept such great love.'

'Great love surely expects nothing.'

'No, you're right. But it suffers more. Living one's sweetheart's life every second of the day as if it were one's own. Anyone who accepts great love is the greatest captive, unless they choose to be a monster and soul destroyer.'

'And is that why you haven't the courage to accept great love? But you yourself dare to love... surely that too is internal captivity...?'

'I live without love, it suits me better.'

'But how can you know there isn't some great love and suffering destined for you out there, that you know nothing of...?'

'No,' said Norkko sternly.

'Well, you just don't know.'

But in the same instant Mirdja was afraid Norkko might misinterpret her words to mean she was speaking of herself. So she added quickly:

'I mean you said you might have had someone precious and dear, to whom you could give everything that you cannot bring yourself to sell. Things like that always leave a trace on one's soul...'

But Mirdja became embarrassed by her words, thinking she might have spoken out of turn, as she remembered what Runar had said about his sister.

'There are always good people to be found in this world, who are willing to listen to the sorrows of those with heavy hearts...'

They fell silent.

'I'm glad you are Runar's friend,' said Mirdja after a while. 'Couldn't you be my friend too?'

'No,' Norkko answered drily.

Mirdja did not dare ask why... An unprecedented sense of impotence made her strangely docile in the presence of this clumsy, small man.

And Norkko turned his back on her and left the room.

But after this incident Mirdja was quite changed. She moved around the house quietly, almost timidly. She had thoughts she had never had before. She saw Runar, Norkko, and the whole world in a completely new light. But Norkko was in her thoughts too often, this she noticed. And she wished she could have been one of those good people to whom Norkko would have offered the poetry of his soul.

They never really spoke again. But they often found themselves furtively observing one another. And Mirdja always rapidly dropped her gaze when this happened.

Then Norkko left.

And after he had gone, Mirdja felt a huge void around her. She had grown accustomed to him. He had become almost a necessity, as her daily spectator. And now he was gone. The mystery of him remained unsolved, the man's heart was cold and closed on departure...

She sometimes thought it would be better if Runar were out of the way.

But then she regretted it immediately and prayed in her heart for a long, happy life for Runar.

'Runar,' said Mirdja one evening about two weeks after their guest had left, 'I don't hate Norkko anymore. He does have a heart of gold. I am glad you have him for a friend! But he doesn't like me...'

'He is gruff with strangers... He needs time...'

But Mirdja nevertheless remembered Norkko with special fondness. Because he had once again raised Runar in her esteem. — It was only Mirdja's feminine nature, with its selfishness and vanity, that still bore a silent grudge. It would have desired revenge. Revenge of the worst kind: by making him the recipient and bearer of the greatest love — and thus the greatest captive.

XI

∽

But then all is forgotten little by little. And nothing new happens again.

The years flit by imperceptibly... What more could there be to perceive, Mirdja and Runar are already elderly.

All the tall, dangerous flames of youth have been quelled long ago. The couple's domestic drama has grown increasingly subdued and melancholic, the tenderness of their ever-growing love has become increasingly enduring.

And whenever the fire in the hearth blazes and a blizzard blows outside, they sit curled up together like frightened children... And by the fireside they would tell each other remarkable tales from their lives, so remarkable that no one in the whole world would believe them to be true. But they are like children. They believe in their own fantasies...

This is the kind of thing they say:

'I didn't take you into my life to be its emotion, but its knowledge,' Mirdja says. 'When I first saw you, I had already stopped looking for happiness, stopped believing in happiness... I awaited life ahead of me as an observer awaits, quietly, coldly, and personally disinterested... What more disappointments could I possibly encounter? Like you... The tranquillity on your brow is the tranquillity of a betrayed conscience... Isn't it? You thought you had found your happiness with me, but I wasn't happiness. You thought you had found richness and beauty in me, but I was neither. You thought you would be able to look into deep waters, but they dried up like slender creeks running into the great sands of the desert.'

'Yes Mirdja. One thing is true about what you say. I have killed you... Do you really think I haven't been painfully and terribly aware of that all these years; how my presence impoverished you, froze the blood in your veins, cut the wings of your imagination, shot down your wonderful birds in flight, and murdered the poetry in you by daily starvation! My God, what have I done to you!'

'Don't talk like that. You have been my whole life, wonderful and painful like the truth of life itself. You see, if my birds grew weary in flight, they did so because they were never meant for the sky, they never had the span of an eagle. If my beauty faded, it's because it was never real, if my poetry ran out, it's because I was never a true poet. I was a dilettante, by blood, by destiny... But before I learned to understand this, I was harsh and bitter, I blamed the heavens and everything under the sun for my own failings... It was you who taught me to see the truth... I was never anything...'

'And that's what I've taught you, that sad, artificial truth! Like it or not, your words slyly point to the same thing: I have killed you...'

'You mustn't say that, Runar, you mustn't. Do you still not know me? Do you still see mirages of ancient long-extinguished fires before your eyes, you great big child! How can you kill something that never existed...'

'It did exist... An artist too has an age of childhood within the human soul, a moment which quivers between life and death. Its first prayer is frail and quiet and more sensitive to the touch than that of a silent water lily opening its petals at night... And the great prayer of a few such souls, their great lament at such times, cries out towards the loneliness... They pray for its great and exalting, infinite expanse to be their only sun... When I first saw you Mirdja, your eyes carried the same prayer, the artist in you prayed so... I didn't believe in your longing, and you yourself wished to defy it... And now it's too late... And it all could have been so different. What have we done to each other!'

'Ah my poor friend, how deep is your disappointment, even now! I have torn all your beautiful dreams to shreds and have been unable to create anything with which to replace them... I made you feckless. You who aspired to divine dreams, you stopped aspiring...'

'You are what I always sought. Why seek further?'

'And you are the only thing I ever wanted from the world. What further need do I have of the world...? Have you noticed how good things are now that we are no longer seeking and aspiring to anything. I am no longer bitter, have you noticed? All the pain and disappointment, all the shattered and shipwrecked dreams have disappeared under a blanket of conciliatory peace...'

'Yes, the peace of death, the peace of quiet wisdom in old age, which states: "Consider, all is vanity."[145] Solomon was a great decadent.[146] So what! They too were able to spread their blessing across the world in their day, the eternal peace of emptiness and destruction. The cold, icy fragrance of Nirvana...[147] Which spreads like a sweet balsam to feverish brains and scorched souls...'

'Yes, no mad aspiration, despair, or restlessness can outstrip Solomon,' Mirdja laughs. '"Consider the work of God: for who can make that straight, which he hath made crooked?"[148] That's surely a message for me!'

'There's more too. "Sorrow is better than laughter: for by the sadness of the countenance the heart is made better."'[149]

'My heart has been made better. I don't need any more sorrow...'

'I am your sorrow, Mirdja.'

---

[145] Ecclesiastes 1. 2: 'Vanity of vanities, saith the Preacher, vanity of vanities; all is vanity.'
[146] See note 22, p. 74.
[147] See note 69, p. 124.
[148] Ecclesiastes 7. 13.
[149] Ecclesiastes 7. 3.

'You are my healer, Runar. Before you I was broken and stumbling, now I am whole and happy… You were always stronger than me after all…'

'In what way?'

'In love. Now I know what love is…'

'What is it?'

'The greatest of all…[150] And I love you Runar…'

'I have waited for those words all my life. Now I am ready to die…'

This is the kind of conversation they have. And when they are silent, they look into each other's eyes and smile with the same happiness and the same thoughts…

Those great big children curled up together!…

And the fire in the hearth blazes at their long overdue happiness…

[150] 1 Corinthians 13. 13: 'And now abide faith, hope, love, these three; but the greatest of these is love.'

XII

But the newly awakened, miraculous childhood of Runar and Mirdja is not limited to dreams and fantasies shared in the gloaming. It calls for everything that childhood generally calls for: playfulness and prattling, the unbridled freedom of a clear conscience, and sunny, carefree joy…

And so they play and prattle from morn till night only to begin again the next morning…

No child in the world plays as sweetly as Mirdja. No child in the world has a laugh so like a bell and eyes so bright and clear.

'It is nature's masterful deception,' says Runar, 'that you are still a child. Why are you still a child Mirdja?'

'Because,' answers Mirdja, 'my real childhood was cut short. I never had the chance to play when other children played. It left a permanent urge to play in my soul, and the residue of fairy tales in my eyes… The child in me is still alive, it's true, a hundred-year-old child… Longing to be caressed and comforted… Longing for her mother's gaze which she has never seen, or her father's hand, which she has never held… She wants to pray to the stars and believe the flowers are her sisters… You are now my mother and father and star and flower…

'My darling, little Mirdja,' Runar says, and is happy.

XIII

~

G ames and fairy tales continue to gain sway, but the shadow of death is growing longer…

For Mirdja and Runar are both quite unwell…

They notice this themselves eventually, but with dread in their hearts they conceal their observations from one another. For they do not wish to acknowledge it after all, they are desperate to silence the ghastly spectre of death in their midst. They try not to dwell on it and yet they live every moment in careful examination of each other, filled with grim, mounting suspense. For what can they do! Strange, terrible things are happening between them, and it makes them think of things they would rather not.

One evening Runar and Mirdja are sitting together on the sofa. Silence reigns absolute in the room. And in the dusk, they are each preoccupied with their own oppressive thoughts…

Ghastly is the evening twilight of loneliness penetrating the heart… Even though they are two…

Mirdja begins to observe Runar again, furtively, fearfully. Who are they really, the two of them? Why were they sitting there in silence…? But why should they talk for that matter?

Which one of them was a ghost?

Suddenly Mirdja is startled by something. She takes another look at her husband, and with a bloodcurdling shriek she collapses in a heap…

She has had a horrid, horrid vision…

Runar is frightened… He lifts Mirdja into his arms but she bites and kicks and her whole body shakes and trembles…. Runar carries her to bed by force…

'What's wrong with you? What happened?' he asks her anxiously.

But Mirdja just stares at him unconsciously and her face contorts once again in a spasm of terror…

It is only the next day she can speak of her vision:

'I saw us differently at that moment… You were a skeleton, just risen from the grave. Your empty eye sockets stared blankly, your bones rattled… I was sitting next to my dead husband… I… and do you know who I was? I was a madwoman, with incurable brain and heart disease… That was us, that's who we were in that terrible split-second. And that is who we are to become,' Mirdja adds quietly as she trembles. 'I believe that. It was a vision of the future…'

'Don't strain your nerves so, my darling little Mirdja,' says Runar. But in his heart the same image takes hold, and he tries to guess which one of them will die first.

But Mirdja hasn't told him everything. Not that there were times she had wished for Runar's death and that now she is expiring under the burden of her deep-felt guilt...

She no longer has a moment's peace. The prediction, the image follows her everywhere. And new, similar images appear constantly in her path. She no longer dares to let her gaze rest in one spot. She must keep blinking and moving and fearing...

But it is the fire she must fear the most. It is full of pictures... And people... Who would suddenly turn into skeletons... But the darkness and loneliness are terrifying too.

And whenever Runar would leave the house, Mirdja felt like clinging to his coat, firmly, relentlessly, to prevent him from leaving... But then she would pull herself together and try to conceal her madness... Though the fear and pain of death are already driving her frantic...

And then once, Runar happens to return home to find her huddled under three coverlets in the smallest corner of her room, curled up like a dog...

This is how it came about:

Mirdja had been sitting alone... The evening had been drawing in, growing darker. She had been staring into the darkness... Then the maidservant had entered and placed a large, white-eyed funereal confection on the table in front of Mirdja.[151] She thought that Madam had dropped some old memento... Mirdja could not utter a single word, she had merely stared at that horrifying black confection, and it had stared back at her with its single white eye. And she was overcome with stifling terror. She wanted to hide the item. She carried it around the house but couldn't find a suitable hiding place. Every object seemed too precious to her, to have that foreboding eye placed under it... In the end, she burned it... But then the fire had stared out at her like a huge, giant funereal confection, at which point Mirdja, driven by unbridled terror, had rushed to hide in the corner, pressed herself against the wall, and wrapped herself in coverlets...

The shadow of death is growing longer...

In the end, they take each other to the doctor.

The doctor examines them both, a little at a loss for words. For in his heart, he would pronounce them both terminally ill... And he can see they only make each other worse.

Carefully he suggests travel and solitude.

But then Mirdja has a hysterical fit and through her tears she cries:

'You are not a real doctor! You cannot treat the soul! You cannot see that we have searched for one another our whole lives and only now found each

---

[151] A funereal confection was a Finnish and Scandinavian tradition: sweets in black wrappers, often with a white decoration, were offered to guests at a funeral.

other. You cannot see we have the same soul. We cannot be separated now.'

You are moving towards your separation, thought the doctor, but there is nothing I can do for you anymore...

And the ailing pair leave as they had come... To carry on with their lives, which is never again to witness a single healthy moment...

It is little more now than the ever-fading breath of one who lies dying, than the gentle, uneven ebb of a waning fire...

DEATH KNELL

~

Dark and lonely…
       A lonely candle faintly illuminates the room of a lonely woman… A woman in black… A woman not well…

Mirdja stares and stares…

A whole lifetime of reflection is concentrated in the rigid pain of her fixed stare. There is nothing else left…

The candle burns lower and lower. White wax patterns gather along its length. So white and delicate… Just one now — a trickle. It gradually builds up, growing longer and thicker — just like loneliness. Staring makes it grow bigger — just like loneliness. And it swirls in a never-ending ring… Flowing eternal. Another old chestnut. The circle signifying eternity…

Dear God, everything is so old, all been and done before!

And of course, Mirdja too and Mirdja's fate is old, all been and done before! She had been nothing but a pale replica, an heiress who went about with her arms full of antediluvian goods and chattels. And yet all that effort to be and do something new! How petty and ridiculous to be born a human being! Spent in full bloom, one foot in the grave before life even begins!

Not one single new idea ever manifested itself throughout Mirdja's lifetime. A lot of hot air, a lot of grand words bandied about, but all borrowed, plucked from the detritus and catacombs of centuries past…

What ragpickers we are, we human beings!

But our universal sense of emptiness is not enough to bring us close together. It will always be lonely and dark around us — no matter what.

Lonely and dark…

The wax shape suddenly buckles in total silence.

But Mirdja feels as if the room is blown asunder and she leaps to her feet with a feeble cry.

And then…?

Nothing new as usual…

The candle burns lower. Mirdja stares…

*

She can hear it again now, that horror. — The death knell. — The boom is heavy and disheartening in Mirdja's ears.

She would like to scream and shout. To grab the bell-ringer's hand, to hit out, to tear and bite and scratch…

Why must they ring those terrible, thundering bells which Mirdja has hated all her life with a violent, mistrustful aversion!

They always transport her to an oppressively grey autumn day... Mist and melancholy in the air, murky slush on the ground... Head bent... Heavy footfall — Ding... dong — Grey footfall — Sink into the earth, we will sink you! — Ding... dong — We are your nightmare. — We will not allow you to step lightly. Lightness is a sin. — Ding... dong — The world is a vale of sorrow — Ding... dong...

All her life Mirdja has hated church bells, for they have always felt like the nails of crucifixion hammering into her delicate soul.

But now, they also recalled the most morbid moments of her life, the most painful separations. To the peal of such bells did she walk to her uncle's and her husband's graves... How long ago now? Ah, she does not wish to think about it, no, no... She wouldn't know anyway... And it would just make her sad... Or no, even the sadness is gone... There is nothing left at all. She has cried her eyes dry, mulled her thoughts numb, grieved her grief all away. Only weariness remains... And one thing she has learned from all of this: 'The day of death is better than the day of birth.'[152] Is this idea, springing from the mind of that strange wise man, to be her very last thought...?

Mirdja jumps to her feet, stamps her foot, and then collapses again. Those terrible bells!

Then she sits staring again...

She has a vision of her own funeral. That pious old fellow reading something from his book... Anna, the kind simpleton, crying because to do so is good manners... The rest are strangers, people who have come out of curiosity... none of them have known her, none of them miss her... Rolf is the only one who would but he is out in the world and doesn't know she has passed. And the others, those who have come out of curiosity and obligation, they curse the winter frost and the long service. And Mirdja feels so sorry for them, with their dutifully bent profiles, their miserably distorted facial muscles. What a lot of trouble they go to, for the sake of a complete stranger... but on the other hand, Mirdja thinks, if she shot herself in the chest now, which would be the wisest thing to do, they would crack her skull open in order to prove her insanity...

She would like to be present at the post mortem to declare: abnormal development, completely abnormal. Caused by mental instability...

*

Mirdja has overheard people referring to her as mentally ill. And she has simply nodded: yes, yes that's right, my mind has been very unwell...

[152] Ecclesiastes 7. 1: 'A good name is better than precious ointment; and the day of death than the day of one's birth.'

Mirdja has also heard them use the term: mad fool. But this she has brushed aside: no, I am much wiser than I used to be, much wiser...

For Mirdja spends whole nights now conversing with wise spirits.

But the discussions are harsh, mercilessly harsh. Which is why Mirdja fears their trenchant wisdom, fears those long, sleepless nights that she knows so well, but which have lately acquired their own uncanny dreams and foul language.

Mirdja has visions and hears the shadows talking. And she even converses with her own shadow, they converse aloud, long conversations in the terrible silence:

'You have no cause to reproach the god of destiny for being harsh. Two people have died. What of it? People die every minute. Did these mean more to you than all the others?'

'The only ones I loved.'

'The only ones who loved you, you mean. You yourself have never loved. Have you forgotten? You've always known this and nevertheless you've always lied and smothered other souls with your lies...'

'I lied? I, who have always warned others against me, forbidding them to touch me for fear they may unwittingly fall prey to my trap and then accuse me of poaching! I have always told the truth and yet you accuse me...'

'You are afraid of accusations, Mirdja. Fine. But I accuse you anyway: When your lips said "don't touch" your voice was a caress: "touch me, touch me!" You seduced and excited on purpose, and yet you wished to retain the emotionless victory and invincibility of a sophist. Shame on you Mirdja!'

'Could I help it! There was magic in me. And I was a bad person. I would have liked to be different but I couldn't be.'

'Liar, liar! You have never in your life wanted to be anything other than what you are. You have never considered yourself a bad person... On the contrary, the most wonderful individual of all. And yet you were just one of those people who are like sounding brass or tinkling cymbal.[153] Do you know who they are?'

'I am not one of them. I have loved.'

'Why then, did you murder them?'

'I? Committed murder?'

'Yes, don't even try to claim they died of natural causes. Well, well, my double murderess, at least you blench. You see you cannot hide anything from me. I know everything. You left the one person you should never have left, you claimed the one person you should never have claimed... You killed the first by leaving him starving in his soul and mad with loneliness, the second you killed by even crueller methods... Oh how great was your love for them!'

[153] 1 Corinthians 13. 1: 'Though I speak with the tongues of men and of angels, and have not charity, I am become as sounding brass, or a tinkling cymbal.'

'Yes, I did love them. And now I am crushed...'

'All your life you sought to be proud and alone, and now you can't stand the solitude after all. You poor wretch!'

'I loved them. And even now some irrepressible power draws me to my love...'

'They are deceased, you admirer of grand words, you self-seeker...'

'I loved them. I want to atone for the sake of the deceased.'

'And you think that a whole lifetime of selfishness can be atoned for with a single, belated sacrificial fantasy?'

'I loved them but my love was of the wrong kind. It is only now that I've found it...'

'That can only be granted by the great man of Nazareth...[154] But you wouldn't know him...'

Mirdja tosses and turns in bed, feverish and hallucinating, and great beads of anguish roll from her brow. Her eyes have the dull, glazed look of one who sees spirits...

And such spirits, such unprecedented visions!

Mirdja sits up in bed. Her eyes are burning, piercing... She distinguishes a glow in the darkness. She recognizes a tall, clear brow, deep eyes, a halo...

But suddenly everything dims. A paralytic blow strikes her down again...

She lies numb and sees nothing more.

Mirdja is sick to her soul.

*

It's always quiet in the cemetery, but quieter still when dusk has just fallen, when the shadows grow longer by the minute and the age-old crosses stand waiting in the lull of twilight.

It is the moment when the living have already moved on, and the dead have not yet awakened. It is the moment when the silence is greatest. And it is the moment Mirdja loves best.

This is when she wraps herself in a long white shawl and steals noiselessly, surreptitiously out of her front door, as if to a lovers' tryst.

She looks tentatively around. She is wary of the groundsman who sometimes stands by the gate. She is afraid of the slumbering coachman, sitting stock-still on his box seat. She is even afraid of the friendly little dog which lives in the residential building and accidently follows her now and then.

They keep watch on her, all of them, whenever she wants to go and see her beloved without anyone knowing. Swift of foot and heart pounding, Mirdja hastens to the cemetery.

There at last she can be alone, for she has reserved this quietest of moments for herself.

---

[154] Luke 24. 19: 'Concerning Jesus of Nazareth, which was a prophet mighty in deed and word before God and all the people.'

This is her moment. The moon shines silver, the shadows lie tall, and Mirdja arrives, her lips parted like a woman rushing to be kissed...

All is translucent between heaven and earth. The same cool translucence pierces the soul.

> 'The moon shines bright,
> the dead ride light,
> be the maid not afraid?'[155]

Every night the spirits ask the same question, every night Mirdja gives the same answer: no, not I, not I...

She spots the mound she seeks from afar. It glimmers more eerily than any other mound in the whole world. Ah, there it is, her church...

But suddenly Mirdja stops in her tracks. And she is about to cry out as if piqued by jealousy, or anger or wounded love... This has never happened before. But in the same moment she quashes her welling emotion. They surely belonged to the living, those two whose shadows loomed from the holy ground. And Runar and Mirdja, they were spirits, it did not do for them to take offence at mortals...

So Mirdja creeps forwards on tip-toes, ever so quietly... She hides behind a large tombstone to watch the young couple by Runar's grave.

She sees the woman pluck a rose for the man...

It was the same rose she had brought for Runar last time... Light as a bubble it now lilts in the limpid moonlight. But Mirdja knows that by the light of day it is a heavy, ominous red, like the blood in her sick heart...

Why did it never occur to her to give Runar a rose when they were still alive together, like it occurs to others, to the wise, the happy!

At first Mirdja assumed the man was a brute and the woman cheap, but now suddenly it seemed to her that everything was as it should be, as it was meant to be. They were as sacred as love itself right now, those two animals. And their love required the plucking of that large, ominous rose, wherever it happened to grow. How happy that man must be!

And suddenly, like a ghost rising from the grave, Mirdja swoops before them shouting: 'Pluck the roses, pluck them all and offer them to each other! Then you may rest in peace after your death. You won't have to haunt the world as I do, I who have never once in my life offered anyone a rose...'

---

[155] The verses allude to the Lenore cycle or Lenore motif (also known at the 'Spectre Bridegroom' motif) from European folklore, which has been used extensively in art and literature. The words of the Finnish ballad were written by Eino Leino for a play on which he worked during the period of his intense friendship with Onerva. The play was ready in the summer of 1905 but it was never published during Leino's life. The poem was eventually included in Leino's last collection of poems, *Pohjan yhteys* ('Northern bond', 1924), under the title 'Manamansalo' ('Manamansalo island').

The girl screams and the man drops the rose. And they scurry off as if the Devil were on their heels.

What odd people! Why did they run? It wasn't at all nice of that man to throw away the great ominous rose… Not nice at all…

And Mirdja bends over, looking for the discarded rose for some time. Then she returns it to Runar's grave.

Can you see, Runar, she says, I do know how to love after all. I have finally discovered what great love is, love whose happiness lies in giving… But now you are the one who is cold and motionless and distant, as I used to be when you loved me…

And all of a sudden Mirdja remembers the tale of a man who was in the grip of a great fever one frightful, stormy night, and he trekked to the next parish, climbed into the churchyard and broke into the tomb of a recently deceased young maiden… What must he have felt?

And then she speaks aloud again: How wonderful you were, Runar, when you died, your skin as white and smooth as marble! How lofty and unattainable was the great majesty of your death!…

What must that man have felt, to break into a dead maiden's tomb…?

It's odd being the wife of a dead man, Mirdja repeats over and over.

Never before has she felt the presence of her husband as strongly as she does now that he is no longer there. Never before has she felt her love to be as everlasting and faithful as now, loving a dead man.

She even enjoys the harrowing burden of her loneliness, as a lover enjoys the suffering of love…

'What happens to all the harlots in old age? No one knows,' Mirdja remembers someone saying once. This thought suddenly flies into her head. She too is now old and forgotten, she who in her youth enjoyed palpable fame, who was expected to make an immortal name for herself… What was she? At any rate, her fate is no better than a harlot's. She had a glorious youth, but no one knows what happened to Mirdja in old age.

Everything is so far in the past now. Everything before the onset of old age. Impossible for anyone to remember any of it. Even Mirdja herself remembers nothing… It must have been someone else who enjoyed palpable fame in their youth…

But how is it that Mirdja knows that this someone had been to Paris and when she sang, her voice had once brought tears to the eyes of her elderly singing instructor…? And that the song went:

'Dans les chaleurs d'orage
je chevauchais toujours,
Forét! Forét sauvage,
où donc sont mes amours?
Personne ne passait
dans le triste sentier.

Si j'appelais,
qui répondrait?
Personne.'[156]

'No singing in the street,' a policeman remarks.

Mirdja looks at him, astonished.

Is this a street? Yes, that's right, everything outside the holy mound is a street or a road.

And she turns away haughtily.

Little does he know, Mirdja thinks, that I could have sung in the most magnificent concert halls in the world, had I so wished…

But she quickly turns back again:

'I'm sorry, officer, I was mistaken. I am not a singer after all, only a dead man's wife…'

The policeman looks pityingly at the madwoman.

*

For a long time Mirdja achieves peace and light from the thought: I am a dead man's wife. But then she finds that even this is a lie.

I have no children, she tells herself. How can I be Runar's wife after his death, when I wasn't his wife while he lived… I really have lived like a harlot. I have no children…

From the moment Mirdja hits upon this notion, her restlessness and her quest begin again. She wanders longingly, in search of the child she never had…

With a child she could still be Runar's wife, with a child she could achieve atonement and redemption and true love.

But now there is none of that. And she has committed a terrible sin. Even the chance of a child she discarded in her horribly selfish youth…

And she begins grieving for her child as if it were dead. She begins seeking out women with children. She follows them, worships them, watches them with admiration and envy and regret…

There is a poor wife walking hand in hand with a small boy. Mirdja approaches them.

'Do you love your child?' she asks.

The woman looks at her in amazement.

'Would you like to lose the boy?'

'No, ma'am.'

'If he were drowning, would you jump in after him?'

'I wouldn't be scared of the water, if it was an emergency.'

---

[156] 'In the heat of the tempest | I continued to ride | Forest! Wild forest, | where do my lovers abide? | No one ever passed by | along the sorry path. | If I gave a cry | who would reply? | No one.' (French.) The incorrect spelling of 'forêt' is Onerva's own.

'Even if you yourself might drown?'

'He's my boy after all…'

'Is it for him you live?'

Again the woman stares at Mirdja, speechless.

'I mean,' Mirdja continues hastily, 'is there anything more precious to you in life than your child? Would you exchange him for a great ideal or fame or beauty or money…? Or would you give him to me, so you could stop worrying, if I promised to raise him?'

The woman fearfully observes the strange look in Mirdja's eyes, and instinctively draws the child to her.

'I wouldn't give my child away for anything in the world,' she says.

Mirdja walks away, with a curious smile on her face.

Ah, at last she has found the answer to humanity's purpose. A child, a child…

A child is more than all the ideas and mad ambition in the world. Worth more than gold and fame, more than life itself. Therein lay true love…

And it represents the greatest, the highest cause to everyone except Mirdja, who never recognized its essence, and threw it away…

But from that moment on Mirdja thinks more about the child than about Runar. She invents the child from birth, through every moment unto death. And this non-existent death is more agonizing to her than anything she has ever seen…

So what is her child like? Good like Runar, or criminal like Mirdja? Surely criminal. How else would she achieve the happiness of atonement and forgiveness that comes with suffering? And Mirdja almost wishes her child were a criminal…

A few days later, she is walking through the town's remote, poorer quarters, seeking out long-suffering mothers with her eyes and her heart… And there are plenty of them…

Once Mirdja sees a young man being led in handcuffs. He had wounded someone in a drunken brawl… It is a sorry sight. For his old grey-haired mother walks behind him in despair… And her thin lips keep muttering the same phrase: 'God help thee and grant thee mercy, my dear son, my dear son…'

And this is a mother whose son has perhaps been harsh-spoken, brutal, and cruel to her!

But Mirdja forces her way through the crowd to the old woman and drops to her knees at the woman's feet…

This causes a commotion.

'Take her away, she's deranged!', people start shouting. 'She's a madwoman!'

'It is you who are mad,' Mirdja shouts back, 'you who must climb to Calvary before you can find your God![157] Every great suffering can serve as a

---

[157] The place where Jesus was crucified, as mentioned in Luke 23. 33.

Mount of Transfiguration.[158] A person dies, but God is born in that moment. Can you not see God before you? Look at this woman's suffering! Look at the holy mother! Go down on your knees, good folk! You will see God...'

Mirdja is carried off.

*

Mirdja is taken to Lumiluoto.

A quiet young woman is assigned as her companion...

But Mirdja cannot understand what this stranger is doing in her home.

'I've never seen a woman before,' Mirdja says. 'I could almost be afraid of you if you weren't so uncommonly kind.'

But then she winces.

'Your name isn't Anna, by any chance?' she asks. 'All kind people are called Anna...'

'My name is Martta.'[159]

'I see... Never mind... Anyway, it's a good thing your name isn't Anna... very good... But you are a woman, aren't you?'

'I am.'

'That's good. I have not seen a woman before. But do you have children?'

'No.'

'That's good... For in that case you would be God and I would be afraid of you. Did you know God is to be feared? I have always feared God. It's good that you are with me. But make sure you don't light the fire, it has such evil eyes. It's a shame you're not God. Then you could destroy the fire and its evil eyes... You are so kind, even though your name isn't Anna...'

*

The madwoman of Lumiluoto has only one passion: drawing. All day long she draws, and only eyes. The tablecloths and floors, covered in eyes. The curtains and wallpaper, covered in eyes...

She is looking for her child's eyes, she says. But the more eyes she draws, the more she is afraid of them.

'I want to burn them all, they look at me so wickedly!' she would cry.

But in the very next moment she would lament:

'Wretch that I am, I'm not a proper mother at all, for wanting to burn her child... No, no I haven't the courage. I have to suffer their wicked stare...'

---

[158] The mountain where Jesus was transfigured, becoming radiant in glory, as described in Matthew 17. 1–9.

[159] In the Bible, Anna is the only named prophetess, mentioned by Luke. According to tradition derived from some apocryphal writings, Anna is also the name of the Virgin Mary's mother. According to Luke and John, Martha is one of the two sisters who supported Jesus. Her name has come to symbolize care and concern for others, hospitality, maturity, strength, and common sense.

And she would inch furtively towards a pair of eyes, then collapse under their gaze and dare not get up…

Suffer them she must…

But one day, a small fire is kindled in Mirdja's room…

*

The sick mistress of Lumiluoto is sometimes paid a visit.

Once, even Norkko visits.

'You are Runar's friend,' says Mirdja. 'Runar is not home. But why are you so grave? Ah yes, you are grieving the sister, I the brother. We have something in common after all. Couldn't you be my friend too?'

'Your friend,' Norkko articulates, drawing closer.

'No, don't approach me,' Mirdja screeches, and with the agility of an animal she rolls into a ball. 'Don't approach! I have nothing in common with any man. I am very faithful, though you don't believe me. It is a hundred years since I was the odalisque,' she sobs. 'I have learned to pray. One white prayer, two black prayers, then another great white prayer, white prayer…

You see, when you love the dead, you have to know how to pray, and differently, not like before, and you have to love differently too. And we have sworn to love each other for seven thousand years… Not ordinary years… but seven thousand of God's years.[160] Do you see…? But that's right. We both love the dead…'

'Yes, the dead,' Norkko answers and turns away, a tear running down his cheek…

*

It becomes more and more difficult to visit Mirdja.

She is afraid…

Once she thought she saw a glimpse of Rolf and she was so terrified by this that she dared not move for two weeks.

But then once Mirdja even asks for Rolf…

And she receives him stiffly, motionless, with her head held high.

'Someone has told me you are a wise man, but I do not believe it. Or can you tell me how to find a small black peppercorn in tar? You cannot. But my uncle could have. Be gone, be gone! You are not a genuine wizard. I need a genuine wizard. I need to know who stole my child…'

But then Mirdja suddenly recoils, backs away until she is pressed against the wall, her eyes filled with darkness and terror.

'Why are you here now, when you have never been before? I am not a

---

[160] A reference to the theory that, in the Bible, the seven-day week is a pattern that applies to time on a grander scale, inferred from II Peter 3. 8: 'But, my beloved, do not forget that with the Lord, one day is as a thousand years and a thousand years is as one day'.

harlot even if I don't have a child, I am the real wife of a dead man. But I don't know where my child is…'

And Mirdja begins to sob and wail, and her body has suddenly fallen limp and lifeless…

'It was good of you to come now… No, now I remember, you shouldn't have come… no. I must not be allowed comfort, I have to suffer.'

Mirdja regains her initial stiff composure. The soul blazing in her big eyes is unrecognizable as she lifts her gaze to the ceiling, and she speaks not another word…

*

The feeble-minded should be wary of wandering the marshes alone.

The marshland is an enchanted wilderness full of mysterious voices, intoxicating smells, and visions, especially visions… The mists gather there to frolic. To acquire whimsical shapes and ghostly outlines. And the marsh herbs, the world's most pungent, release their wild and savage reek into the nostrils of anyone who ventures to defy the enchantment. And the moss beckons and the cottongrass whispers: 'take a seat, take a seat!' And the woodcock warbles, and the quagmire beguiles into its lap…

The feeble-minded should be wary of wandering the marshes alone…

But Mirdja hoists her hems upon her shoulders and tramps a few leagues into the swamp.

And when the woodcock warbles, Mirdja says: that is my child crying…

And when the brume thickens into a phantom which comes alive, Mirdja whispers: that is my child pointing the way…

And when the wild herbs and moss cushions combine forces to draw her into the mire she smiles: that is my child's spirit drawing me on…

And she sits down on the softly sinking wet moss, to await her child.

The cold mist rises to embrace her. The hoarfrost creeps over her and covers her with its white shroud…

The marsh herbs reek…

CONTEMPORARY REVIEWS

~

Review by V. A. Koskenniemi in *Aika*, 23, 1 December 1908

L. Onerva: Mirdja. Novel. — Otava, Helsinki 1908.[1]

Mirdja is a Finnish female student. But not one of the ordinary ones: she is a romantic, an individualist, and a 'Nietzschean'. And above all: she is erotic to the tips of her fingers. She wants to 'experience life in love's sweet breath', she looks with disdain upon the bourgeoisie, 'who don't appreciate the emotional evermore of fleeting seconds, the glorious musical beauty of the blink of an eye.' She is Don Juan in female form. She is every mother's nightmare and every student's infatuation. Her conquests among the city's 'bohemians' are numerous. The student Eino Kailo is a mediocrity whom she seems to love for a while, and then casts aside like an old glove. Her attention is captured for longer by Rolf Tanne, a man with an 'interesting' past who also has the gift of the gab: 'Not even the most resilient of men can resist the burning glimmer in your eyes and the delicate, soft, sultry sway in your step. You were born to be a *bayadère*.' But even Rolf Tanne fails to attach himself to Mirdja more permanently. Because Mirdja's spirit burns for new affairs. One such is with Mauri Etso, who we learn is 'strong, sure and sound, hot-blooded and passionate in love'. Next in line is Eero Selinä, who has ruined himself with drink. He is 'terribly talented' but since his Bachelor's degree he has done nothing but drink absinthe. He refers to himself and his social circle as 'we decadents'. However, his schoolboy infatuation with Mirdja and his youthful rhetoric lead us to believe his world-weariness and decadence are not of the severest kind. After Selinä's exit, onto the scene steps Torild, an artist with whom Mirdja has a brief moment of bliss. After him comes the 'half-lunatic' painter Bengt Iiro and finally the schoolteacher Runar Söderberg, whom Mirdja ends up marrying. The marriage is unhappy, both parties

---

[1] This largely negative review of *Mirdja* was written by Veikko Antero Koskenniemi (1885–1962), an influential conservative Finnish critic, poet, and professor of literature. Koskenniemi began his career as a Parnassian and was a great admirer of classical antiquity and J. W. Goethe, whom he considered his model and whose work he translated into Finnish. Decadence and most other *fin-de-siècle* and modernist trends did not meet with his approval. In the interwar period his conservative orientation developed into strongly right-wing sympathies. The cultural journal *Aika* (1907–1922) also had a conservative profile, representing the voice of the conservative Old Finnish Party. Koskenniemi was the editor-in-chief of *Aika* from 1913 to 1922. The review shows that *Mirdja* did not correspond to Koskenniemi's classical ideals and taste.

torment both themselves and their partner and the outcome is that Mirdja loses her mind.

I imagine that the author's purpose was to create a modern psychological novel in which the thematic imagery draws on the depths of human passive eroticism and imagination. In particular, she seems to have enjoyed exploring woman's love life in graphic detail. The subject itself is not unrewarding and, treated by a woman, it moreover acquires a special fascination in the reader's eyes. For although it is quite wrong to suppose that only a woman can properly understand and depict her sex, nevertheless it cannot be denied that one would also like to read a woman's description of woman sometimes. In *this* sense, I think that even 'Mirdja' can prove interesting.

But as an *artistic* achievement, I feel there is not much to commend the work. It seems as if the author embarked on her novel without any solid concept or even much of an outlying plan; the events and topics in this tale seem to follow on from one another, how can one put it, by Divine Providence. For this reason, the dimensions of real life are confused, the essential is over-shadowed by the inessential, and many trivialities are blown out of all propor-tion. Thus, Mirdja's repeatedly similar romantic fantasies page after page, and her pseudo-psychological ponderings, certainly do try the reader's patience. The reader is further wearied in this book by the fact that the author rarely describes any concrete situations for the reader's imagination to gain a foot-hold, or even a moment's repose during this wild death ride, a term which can also serve as a metaphor for the author's style of expression, both in the nature of its tempo and in the unhappy fate that awaits the novel's protagonist. The airy abstraction of the author's style also fails to make the characters life-like. Not even Mirdja is life-like, as the author has put all her effort into describing Mirdja's moods, impressions, and yearning for love, in other words those most basic aspects of depiction, and largely forgetting those aspects which elucidate a person's individuality and character. And this is even more true of the objects of Mirdja's infatuations, whose words, on the few occasions when they do speak, tend to be more or less in the same vein. In view of this, I suggest it cannot be said that the author has successfully fulfilled the psychological task she set for herself.

This is not to deny, however, that Mirdja does contain instances of good psychological observation. For example, the description of married life between Mirdja and Runar, with its incessant mutual torment, feels extremely well observed, as does Mirdja's final descent into madness. This last develop-ment also offers some small concession to those readers — of which there are no doubt many — who found it difficult to accept the spiritual, or should I say moral, outlook that seems to prevail throughout the first part of the book. There are also some individual moments of astute characterization to be noted here and there in the novel. I feel the following remark to be quite accurate, made by one of Mirdja's admirers in the middle of one of his eulogies: 'But you Mirdja, you can give it all away, suffer everything, cast yourself aside — *and yet remember nothing after the fact*.' I suspect that Otto Weininger,[2] expert on the female psyche, would have rubbed his hands in delight at Rolf Tanne's remark.

All in all, the impression left by this almost 500-page novel is that of a hopelessly long, embarrassing, and tedious monologue. The author did not possess sufficient imaginative power to elevate her vision into an objective depiction of people and life. Perhaps the author also lacked sufficient spiritual freedom to view life calmly, broadly, and profoundly.

V. A. K. (Veikko Antero Koskenniemi)

*

Review by Aarni Kouta in *Helsingin Sanomat*, 138, 18 June 1908[3]

It is with some considerable curiosity that one approaches L. Onerva's new book. One recalls the writer's debut, that little poetry edition entitled 'Disharmonies',[4] whose short verses introduced a haughty spirit, defiant and disdainful, seeking to break new ground. The book was nothing striking in itself, after all four years ago Finnish literature was already at the height of its 'Sturm und Drang'[5] period. And by no means did all of these verses crystallize into fully fledged art, into complete and pure creations; there was much about them that was jarring, uncertain, fumbling, the kind of expression that did not well up from the inner compulsion of the author's personality, that was not inextricably linked to it. But 'Disharmonies' did contain a number of

---

[2] Otto Weininger (1880–1903) was a philosopher of Jewish origin born in the Austro-Hungarian empire, whose major work was *Geschlecht und Charakter. Eine prinzipielle Untersuchung* (*Sex and Character: A Fundamental Investigation*, 1903). Many *fin-de-siècle* women writers responded to Weininger's anti-feminist views, later often interpreted within the framework of a crisis of masculinity and fear of women's emancipation. According to Weininger, genius is the preserve of men since women's life is consumed with the sexual function. For him all people are composed of both male and female substance, being naturally bisexual, but psychologically everybody has to be either a man or a woman. Weininger's thoughts were influential all over Europe, including in Finland. L. Onerva was familiar with Weininger, as is shown by the fact that she owned his posthumously published *Gedanken über Geschlechtsprobleme* ('Thoughts on sexual problems', 1907) and wrote ironically apocryphal Weininger aphorisms (see Kortelainen, *Naisen tie*, p. 167).

[3] This positive review of *Mirdja* was published in the daily *Helsingin Sanomat*, today the largest subscription newspaper in the Nordic countries. The predecessor of *Helsingin Sanomat* was *Päivälehti*, founded in 1889 by the liberal Young Finnish Party. The first number of *Helsingin Sanomat* came out in 1904. The author of the review, Aarni Kouta (1884–1924), was L. Onerva's friend as well as being the Finnish translator of Ibsen, Strindberg, and Nietzsche. He was the author of strongly Nietzschean poetry, such as the 1905 collection *Tulijoutsen* ('Fire swan'), and was also known for his intense interest in esotericism. See Introduction.

[4] *Sekasointuja* (1904).

[5] See note 41, p. 102.

harmonious verses too, here and there a cultivated personality showed through, lyrical moods and feelings rang out. Now the poet behind 'Disharmonies' has published a novel of nigh on 500 pages. So it is only natural that one rushes to examine the work with curiosity, to see how and by which methods this author of short verse takes command of a broader perspective.

The work is indeed grand in its scope. It is the depiction of a soul at odds with others and its environment, a soul which cannot accept and will not conform to prevailing conditions, one which suffers in the face of society with its norms and mores, and in the face of conventionalism and subjugation in general. It is a searching, fumbling, provocative, and fastidious soul, for whom each find is followed by disappointment, then a new quest, followed by a new find and disappointment, from which to walk away cold and disaffected. The novel's protagonist has artist's blood running through her veins, the blood of an artistic lineage whose members have never yet borne fruit, and neither does Mirdja. She is whole, but in the next instant she is broken into shards, she collects herself only to splinter apart again. The author describes this soul's development and its various forms of expression with great psychological precision. We follow a young woman who shatters society's and its supporters' concepts of conventionality, who philosophizes in restaurants with young decadents, who indulges in feverish, almost morbid sensual moods, who practises a lifestyle of erotic freedom, who builds and breaks relationships. The first part of the novel is a strange concoction of moods and atmosphere, toying with ideas, lifestyle, and love. And the author has managed to cement all this into a fully artistic form. The style is full of finesse and frivolity, a symphony of words, tones, and images, it is light, translucent, and restlessly staccato. There is much lyrical beauty, much magnificent, nuanced depiction of both the external surroundings and the inner soul.

Gradually Mirdja grows tired of this environment and its inhabitants, and she withdraws into solitude, firstly at her uncle's in Lumiluoto, and then by going abroad. This is also a period of quest, but now she is searching for her inner self. When, after some time, she finally returns to her native country, she meets a certain professor Söderberg, and a tender union of souls is born between them. Mirdja is tired, she longs for rest and happiness, and thinks she will find it in marriage. She makes peace with herself, or rather, she deludes herself and makes peace with society and the church, entering into holy matrimony. But the deceptive peace and happiness turn out to be too fragile an illusion, it soon shatters, and the surrounding environment, society with its expectations and representatives, weighs her down even more than before, it has become the air she breathes, brushing against her at every turn, forcing her into direct contact with it. This ruins everything, everything fills her with anger and rage, her marital and family happiness is broken, Mirdja withers, she torments herself and torments her husband to the point of sickness, exhaustion, and death, and she herself loses her reason. The end of the novel is a work of gravity, gravely intense, mature art, grave in its words of anger and pride, grave in its psychological precision.

We have already touched on the book's style and composition in this review. The style is indeed the work's strongest merit, it demonstrates that we are dealing with a mature artist, one of sensitive inclination, who is able to capture different atmospheres in words and images, who is able to set in poetic rhythm the fluctuations and flashes of different moods. We are tempted to call the author's style lyrical, to call her inclination a lyrical one. This poetic tour de force reaches its climax in the final section of the work, entitled 'Death Knell'. This section is deeply felt, beautiful poetry, and demonstrates the author's finesse and precision. The poetic substance is age-old, sung and spoken before, but the author's instinct has not led her astray. She does not err into vacant sentimentality, although the danger and opportunity for it are ever present; she has created a poetry in which the crucial developments are new, creating a unique atmosphere and mood. And this can also be said of many other sections of the book.

We hope that all lovers of literature will rush to discover this new work, it deserves attention for the gravity of its endeavour and its art.

The book is pleasantly bound and most reasonably priced.

A-i K-a (Aarni Kouta)

MHRA JEWELLED TORTOISE

The 'Jewelled Tortoise', named after J.-K. Huysmans's iconic image of Decadent taste in *À rebours* (1884), is a series dedicated to Aesthetic and Decadent literature. Its scholarly editions, complete with critical introductions and accompanying materials, aim to make available to students and scholars alike works of literature and criticism which embody the intellectual daring, formal innovation, and cultural diversity of the British and European *fin de siècle*. The 'Jewelled Tortoise' is under the joint general editorship of Stefano Evangelista and Catherine Maxwell.

To sign up to the series mailing list, email jewelledtortoise@mhra.org.uk.

Previously published:

Walter Pater, *Imaginary Portraits*
Edited by Lene Østermark-Johansen

Arthur Symons, *Spiritual Adventures*
Edited by Nicholas Freeman

Arthur Symons, *Selected Early Poems*
Edited by Chris Baldick and Jane Desmarais

Decadent and Occult Works by Arthur Machen
Edited by Dennis Denisoff

Mathilde Blind, *Selected Fin-de-Siècle Poetry and Prose*
Edited by James Diedrick

Hubert Crackanthorpe, *Selected Writings*
Edited by William Greenslade and Emanuela Ettorre

Michael Field, *'For That Moment Only' and Other Prose Works*
Edited by Alex Murray and Sarah Parker

Decadent Writings of Aubrey Beardsley
Edited by Sasha Dovzhyk and Simon Wilson

George Moore, *Confessions of a Young Man*
Edited by Matthew Creasy

www.tortoise.mhra.org.uk

www.ingramcontent.com/pod-product-compliance
Lightning Source LLC
Chambersburg PA
CBHW020811020726
47495CB00008B/2685